T0360273

Special EDITION

Believe in love. Overcome obstacles. Find happiness.

A Beach House Begining
RaeAnne Thayne

A Beauty In The Beast
Michelle Lindo-Rice

MILLS & BOON

A BEACH HOUSE BEGINNING
© 2024 by RaeAnne Thayne LLC
Philippine Copyright 2024
Australian Copyright 2024
New Zealand Copyright 2024

First Published 2024
First Australian Paperback Edition 2024
ISBN 978 1 038 91744 7

A BEAUTY IN THE BEAST
© 2024 by Michelle Lindo-Rice
Philippine Copyright 2024
Australian Copyright 2024
New Zealand Copyright 2024

First Published 2024
First Australian Paperback Edition 2024
ISBN 978 1 038 91744 7

THE TEN-DAY BARGAIN
© 2024 by Michelle Lindo-Rice
Philippine Copyright 2024
Australian Copyright 2024
New Zealand Copyright 2024

First Published 2024
First Australian Paperback Edition 2024
ISBN 978 1 038 91744 7

Published by
Harlequin Mills & Boon
An imprint of Harlequin Enterprises (Australia) Pty Limited
(ABN 47 001 180 918), a subsidiary of HarperCollins
Publishers Australia Pty Limited
(ABN 36 009 913 517)
Level 19, 201 Elizabeth Street
SYDNEY NSW 2000 AUSTRALIA

MIX
Paper | Supporting
responsible forestry
FSC® C001695

A Beach House Beginning

RaeAnne Thayne

MILLS & BOON

Dear Reader,

What an honor it is to be part of Harlequin's 75th anniversary celebration. No other publisher has so consistently been focused on stories of people opening their hearts to love, despite all the many obstacles they may face. For decades, Harlequin has been gracing bookshelves around the world with enchanting stories filled with swoon-worthy heroes and captivating heroines. I'm delighted to play a small part in remembering all the things that make Harlequin books so special—the promise of love, the thrill of unexpected twists and the satisfaction of happily ever after.

The anniversary celebration seemed a perfect chance for me to finish off my Women of Brambleberry House series. Through the six books in the series, I have come to adore this rambling old house by the seashore. Returning to it feels like coming home for me and I hope my readers feel the same. I have loved revisiting old friends and making new ones!

Thank you for being part of this incredible journey, and here's to many more years of shared stories, cherished moments and the enduring power of love.

All my very best,

RaeAnne

DEDICATION

To all the hundreds of people at Harlequin
who work with such passion and heart to get our books
into the hands of our amazing readers. Thank you!

Chapter One

"Jenna? Are you still there?"

Jenna Haynes slowly lowered herself to one of the kitchen chairs of her apartment on the second floor of Brambleberry House. Her cell phone nearly slipped from fingers that suddenly trembled.

"I...yes. I'm here." Her voice sounded hollow, thready.

"I know this must be coming as a shock to you." Angela Terry, the prosecuting attorney who had worked on the Oregon part of her case, spoke in a low, calming voice. "Believe me, we were all stunned, too. I never expected this. I'm sorry to call you so early but I wanted to reach out to you as soon as we heard the news."

"Thank you. I appreciate that."

"Seriously, what a shock. It's so hard to believe, when Barker was only halfway through his sentence. Who expects a guy in the prime of his life to go to sleep in his cell one night and never wake up? You know what they say. Karma drives a big bus and she knows everybody's address."

Jenna didn't know how to answer, still trying to process the stunning news that the man she had feared for three years was truly gone.

On the heels of her shock came an overwhelming relief. A man was dead. She couldn't forget that. Still, the man had made her life a nightmare for a long time.

"You're…you're positive he's dead?"

"The warden called me to confirm it himself, as soon as the medical examiner determined it was from natural causes. An aneurysm."

"An aneurysm? Seriously?"

"That's what the warden said. Who knows, Barker might have had a brain anomaly all along. What else would cause a decorated police officer to go off the rails like he did and spend years stalking, threatening and finally attacking you and others?"

Jenna fought down an instinctive shiver as the terrifying events of two years earlier crawled out from the lockbox of memories where she tried to store them for safekeeping.

Dead. The boogeyman who had haunted her nightmares for so long was gone.

She still couldn't quite believe it, even hearing it from a woman she trusted and admired, a woman who had fought hard to make sure Aaron Barker would remain behind bars for the maximum allowable sentence, which had been entirely too short a time as far as Jenna was concerned.

Jenna didn't know how she was supposed to feel, now that she knew he couldn't get out in a few years to pick up where he left off.

"I hope I didn't wake you, but I wanted you to know as soon as possible."

The concern in her voice warmed Jenna. Angela had been an unending source of calm and comfort, even during the most stressful of times during the trial.

"No. I'm glad you called. I appreciate it."

Slowly, her brain seemed to reengage and she remembered the polite niceties she owed this woman who had fought with such fierce determination for her.

"You didn't wake me," she assured Angela. "I have school this morning."

"Oh good. I was hoping I didn't catch you while you were sleeping in on your first day of summer vacation or something."

"One more week for that," Jenna answered. "I'm just fixing breakfast for Addie."

"How is my little buddy? Tell her we need to get together soon for a *Mario Kart* rematch. No way can I let a seven-year-old get the better of me."

"Eight. She turned eight last month."

"Already? Dang. I can't believe I missed her birthday. I'll have to send her something."

"You don't have to do that, Angela. You've done so much already for us. I can never thank you enough for everything. I mean that."

"Well, we still need to get together and catch up. It's been too long."

"Yes. I would love that. I'll only be working part-time at the gift shop this summer so my schedule is much more flexible than during the school year."

"We'll do it. We can have Rosa join us. I'll set up a text string and we can work out details."

"Thank you for telling me about Aaron."

"I know you had been worrying about his possible release next year," the other woman said, her voice gentle. "I hope that knowing he can't ever bother you again goes a little way toward taking a weight off your heart."

"It does. I can't even tell you how much."

They spoke for a few more moments before ending the call with promises to make plans later in the summer.

Jenna set her phone on the table slowly, released a heavy sigh and then covered her face with her hands.

Dead.

She didn't quite know how to react.

Since the arrest and conviction eighteen months ago of the man who had tormented her for years, she had been bracing herself for the moment when he might be released, when she might have to pick up her daughter again and flee.

She had hated the idea of it.

Brambleberry House, this beautiful rambling beach house on the dramatic coastline of northern Oregon, had become a haven for them. She had finally begun to rebuild her life here, to feel safe again and…happy.

Lurking at the edge of her consciousness, though, like the dark, far-off blur of an impending storm, was the grim realization that someday she might have to leave everything once more and start again somewhere else.

Now she didn't have to.

She wiped away tears she hadn't even realized were coursing down her cheeks.

He was gone. They were free.

"What's wrong, Mom?"

She turned to find her daughter in the doorway, wearing shorts, a ruffled T-shirt and a frown.

Jenna gave a laugh and reached for Addie, pulling her into a tight hug.

"Nothing's wrong. Everything is terrific. Really terrific."

Her perceptive child wasn't fooled. She eased away, narrowing her gaze. "What's going on?"

Jenna didn't want to talk about Aaron Barker. She didn't want Addie to have to think about the man who had threatened them both, who had completely upended their lives simply because he couldn't have what he wanted.

"Nothing." She gave a reassuring smile. "I'm just happy, that's all. It's a beautiful day, school will be out next week and summer is right around the corner. Now hurry and finish your breakfast so we can get to school. I could use your help carrying the cupcakes for my class."

Addie still didn't look convinced. Sometimes she seemed

far too wise for her eight years on the earth. Apparently she decided not to push the matter.

"Can I have one of the cupcakes? You said I could when we were frosting them last night."

The cupcakes were a treat for her class, a reward for everyone meeting their reading goals for the year.

Jenna pointed to the counter, at a covered container near the microwave. "I've got two there for us. I was going to save them for dessert later tonight after dinner, but I suddenly feel like celebrating. Let's have a cupcake."

Addie's eyes widened with shock and then delight. She reached for the container and pulled out one of the chocolate cupcakes, biting into it quickly as if afraid Jenna would change her mind.

"You still have to eat your egg bites and your cantaloupe," Jenna warned.

"I don't care. Cupcakes for breakfast is the best idea ever."

She couldn't disagree, Jenna thought as she finished hers, as well as her own healthier breakfast. Still, the call was at the forefront of her thoughts as she hurried through the rest of her preparations for the school day.

Twenty minutes later, she juggled her laptop bag, a box of cupcakes and a stack of math papers she had graded the evening before.

She couldn't help humming a song as she walked out of her apartment, Addie right behind her.

A man stood on the landing outside her apartment, hand on the banister. He was big, dark, muscular, wearing a leather jacket and carrying a motorcycle helmet under his arm.

For one ridiculous moment, her heart skipped a beat, as it always did when she saw her new upstairs neighbor. Her song died and she immediately felt foolish.

"Morning," he said, voice gruff.

"Um. Hi."

"You've got your arms full. Can I help you carry something?"

"No. I've got it," she said, her voice more clipped than she intended.

His eyes darkened slightly at her abrupt tone. Something flickered in his expression, something hard and dangerous, but he merely nodded and gestured for them to go ahead of him down the stairs.

Did he guess she was afraid of him? Jenna had tried to hide it, but she strongly suspected she hadn't been very successful.

"Come on, Addie."

Her daughter, who seemed to have none of Jenna's instinctive fear of big, tough, ruthless-looking men with more ink than charm, smiled and waved at him.

"Bye, Mr. Calhoun. I hope you have a happy day."

He looked nonplussed. "Thanks. Same to you."

Jenna led their little procession down the central staircase of Brambleberry House, which featured private entrances to the three apartments, one on each floor.

As she hurried outside, she couldn't help wondering again what Rosa Galvez Townsend had been thinking to rent the space to this man.

She had heard the rumors about Wes Calhoun. He had a daughter who attended her school, and while Brielle was a grade older and wasn't in Jenna's class, the girl's teacher was one of Jenna's closest friends.

Teachers gossip as much as, if not more than, other populations. As soon as Wes Calhoun rode into town on his motorcycle, leather jacket, tattoos and all, Jenna had learned he was an ex-con only released a few months earlier from prison in the Chicago area.

Learning he would be her new upstairs neighbor had been unsettling and upsetting.

Rosa—who functioned as landlady for her aunt Anna and Anna's friend Sage, owners of the house—assured her he was a friend of Wyatt, Rosa's husband, and perfectly harmless. He had been wrongfully convicted three years earlier and had been completely cleared, his record expunged.

That didn't set her mind at ease. At all. She would have found the man intimidating even if she hadn't known he was only a few months out of prison.

She hurried Addie to her small SUV, loaded the cupcakes into the cargo area and made sure Addie was safely belted into the back.

As she slid behind the wheel, Jenna watched Wes climb onto his sleek, black, death trap of a motorcycle parked beside her and fasten his helmet.

While he started up the bike, he didn't go anywhere, just waited, boots on the driveway. He was waiting for her, she realized.

Aware of his gaze on her, steely and unflinching, she turned the key in the ignition.

Instead of purring to life, the car only gave an ominous click.

She tried it a second time, with the same results, then a third.

No. Oh no. This wasn't happening. She was already running late.

Normally she and Addie could ride bikes the mile and a half to the school, but not when she had two dozen cupcakes to deliver!

Hoping against hope, she tried it a few more times, with the same futile click.

"What's wrong?" Addie asked.

"I'm not sure. The car isn't starting, for some reason."

A sudden knock at her window made her jump. Without power, she couldn't lower the window, so she opened the door a crack.

"Having trouble?" Wes Calhoun looked at her with concern.

She wanted to tell him no, that she was a strong, independent woman who could handle her own problems. But what she knew about cars could probably fit inside one spark plug. If cars even had spark plugs anymore, which she suspected they didn't.

"You could say that. It won't start. I'm not getting anything but clicks."

"Sounds like it might be your battery. Do you know how old it is?"

"No. I bought the car used two years ago. It was three years old then. I have no idea how old the battery is. I do know I haven't replaced it."

"Pop the hood and I'll take a look at it."

"You don't have to do that. I can call road service."

He gave her a long look. "You seemed in a hurry this morning. Do you have time to wait for road service? If it's your battery, I can give you a jump and get you on the road in only a few minutes."

She glanced at her watch. The phone call with Angela had thrown off her whole morning schedule. She was already going to be late, without adding in a potentially long wait for road service.

"Thank you. I would appreciate a jump, if you don't mind. Can you jump a car with a motorcycle, though?"

"I don't know. I've never tried. I was talking about my truck."

He had an old blue pickup truck, she knew. He drove that on the frequent days of rain along the Oregon Coast.

"Right."

"Let's take a look first under the hood. Can you pop it for me?"

She fumbled beneath the steering wheel to find the right lever that would release the hood, then climbed out just as Wes was taking off his leather jacket and setting it on the seat of his motorcycle.

The plain black T-shirt he wore underneath showed off muscular biceps and the tattoos that adorned them.

As he bent over the engine, worn jeans hugging his behind, his T-shirt rode up slightly, revealing a few inches of his muscular back. Her stomach tingled and Jenna swallowed and looked away, appalled at herself for having an instinctive reaction to a man who left her so jumpy.

"Yep. Looks like you need a new battery. I'll give you a quick jump so you can make it to work. If you want, I can pick up another battery and put it in for you this evening."

Jenna tried not to gape at him. Why was he being so nice to her, when she hadn't exactly thrown out the welcome mat for him?

"I...that would be very kind. Thank you."

"Give me a second to pull my truck around."

"What's wrong with the car? Is it broken?" Addie asked from the back seat after Wes moved to his pickup truck and climbed inside, then started doing multiple-point turns to put it in position for jumper cables to reach her battery from his.

"The battery is dead. Our nice neighbor Mr. Calhoun is going to try to help us get it started."

"I can't be late today. I have to give my book report first thing."

"Hopefully we can still make it in time," she answered, as Wes turned off his truck and released the hood latch, then climbed out, rummaged behind the seats for some jumper cables and started hooking things up.

"What do I need to do?" she asked, feeling awkward and clueless. She had needed to have a vehicle jumped a few times before, early in her marriage, but Ryan had always taken care of those kind of things for her. She should have paid more attention to the process.

"Nothing yet. I'll tell you when to try starting it again."

He hooked up the cables, then fired up his truck before

coming back to her car. "Okay. Let's give it a go and see what happens."

Mentally crossing her fingers, she pushed the ignition button. To her vast relief, the engine turned for a second or two, then burst into life.

"Yay!" Addie exclaimed. "Does that mean we don't have to walk to school?"

"We would have found a ride somehow," Jenna assured her. "But it looks like we've been rescued, thanks to Mr. Calhoun."

"Thanks, Mr. Calhoun. I have to give a report this morning on a book about bees and didn't want to be late."

"You're very welcome. You can call me Wes, by the way. You don't have to call me Mr. Calhoun."

Her daughter beamed at him, unfazed by that hard, unsmiling face. "Thanks, Wes."

"You can as well," he said to Jenna. Their gazes met and she couldn't help noticing how long his dark eyelashes were, an odd contrast to the hard planes of his features.

"Thank you, Wes," she forced herself to say. "I really appreciate the help."

"It was no problem. I'll grab a battery for you today. Do you have jumper cables, in case your car doesn't start after you're done at school today?"

She was relieved she could answer in the affirmative. "Yes. I have an emergency kit in back with flares, a flashlight and a blanket, along with a few tools and jumper cables."

"Good. With any luck, you might not need them."

"Thanks again for all your help."

He shrugged. "It's the kind of thing neighbors do for each other, right?"

His words filled her with guilt. She hadn't been very neighborly in the two weeks since he had moved in. She hadn't taken any goodies over to welcome him and did little more than nod politely in passing.

Was he being ironic? Had he noticed how she went out of her way to avoid him whenever possible?

She hoped he didn't notice how her face flushed with heat as she mustered a smile that faded quickly as she backed out of the driveway and turned in the direction of school.

Wes watched his pretty neighbor maneuver her little blue SUV onto the road toward the elementary school.

When he was certain her vehicle wasn't going to conk out on the road, he returned his pickup to its customary spot and climbed back onto his Harley.

It might be easier to take the truck today but he was in the mood for a bike ride, which was just about the only thing that could do anything at all to calm his restlessness.

That was an odd turn for his morning to take, but he was happy to help out, even if Jenna Haynes looked at him out of those big blue eyes like she was afraid he was about to drag her by her hair up the stairs to his apartment and lock her in his sex dungeon.

He might have found her skittishness a little amusing if he hadn't spent the past three years in company with people capable of that and so much worse.

It still burned under his skin how she and others considered him. An ex-con. Not an innocent man wrongfully convicted because of a betrayal but someone who had probably been exactly where he belonged. Even if he hadn't done the particular crime that had put him behind bars, he was no doubt guilty of *something*, right?

He hated it, that pearl-clutching, self-righteous, condemnatory attitude he had encountered since his release. After two months on the outside, he was still trying to adjust to the knowledge that his slate would never be wiped completely clean, no matter how many neighborly things he did.

He couldn't be bothered by what Jenna Haynes thought of

him. What anybody thought of him. He had clung to sanity in prison by remembering that he was not the man others saw when they looked at him.

He lifted his face to the sun for just a moment before shoving on his helmet. He couldn't get enough of feeling the warmth of it on his face or smelling air scented with spring and the sea.

Clutch your pearls all you want, Ms. Haynes, he thought. *I'm alive and free. That's enough for today.*

He drove his bike through light traffic to Cannon Beach Car and Bike Repair, the garage where he had been lucky to find a job after showing up in town with mainly his bike, his truck and the small settlement he had received from the state of Illinois.

He had just parked the bike and was taking off his helmet when a tall, dark-haired and very pregnant woman climbed out of a silver sedan and hurried over to him.

Wes sighed and braced himself, not at all in the mood to have a confrontation with his ex-wife that morning. Though they had a generally friendly relationship, he couldn't imagine why she would show up unless she was mad about something. Not when she could have called or texted for anything benign.

"There you are," Lacey exclaimed. "I thought you started work at eight."

He looked at his watch that read eight oh five. "I had a neighbor with a dead battery. It took me a minute to get the car started. What's up? Have you been waiting for me? You could have called."

"I know. But I had to run next door anyway to pick up something at the hardware store after I dropped off Brielle at school, so I figured I would stop here first to talk to you while I was out."

He really hoped she wasn't about to tell him her husband had been transferred again, after only being moved here a year ago to become manager of a chain department store in a nearby town.

Wes liked it here in Cannon Beach. He liked running on the beach in the mornings and sitting in the gardens of Brambleberry House in the evenings to watch the sun slide into the water.

He liked his job, too. He had worked in a neighborhood auto mechanic shop all through high school and summers during college and definitely knew his way around an engine, motorcycle or car.

Did he want to do it forever? No. As much as he had admired and respected the neighbor who had employed him—and all those who worked with their hands—Wes didn't think working as a mechanic was his destiny. He still didn't know what he wanted to do as he worked toward rebuilding the life that had been taken from him. But for now he had found a good place, working with honest, hardworking people who cared about treating their customers right.

It paid the bills and was challenging enough not to bore him, but not overwhelming as he tried to ease back into outside life.

"What's going on?"

He could see his boss, Carlos Gutierrez, and his brother Paco watching them through the small front window of the shop.

"You know you don't always have to cut to the chase, right?" Lacey looked exasperated. "We're not having a quick conversation between prison bars anymore. A little small talk would be fine. You could say, *Hi, Lacey. How are you? How's the house? How's the baby?*"

Wes worked to keep his expression neutral. He might have agreed with her, except their marriage hadn't exactly been filled with small talk, even before his arrest.

"How are you feeling?" he asked. He had learned a long time ago it was best to try humoring her whenever possible.

Lacey was a devoted, loving mother to their daughter and he still considered her a dear friend. If circumstances had been different, he would have tried like hell to keep their marriage together.

Still, he couldn't help being more than a little grateful her sometimes volatile moods were another man's problems these days.

"I'm good. Huge. I can't believe I still have ten weeks to go before the baby comes."

They had been divorced for two and a half years. She had remarried her childhood sweetheart a year almost to the day their divorce had been finalized and was now expecting a son with Ron Summers.

Wes was happy for her. When he had little to do but think about his life, it hadn't taken long for Wes to recognize that his marriage to Lacey had been a mistake from start to finish. He had been twenty-one, about to head off overseas with the Army and she had been eighteen and desperate to escape an unhappy home life, with an abusive father and neglectful mother.

They hadn't been a good fit for each other. He could see that now, though both of them had spent years trying to deny the inevitable.

One good thing had come out of it. One amazing thing, actually. His nine-year-old daughter, Brielle. She was his heart, his purpose, his everything.

"That's actually why I'm here. Ron has the chance to take a last-minute trip to Costa Rica for work. He'll be gone ten days and he wants me to go with him, if I can swing it. This is my last chance to travel for a while, at least until the baby is older."

"Sounds like fun," he said, trying to figure out where he came in and why she had accosted him at his workplace to deliver the news.

"The problem is that I can't take Brie. She doesn't have a passport and there's no way to get one for her in time."

Ah. Now things were beginning to make sense.

"Is there any chance she could come stay with you while we're gone?"

A host of complications ran through his head, starting with the building just beyond her. The Gutierrez brothers had been good to him. He couldn't just leave them in the lurch to facilitate his ex-wife's travel plans.

He worked full-time and would have to arrange childcare. Brielle was nine going on eighteen and likely thought she was fully capable of being on her own while he worked all day. Wes definitely didn't agree. But he couldn't bring her down here to the garage with him all day, either.

He would figure that part out later. How could he turn down the chance to spend as much time as possible with his daughter, considering all the years he had missed?

"Sure. Of course. I would love to have her."

Lacey's face lit up with happiness, reminding him with painful clarity that it had been a long time since they had been able to make each other happy.

"Oh, that's amazing. Thank you! Brie will be so excited when I tell her. The alternative was staying with my friend Shandy and she has that five-year-old who can be a real pistol. Brielle will much prefer staying with her dad."

He could only hope he was up to the task. "When do you leave?" Wes asked.

"Next Friday. The last day of school."

It would have been easier if she were leaving during the school year, when he would only need to arrange after-school care until his shift was over, but he would figure things out.

He couldn't say no. He had moved to Cannon Beach, following Lacey and her new family, in order to nurture his relationship with Brielle. He couldn't miss what seemed to be a glorious opportunity to be with her.

"No problem. We'll have a great time."

"You're the best. Seriously. Thanks, Wes."

She stood on tiptoe and kissed his cheek, and as her mouth brushed his cheek, Wes couldn't help wishing that things could have worked out differently between them.

He couldn't honestly say he regretted the end of a marriage that had been troubled from the beginning. He did regret that the decisions made by the adults in Brielle's life complicated things for her, forcing her to now split her time between them.

"You do remember that today is Guest Lunch at the school, right? Brie said you were planning to go. If you're not, I'm sure Ron could swing by on his lunch break."

He really tried not to feel competitive with his daughter's stepfather, who seemed overall like a good guy, if a little on the superficial side.

"I'll be there," he answered, hoping the day wouldn't be inordinately busy at the shop.

The Gutierrez brothers were great to work with, but an employer could only be so understanding.

As he watched his ex-wife drive away, the second time he had been caught in the wake of a woman's taillights that morning, he was reminded of Jenna Haynes and her car trouble.

If he were swinging by the school anyway for lunch, he might as well take a car battery with him and fix Jenna Haynes's car. It was an easy ten-minute job, and that way she wouldn't have to worry about the possibility of it not starting after school.

He told himself the little burst of excitement was only the anticipation of doing a nice, neighborly deed. It had nothing to do with the knowledge that he would inevitably see Jenna again.

Chapter Two

"Stay in line, class. Remember, hands to yourself."

Jenna did her best to steer her class of twenty-three third-grade students—including three with special learning needs and Individualized Education Programs—into the lunchroom with a minimum of distractions.

The day that had started out with such stunning news from Angela had quickly spiraled. Her dead battery had only been the beginning.

As soon as she reached the school, she discovered both of her paraprofessionals, who helped with reading and math, as well as giving extra attention to those who struggled most, had called in for personal leave. One was pregnant and had bad morning sickness and the other one had to travel out of town at the last minute to be with a dying relative.

Jenna completely understood they both had excellent reasons to be gone. Unfortunately, that left her to handle the entire class by herself, and her third-grade students were so jacked up over the approaching summer vacation—or maybe from the sugar in her cupcakes—that none of them seemed able to focus.

One more week, she told herself. One more week and then she would have the entire summer to herself.

The previous summer, she had taken classes all summer to finish her master's degree, as well as working nearly full-time at Rosa's gift shop, By-the-Wind.

She didn't feel as if she had enjoyed any summer vacation at all.

She wasn't going to make that mistake again this year. Though she still had two more classes to go before earning her master's degree, she had decided to hold off until after the summer, and she had told Rosa she couldn't work as many hours at the gift shop.

Addie was growing up and Jenna wanted to spend as much time as possible with her daughter while Addie still seemed to like being with her.

"Don't want spaghetti." The sudden strident shout from one of her students, Cody Andrews, drew looks from several students in the cafeteria. Some of the adult guests having lunch with their students also gave the boy the side-eye.

Jenna felt immediately on the defensive. Cody, who had been diagnosed with autism, was an eager, funny, bright student, but sometimes crowds could set him off and trigger negative behaviors.

He had seemed to have a particularly difficult morning, maybe because Monica, the aide he loved dearly, wasn't there.

"Do you want to get pizza from the à la carte line?" she asked him, her voice low and calming.

"No. I don't like pizza." That was news to her, since his favorite food was usually pizza and he could eat it five days a week without fuss.

"What about chicken tenders?"

He appeared to consider that for a long moment, his blond head tilted and his brow furrowed. Finally he nodded. "Okay. I like tenders."

The lunchroom was crowded with parents and friends of the students who had come for their monthly Lunch with a Guest activity.

She strongly suspected another of the reasons for Cody's outburst might have something to do with that. His parents were recently divorced and his father, who used to come have lunch with him every month, had moved two towns over.

Normally she didn't eat with the students, preferring to grab a quick bite at her desk while they were out at recess, unless she was on playground duty. But because Cody was being so clingy, she had decided to bring her sack lunch to the table. Now he slid in next to her with his tray of nuggets.

She waved to a few of the parents, then pulled out her sandwich just as she felt the presence of someone behind her.

She turned and was astonished to discover her upstairs neighbor standing beside his daughter, Brielle. He was holding a tray that carried both their lunches.

"Hello."

In boots, jeans and the same black T-shirt he had been wearing earlier in the day, he looked big and tough and intimidating. Completely out of place in an elementary school lunchroom.

He should moonlight as a bouncer at a biker bar, since nobody would dare mess with him.

"Hi, Mrs. Haynes. This is my dad." Brielle, his daughter, beamed with pride.

"I know. I've met him. We're neighbors."

"This is his very first time coming to one of the Lunch with a Guest days."

She forced a smile. "Welcome. I hope you enjoy yourself."

"So far so good. It's pizza. What could go wrong with pizza?"

He obviously had not tried the school pizza yet, which could double as a paperweight in a pinch.

Jenna was disconcerted when Wes pointed to an empty spot down the row from her. "Is it all right if we sit here? There doesn't seem to be room with Brielle's class."

It was always a tight squeeze in the small lunchroom when each student brought a guest. Parents ended up finding spots wherever they could. She gestured to the empty spot. "Go ahead."

She was fiercely aware of him as she finished her sandwich.

"I have a dog," Cody suddenly announced. "Her name is Jojo, and she's white and brown with white ears and a brown tail. Do you want to see?"

Jenna realized with some alarm that the boy was talking to Wes in particular, unfazed by his intimidating appearance.

"Um. Sure."

Cody pulled out the small four-by-six photo album he carried with him all the time in the front pocket of his hoodie, a sort of talisman. He opened it and thrust it into Wes's face, far too close for comfort.

"Wow. She's very pretty," Wes answered.

"Does she do any tricks?" Brielle asked, genuine curiosity in her voice as she peered around her father's muscular arm to see the photograph.

"She comes when I call her and she sits and she can roll over."

"I wish we had a dog," Brielle said, a hint of sadness in her voice. "We have a cat, though, and it's the best cat in the whole world."

Jenna thought the interaction would end there, as Cody could be quiet and withdrawn with strangers. She was surprised when the boy turned the page of his well-worn photo album to show other things that were important to him in his life. His bedroom. His bicycle. His father, who had walked out the previous year.

She might have expected Wes to turn his attention back to his daughter. That was the reason he had come to lunch, after all, to spend time with Brielle. Instead, he seemed to go out of his way to include the boy in their conversation.

She couldn't help being touched by and grateful for his efforts, especially because it allowed her a chance to interact with some of the other students who did not have a guest with them for various reasons.

As soon as the children finished lunch, they were each quick to return their trays to the cafeteria and rush outside for recess.

Brielle seemed to take her time over the meal, probably to spend more time with her father. Cody was the last to linger at the table, apparently enjoying his new friends too much to leave.

When he left to go out to recess, watched over by the playground aides, Jenna rose as well.

"I brought over a battery for your car," Wes said abruptly. "I can switch it out for you before I head back to the garage. I thought that might be better so you don't have to worry about needing a jump again after school is out."

This man was full of surprises. "Really? You would do that on your lunch hour?"

He shrugged. "It's no trouble. Will take me less than ten minutes. Brie can help me. She loves to work on cars, don't you?"

His daughter beamed. "Yep."

"I will need your car keys, though."

"They're in my classroom. I'm about to head back there, if you don't mind following me."

"Not a problem."

He and his daughter walked with her, Brielle chattering happily with her father. She didn't seem to mind his monosyllabic responses.

As they made their way through the halls, Jenna couldn't help but be aware of Wes. She was a little surprised to realize she had lost some of her nervousness around him. It was very difficult to remain afraid of a man who could show such kindness to a young boy who could sometimes struggle in social situations.

"Thank you for helping with Cody. He's having a pretty tough time right now. Guest days are sometimes hard on him. You helped distract him."

"I didn't do much. We just talked about his dog."

She wanted to tell him the conversation obviously meant much more to the boy, who was deeply missing his father, but she didn't want to get into Cody's personal problems with him, especially not with Brielle there.

"The distraction was exactly what he needed. Thank you."

Wes didn't quite smile, but she thought his usual stern expression seemed to soften a little. "Glad I could help. About those keys…"

"Yes. I'll get them."

She opened her classroom and headed for the closet where she kept her personal effects. After digging through her purse, she pulled out her key chain with her car fob.

"Here you go," she said.

He held his hand out and she dropped the keys into it, grateful she didn't have to touch him for the handover.

"Thanks. I'll bring them back when I'm done."

"Do you need my help out there?"

"No. We got it."

"Thank you."

The words seemed inadequate but she did not know what else to say. As soon as Wes and Brielle walked out the side door closest to the faculty parking lot, her friend Kim Baker rushed out of her classroom across the hall, where she taught fifth grade.

"Who is that?" Kim asked, eyes wide. "I must know immediately."

"My neighbor."

"*That's* the serial killer?"

Jenna winced, feeling guilty that she had confided in her dear friend after she found out Wes had recently been released from prison.

"He's not a serial killer. I never said he was. He was in prison for property crimes. Fraud, extortion, theft. But Anna and Rosa assure me he was exonerated."

"There you go, then. You should be fine."

"Especially since I have nothing to steal."

"You and me both, honey. We're teachers." Kim looked in the direction Wes had gone. "I have to say, I wouldn't mind having that man on top of me."

"Kim!" she exclaimed.

"Living upstairs," her friend said with a wink. "What did you think I meant?"

She rolled her eyes. "You're a happily married woman. Not to mention soon to be a grandmother."

Kim was only in her midforties but had married and started a family young. Her daughter was following in her footsteps, married and pregnant by twenty-two.

"I am all those things, but I'm not dead. And he is way hotter than you let on, you sly thing."

Jenna could feel her face flush. She hadn't told Kim much about Wes.

"I am curious about why your sexy new neighbor is stopping by in the middle of the day to talk to you. Is there something you're not telling me?"

"No!" she exclaimed quickly. "Nothing like what you're thinking. He jumped me this morning."

"Go on," Kim said, eyes wide with exaggerated lasciviousness.

Jenna let out an exasperated laugh. "My car died, I mean. He jumped my battery. He offered to fix it tonight, but since he was coming by the school today to see his daughter for lunch, he offered to fix it now."

To her vast relief, this information was enough for Kim to drop the double entendres. "That is really nice of him."

"Yes. It is."

"And you're sure that's all?"

"Yes," she said, more forcefully this time. "He's been very kind. That's all."

Kim made a face and reached for Jenna's hand, her features suddenly serious.

"I'm only saying this as your friend, but I can't think of anyone else who deserves to have their battery jumped by a sexy guy. And if he's kind and thoughtful, all the better."

The genuine concern in her voice touched Jenna, even if she didn't agree with the sentiment. She was deeply grateful for the many friendships she had made since coming to Cannon Beach. The people of this community had truly embraced her and welcomed her and Addison into their midst.

She still could not quite believe she was now free to stay here as long as she wanted.

"I appreciate the sweet sentiment, Kim, but I'm fine. Completely fine. I have everything I need. A great apartment, a job I love, Addie. It's more than enough. I don't need a man in my life."

And especially one who intimidated her as much as Wes Calhoun.

Kim did not look convinced, but before her friend could argue, Wes returned to Jenna's classroom, on his own this time instead of with his daughter.

He set Jenna's keys on the edge of her desk. "Here you go. She's running great now. Started right up. Looks like you're due for an oil change, though. You're going to want to get on that."

"I will. Thanks. What do I owe you for the battery?"

He looked reluctant to give a number but finally did, something that seemed far less than she was expecting.

"What about labor?"

"Nothing. There was really no labor involved."

She wanted to argue but couldn't figure out how in a gracious way. "Thank you, then," she finally said. "I'm very grateful."

She would have said more, but the bell rang in that moment and children began to swarm back into the classroom from the playground.

"Glad I could help," he answered. "I'll let you get back to your students."

"I'll settle up with you this evening, if that's okay."

Again she had the impression he wanted to tell her not to worry about it, but he finally nodded. "Sounds good. See you later."

Two students approached her desk to ask a question about the field trip they were taking on Monday to the aquarium in Lincoln City. By the time she answered them, Wes had slipped away.

Chapter Three

"I love, love, *love* pizza night!"

Wes smiled at Brielle, her face covered in flour and a little drip of tomato sauce on her nose. She wore an apron that matched the black one he wore on the rare occasions he cooked. Those occasions mostly consisted of Friday nights, when Brielle came over for her weekend visitation. Their tradition had become centered around pizza night, where they would spend an hour or so making their own pizzas and then would watch a show of her choosing.

The few days he had the chance to spend with Brielle were the highlight of his week. Even when they didn't do anything more exciting than hanging out at his apartment and playing board games, Wes found himself happier than he believed possible three months earlier.

This moment—in his warm kitchen with rain pattering down outside and his daughter giggling at the kitchen table as she made a face on her pizza with pepperoni—seemed worlds away from his life the past three years.

Rich and sweet and filled with joy.

He had been given a second chance and didn't want to waste a minute of it.

"Only one more week of school. Can you believe it?"

Brielle shook her head. "No. And I also can't believe I'm

going to be in fifth grade next year. I hope I get Mrs. Baker. She's super funny."

He had met the woman the day before when he had returned Jenna's key to her classroom, he remembered.

While he was thinking about things that seemed far away from prison life, Jenna Haynes was the epitome.

She was lovely as a spring morning, her life worlds away from the darkness and ugliness he had been forced to wallow through in prison.

As lovely as he found her, he would be wise to remember they likely had nothing in common. He was darkness to her light, hard and jaded and cynical in contrast to her sweet innocence.

And she was terrified of him. He couldn't forget that part.

"Looks like we made too much dough. What are we going to do with it?"

"We can make another pizza!" Brielle said with a grin.

"We can do that, but that means we're going to have a lot of leftovers to eat the rest of the weekend."

"We could invite someone over," she suggested. "What about Mrs. Haynes and Addison? I can't believe they lived downstairs all this time and I never knew until today."

He hadn't exactly been holding out on Brielle. He simply hadn't thought to tell her before now about his neighbors.

He had only been in Brambleberry House for two weeks, after spending his first several weeks in the area paying a ridiculous amount for a tiny studio with a short-term lease, until he had found this place available. This was only his daughter's second weekend staying here with him. She had been delighted when he mentioned the other building tenants.

"Mrs. Haynes is super nice. I don't have her but my friend Reina does, and she really likes her," Brie had said when he told her.

"What about her daughter? Do you know her?"

"She's only in third grade, but we have the same recess so we play soccer sometimes. She's super fast. And she's funny!"

A good sense of humor seemed to be the barometer by which Brielle judged everyone. He couldn't disagree.

"So can we take them our extra pizza?" she asked now.

He was trying to come up with a good excuse to refuse when his doorbell rang.

Wes frowned, instantly on alert. Prison had given him a strong dislike of surprises. He wasn't expecting anybody, but maybe Lacey had forgotten to send something with Brielle for her overnight stay. Vitamins or extra socks or something.

"I'll get it," Brie sang out, rushing toward the door.

Wes hated that his life experience made him constantly brace for trouble.

He followed Brie, ready to yank her back to safety if necessary as she opened the door.

It wasn't trouble. At least not the sort he had become used to. His neighbor and her daughter stood on the landing to his apartment.

"Hi, Mrs. Haynes. Hi, Addie," Brielle said.

"Hi, Brielle." Addie beamed at his daughter.

The two girls looked very different. Addie had blue eyes and blond curls while Brie had long straight dark hair, which she usually wore in a ponytail or braid.

"It smells delicious in here," Addie exclaimed, giving a dramatic, exaggerated sniff. "What are you making?"

"Pizza." Brie grinned. "We make the dough and everything. My dad is the best pizza maker. He learned from my grandpa, who died when my dad was a kid. Isn't that sad?"

"My dad died when I was a kid, too. I was only four."

"I'm sorry." Brielle hugged the other girl, which seemed to touch Jenna.

So Addison's father had died. He had wondered if the man was still in the picture somewhere.

He gave Jenna a look of sympathy, which she met with a strained smile.

"Pizza is a great skill," she said. "We brought you dessert, then. Sugar cookies."

Brielle's features lit up. "Wow. Thanks! I love cookies."

"Here you go," Addie said, handing over a plate covered in pastel-frosted flower cutout cookies that looked like spring.

"You didn't have to do that," Wes said.

She had already paid him for the battery, a check in an envelope she had left tucked in the door frame of his apartment. He was more than a little embarrassed that he had noticed the envelope smelled of strawberries and cream, like Jenna.

"It's the least I can do to thank you for all your help with my car yesterday. I know cookies are poor recompense for giving up part of your lunch hour, but I didn't know what else you might enjoy."

"Home-baked cookies are always a treat. I don't get them very often."

"Well, I hope you enjoy them."

"How is the car running?"

"Great. Everything has been perfect."

"I'm glad."

They stood awkwardly for a moment as he fought the urge to brush the pad of his thumb over that slight tinge of pink rising on her cheekbone.

Brielle saved him from doing something so foolish. "Hey, Dad. Can Addie and her mom stay for dinner? You said we had too much pizza to eat ourselves."

The awkward level had now ratcheted up to a ten.

"I'm sure they have other dinner plans," he said quickly.

"We don't," Addie said. "Pizza would be great!"

"We were going to heat up some soup from the freezer, remember?" Jenna said, not meeting Wes's gaze. "We were just saying how soup is just the thing for a stormy night."

As if on cue, lightning arced through the sky, followed by a sharp crack of thunder that made both girls shriek in surprise, then giggle at each other for their shared reaction.

"I like soup, Mom, but I would rather have pizza," Addie said. "It smells soooo good, doesn't it?"

"We really do have more than enough dough and toppings," Wes said. "We were just trying to figure out what we were going to do with it when you knocked on the door. It was perfect timing."

Another bolt of lightning flashed outside and rain began to pelt the window.

It was beyond comforting to be here inside this warm apartment in the big, rambling house by the sea.

"It does smell good," she admitted.

"And tastes even better," he said, not bothering with false modesty. He had very few skills in the kitchen and was justifiably proud of his pizza dough, a recipe his father had perfected over the years before he died.

"All right," she finally said. "If you're sure we won't be imposing on your time with your daughter."

"Not at all," he assured her. "We were just about to put the toppings on, if you want to come and choose what you want."

She followed him to the kitchen of his apartment, which Wes had considered a decent size. He wasn't sure exactly how it seemed to shrink with the addition of another child and a small woman.

"How can I help?" Jenna asked.

How long had it been since he had shared a meal with a woman besides his daughter? He honestly couldn't remember.

"You could throw together the salad, if you don't mind. I've already rinsed the lettuce and it just needs to be tossed."

"I can do that."

She crossed to the sink and washed her hands then went to work ripping leaves from the romaine and green lettuce heads he had purchased earlier that day before picking up Brielle from her mother's.

"What do you like on your pizza?"

"I'm not picky. What do you usually have?"

"Brie is a big fan of plain cheese and pepperoni. I typically go for margherita, with crushed San Marzano tomatoes, fresh mozzarella, basil and a splash of olive oil."

Her eyes had widened during his geek-out about pizza and she gave a surprised laugh. "That sounds really delicious. Addie will probably be happy with the pepperoni as well."

"Perfect. So two margherita and two pepperoni. I can only cook two at a time on my pizza steel so let's do the girls' first. They don't take long."

"Okay."

While he formed another ball of dough into pizza crust for Addie, then enlisted the girls' help to add the sauce, mozzarella and pepperoni, Jenna began slicing cucumbers and tomatoes to add to the salad.

This was nice, he thought as the girls went to work setting the table. He had bought a kitchen-in-a-box set of plates and silverware and serving utensils that supposedly contained everything a person needed to set up a basic kitchen. Now he wished he had sprung for something nicer.

Once the girls' pizzas were in the oven, he went to work with the other two balls of dough, expertly shaping them and adding the toppings. Jenna watched him work, her expression interested.

"You really do know what you're doing."

He gave a rueful smile. "I'm kind of a pizza geek. My dad spent a year working in Italy at a pizza place during a gap year of college and he taught me a few secrets."

"Brie said you were only a child when he died."

He didn't like remembering the pain of that time. "Ten. He moved from making pizza to opening his own restaurant in the little town outside Denver where he grew up. One night after closing, a couple of drifters broke in, thinking the place was empty. They shot my dad and took off with what was left in the cash register after he'd already made the deposit for the night. Thirty bucks in change."

"Oh. I'm so sorry."

The soft sympathy in her voice, in her expression, seemed to seep through him and he wanted to bask in it.

Embarrassed, he quickly changed the subject as he ripped a couple of basil leaves off the plant he bought at the supermarket.

"I can't get enough of smelling fresh basil," he said as he sprinkled the herb atop the two margherita pizzas. "Sometimes I want to just bury my face in it. Amazing, the things you never realize you missed."

Oh wow. He was just full of brilliant conversation. First he dropped his father's long-ago murder into the conversation, then he started gushing about herbs. He wouldn't be surprised if she scooped up her daughter and went rushing back downstairs, away from the weirdo with a basil fetish.

Instead, she was looking at him again with that same soft compassion. "How long were you…in prison?"

"Three years, two months and five days."

He didn't look at her as he turned on the oven light to check the girls' pizzas.

It didn't matter that he had been cleared of any wrongdoing. The damage was done. He would never get that time back and his reputation would never fully recover.

Guilty or not, he had spent more than a thousand days in prison. Had seen things he couldn't unsee. Cruelty between inmates, intimidation and abuse by guards, people treated more like cattle than human beings until they gradually began to lose their humanity altogether.

He was a different person than he'd been the day he had been arrested.

"I'm not sure what should be the appropriate response to that," she admitted after a moment. "*I'm sorry* doesn't feel at all adequate."

He shrugged. "It happened. It's done. I'm still trying to figure out what comes next."

He wasn't sorry to change the subject again. "Looks like these are ready to come out."

He pulled out the two pizzas, happy to see the crust bubbly with air pockets, then slid the other two into the oven.

"These other pizzas will only take a few minutes. Since the girls' pizzas have to cool down first before they can eat them without burning their tongues, why don't we start with the salad and vegetables?"

He had already prepared a relish plate as it was the only way he could persuade his daughter to eat a few vegetables.

The next few moments were busy finding beverages for everyone and taking the girls' pizzas to the table.

Soon, his timer went off to remove the other pizzas from the oven. He was delighted by the surprise and pleasure on Jenna's expression.

"That looks absolutely delicious."

"I hope it tastes even better."

The girls chattered away about school around mouthfuls of pizza, while he and Jenna worked on their salads. Finally, she picked up her first piece of pizza. He felt silly, but couldn't help holding his breath until she took a bite. The sound of delight she made was gratifying.

"Wow," she exclaimed. "That is really delicious. The flavors come together so perfectly. I'm afraid I might never be happy with pizza delivery again."

"That's the problem with making your own pizza. If you do it right, it kind of ruins you for anything else."

He couldn't help staring at her mouth as it lifted into a slight smile. What would it be like to have her give him a full-fledged smile? Even better, a laugh?

He shouldn't be wondering about that, Wes chided himself. He and Jenna Haynes were simply neighbors, though he wanted to think maybe after the past few days, she would no longer watch him out of those nervous eyes, like he was a mountain lion crouched to pounce on her at any moment.

Her life felt so surreal sometimes, the reality often more bizarre than anything her imagination could conjure up.

A few weeks ago, Jenna would never have believed she would find herself having dinner with her intimidating new neighbor and his daughter.

Or that she would enjoy it so much.

The pizza was delicious, probably the best she'd ever had. And though Wes Calhoun seemed to be going out of his way to be friendly, she still sensed a wary reserve in him.

He seemed to measure each word as carefully as he probably did the flour in his father's pizza dough recipe.

Did he ever completely let down his guard? She doubted it.

She was fine with that. She had to be, since she had her own protective barriers firmly in place.

"Thank you," she finally said, after she had eaten every single bite of her personal-sized pizza. "That was truly delicious."

"It was super good," Addison agreed. "Mom, you should take lessons from Brie's dad on how to make pizza."

She raised an eyebrow. "Should I?"

"You make good pizza," her daughter quickly said. "But Mr. Calhoun makes *really* good pizza."

"He truly does."

"I'm happy to teach you all I know. Which should take maybe five minutes. It's all about not skimping on the quality of your ingredients and putting a little advance thought into it."

"I'll keep that in mind. Thank you again for sharing your pizza night with us."

"You're welcome to come back again the next time we make it," Wes said. "Every Friday night is pizza night. We might even have to do it more than once a week. Brielle is going to be with me full-time for the first few weeks after school gets out, and I don't have that many other specialties. I expect we will have the chance to enjoy a lot of pizza."

"My mom is going to Costa Rica," Brie said. "I think she should take me, but she says she can't because I don't have a passport."

"You'll get another chance to go on a trip with your mom and stepdad," Wes assured his daughter. "Meantime, you get to hang out with me and do all kinds of fun things."

"We can definitely plan some times for you two to hang out while you're staying at Brambleberry House with your dad. It will be great for Addie to have someone her age here."

"My friend Logan used to live downstairs on the first floor, but he moved away with his dad *forever* ago."

"I know Logan. He's nice."

"He is," Addie agreed. Suddenly her eyes widened with excitement. "And guess what? As soon as school is out, we're getting a dog! I've been begging and begging for one, and Mom finally said we can go to the shelter next week to find a rescue."

"Lucky!" Brielle exclaimed. "I always wanted a dog. We just have a cat. What kind are you getting?"

Addie shrugged. "I don't know. We haven't picked it yet. Whichever one needs a home most, I guess."

Jenna did her best to ignore the misgivings she still felt about taking on a pet. She knew full well how much responsibility it would be, adding a dog to their family. But now that she knew for certain they wouldn't have to pack up and disappear again, as she had feared for so long that they would have to do when Aaron Barker was released from prison, she could no longer think of any more excuses.

Addie had been through so much in her short life. Losing her dad. Having to uproot her life and escape here to Cannon Beach. Living for more than two years with a jumpy, scared-of-her-own-shadow mother.

Agreeing to her daughter's relentless pleas to add a dog into their lives felt like the least Jenna could do for her.

"You're so lucky!" Brielle exclaimed. "Can I play with him or her?"

"Anytime you want," Addie said. "You could even help me take him for a walk, if you want. Dogs need a lot of exercise. That's what my mom says."

"Your mom is right," Wes said. "The happiest, healthiest dogs get exercise at least a few times a day."

He sounded like an expert. She really hoped so, since she had no idea what she was doing. Maybe he could give her advice.

While the girls chattered more about what kind of dog was best, Jenna turned again to Wes.

"Thank you again for the pizza, though I just realized that I owe you even more now."

"How's that?"

"First you kindly go out of your way to change my car battery, then you make us the best pizza ever. All I've done in return is bake you a batch of cookies."

"They were delicious cookies, though. I'm sure between Brie and me, they will be gone by morning."

"Cookies hardly compare. You make it tough for a woman to clear her debt to you."

He gazed down at her, something in his expression suddenly that made her cheeks feel hot.

He blinked it away and returned to a polite smile. "You don't owe me anything in return. Cookies are more than enough."

She did not necessarily agree, but couldn't immediately

think of anything she could do to repay him for his kindness. She would have to give it some thought.

"Come on, Addie. It's almost bedtime."

Her daughter predictably groaned but headed for the stairs. "See you later," she called to Brielle.

"Good night." Jenna gave one last smile as she followed her daughter down the stairs.

On the positive side, she suddenly realized, the evening together had gone a long way toward reducing her fear of Wes. It was tough to be nervous around a man who obviously adored his daughter and who found such simple pleasure in the smell of fresh basil.

Chapter Four

"This is the one, Mom. He's perfect. We have to get him."

Jenna looked at the floppy tan puppy in her daughter's lap, all paws and ears and big, soulful eyes. She was watching firsthand the process of two creatures falling in love. The dog couldn't seem to keep his eyes off Addie and her daughter was clearly already long gone.

"He's the cutest dog ever. The very best dog. Please, Mom!"

She had envisioned them leaving the shelter with a small older dog. A Chihuahua or a little Yorkie, some kind of petite, well-trained lapdog who didn't bark or chew or make messes all over the floor.

"He was one of a litter of six mini goldendoodles that were found abandoned down near Manzanita."

The shelter volunteer helping them, a woman in her forties with a name tag that read Pam, gave the dog an affectionate pat. "We've adopted out all but him. You could call Theo here the last man standing, I guess."

"Hi, buddy. Hi."

The clever dog licked Addison's cheek, completely sealing the deal, as if he knew exactly which of them really held the power in this situation.

Jenna was suddenly quite certain there was no possible way on earth she would be able to get out of here now without taking along this dog, who literally met none of the qualities on her own personal wish list.

Her daughter clearly loved him. That was the most important thing, she reminded herself. Jenna would simply just have to figure out how to readjust her own expectations.

"How old is he?" she asked Pam.

"We can't say for sure," the shelter worker said. "The vet thinks maybe three to four months? They were weaned puppies when they were found and he's been here a month. That's just an estimate, though."

"Why would anybody abandon a litter of puppies?" Addie looked horrified, her arms tightening around the dog as if to protect him.

Because people can be selfish and cruel sometimes.

She didn't want her daughter to learn that lesson yet, so Jenna only shook her head sadly. "Who knows?"

"I wish I understood it," Pam said. "I can't comprehend how anyone could think a litter of puppies would be better off there, in the middle of a forest, than here at our shelter. It makes no sense to me."

"Me neither." Addie hugged Theo, her cheek pressed against the dog's fur. "Nobody's going to leave you anywhere now, Theo. I promise. You're coming home with us. You'll love our house. We even have a ghost!"

Pam looked startled. "A ghost?"

Jenna gave a rueful smile. "We live in an old beach house. Brambleberry House? You might know it."

"Oh yes. That wonderful place on the edge of town."

She nodded. "Some of the previous residents are convinced we have a benevolent spirit who watches over all those who live in the apartments."

She still wasn't convinced and found it amusing that her friends Rosa and Melissa spoke about Abigail as if she were an old friend, though she had died more than a decade before either woman had lived in the house.

"A ghost!" Pam looked enthralled. "Oh, that's lovely. How about that, Theo? Want to live in a house with a ghost?"

The dog's tongue lolled out and he actually looked enthusiastic, but that could have been more evidence of his growing adoration for the girl holding him.

"Is he trained at all?" Jenna hated to ask but needed to know what challenges she might be facing.

"He's getting there. He's not a hundred percent but he is very smart, and it shouldn't take him long to learn how to follow some basic commands, as soon as he adjusts to the routine of your house."

"I can't wait!" Addie's eyes glowed. "I'm going to teach him to sit, to roll over, to shake hands and to catch a ball in the air like my friend Logan's dog can do."

"Those all sound great but first things first," Jenna said. "We need to start with teaching him not to go to the bathroom inside the house. After that, we can work on the other commands."

"We can provide you with some great websites and other resources that give good training advice," Pam said. "We can also connect you with a few places locally that offer puppy training classes."

"That would be very helpful," Jenna said, again trying to push down her misgivings. She could handle this. She certainly had done harder things in her life than train a puppy.

"So have you decided for sure?" Pam asked.

Jenna gestured to her daughter and the dog. "I think these two have decided for me."

"Oh great. And since you've already been approved for adoption, you can take him home with you today, if you'd like. We do have a few forms for you to fill out. Addison, would you bring Theo with you to my office?"

"Yes!" she exclaimed. Pam provided a leash from a hook on the wall and Addie attached it to the dog's collar, then proudly walked with him down the hall to a small office decorated with pictures of dogs and cats and their happy new humans.

A half hour and several signatures later, they walked out of the shelter with their new family member padding happily beside them.

All her misgivings came flooding back as she loaded Addie and Theo into the car. What had she done? She went through days when she felt as if she could barely take care of herself and her child. Adding another living creature to her responsibilities suddenly felt overwhelming.

"Can I go show Mr. and Mrs. Anderson downstairs? Theo also has to meet Sophie. Do you think they'll be friends?"

The retired couple who lived in the first-floor apartment of Brambleberry House had a very cute—and very spoiled—toy poodle.

"I'm sure they will be great friends." She hoped, anyway. "The Andersons left this week for their trip, remember? They left Sophie with their friend in Portland."

"Oh right."

"We're going to have to pick up some supplies before we can take Theo home. Toys and food and a crate."

She probably should have purchased all that in advance before taking home the dog, but she had been so busy wrapping up end-of-year school details, she hadn't thought that far ahead.

"Can we take him into the store?" Addie asked. "I don't want to leave him alone in the car."

"No," she agreed. "We shouldn't do that. I know they let dogs into the pet store. We'll go there."

They parked at the pet store and headed inside, after stopping long enough for Theo to raise his leg on a fire hydrant conveniently placed near the door.

It didn't take long to fill a shopping cart for the puppy. At this rate Theo would be as spoiled as Sophie, she thought.

They had nearly finished finding everything on the quick list they had made before coming inside when Addie suddenly exclaimed with delight. "Mr. Calhoun! Hi, Mr. Calhoun!"

Jenna whirled around and found her upstairs neighbor walking through the pet store with a bag of cat food.

"Oh. Hi."

She hadn't seen Wes since pizza night, nearly a week earlier, except for a few brief waves of greeting in passing. She had somehow forgotten how big and tough and intimidating he looked.

And gorgeous.

She hadn't forgotten that part.

She could feel her face heat and hoped he didn't notice.

"Wow." He looked down at the gangly dog. "Looks like you've got a new friend."

"This is Theo. He's the best dog ever. And he's our very own dog now! He gets to come home with us."

"That's very cool. Hi, Theo. Nice to meet you." Wes crouched to the same level of the dog and reached out a hand, which Theo investigated with a sniff followed by vigorous tail wagging.

"I think he likes you," Addie said, beaming.

"Hey, bud." He scratched the dog's ears and under his chin, which seemed to earn him Theo's instant adoration.

"I didn't know you had a cat," Jenna said, gesturing to the food bag.

"I don't." He straightened. "But we've got a couple of strays that hang out at the shop. They're good mousers but I still like to leave a little food for them. Plus I guess I'll be cat-sitting for a couple weeks as Brie is bringing along Murphy when she comes to stay with me."

"That's nice of you."

He shrugged. "If I have to take a bad-tempered elderly cat

as part of the package in order to hang out with my daughter, it's worth the sacrifice."

He looked back at the dog. "You say his name is Leo?"

"Theo," Addison corrected. "The nice lady at the shelter said his real name is Theodore because he looks like a teddy bear but they didn't want to call him Teddy so they call him Theo."

"Nice name."

"I hope he doesn't bother everyone at Brambleberry House," Jenna said. "The shelter said he's not one to bark a lot."

"He'll be great, I'm sure. I'm not worried. I hardly ever hear the neighbors' little poodle."

She decided not to point out that Sophie lived two floors below him and had been gone for a week, where Theo would be just downstairs one flight all the time.

"Fingers crossed," she said.

He glanced into their cart. "Looks like you have everything you need to take the dog home."

"And then some, right? I'm afraid we've gone overboard."

"You can never have too many tennis balls when it comes to dogs. I can help you load your supplies into your car after you check out."

She was a tough, independent woman who had been forced by circumstance to learn how to stand on her own two feet. Still, it was nice to have the option to lean on someone once in a while.

"That would be really helpful. Thank you."

As he only had one item, he checked out first, then waited while she did the same. The final tally made her gulp. Having a pet was not a cheap undertaking.

When her items were bagged and she had paid for them, all three of them walked outside.

"When is Brielle coming to stay with you?"

"Tomorrow night."

"How exciting. I bet it's going to be wonderful to have her there."

"Sure. It should be great."

She thought she picked up a note of hesitation in his voice, but she didn't have a chance to ask him about it before they reached her SUV.

She popped the cargo gate and he helped her load all their supplies into the back, including the heavy bag of puppy food.

"Thank you. I really appreciate your help."

"My pleasure."

He gave a smile, or as close to one as he seemed to offer. It wasn't really much of a smile, mostly just a small lifting of his mouth, but it still made her toes tingle.

"I guess we will see you."

"Yes. Leave the dog food by your car and I can carry it upstairs for you."

She could manage, but it seemed ungracious to refuse. "Thank you. I appreciate that."

"See you later, Addison. Bye, Theo."

Addie waved and Theo wagged his tail with delight.

After she made sure Addie had her seat belt on, Jenna drove away, wondering how on earth she had shifted from fear to this wary fascination in such a short time.

Wes had never smoked but some nights, he really longed for a cigarette.

He knew there were guys in prison who had picked up smoking there as a way to relax and beat the boredom. He had preferred other methods. Working out, reading. Studying.

He had taken Spanish lessons in prison as well as a couple of community college history and rudimentary law classes. He also volunteered for a couple of service programs.

Anything he could do not to sit in his cell and feel sorry for himself and angry at the world.

Now he had the freedom to do whatever he wanted, whenever he wanted. Maybe that was why he felt so…restless. He still didn't quite know what to do with that freedom.

He thought the hour run he had taken earlier might ease this edgy discontent. It hadn't, nor had the long, pulsing, delicious shower after.

He ached for something but wasn't sure what.

After changing channels a dozen times, picking up his book, then putting it back down, scrolling on his phone through news stories he didn't really care about, he decided to take a ride on his bike down the coast. Maybe a little sea air on his face would calm him.

He walked down the two floors of Brambleberry House, sensing, as he sometimes did, the faint, barely perceptible smell of flowers on the stairs.

Rosa Galvez Townsend, who had rented him the apartment, had told him there were rumors that a benevolent spirit walked the halls of the house, the ghost of a longtime owner of the house, Abigail Dandridge.

She had died with no direct heirs and had left the house to two friends and tenants of hers.

She apparently had loved the house so much she had not wanted to leave.

He remembered staring in disbelief at the woman, who had given him an embarrassed sort of laugh. "You do not have to believe it. Most people don't. But I felt like it was only fair to warn you about the rumors before you move in."

A hint of flowers on the stairs was not exactly a convincing argument. Even if there had been a real ghost, how could he pass up a beautiful apartment in a rambling old house on the seashore? He had no problem putting up with the random scent of flowers and the occasional waft of cold air that seemed to come out of nowhere.

As he walked outside, the night smelled of lilacs and lavender, with a salty tang from the Pacific fifty yards away.

And he was not alone in the Brambleberry House gardens, he realized. Jenna stood in the grass, holding the leash of her gangly new puppy.

She spotted him coming onto the porch and waved.

"Hello. Don't mind us. This is about our tenth trip outside this evening. We're working on potty training. I'm not quite sure Theo understands the concept completely yet, so I imagine we'll be coming out frequently to reinforce. So much for my relaxing summer vacation, right?"

She smiled, a white flash in the moonlight, and his entire body seemed to tighten.

"He'll figure it out," he said. "Consistency is the key to training puppies."

She moved closer, and he could smell the scent of her, an intoxicating mix of strawberries and vanilla and sunshine.

"You sound like you have some experience in that area. Have you trained many dogs?"

For a brief moment, he debated how much to tell her and finally decided there was no good reason to withhold the information.

"I was part of a canine training initiative in prison. We did the initial basic training with puppies that might eventually become service dogs. I was lucky enough to have three great puppies during my time. All of them eventually graduated and are working as trained service animals now."

"That sounds like a wonderful program."

The dogs had truly been lifesavers to him, bringing peace and comfort and purpose during those dark years.

"It was a good fit. You have a bunch of people with nothing but time on their hands. That's what dogs need most, especially in the beginning."

He missed those puppies. He had given his heart to each

of the three dogs he had worked with in prison and had been gutted when it was time to pass them on for the next phase of their training.

Now that he was on the outside, Wes had been thinking about getting a dog of his own, though he wasn't sure he was ready to start over with another pet.

He supposed some part of him still worried things might change in a heartbeat, that something could happen to throw his life back into chaos. He didn't know what that might be, but didn't want to take any chances that he might not be ready for that kind of complication and commitment.

That was the main reason he was working as a mechanic at the Gutierrez brothers' shop. He was good at it, for one thing, but he also needed something fairly straightforward to do right now while he tried to figure out the rest of his life.

Before his arrest, he had been running a highly successful security company in Chicago with thirty employees and multimillion-dollar contracts.

All of that had disappeared in a blink. The company. His life savings. And most of his trust in humanity, Wes had to admit.

He wasn't sure he had the bandwidth right now to start over and rebuild everything from scratch.

He knew he had to start somewhere, but he had no idea where the hell that somewhere might be.

He wasn't about to spill his angst all over Jenna Haynes. If she knew the tangled morass of his brain, she would probably be more afraid of him than she had been when he first moved in.

She didn't seem as afraid of him now.

He found that awareness both exhilarating and vaguely terrifying.

Some part of him wanted to warn her she had every right to be afraid. Around her, he felt like the proverbial Big Bad Wolf.

He wanted to swallow up a sweet thing like Jenna Haynes in one delicious bite.

"I could use any pointers you have with Theo here," she said before he could tell her any of those things. "This is my first time training a dog. My first time being responsible for any pet, actually."

He raised an eyebrow. "You didn't have a dog growing up?"

"No. Believe me, I wanted a dog desperately but it never quite worked out."

"Why not?"

"I grew up with a single mom, with no dad in the picture," she said after a slight hesitation. "I don't even have a name, since he took off before I was born and my mom didn't like to talk about it. Mom always worked two jobs to support us, and she didn't think it would be fair to have a pet when we weren't home very often to take care of him. Also, money was invariably tight so she could never quite justify the cost of pet food or vet bills when she was working so hard just to take care of us."

"Is that one of the reasons you gave in to Addie's pleas, even though you're nervous about taking on a dog? Because, like most parents, you want to give her what you always wanted but never had?"

Her gaze sharpened at his insight. "Yes. That's exactly why. Good guess, Dr. Calhoun. I must say, I feel a little called out right now."

He gave a short laugh. "I'm not all that brilliant. I only understand it because I'm the same way. I told you my dad died when I was ten. I missed him fiercely when I was a teenager, so I'm determined to be as present as possible in Brie's life. To the point of being obnoxious about it."

Wes paused, then added, "What about after you married? Why didn't you get a dog then?"

"Multiple reasons, I suppose. We wanted one but our first apartment didn't allow pets. We moved into our first home after we had been married two years, but I was pregnant at the time and we decided to wait a bit until adding a pet into the mix, on top of first-time home ownership and new parenthood."

"Sounds sensible."

"Sometimes I wish we hadn't been so sensible. I only had six years with Ryan. We should have done all the crazy things we dreamed about. Flown to Paris. Quit our jobs and lived on the beach in Mexico for a time. Gotten a puppy. Or a half dozen puppies."

Life's cruelties never ceased to infuriate him. A sweet woman like Jenna deserved to have a long and happy life with the man she loved. "How did your husband die?"

"Cancer. Melanoma. He was only thirty."

"That's tough."

"Yes. Addie was barely three when he was diagnosed. He died a year later. It was a very painful time."

"I'm sorry," he said, the words feeling painfully inadequate.

"Thank you. But I've learned since Ryan died that everybody has something, you know? I don't have the monopoly on pain."

He knew so many people who could take a lesson from her, who considered themselves permanent victims of whatever hardship that came their way and refused to accept that someone else might be struggling, too.

"What about you?" she asked, obviously eager to change the subject. "Did you have dogs when you were growing up?"

He nodded. "When I was young, we lived on the small hobby farm where my dad grew up and there were always dogs around. We didn't really have house pets but we always had horses and dogs and chickens."

"Oh, that sounds lovely."

"It was a pretty good childhood, for the most part. Then my dad died and my mom couldn't keep up with things. She sold the restaurant and the farm and we moved to the Chicago area to be closer to her family."

How differently might his life have turned out if his father had not died? Wes probably would have stayed in the Denver area. He might even still be there.

Instead, they had moved to Chicago, where he had struggled in school and became friends with people who hadn't always had his best interests at heart.

Wes had been involved in a few scrapes during his teen years and had even served a brief stint in youth corrections.

He might have continued on that path, except he had one teacher who had given him the straight truth about the dead-end direction he was headed. For some reason, Wes had listened.

He had determined to change his life. He had enlisted in the Army, where he had worked first as a mechanic and then as a military police officer. He had met and married Lacey while he was still in the service and taken her first to Germany and then to Japan.

Even before he got out, he and a buddy had decided to start a security business. Hard work and determination had turned their fledgling enterprise into a success beyond his wildest dreams.

And then everything had changed.

"Were you going somewhere?" Jenna asked.

It took him a moment to realize she was referring to his leathers and helmet. He suddenly didn't feel like taking a ride anymore. He wanted to stay here with her in this moonlit garden and enjoy the sound of the waves and the scent of a lovely woman beside him.

That was a dangerous road. He would be much better off climbing on his bike and riding off into the night.

"I was going to take a ride. Nowhere special. I do that

sometimes. It's cliché, I know, but I like to feel the wind on my face."

"I've seen you leave at odd hours and wondered where you go."

He wasn't sure how he felt to know she had watched him from her window as he sped off into the night, trying to outrace demons that always seemed to be racing right behind him.

"How long ago did you lose your husband?"

"It's been four years now. I can hardly believe it's been that long. It feels like only yesterday. Addie has spent half her life without her father. She hardly remembers him, which I find so sad. Ryan was a wonderful father and adored her from the moment she was born."

"She won't completely forget. Ryan is part of her, just as she is part of him."

"You're right. I see him sometimes in the way she loves to read every sign we pass on the road or tilts her head when she's studying something she doesn't quite understand."

"He lives on in her."

"Yes."

She was pensive for a moment, then smiled. "I'm sorry I kept you from your ride. Thanks for the encouragement with Theo. Don't be surprised if I become annoying and bring you all my many questions."

"You shouldn't expect veterinarian-level answers," he warned. "I spent a year training puppies. That's the extent of my knowledge."

"That gives you a year more experience than I have."

Her smile flashed in the moonlight, and he had to curl his hands around his helmet to keep from crossing the space between them and reaching for her.

"I'm happy to help with whatever I can do."

"Thank you. Good night. Enjoy your ride. And I apologize

in advance if Theo and I make too much noise going in and out at all hours."

"Don't worry about that. I can't hear anything up on the third floor except the wind."

"Are you sure you're not hearing Abigail? If you smell freesia, that's supposed to be her."

He raised an eyebrow. "Do you really buy into all the ghost stuff?"

She shrugged with a rueful smile. "Originally I was skeptical when we moved into Brambleberry House. Since then, I don't know. I'm less skeptical, I guess. I hope that doesn't make me sound too out-there. I don't usually believe in that sort of thing, but for some reason living in Brambleberry House leaves you open to all kinds of ideas you might once have thought were unlikely, bordering on ridiculous."

"I'm surprised there wasn't a ghost clause in my rental agreement."

"Did you read all the fine print? There might have been. I don't know. It's been more than two years since I signed my agreement, and to be honest with you, when I moved in, I didn't care if there were a *dozen* ghosts living here. Addie and I just needed a safe place, which we certainly found here in Cannon Beach."

He frowned. A safe place? Why? What had threatened them? Her words did certainly explain her general air of unease, especially around him.

Was she still running? Somehow, he didn't think so.

Even in the short time he had known her, she seemed calmer than she had in the beginning, when he first moved into the apartment. Maybe that was only because she had come to know him a little.

He wanted to press her, but she certainly looked as if she regretted saying anything at all.

"I hadn't realized how late it is," she said quickly, confirming his suspicion. "I should go back in with Addie. Thank you again."

"You're welcome. Good night."

He gave the dog one last pat. "Good night, Theo. Be good."

"Considering he's already chewed up one of my flip-flops and a pair of Addie's socks, I think we're past that."

"He'll outgrow the chewing. Get him a couple of nonrawhide bones he can chomp on. Or you can freeze some wet puppy food in one of those sturdy chew toys you bought at the pet store and give him that. When he's outside, of course, where he can keep the mess in the grass."

"I'll keep that in mind. Thanks. Come on, Theo."

With that, she hurried back inside the house, leaving the scent of her, strawberries and cream, floating on the breeze. Along with lilacs and...was that the smell of freesia? He wasn't sure he even knew what that was and didn't know how to find out. Maybe he would have to make a trip to the garden center to see if they had any of the flowers so he could do a scent test.

The concept made him roll his eyes at himself. Was he really buying the idea that the house might be haunted?

It didn't matter. He was staying put, no matter how many ghosts the house might hold.

Jenna hurried up the steps to her apartment and closed the door behind her. Theo plopped down immediately, as if their trek out to the garden had completely sapped him of all energy.

She could only hope.

"You had better sleep all night now," she said sternly. "I don't feel like going out there at 2:00 a.m."

The puppy yawned, stretched and closed his eyes, right at her feet.

"Nope." She scooped him up. "You need to sleep in your crate."

She set him in the large crate the shelter had suggested. Theo seemed completely comfortable in the space. He immediately curled up on the soft blankets she had folded into the corner.

She could only hope she would sleep as well, but something told her she might be up for a while, remembering that conversation with Wes.

Had she really blurted out that she believed in ghosts?

The encounter played back through her mind, and she suddenly realized something that had been haunting the edges of her subconscious since he moved in.

Wes Calhoun was lonely.

She did not know why she had that impression, but she was suddenly convinced of it. He had come out of the house with a glower she wasn't even sure he was aware of. Nor did she think he realized how that glower had lifted when he spotted her and Theo.

Poor man. He had moved to Cannon Beach to be closer to his daughter and likely knew few people except those he worked with and his ex-wife and her new husband.

She understood where he was coming from. She had certainly felt alone when she first moved to town, though she had had Rosa, her dear friend from college.

Rosa had convinced her to come here in an effort to escape the numbing terror she had lived with for months because of Aaron Barker.

She thought she had fled far enough away so that she and Addie would be safe here in Cannon Beach. Aaron had no idea one of her dearest friends lived here. She knew she hadn't mentioned Rosa during any of their three dates, before she broke things off when his obsessive control began to manifest itself.

She had been wrong about being safe here in Oregon.

By a cruel twist of fate, an accident, really, he had discovered where she had fled and had followed her here, with horrifying consequences.

She pushed the darkness away. She could not let him intrude further in her life. She had already given him far more than he deserved. He was gone now. She was safe, at least physically.

She had attended counseling after Aaron had ultimately been arrested. She had worked through much of her trauma from the long months of relentless anxiety. She had come far, especially if she could chat with a big, dangerous man in a moonlit garden beside the sea.

She hadn't been completely comfortable, but she suspected that might have to do with her growing awareness of him as more than simply her neighbor.

The man seemed in dire need of a friend, someone he could turn to when the nights seemed long and empty.

She wasn't sure she could be that person, nor could she completely understand why she suddenly wanted to try.

Chapter Five

Why, oh why, did she always end up having to carry her groceries into the apartment during a fierce downpour?

Was she a victim of poor planning or merely fickle weather?

When she had set off for the grocery store that Saturday morning after dropping Addie off at a birthday party, the sun had been shining and the birds had been singing. Yes, she knew a storm lurked on the horizon. She couldn't miss those dark clouds gathering offshore. But she hadn't expected it to hit so quickly or with such ferocious fury.

Now she sat in her car in the driveway of Brambleberry House, waiting for the weather to cooperate and the rain to slow at least enough that she could carry a few bags inside without becoming completely drenched.

She also had to let out Theo, whom she had left in his crate inside her apartment.

She had just about decided to run for it anyway when a sudden knock on her window startled her. She gasped at the unexpected sound and momentary fear pulsed through her as she saw the large, hulking shape of a man standing outside the door.

He shouted something she couldn't quite hear over the noise of the storm. Lightning flashed nearby, followed almost immediately by thunder. So close!

The instant she recognized Wes standing outside her car with a large umbrella, her instinctive panic eased.

She opened her door just a crack. Even in the small space, rain poured in.

"Do you need help? I saw you pull in from upstairs. When you didn't go into the house, I was worried something might be wrong."

"Yes, something's wrong. We're in the middle of a hurricane, in case you didn't notice."

He chuckled, a deep, pleasing sound that drifted to her even over the tumult of the storm.

"This is not a storm. I've been in actual hurricanes when I was in the Army stationed in Florida. This is only a little squall."

"It's still enough to soak my groceries. I don't feel like eating soggy bread for a week. I was waiting for it to let up a little."

"Makes sense. You could do that, if you want to. Or I brought you out an extra umbrella. You can run up to the porch with it and I'll grab your groceries."

"Thank you. I usually keep a few in my car, but Addie and I both used one last time we had a big rain and I think I left them inside the apartment."

"Open the back of your car and head inside. I'll grab as many groceries as I can."

"I can grab a few bags, too."

Why had she picked today to do the big grocery shopping, her monthly trip when she stocked up on the necessities they used most?

Oh yes. She remembered. Because as much as she adored her daughter, shopping with Addie usually took twice as long. Her daughter liked to look at every book on the racks, every possible cookie at the bakery and each little item in the tempting little toy section.

She scooped as many bags as she could carry in one hand while juggling the umbrella in the other and hurried up to the porch, where she quickly entered the security code on the front door.

Wes was close behind her. He didn't bother with the umbrella, she noted. He simply sprinted inside so the reusable shopping bags filled with groceries didn't have much time at all to become drenched.

"Is that everything? I can go back out."

He held up both hands, where she saw he had at least three shopping bags in each. "This is everything. One question. Are you planning for the apocalypse?"

She shook her head. "I'm on a teacher's salary and only get paid once a month. When I grocery shop, I try to buy in bulk and freeze food to make it last."

She supposed she hadn't ever really lost the fear that she would never have enough to provide for her daughter, which she knew was a lingering worry from her insecure childhood.

"Thank you for bringing it in and helping me keep everything dry. I can take it up the stairs from here."

He gave her a look that showed he clearly took offense at her suggestion. "I've got it. I haven't had a chance to go on my run today, since I had to take Brielle shopping for a friend's birthday present, so I'll count this as my workout for the day."

He hefted the bags high, which made her smile. The gloomy day suddenly felt much brighter. "Brielle must be at Carly Lewis's birthday party, too."

"Apparently it's the social event of the weekend."

"Of the whole month, according to Addie. She was thrilled to be invited to an older girl's party."

"I can imagine." He made it up the stairs without a sign that carrying the heavy bags was any exertion at all.

"So Brielle's mom has left the country?" she asked as she opened her apartment door for him.

"Yep. I'm flying solo. It's a little daunting to know I'm alone right now in the parent department. Lacey is now two thousand miles away. If I had a problem, I know I could always reach out to her, but it's more than a little intimidating to realize I'm on my own."

"You'll be fine."

"I hope so. The prospect of two weeks of being on my own with Brie gives me even more respect for single parents like you, who do this alone all the time."

She smiled as she started putting groceries away. "I'm lucky. Addie is easy."

"So far. The girls haven't hit their teens yet."

She groaned, not wanting to think about how fast her child seemed to be growing up.

From his crate, Theo whined to be let out. She winced. She was a terrible dog mom. She should have done that first thing. "Oh shoot. I'd better take him outside. He's been in his crate for an hour while I went shopping."

"Why don't I take care of that and you can keep putting away your vast quantities of vegetables?"

"That would be great, actually."

"I'll take him out to the fenced area of the garden. That way we won't need the leash, especially since I don't expect he'll be that crazy about hanging out in the rain, either."

"We call that the dog yard, since that's where the Andersons put their little Sophie."

The entire Brambleberry House property had a wrought-iron fence surrounding it, but it was open in front for the driveway. The completely fenced area adjacent to the house was the perfect size for Theo.

She had just finished finding room in her refrigerator for the rotisserie chicken she planned to shred and use in multiple recipes when she heard a sharp rap on her apartment door.

She hurried to open it for Wes and Theo, both of them drenched.

"Oh my! What happened to the umbrella?"

"It broke in the wind ten seconds after I walked outside."

"You're soaked. Let me find you a towel."

She grabbed two—one for Wes and one for Theo.

"Thanks," he said as Jenna picked up her dripping dog and began rubbing him briskly with the towel, trying not to notice how Wes's blue T-shirt clung to every hard muscle of his chest.

He dried off his hair, not seeming to care that the towel left the ends tousled and sticking up in random directions.

He looked as if he had just climbed out of the shower.

Her shower.

She swallowed and turned her attention back to the dog. She did *not* want to go there, even in her imagination.

"You seem to know what you're doing in the kitchen."

"You mean because I bought a little of everything at the grocery store?"

"Yes. Plus I think you have some things there I've never even heard of."

"I like to cook. I don't have a lot of time during the school year so summer gives me a good chance to experiment and try some new recipes."

"I should do that. I'm sure Brielle will quickly get tired of eating pizza or going down to the taco truck on the beach."

"Who could ever get tired of that? We love pizza and tacos."

His mouth lifted into a slight smile that made her suddenly aware that they were alone here in her apartment, without either of their girls.

And she was suddenly aware that he was an extremely attractive man.

"We should grab tacos together sometime while I have Brielle with me full-time."

She swallowed, her mind racing. Was he asking her out? Panic raced through her. She wasn't ready. Not to date again, to allow herself to be vulnerable again. She wasn't sure she would ever be ready.

Just before she would have made some excuse, common sense reasserted itself. He was not asking her out on a date. He was suggesting that, as two single parents, they share a meal together with their children.

She swallowed. "That would be good."

"How about midweek? That's when I get really tired of coming up with something to cook."

"We could probably make that work."

"Great. I'll be in touch."

She remembered suddenly the loneliness she had sensed in the garden, when they had talked in the moonlight.

Wes had been incredibly helpful to her on several occasions. The least she could do was repay the favor, even if it meant stepping outside her comfort zone.

She hesitated, then plunged forward. "I could also show you how I make a few of my basic recipes. I'm far from an expert but I do have a few specialties and I'm always happy to share. It would be the least I can do, after everything you've done to help me the past few weeks."

"You don't owe me anything. But I'm sure Brielle and I would both appreciate a few new recipes to add to the mix."

"We're having lasagna tonight," she said, then went on before she could change her mind. "I have a good recipe for an easy roll-up lasagna that's delicious and Addie never even notices the spinach I slip in. You and Brielle are welcome to join us, if you don't have plans. Consider it my way of paying you back for pizza the other night and also for sacrificing your comfort for my groceries. We could say around seven."

If he was surprised at her invitation, he hid it well. "That would be great. Thank you. I was trying to figure out what to fix for dinner."

"That's one of the hardest things about being a parent. I hate the idea of having to make that decision every single day for the rest of my life until Addie goes to college."

"I hear that."

"On the other hand, I try to remember to be grateful that I'm not like my mother and I've never had to worry that my child will go hungry."

"That's a good way of looking at things."

He gazed down at her, that half smile playing around his mouth. She shivered at the intense light in his eyes and had to hope he didn't notice.

The moment seemed to stretch out between them, soft and seductive.

What would she do if he kissed her right now? Would she be afraid and pull away? Or would she sink into his arms, surrender to the heat simmering between them?

She didn't have the chance to find out. He didn't kiss her. Instead, he broke the connection between them, a small muscle flaring in his jaw.

"I should go change into dry clothes so I can pick up Brielle."

She glanced at the clock on the mantel, an odd combination of relief and disappointment coursing through her.

"Oh, you're right. I can't believe it's that late. There's no reason for both of us to go. I can pick up the girls, if you want."

He nodded, a little tersely. "Okay. That works. I guess we'll see you at seven, then."

She wasn't quite sure what happened next. She only intended to walk him to the door. One moment they were moving together in that direction and then suddenly Jen thought she caught the vague scent of freesias swirling in the air. At the same time the puppy moved across her path. She caught herself just in time from tripping over him but the awkward movement left her unbalanced.

She was going to trip anyway, she realized in a split second. She reached out instinctively, blindly, to brace herself, and her hand encountered damp cotton covering warm, solid muscle.

"Whoa," he exclaimed. "Careful."

His arms came around her and held her upright. She stared up at him, this man whose intimidating looks concealed emotions she suspected ran deep.

All of him was hard, dangerous, except his mouth. That was soft, mobile. Enticing.

She stared at his mouth, just inches from her own.

She wasn't afraid of him kissing her. She *wanted* him to.

The realization left her more off-balance than stumbling over a puppy.

She wanted to wrap her arms around him and taste and explore that mouth that often looked so stern.

She held her breath, waiting, aching. For a long moment, they gazed at each other, the only sound in her apartment their combined breathing.

Before she could do something foolish like reach up and instigate the kiss, take what she suddenly wanted, Jenna came to her senses.

No. She couldn't do that. She was not in the market for a relationship, and she was certainly not in the market for a relationship with a hard, dangerous man like Wes Calhoun.

She quickly stepped away, pulling her hands together so that he did not see them trembling. "Thank you. I'm not quite sure what happened there. Maybe there is something slippery on the floor."

If she didn't know better, she would almost think Theo had tried to trip her on purpose. She could not say that, of course. It sounded ridiculous. Anyway, why would her sweet puppy do such a thing?

That muscle flexed in his jaw again. "I'm glad you didn't fall," he said.

"So am I. Thanks for catching me. I really don't need any broken bones to start out the summer."

"Watch out for wandering puppies."

"I'll do that. I'll let Carly's mom know I'm taking Brielle home, but she might want to text you to make sure it's okay."

"Sounds good. Thanks. I guess I'll see you tonight, then."

Anticipation curled through her, sharply sweet. "Yes. See you then."

By then, she would try to have a much better hold on this burgeoning attraction to a man she knew she shouldn't want.

He had to stop doing this.

Wes hurried up the steps toward his apartment, for the first time feeling the chill of his damp clothing.

He was a glutton for punishment. Jenna Haynes was not the woman for him. He knew that. She was sweet, warm, nurturing. Innocent.

They couldn't have been more different. He possessed exactly none of those qualities.

That didn't stop him from wanting her anyway.

Some part of him had responded instinctively when she stumbled. He had reached for her and had wanted to pull her tightly against him and keep her safe from any harm.

He had almost kissed her. The urge had almost overwhelmed him.

Fortunately, he came to his senses in time, seconds before he would have pressed his mouth to hers.

Kissing her, unleashing his hunger, would have changed everything.

They were forging a fragile friendship, one he was beginning to cherish. He liked talking with her. She was smart, funny, kind.

While he might yearn for much more than a friendship, he knew it was impossible between them. He had to get over it.

She seemed to have lost her outright fear of him, but that didn't make her less wary. She jumped if he accidentally touched her and she still watched him as if not sure how he would react to any given situation.

Why was she so nervous? Okay, yes, he looked tough. He could see himself in the mirror every morning when he shaved. He knew he appeared intimidating and fierce. He had put on muscle in prison, not really as protection or defense but mainly as a distraction.

He might have hoped Jenna would know him enough by now to understand he would not hurt her—or any woman, for that matter.

Maybe her unease didn't have anything to do with him.

If she had not spoken of her husband in such affectionate terms, he might have thought she had been a victim of domestic abuse. That could still be the case, though somehow he doubted it.

Her secrets were her own, he reminded himself. Everyone had them and if Jenna was not interested in sharing hers, he could not fault her for that.

She seemed willing to be friends. She had invited him and Brielle to dinner, after all, and had agreed to take their girls out for tacos some other time during the week.

Could Wes put away his growing attraction for her and be content with only a friendship?

What choice did he have?

He liked being with her. Maybe in time she would trust him enough and would begin to relax a little more in his presence.

He had very few friends here in Cannon Beach. He didn't want to lose this one, even if that meant shoving down his growing attraction for her.

Chapter Six

Later that evening, Wes sat at Jenna's dining table, feeling distinctly uncomfortable.

The food was delicious, pasta in a creamy spinach and tomato sauce with a tossed salad and fluffy breadsticks.

The conversation was fine, too, with the girls chattering away and carrying most of it.

Still, he was aware of a vague feeling of unease.

This felt entirely too domestic, the kind of warm, enjoyable scene that he had dreamed about through all the long months he spent on the inside.

His own marriage had never been this cozy. He and Lacey had been a bad combination from the start. She had been so young, not at all ready for marriage but eager to escape her difficult family.

He had liked her more than most of the women he'd dated. When she had become pregnant about four months after they started dating, despite their use of protection, they both decided marriage was the best course of action.

She had lost the baby a week after their wedding at the county clerk's office in North Carolina, where he had been stationed at the time.

He had once cared about her. Or told himself he had, anyway. Having Brielle two years later had been a joy for both of them, going a long way toward erasing much of the pain of that first miscarriage. But somewhere along the way they had both realized they weren't a good fit and had been talking about ending the marriage before he had ever been arrested.

He knew he had been a lousy husband and blamed himself for the breakdown of their marriage.

He had been a workaholic, completely focused on building up his business. At the time, he told himself he was doing everything for Lacey and Brielle. Lacey had begged him to slow down, to spend more time with them, to help her out more around the house and with their child.

He had made empty promises, again and again, but he hadn't changed.

In prison, he had finally acknowledged to himself that he had always held part of himself back from the marriage. He had never let himself be vulnerable with Lacey, had never truly opened his heart to her.

He had seen how devastated his mother had been after his father's murder, and maybe some part of him had internalized that and prevented him from completely letting down his guard.

Even if he had, he wasn't sure they ever could have healed all that had been withered because of neglect.

By then, Lacey had already reconnected with her childhood sweetheart. She was now very happily remarried, expecting another child with her new husband.

She had found in Ron Summers all that Wes hadn't been able to give her.

When he saw how happy they were together, Wes had decided he had been the problem all along, as he suspected. He sucked at marriage, apparently. Maybe he should just stick with being the best possible father to Brielle to make up for lost time and leave domestic bliss to others more suited to it.

This, though. This felt so comfortable here in Jenna's apartment, easy and natural and soothing. Rain clicked against the windows and the puppy snored at the girls' feet. As she listened to the girls' steady conversation, Jenna smiled with a warmth that made something in him ache with cravings he thought he had buried long ago.

"That lasagna was delicious, Mrs. Haynes," Brielle said.

"We did a good job on it, didn't we? Thanks for helping me. All of you. We have so much left over—you can take some home and put it in the freezer for another day."

"Good idea."

Dinner prep with her had been a delight as she showed the girls with calm patience how to make the sauce and then layer the ricotta and spinach sauce on the noodles before rolling it up into pinwheels on the pan.

"You did most of the work with dinner," he said now to her. "We can clean up."

"We left the kitchen a mess, though."

"We don't mind the work, do we, girls?"

The girls looked as if they minded very much but they didn't argue, simply went to work clearing away the table and carrying the dishes to the sink.

The cleanup did not take as long as Jenna seemed to think it would. After they had finished, Brielle and Addie asked if they could play a new board game Jenna had recently purchased.

He couldn't come up with an excuse, since he had nothing else planned for the evening with his daughter and it was too early for bedtime.

The game was fun and challenging and much giggling ensued as they tried to figure out the rules.

"Looks like Theo needs to go out," Jenna said after the second round. "You three keep playing. I'll take him out."

"It's still raining, though," Addie pointed out.

"Yes. We live in Oregon. It tends to do that. But unfortunately for us, dogs still need to go outside occasionally, especially when they're being trained."

"I can take him," Wes offered.

"You're the one who told me how important consistency is in puppy training, remember? I need to reinforce the training. I don't mind."

He rose from the table, undeterred. "Can I come with you anyway? After all those carbs, I could use a stretch."

He wasn't lying. For reasons he wasn't ready to explore, his muscles felt tightly coiled. She hesitated briefly then nodded. "Will you girls be okay in here? We'll just be outside for a few moments."

Addison rolled her eyes. "I'm eight and Brie is nine. We're fine. Can we play *Mario Kart*?"

"Fine with me. We won't be long."

The girls were already moving to the sofa and pulling out the game controllers as Jenna reached for her raincoat. Wes took the coat from her and held it out, manners drilled into him by his mother coming to the fore.

"You don't have a raincoat?" she asked as they headed for the door.

He shrugged. "I have one but it's upstairs. I'll be fine. I'll stay on the back porch."

He would actually welcome a little rain right now to cool his skin and his overheated imagination, though he didn't share that information with her.

She picked up a small towel he assumed was for wiping down the wet dog and handed Wes an umbrella from a container by the door. When she opened the door, Theo trotted happily down the stairs to lead the way.

The rain had slowed to a drizzle, he saw when they walked outside to the rear of the house and the dog yard. The moon even peeked out from behind the clouds to cast a pale light onto the shrubs and flowers.

She inhaled deeply as she walked down the steps with the

gangly puppy still leading the way. "Oh, I love that smell. Don't you?"

He drew in night air scented with rain and flowers and the sea.

"It's nice," he had to agree.

"When I was a kid, we lived in one apartment building that had a very small playground with a patch of grass no bigger than one of the flower gardens here. I still loved to go out every time it started to rain and stand on that little patch of grass to sniff the air. My friends all thought I was weird."

"I don't think you're weird."

Funny, warm, appealing. Definitely not weird.

"Since I've moved to Cannon Beach, I've decided everything smells even more delicious here, when you add in the ocean and all the pine and cedar trees around, plus the Brambleberry House flowers. It's magical, isn't it?"

She was magical. Wes found her sweet and refreshing and unforgettable. How was any man supposed to resist her, especially a man who had known far too little sweetness recently?

He could not disagree about the air. It was intoxicating. Something told him he would never be able to smell this particular combination of scents, rain and flowers and the ocean, without thinking of this night and this woman.

"The first night after my release, we had a rainstorm. I stood outside my motel for at least an hour and just relished the rain on my face."

It was an admission Wes suspected he could not tell anyone else on earth. Somehow he knew Jenna would understand.

She said nothing for a long moment, attention fixed on the dog, who was currently sniffing the base of a Japanese maple. Finally she turned to face him, eyes solemn and her features sad.

"Why were you in prison, Wes?"

The question seemed to come out of nowhere, like a sudden unprovoked attack from his six that left him momentarily breathless.

He owed her an answer.

He wanted to tell her all of it. At the same time, he wanted to pretend it had never happened.

"I trusted the wrong person," he finally said. The words sounded naive and unbelievable, even to him. Was it any wonder a jury of his peers had not believed them either?

He wished he didn't have to talk about this. He wanted to stand in this delicious-smelling garden and enjoy the simple pleasure of talking to a lovely woman. But the past was part of him now, an inescapable imprint on his personal story, and he suddenly wanted her to know.

"I told you I served two tours in the Army as an MP. Military policeman. When I got out, I got a job providing private corporate security. After a year or two of that, I ended up starting a company doing the same thing with a good friend, another MP I served with. Anthony Morris."

Even mentioning Tony's name left a bitter taste in his mouth, pushing away the remaining sweetness of the boysenberry pie they'd had for dessert.

"Tony was my best friend in the service. I thought I knew him. I trusted him. But unfortunately, the man I thought I knew didn't exist. He said all the right words about honor and integrity but lived a completely different reality. Somehow he managed to conceal it from me and our clients, smiling to our faces while filling his pockets with anything he could find."

"He was dirty?"

"To the core. The whole reason he wanted to start Mor-Cal Security was to use our clients, people who trusted us, as his personal booty chest. He didn't steal just a few things, either. The extent of it was staggering. He stole something from every single client. Large or small. Trade secrets. Account information. Personnel records. Even loose change. Whatever he could pocket or sell to the highest bidder. He was an equal opportunity thief."

That helpless rage swept over him again. "And I was stupid enough to hand him the keys. Literally and physically. I never imagined he would betray our clients like that. Betray *me* like that. I didn't believe him capable."

Maybe he deserved to go to prison for being so unbelievably stupid. But if everyone who trusted the wrong person ended up in prison, there would be no room for the actual criminals.

"People can be capable of all sorts of things we never imagine."

Her tone was tight, resigned, making him wonder who could possibly betray someone like Jenna.

"You are right, unfortunately. If I had given it any thought at all, I would have figured a guy whose life you saved in the middle of a firefight is not going to screw you over a few years later."

Her features softened with compassion. "Oh, Wes. I'm sorry."

Her compassion seeped into all the cold places, taking away a little of the chill from the memories. "I should have suspected something was up, but he handled all the finances. He was the brains, I was the muscle. I was just glad I could help my mom and my sister out a little and buy a nice house for Lacey and Brie, after they put up with years of base housing."

"When did you start to suspect?"

He sighed, remembering the bitter shock. "When I was arrested for grand theft. I denied everything, of course. I thought the feds had made the whole thing up. Tony would explain everything, I told them. Then I discovered Tony had fled to South America, leaving me swinging in the wind. Everything traced back to me. He had cleverly covered his tracks and created a false trail that led straight to my door. From the outside, it looked as if I had planned and orchestrated everything and that he had escaped only to protect himself from me when he uncovered the truth."

"Oh no."

"Right. Tony had completely set me up and I was too naive to see what was happening."

"You must have been in shock when you figured out what was really happening."

"You could say that. He was the closest thing I had to a brother, you know?"

She placed a comforting hand on his arm and he gazed down at her fingers, small and pale in the moonlight. Did she feel this pull between them, the same magnetic force of the moon directing the tides?

"Is he still on the run?"

He shook his head with a grim satisfaction. "A couple of my Army buddies went down and found him about a year ago. They dragged him back to face the consequences. He eventually ended up coming clean and admitted I wasn't involved. The prosecutors didn't buy it, but my attorneys fought like hell to find the evidence to exonerate me. Which is how I can be standing here today enjoying a rainy evening with you."

"So in the end Tony did the right thing?"

"Only because he was backed into a corner and had no choice. Don't paint a rosy picture of him, Jenna. He was a bastard who only admitted the truth after he was caught, in hopes that it might mean a lighter sentence for himself. He was only too happy to let me rot in prison for something I didn't do."

The bitterness in his voice made Jenna want to wrap her arms around him and hold him close to ease some of the vast pain of betrayal.

"I'm so sorry that happened," she murmured. "But at least you learned you had good friends you could count on."

He somehow managed a rusty laugh. "Are you always such an optimist, Mrs. Haynes?"

"Oh, no," she assured him. "Far from it. I've just learned the value of good friends over the years. I would have been lost without them."

He gave her a searching look, and she wondered how much truth she had revealed with her words. She wanted to tell him what had happened with Aaron but now wasn't the time, after he had unburdened himself about something much darker from his own history.

She couldn't think of anything else to say and realized they had been standing for a long moment, gazing at each other silently.

He was an extraordinarily good-looking man. Once a woman could see beyond his intimidating size and fierce features, she began to notice other things. The softness of his mouth. The firm line of his jaw. Those intense blue eyes fringed with long dark eyelashes.

She felt hot, suddenly, as if she had stood too long in front of the little electric fireplace in her bedroom.

"The rain has stopped."

He blinked and looked around. "Yes."

"When I'm going through hard times, I try to remind myself that, just like a rainstorm, nothing lasts forever. Pain and betrayal eventually begin to fade."

"Has your grief for your husband faded?"

He seemed genuinely interested, so she didn't answer with the trite response she might have otherwise. "I don't know if it will ever fade completely. But it has…mellowed over the years. I no longer feel devastated every time I think of Ryan. I now can remember the good times as well as the bad. We had several wonderful years together and I will always treasure them. And he gave me the greatest gift of all, Addie."

"He was a lucky man."

Something in his voice, some odd, yearning note, drew her gaze. He was looking down at her with an expression that made her catch her breath.

He wanted to kiss her.

She recognized the hunger deep in her soul because she shared it. It seemed so odd—so wrong—to be talking about her husband to a man who was completely unlike him but who made her ache with awareness.

"I should…" She pointed vaguely to the house, to the door. The girls were waiting upstairs, she reminded herself.

"Yes," he answered.

He didn't look away, though, merely continued watching her. She drew in a ragged breath, intending to call to the dog, but the words died in her throat.

When she tried to analyze it later, she wasn't sure which of them moved first. One moment, they were staring at each other in the garden, the next, they were reaching for each other.

His mouth was cool and tasted of berries but the rest of him was warm. Deliciously warm.

He kissed her with a raw hunger that took her breath away. His mouth moved over hers as if he wanted to memorize every dip, every curve.

Her arms rested against his chest and it took her a moment to realize he was shaking slightly. Not from cold. From hunger.

Jenna found something incredibly powerful and also deeply terrifying to know this man could tremble with desire because of *her*.

The rain started up again, just a cool mist that landed in her hair. She didn't care. She wanted to stand here forever and go on pretending the rest of the world didn't exist.

He was the first to pull away. She wasn't sure what brought him back to his senses. One moment, his mouth was tangled with hers, the next, he had eased away and gazed down, his breathing ragged and his expression dazed.

"I'm sorry, Jenna. I didn't mean to do that. I've been telling myself all evening that kissing you would be a mistake."

All evening? He had been thinking about kissing her *all evening*? She didn't know what to think, what to say.

"Yes. You're right. It was a mistake."

As soon as she said the word, she thought she saw a flicker of something in his gaze reflecting from the landscaping lights, something that looked almost like…hurt.

He had been the one to say the words first and she could not disagree. They were completely wrong for each other. She was finding herself increasingly drawn to the man. But she knew nothing could ever come of it.

"Let's just blame the moonlight. It's lovely out here, especially after the rain. It's hard not to be…carried away by the moment."

She couldn't look at him as she spoke, hoping he didn't see remnants of her desire on her features.

"We should go in. The…the girls."

Without another word, she scooped up Theo, grabbed the towel off the porch swing and let herself into a house that suddenly, oddly, felt colder than the garden had, almost disapproving.

Jenna hurried up the flight of stairs to her apartment, drying the confused dog as she went.

With each step, she wondered what she had been thinking to kiss him with so much…passion.

That wasn't her.

Or maybe it was.

It was a disconcerting thought.

Maybe there were parts of herself she had never had occasion to explore before, needs and desires that had always seemed warm and comfortable and…*muted* during her marriage to Ryan.

Maybe she was like that ocean out there. On a calm afternoon at low tide, only tiny waves licked at the sand. When conditions aligned, though, and storms blew in, the ocean could be mighty and powerful. Terrifying.

She sensed this thing between her and Wes would be like that—wild, passionate, fierce.

And that she would quickly find herself in over her head.

The rain began in earnest again as Wes watched Jenna hurry into the rambling old Victorian house. Drops slid down his collar, soaking him quickly. But he ignored it, too busy cursing himself for letting his base instincts take over.

After he had kissed her, she had almost looked *afraid*. Did she think he would hurt her?

He had completely screwed up everything.

Why had he kissed her?

He should have simply tamped down his attraction to her, as he had been doing for a long time now.

Maybe he had wondered on some level if kissing her could prove to her he was absolutely no threat to her.

How ridiculous. If he had given her a mild, restrained sort of kiss, that might have been the case, but he had kissed her as if she were his last meal.

Why was she so afraid? She had said something earlier that evening that might have been a clue. He closed his eyes as more rain slithered down his collar.

Who had hurt her? And where was the bastard now, so Wes could make him sorry?

He let out a breath. Her reasons for being jittery around him didn't matter. Nor did it matter if she was actually afraid of *him* or simply of any man.

He had done nothing to ease that fear. By kissing her, giving in to the heat and the hunger, he had only provided her with more reason to be nervous in his company.

How could he help himself? He was finding Jenna increasingly difficult to resist.

It wasn't simply a physical attraction to her, a hunger that kept him up at night and left him aching and empty.

He was quickly developing a thing for her.

Wes curled his hands into fists.

Could he be any more pathetic? He was falling for a woman he couldn't have.

Jenna Haynes was soft and gentle and kind, all the things that no longer fit into his world.

Wes let out a breath, chilled and damp, though he had moved to the porch, out of the drizzle.

As difficult as he knew he would find it, he had to go back up the stairs to Jenna's apartment, for Brielle if nothing else.

He had to forget about that kiss, about his aching hunger for her and about his growing feelings he knew were doomed to remain unreciprocated.

As he made his way up the stairs, he had the strange feeling that the house responded to his turmoil somehow.

He shook his head at his own foolishness. It was a *house*, for heaven's sake. Four walls, a foundation, a roof. It didn't have feelings and certainly couldn't offer sympathy.

When he reached her apartment, his knock was answered almost immediately by Brielle.

"There you are. Did you get lost out in the rain?" his daughter teased.

Yeah. Something like that.

"It's a pretty night. I was just enjoying it."

Jenna sat in an easy chair, watching the girls playing *Mario Kart*. She had Theo on her lap, almost like a shield.

When her gaze met his, the uneasy apprehension in her expression hit him like a blow coming out of nowhere in the exercise yard.

What did she think? That he was going to rush into the room and kiss her again?

"We're almost done with this race, Dad. Do you want to play?"

"We should head off, kiddo. It's getting late and we have to get ready for camp on Monday."

Jenna's daughter lit up. "Hey, I'm going to camp Monday, too. Are you going to science camp?"

Brielle nodded. "My mom signed me up before she even knew she was going to be out of town. I hope it's not lame."

Addison gave her a look of astonishment. "Science camp is not lame at all! It's way fun. I went last year and we always did cool things. Experiments and kayaking and bird-watching and stuff."

"I really do think you'll have a wonderful time," Jenna assured his daughter with that warm smile she seemed to give to everyone but him. "Addie loved it last year. She couldn't stop talking about it. She's been looking forward to it all year."

"I hope so. I'm happy you'll be there. At least I'll have one friend," Brielle said.

"You'll have lots of friends," Addie said breezily. "A lot of the kids from school went last year and I'm sure they'll go again. But we can totally be camp buddies!"

"Definitely!" Brielle said with a grin. Wes thought again how grateful he was that his daughter seemed happy and well-adjusted, despite the divorce and his incarceration.

She was a curious child who was kind to others and made friends easily.

"If you want, I'm happy to take Brielle to camp Monday and I can pick her up again as well. And she's more than welcome to hang out here after camp, until you're done with work."

"That's a lot to ask of you for two weeks."

"Not at all. I know how hard it is to be a single parent, trying to coordinate schedules. I don't mind at all."

He had been trying to figure out how he was going to manage things. He had already talked to the Gutierrez brothers, who were willing to be flexible with his schedule, but Wes hated to take advantage after they already had been so good to him.

At the same time, he needed to stay away from Jenna so he could work on getting rid of these inconvenient feelings he was developing for her. Arranging his life so he was guaranteed to see her at least twice a day probably wasn't the solution.

What choice did he have, though? All his efforts to find someone to stay with Brielle for the hour between camp and the end of his shift had come to naught.

"That would actually be really helpful, unless I can find someone else tomorrow. I was trying to figure out how to squeeze in everything. I was planning to go in late and come home early to work around her schedule."

"You don't have to try. I'm more than happy to help."

"Thank you."

She still hadn't met his gaze directly, he realized, except for that first brief moment.

"Thank you also for dinner," he said. "I definitely need the lasagna recipe to add to my rotation."

"No problem. I can share it with you, if you want to give me your email."

She handed him a notebook and he quickly wrote down the email address he rarely used.

"I'll send it later tonight."

"Thanks. I'll watch for it. Let's go, Brie. Looks like the race is over."

His daughter sighed, clearly reluctant to leave her new best friend.

"Bye, Addie. Maybe I'll see you tomorrow."

"For sure on Monday."

The girls hugged as if they were each heading off on different long sea voyages, and Wes had to hide a smile. He caught Jenna's gaze, finally, and saw that she was smiling, too.

She quickly shifted her gaze back to the dog in her lap, leaving Wes feeling slightly bereft.

Bad enough that he had kissed her, when he had every intention of keeping his attraction to her bottled up.

He really hoped he hadn't completely ruined a friendship he was beginning to cherish.

Chapter Seven

"What time will Brielle be here?" Addy asked for what seemed like the hundredth time that morning.

Jenna sipped her tea, frustrated with herself for the butterflies jumping around in her stomach. She had awakened filled with a mix of anticipation and nervousness about seeing Wes that morning when he brought his daughter down the stairs.

She could not stop thinking about the kiss the other night.

The memory of it seemed seared into her subconscious. Every time she closed her eyes, she recalled the heat of his body next to hers, the strength of his muscles beneath her fingers.

She had wanted more than a kiss.

At some point in the early hours of the morning, she had finally admitted that to herself. For the first time since Ryan's death, she had ached for a man's touch.

For Wes's touch.

Despite two tortured nights of wondering what it might be like, she knew anything more than a heated kiss between them was impossible.

She was the problem.

It was easy enough to tell herself she wasn't ready yet. But Ryan had been gone for four years. While some part of her would always grieve for the future they had dreamed about, she had determined years ago that she couldn't spend the rest of her life aching for something she could never recapture.

She had decided to move on three years ago, when she had first accepted a date with Aaron Barker.

That decision had turned out to be a disastrous one, upending her entire life.

She was only now beginning to put the pieces back together.

She might be fiercely drawn to Wes Calhoun and felt great sympathy for what he had endured, spending three years in prison, wrongly convicted for another man's crimes, but Jenna couldn't picture a future with him.

Wes was rough, hard, dangerous. He rode a motorcycle, ran for miles on the beach, was built like a professional athlete.

What did she have to offer a man like that? Her hobbies included knitting and reading the occasional cozy mystery, not riding on the back of a Harley.

She sighed, more depressed than she had any right to be.

Wes was a very nice man and someday he would find the perfect woman for him. Jenna was more sorry than she would have expected that she couldn't be that perfect woman.

The doorbell suddenly chimed through their unit, distracting her from her thoughts.

Her pulse fluttered like the butterflies in her stomach.

"They're here!" Addie exclaimed, rushing to the door. She flung it open before Jenna could tell her daughter to give her a moment to compose herself.

And there he was.

Everything inside her seemed to sigh as he reached down to greet Theo, who rushed to be the first one to say hello.

Yes, Wes Calhoun was big and hard and dangerous. But his eyes were warm, and the genuine smile he gave both her puppy and her daughter touched something deep inside.

"Good morning, Addison."

"Hi, Mr. Calhoun. Hi, Brielle."

Addie reached a hand to the other girl and tugged her into

the apartment, already chattering about what might be in store for them that day.

Jenna had to say something to him, she told herself. She couldn't stand here all day simply gazing at the man.

"Good morning," she said, forcing a smile to hide her sudden shyness.

"Morning. Sorry we're a little late. We misplaced a tennis shoe."

"I think the Brambleberry House ghost hid it from us," Brielle said from the sofa, where she and Addie were now sitting, heads together, petting Theo. "I swear, I looked in that closet four times before we finally found it, right in front of us."

"But our ghost usually doesn't tease," Addie said, her voice perfectly serious. "I don't know why she would hide your shoe."

Brielle shrugged. "Who knows? Maybe she doesn't want me to go to day camp."

"Or maybe," her father said mildly, "you didn't look hard enough in the closet and your shoe was there all along."

"I did look, though," his daughter insisted.

"Well, you found it and you're here now," Jenna said with a smile. "Did you pack a lunch? If not, I made an extra PB&J."

Wes handed over an insulated lunch bag. "This one is turkey and cheese, along with some carrots and grapes and a small bag of chips."

"Sounds delicious."

"I'm still figuring out the sack lunch thing," he admitted.

"You seem to be doing great."

"I guess I should find my own tennis shoes," Addie said.

"Yes. You should," Jenna said. She had only been reminding her daughter to finish getting ready for the past half hour.

"Maybe the ghost hid my shoes, too," Addie said, looking thrilled at the possibility. "Maybe the ghost doesn't want either one of us to go to science camp. Maybe she doesn't like science."

"Before you start spreading any unfounded conspiracy the-ories about our poor Abigail, go look in your closet," Jenna said.

"You can come help me find them," Addie said to Brielle. "Four eyes are better than two. That's what my mom always says, anyway."

"Okay," the other girl said cheerfully. The two of them hur-ried, Theo close on their heels, toward Addie's bedroom door, decorated with drawings of unicorns and flower gardens, along with the occasional bloodthirsty, jagged-toothed dinosaur.

Their departure left her alone with Wes, she suddenly re-alized.

There was no reason for things to be awkward between them, she told herself. Yes, they had shared a kiss, but they had dealt with it after it happened. Surely they could go back to being friends now, right?

"She's a great kid," Jenna said.

"Yeah. I really lucked out in the kid department. Even with the divorce and all the mess of the past three years, Brielle is great. I thank heaven for it every day."

"Children can be fairly resilient. After my husband died, I was so worried about how it would impact Addie, but she seems to be doing okay, so far."

She couldn't resist knocking on the intricate woodwork of the door frame, which earned her a smile from him.

She did not tell him that while she certainly had worried about Addie losing her father at a young age, she had also stressed about how her daughter internalized their summer two years earlier when they had fled to Cannon Beach. They had been forced to use assumed names, to change their hair color, to be cautious about everyone who came into their tight circle.

She didn't want to share that with Wes, though. That was in the past and she refused to let Aaron Barker take up any more space in her present or her future.

"It's a nice day so we'll probably walk the three blocks to the community center where the camp is based. Is that okay with you? I'm multitasking and walking Theo in hopes of wearing him out so I can get some things done around here today."

"Sounds like a plan. Thanks again."

"The forecast calls for more rain this afternoon, so I'll probably drive to the center to pick them up after day camp."

"I'll be here soon as I can after work."

"No rush. The girls are getting along great and I don't mind having Brielle here at all."

"Thanks. I really appreciate it. I'm definitely going to owe you dinner."

She shook her head. "You don't. This is what friends do for each other, Wes."

His gaze met hers in a searching look that left her slightly breathless.

"I was worried you might not want anything to do with me and Brielle after that kiss the other night."

She studied him, surprised by the note of uncertainty in his voice. Was it possible that he had been left as disconcerted as she was by their kiss?

"Don't be silly. It was only a kiss." She knew that was a vast understatement. It had been much more than that for her. The words *stunning* and *earthshaking* seemed more appropriate. "It shouldn't have happened and we both agree it won't happen again. But it's no big deal."

He didn't answer immediately. "I'll try to keep my hands to myself but I'm very attracted to you and…it's been a long time for me."

His hands had shaken when he touched her, she suddenly remembered. The memory made her toes curl.

"Same here," she admitted. "I guess it's a good thing neither of us is in the market for a quick fling."

"I don't know. I could probably be persuaded."

Her gaze flew to his. Though his tone was sober, there was a sparkle in his gaze, a little devilish glint that made her give a startled laugh.

"So could I, truth be told," she admitted. "But it's not a good idea, right? We're neighbors. Our daughters are friends. I would hate for things to become messy and awkward between us."

After a long moment, he sighed. "I know you're right. But I don't have to like it. It was a really amazing kiss."

She could not disagree.

The girls came out of the room before she could answer.

"Guess what?" Brielle exclaimed. "We found Addie's shoes right away. I guess it was only my shoe that Abigail hid."

"Whew. Good thing." He smiled again at his daughter with so much warmth and affection, Jenna's toes curled again.

"I've got to go. I'll see you all later."

Brielle gave her father a brilliant smile. "Bye, Dad. I'll see you tonight."

"Have fun at camp. Learn all you can about science so you can teach me stuff."

"Okay. But you already know lots of stuff."

"I'm always willing to learn more."

Before he left the apartment, Wes sent Jenna a look that had her wondering exactly what kind of things he knew…and regretting that she would never have the chance to find out.

After she walked the girls to the community center and checked them both into their day camp, Jenna decided that morning was too beautiful to go straight home.

On impulse, she decided to head down to the beach with Theo and walk home along the seashore.

She and Addie had already discovered the dog loved the water. After his initial hesitation, Theo had become a big fan, dancing through the little waves and sniffing every sand mound and seaweed tendril along the beach.

The morning was cool and lovely as they walked along the hard-packed sand close to the water's edge. They certainly weren't alone on Cannon Beach, but it was far from crowded, like it could be on a July afternoon.

A couple of teenagers flew colorful trick kites on the sand and a few hardy souls played in the water, though she considered it still too cold for comfort.

Sometimes Jenna still had to pinch herself to make sure she really was lucky enough to live here, beside the Pacific.

She loved the ocean and found it both invigorating and, conversely, calming.

She wasn't sure if she could ever return to her home state of Utah. While she loved the mountains there, Oregon had mountains, too, whenever she might need a fix.

Utah held plenty of sad memories. She had lost her husband there, had worked to rebuild her life, then had fled, abandoning everything because of one selfish man who didn't know the meaning of the word *no*.

Here in Cannon Beach, she had found peace. Had it been perfect? No. But she had found friends and a community here. Everyone here had been kind to her from the moment she moved into Brambleberry House.

They had nearly reached the beach below Brambleberry House when she spotted a familiar figure moving toward them from the opposite direction with a beautiful Irish setter pacing protectively beside her.

"Rosa!" she called as they approached. "Hello! How are you, darling? And how are you, Fiona?"

"Jenna, my friend. Hello."

Rosa's serene features lit up with happiness. Her friend was round and lovely, her pregnancy giving her a graceful beauty that Jenna loved to see.

"Who is this little sweetheart?" Rosa asked with a smile.

"This is Theo. He's a rescue dog we picked up last week

at the shelter. I've been promising Addie we would get a dog forever. I finally ran out of excuses."

"He is beautiful. I am so happy for you and Addie. She must be thrilled."

"They adore each other," Jenna said. "It's been really sweet to see. How are you feeling? Do you need to sit down? There's a bench over there. Let's stop for a minute and visit. We haven't had the chance to talk in forever."

After a moment's consideration, Rosa nodded and made her way to the bench, where she lowered herself down, still graceful despite her advanced stage of pregnancy.

"I am trying to stay active like my doctor says I must do, but it is not easy at this stage. Every day, moving becomes a little harder."

"I remember too well. I was in my first year of teaching when I was pregnant with Addie. Before she was born, I was so miserable. I wasn't sure I would be able to survive it."

"I am the same. I am ready to turn over the store to Carol."

Their mutual friend Carol Hardesty worked full-time at Rosa's gift shop as the assistant manager. She was competent and efficient but didn't have Rosa's business sense or her creative approach to retail management.

"I'm happy to take a few extra hours during the summer if you need me to," Jenna said. "I can go to three days a week during the busy summer season, if that would help."

Rosa made a face. "It is not necessary. We talked about this. You need to slow down, now that you are done with your school classes. You should take time to enjoy your summer a little bit instead of always working, working, working."

This was the first year of her life that she had decided to take an actual summer break. She still worked twelve to sixteen hours a week at the gift shop, but compared to previous summers, when she had worked full-time and taken extra classes so she could accelerate her advanced degree, that seemed like a breeze.

She knew she would love having time to catch up on projects as well as plan ahead for the next school year.

"I don't mind working, working, working if it will help you out," she said to her friend, to whom she owed so much.

"We will be fine. Do not worry. I have other workers who need the extra hours. You enjoy being with your daughter."

She looked around. "Where is our Addie?"

"Science camp. I am just heading home after walking her and Brielle Calhoun there."

"Brielle. This is Wes's daughter."

"That's right."

"How are you getting along with my new tenant?" Rosa asked.

Jenna remembered the heat of his mouth on hers, the scent of flowers and pine surrounding them as they kissed. She did not meet Rosa's gaze. They had been friends since being paired together as college roommates and Rosa knew her too well. Would she be able to tell the situation had become... complicated?

"He was nice enough to change my car battery a few weeks ago when I had trouble. His daughter is staying with him full-time for the next few weeks while her mother is out of town, so I'm helping out with some gap babysitting."

"That is very neighborly of you. I am sure Wes appreciates your help."

"He seems grateful."

"He is very handsome, do you not think?"

Jenna gave a casual shrug she suspected did not fool Rosa for a moment. "I don't know. I hadn't really noticed. He's just the neighbor who lives upstairs."

Rosa made a disbelieving sound. "I do not believe you. How can any woman not notice a man like that? I am very happily married to my Wyatt and so huge I cannot see my toes right now. And still I would notice someone like Wes Calhoun."

Jenna could feel herself flush. For a moment, she was tempted to confide in her old friend about that kiss two nights earlier and the heated dreams that had left her aching and alone in her bed.

In the old days, they used to wake each other up in their dorm room after dates to talk long into the night. She had told Rosa everything, though she suspected her friend had not ever been entirely truthful with her.

But they were not college students now. She was a grown woman, a respected educator, with an eight-year-old daughter. It seemed undignified, somehow, to dish with her landlady about the gorgeous guy who lived upstairs—even if that landlady was her dearest friend.

On the other hand, she could really use some advice.

She gazed at the dogs, now digging in the sand, probably on the hunt for a crab or some other poor creature.

"Okay," she admitted. "I noticed."

"Ha. I knew it!" Rosa looked inordinately pleased with herself. "I told Wyatt I thought maybe it would be good for you to have such a handsome man living upstairs from you. You spend too much time alone."

Jenna frowned. "Seriously? You were trying to matchmake when you rented the apartment to Wes?"

Her friend tried, and failed, to look innocent. "I would not say matchmake. Maybe just give you a little, what is the word, *nudge*."

Jenna gave Rosa an exasperated look. "I don't need a nudge. And I certainly don't need someone to matchmake for me, especially not with a man like Wes Calhoun."

Now it was Rosa's turn to frown. "How do you mean, a man like Wes Calhoun? What is wrong with him?"

She sighed. "Nothing is wrong with him. As I said, he

seems very nice. He's a good father and clearly loves his child. He has been very kind. He has even given me a few training tips for Theo, who adores him."

Rosa laughed. "See? There you go. Dogs are very wise. They see into the heart of a person. If you find Theo does not like a man, that is when you should be nervous about him."

She wasn't sure she was ready to let a dog vet the men in her life. On the other hand, she also wasn't sure she could trust her own instincts about men, considering what happened with Aaron Barker.

"I don't believe that's scientifically proven, Rosa."

Her friend made a dismissive gesture. "Maybe not science. But I have seen it myself. I would never have considered dating anyone if Fiona did not approve. The men she did not like always proved to be someone I did not like, either."

"But do I really have to base my dating decisions on the opinion of a puppy whose favorite thing in the world seems to be sniffing the behind of any other dog who comes along?"

Rosa laughed. "Fine. You may have a point. What does our Abigail think of him?"

Jenna rolled her eyes at Rosa's mention of the woman believed to haunt Brambleberry House. "I don't know. I'll have to ask her. So far, she hasn't seemed inclined to discuss the matter with me."

"She will let you know if she approves." Rosa smiled, then suddenly winced and rubbed at her protruding abdomen.

Jenna didn't miss the gesture. "Everything okay?"

"Yes. Fine. I am having a few twinges, that is all. For the most part, this has been an easy pregnancy, though Wyatt is nervous enough for both of us."

Jenna adored Rosa's husband, Wyatt, who had temporarily lived downstairs from them when Rosa lived on the third floor. Wyatt was a police detective and she considered him one of the good guys, especially after he had worked so hard to make sure Aaron Barker received a lengthy prison sentence.

They sat for a moment on the beach overlooking the sea. Finally Rosa sighed. "This is so lovely but I should probably go. I have an appointment in a short time."

Jenna hugged her friend. "Take it easy on yourself. And remember that I'm more than willing to help out if you need me to take additional hours at the store."

"I will remember. Thank you, my dear."

Rosa whistled to Fiona, who returned to her side, then the two continued on their walk while Jenna did the same with Theo, heading up the beach toward home.

Chapter Eight

She had come to enjoy this last trip outside before bedtime each night for her and Theo.

With her daughter asleep in her room, Jenna would take the dog down the staircase and out the back door to the fenced dog yard.

In the moonlight, with the murmuring sound of the ocean not far off and the random peeps and calls of the various night creatures who lived nearby, she found it peaceful. Almost meditative.

Once, she had been afraid of the night. Those were the hours when she felt most vulnerable, at risk from a boogeyman whose name she knew all too well.

Since Aaron Barker had been arrested, Jenna worked hard to overcome her fear of nighttime. She wouldn't let him take that from her forever.

Okay, she still walked outside with pepper spray in her pocket. She could be brave and cautious at the same time, couldn't she?

On impulse, tonight she had brought along Theo's leash as well as her phone, where she had a security camera linked up in the living area of the apartment so she could hear if Addie woke for a glass of water. She decided to walk the dog down the beach a short way, only to the water's edge directly west of the house.

As she watched the moonlight dance on the waves, she released a breath, all the pent-up frustrations and concerns of the day floating away on the tide.

She had worked that day at Rosa's gift shop, and her shift had been unusually stressful from start to finish.

The day had started with her catching a shoplifter, her least favorite thing. Worse, the person who had slipped into her purse a handcrafted necklace valued at several hundred dollars turned out to be someone she knew, the aunt of one of her students.

It hadn't been the woman's first offense and not even her first shoplifting incident at By-the-Wind, so Rosa had no choice but to call the police, who had arrested the woman, angry and protesting all the way.

The event had put a pall over her whole day. After her shift and before she had to go pick up the girls from their fourth day at science camp, Jenna had gone to the grocery store to purchase a few things she had forgotten in Saturday's epic shopping trip and had ended up dropping and breaking an entire bottle of pasta sauce.

She had insisted on helping the store employee clean up the mess. As a result, she had been late picking up the girls and had rushed up to the community center to find them waiting on the curb for her.

She hadn't even had the chance to talk to Wes that afternoon when he came to pick up his daughter, as Brielle had rushed away with a hurried thank-you as soon as she saw her father's motorcycle pull into the driveway, eager to tell him about all the things she had learned that day.

Jenna told herself it was for the best. She was thinking about the man entirely too much anyway. It didn't help that for the past four days she had seen him in the morning when he dropped off Brielle and then again in the afternoon when he picked her up.

Each time she saw him, Jenna's awareness of the man only seemed to intensify.

What was she going to do about it?

She sighed. Exactly nothing. She planned to remain friendly with him and keep a safe distance.

"Are you ready to head back?" she asked Theo after a few more moments.

The dog turned its head, tail wagging. At odd moments, she almost felt as if he understood exactly what she was saying. As far as dogs went, Theo seemed unusually intuitive.

Sure. And maybe during those odd moments when he seemed to be staring at nothing in the corner, he was really communing with the Brambleberry House ghost.

She shook her head at herself. He was a great dog but he wasn't some kind of canine medium to the other side.

"Come on, Theo. Good boy."

The dog trotted beside her, already well-behaved on the leash. So far, he was fitting into their little family as if he had been there forever.

She keyed in the password to the locked beach gate and made her way through the garden, pausing occasionally to sniff the lavender and the climbing roses over one of the trellises.

She again felt so fortunate to be living amidst such beauty. Not only were the gardens of the house spectacular, but the view was beyond compare. On stormy nights, she loved watching the clouds roll over the water and seeing the waves churn.

Tonight was calm, though, only a light breeze, lush with the smell of flowers and pine and sea, to send the leaves shivering.

She was nearly to the house when the dark shape of a man stepped down from the porch.

She let out an instinctive shriek and reached for her pepper spray.

"Easy, Jenna," a low voice said. "Easy. It's me. Wes. I didn't mean to alarm you. I had no idea you were out here or I would have given you some kind of warning."

Her chest felt tight and shaky and it took her a moment to catch her breath again. With her heart pounding, she slipped the pepper spray back into her pocket.

"Hello. You startled me."

"I can tell. I'm sorry. Are you okay?"

Heat soaked her face and her skin felt tight and itchy with embarrassment. "Yes. Fine. I was surprised, that's all."

"Are you sure that's all?" He stepped down from the porch and moved closer to her. Jenna fought the urge to back away.

"What do you mean?"

"When I first moved in, I thought something about me was causing you to be so jittery."

She sighed, embarrassed all over again. "It's not you," she whispered. Or at least not *completely* him.

He peered down at her in the moonlight. "I think I'm beginning to figure that out."

He reached out and laid a hand on her arm. She didn't feel threat from him. She felt…comfort.

"Why are you so nervous, Jen? Did someone hurt you?"

His voice was gentle, like a cottonwood fluff floating on the breeze. He sounded concerned, not nosy or intrusive, as if he genuinely wanted to know so that he could figure out a way to help her.

"It's a very long story," she said.

He sat down on the bench there in the garden surrounded by rhododendron, iris, rosebushes. He gestured to the spot beside him, not demanding, only inviting her to share if she wanted to, offering a listening ear.

She wanted to tell him, suddenly.

She did not like to talk about what had happened to her two years earlier, especially nights like tonight when the fear and emotional distress seemed so raw and close.

Yet somehow, she wanted to tell Wes.

After a moment, she lowered herself to the bench beside him, strangely aware of the hard slats of the bench beneath her, the sweetly scented night breeze, the soft knit fabric of her sweater.

"I told you a little about my husband and how he died."

"Yes. I'm sorry again for that."

"I loved Ryan dearly. Together we created the family that neither of us had before. He was a kind man. Not perfect, but perfect for me, if that makes sense."

She glanced at Wes in time to see a muscle twitch in his jaw. "He sounds great," he said.

"He was. I was devastated by his death. So was Addie. I didn't expect to ever date again. But a year after he died, friends pushed me to try online dating. I didn't think I was ready for anything serious, but they persuaded me that I didn't have to marry a man just because I went out on a date with him. It would be good practice, they told me, and would help me figure out what I might be looking for if I ever wanted to let someone else into my heart."

She picked at the cuff of her sweater, unable to meet his gaze. "I didn't want to date anyone. At the same time, I was beginning to feel terribly lonely. I taught all day and then was alone with Addie all evening. I missed adult conversation, especially because Ryan had been sick for so long and hadn't really been a partner for that last year. I thought maybe dating again would distract me from how much I still missed my husband."

"I'm going to assume something went south," he said, his voice low.

She sighed. "You could say that."

She leaned back on the bench, finding an odd sort of strength from Wes's company. How strange, that this dangerous man could make her feel so very safe.

"I met a few guys who seemed nice enough. We went out for coffee or a meal, but things never progressed beyond that. I figured that was enough, then I made one more match on my profile. A man from a nearby town. Aaron Barker."

She couldn't seem to say the name without her whole body tensing. Did Wes notice?

"Aaron seemed very nice on the surface. He was charming and kind. We went for coffee and had a lovely conversation. For the first time, I was tempted to go on a second date with someone. We went to lunch one afternoon. It was pleasant. Enjoyable, even. We talked on the phone a few times and met a few nights later, for dinner this time. After dinner, he walked me to my car and…kissed me."

At this rate, she was going to unravel her sweater, so she forced her fretting fingers to relax.

"It was too soon for me. I got into my car and drove away. Before I could make it home, I had to pull over and be sick."

"Not a good reaction for a first kiss."

She remembered, suddenly, how she had reacted after Wes had kissed her. She had certainly not been sick. She had been achy and hungry and wanted more.

"He called me that night to check that I made it home safely and I…tried to break things off. I explained that I wasn't ready to date yet, that it had been a mistake for me to create a profile on the dating website and that I should not have let my friends push me into it. I tried to be as kind as possible and assure Aaron that he had done nothing wrong. I told him I liked him but that it wouldn't be fair to date him when my own emotions were still so tangled up with my late husband."

"I'm guessing he didn't take it well."

She shook her head. "He refused to listen to anything I said. It was almost as if he didn't hear me. He kept talking about how we clicked and he knew for sure that I felt it as well. I tried to let him down as gently as possible, but he would not listen. Not that night and not the next night when he called me again. He started to became…forceful."

He grew rigid beside her. "Oh, Jenna."

"Not that. He didn't…sexually assault me or anything. He just refused to accept that I didn't want a relationship with him. He would write me love notes, send flowers to me at work, text me endlessly at any time of the day or night. I finally blocked his number, but he would get another number and start all over again. I changed my phone number and my email, but he always seemed to figure out how to connect with me."

"Did you talk to the police?"

"He was the police," she said simply. "He was a patrol officer for a small department in a nearby Utah town. His uncle was the police chief and he wouldn't listen to any of my complaints. Not only that, but Aaron specialized in cybercrime, which made him a tech whiz. He could infiltrate all my social media, my contact info, even my private school email address. I couldn't escape him. This went on for weeks, until I was completely terrified."

"I can imagine."

"And then he went after Addie."

"How?"

The single clipped word contained both shock and hard fury. It should have frightened her, coming from such a fierce man, but somehow only made her want to lean against him and let this man protect her from the world.

"She was in kindergarten and he picked her up from school early one day. I hadn't said anything to my coworkers about what was going on with me. I guess I was too embarrassed. So when he showed his badge to the kindergarten teacher— who was elderly and should have retired years earlier—and told her we were old friends and that he wanted to take Addie to visit her father's grave and pick up a birthday present for me, she didn't blink an eye."

"I hope she was fired," he said, without a note of sympathy in his voice.

"She was retiring that year anyway, so it was all swept under the carpet. Anyway, he returned her to me about an hour after school was out. He kept her just long enough to terrify me and make it clear that he could get to either of us anytime he wanted. I knew I had to leave. He wasn't going to let up. If anything, he was escalating."

"Sounds like it."

"That very day, I happened to get a phone call from my dear friend Rosa."

"Rosa? As in Rosa our landlady?"

"One and the same. We were college roommates. Somehow in the middle of our conversation, I ended up spilling the entire ugly story to her. For so long, I had carried the burden by myself. It felt so good to tell someone else."

"Rosa was a good choice."

"Yes. Her father was in law enforcement so she wasn't naive. She knew what could happen if I didn't take action. She insisted I come to stay with her. She set me up in my apartment, got me a job at her gift shop and basically helped me begin the process of putting my life back together."

"Good for you."

"I can't explain how wonderful it felt to finally start believing I was safe. I really thought Addie and I could make a new start here. I was even thinking about trying to get an Oregon teaching certificate."

Her voice trailed off and she once more gripped her hands together in her lap.

"I take it that didn't happen as seamlessly as you had hoped."

His gentle tone soothed her somehow. The memories were still hard, but they seemed slightly less hard through sharing them.

"Addie and I had a few good months here. We were finally starting to feel safe. And then Aaron found me."

"How?"

"A fluke, really. Apparently someone from his little Utah town came to the coast on vacation and spotted me working at the gift shop. I should have expected it. Many people from other western states come here to enjoy the Oregon Coast. It was my bad luck that one of his friends who had seen a picture of me decided to come to Cannon Beach."

"Did Barker try to come after you?"

She nodded with a shiver she couldn't restrain. The events of that afternoon, here in this very garden, suddenly felt closer than they had since she testified at his sentencing hearing.

"Aaron couldn't understand why I had fled. But he magnanimously told me he was ready to forgive everything as long as I came back with him. When I tried to flee, he… attacked me and especially Rosa, when she tried to protect me. She was so brave. Though she and her dog were both hurt, they still managed to distract him long enough for me and Addie to escape into the house and call 911. I'll never be able to repay her for her courage. She showed far more grit than I did. I was petrified."

"Understandable, after everything you had been through. What happened to Barker? Was he caught?"

"Yes. Rosa hit him with a rock and stunned him. He was still coming to when Wyatt and the other police officers arrived. He was arrested and charged with multiple assault and attempted kidnapping charges. He pleaded not guilty, of course. He would never admit he did anything wrong, but he was convicted and sentenced to serve five years in the state prison system."

"Five years. Hardly seems like enough for what he put you through."

"He was sentenced to five years but was scheduled for a parole hearing in December."

His gaze narrowed. "Was?"

Wes, she had previously noticed, didn't miss much. "Yes. He...he died unexpectedly in prison a few weeks ago. Natural causes. An aneurysm, according to the autopsy."

"Wow. No kidding?"

She nodded. "I finally feel like I can breathe again, you know? For the first time in two years, I can think about the future. In many ways, I feel as if I've been living in suspended animation. Trapped by events beyond my control. I was ready to go into hiding again as soon as he left prison. Now I don't have to. I can stay here in Cannon Beach. We can make this area our forever home. It's liberating."

He looked down at Theo, sleeping at their feet. "Is that what led you to adding a dog to your family?"

She nodded. "I've been in survival mode for so long. It really feels as if Addie and I have been in a constant state of turmoil since Ryan died. We're finally in a good place now. Addie has wanted a dog forever and this seemed like a small thing to do for her, after everything she has endured."

"He seems like a good dog."

"We got lucky. He's really well-behaved and eager to learn."

He petted the dog, and she couldn't seem to stop watching those big, calloused hands.

"So now you know the entire grim story. I don't...trust easily. For obvious reasons."

"Understandable."

"It's easy to fall into the victim mentality. But I don't want to live the rest of my life that way. That is giving Aaron entirely too much power over me. I would rather not have to think about him another moment."

"I'm sorry I dredged up all the bad memories by asking what happened."

She shook her head. "I wanted to tell you. I consider you a friend, and friends share things about their lives with each other, right?"

"I suppose that's true."

"You were honest with me about what happened to you. I should have been honest in return. I suppose I'm a little ashamed that it has affected me so much, when there are others who have been through much worse things. Like you, for instance, convicted for something you didn't do."

"My mom used to tell me not to compare my troubles to anyone else's. I wouldn't want theirs and they wouldn't want mine."

She smiled. "Well, thank you for the sympathetic ear. I'm glad I told you."

"So am I. It only reinforced to me how amazing you are."

She blinked, disconcerted by his words. "Me? I'm not amazing. I told you how terrified I was when Aaron found me. I couldn't think straight. Two years later, I'm still scared of far too many things. I even scream at shadows, as you saw clearly tonight."

"And yet you are inherently kind to your students, to your customers at the gift shop and to random strange men who live upstairs."

He took her hand in his and smiled down at her. Something sparked in his gaze, something warm and glittery, and his throat moved as he swallowed hard.

"Wes."

That was all she said. All she could manage. His gaze met hers and she was unbearably moved when he lifted her hand to his mouth and gently kissed her fingers.

She wanted to kiss him.

An aching hunger bloomed to life, like the rosebushes bursting with color on a June morning.

She looked at his mouth, breathless as she waited for him.

He lowered his mouth and she leaned toward him, heart pounding. At the last moment, he froze, his expression suddenly tormented.

He wouldn't kiss her, she realized. Not only because of what she had told him but because she had been clear that she didn't want more than a friendship with him.

If she were wise, she would count her blessings, gather her dog and rush inside.

She didn't feel very wise right now. Before she could think through the ramifications, she leaned forward, bridging the last few inches between them, and kissed him.

It was as if she had unleashed the storm. He kissed her back with a fierce intensity that pushed every coherent thought out of her head.

Still, she sensed he was holding back. She could feel it in his leashed strength, in the tight control he was keeping over himself.

She wanted that wildness, suddenly. Would this man ever let himself lose control?

She tightened her arms around his neck and tangled her mouth with his, wanting the delicious kiss to go on and on.

Chapter Nine

He was in so much trouble.

As flames of desire licked through him, Wes tried his best to hold on to whatever semblance of control he could manage to dredge up out of the depths of his subconscious.

Jenna tasted so damn good. Like chocolate and cherries and this perfect summer night.

She made a soft, breathy sound deep in her throat and her arms seemed to tighten around him.

He could feel his control slip away, inch by painful inch. All he wanted to do was kiss her, taste her, make love to her.

He traced a hand beneath her sweater, to the warm, luscious skin there. She shivered and arched against his hand, pressing her curves into his chest.

He was aching with need, his brain empty of everything but how much he wanted this woman in his arms, in his bed.

His hand slid from her back to one hip. He wanted to touch those curves she pressed against him.

He was inches from his goal when she made that soft, sexy sound again.

The sound seemed to yank him back to his senses. What the hell was he doing? He had told himself he couldn't do this again. He wanted her too much, though his kissing her again only showed him how very much he was beginning to care for her.

Beyond that, she had just shared with him her harrowing

ordeal. She had been tormented, stalked, terrified by a man who couldn't take no for an answer.

Even though she had made it clear she wasn't interested in anything with him, here he was mauling her in the garden of Brambleberry House, like he was some sort of high school kid making out with a girl behind the bleachers of the football stadium.

He jerked away, disgusted with himself.

She looked small and delicate, lovely as tiny violets springing across the grass in May.

He had spent three years feeling dehumanized, marginalized, discarded.

But he never felt as barbaric as he did right now, taking in the sight of Jenna Haynes staring up at him with huge eyes.

"I'm so sorry. I don't know what came over me."

She blinked a few times and drew in a deep breath. "Why are you apologizing?"

"Because I had no right to kiss you like a starving man who had just been snatched off the streets and plunked down at a table in the middle of a feast."

She made a small, strangled kind of sound. "It was only a kiss, Wes. You didn't attack me or anything. In fact, as I recall, I started things."

He closed his eyes, remembering that heart-stopping moment when she had spanned the distance between them and pressed her mouth to his.

Something told him he would be reliving that moment for a long, long time.

"Maybe," he finally said. "But I took things too far. I shouldn't have, especially after everything you told me about what you've been through. I promise, it won't happen again."

She gazed at him, and he watched as she seemed to regain her composure with every passing second.

She nodded and pressed her lips together, those delicious lips he could have explored all night long.

"Okay," she said. She rose and let out a long breath. "Good night, then. Thanks again for...for listening to me."

She grabbed Theo's leash and the two of them walked into the house, leaving him alone to curse and ache and want.

Jenna walked back up the stairs to her apartment on knees that felt weak, somehow.

She still couldn't quite wrap her head around the realization that she had instigated another kiss with Wes Calhoun.

Hadn't she learned her lesson the first time?

She wanted to blame it on the moonlight or the peaceful garden or the simple release of sharing her story with him finally.

She suspected the real reason for her behavior had nothing to do with that. It had more to do with the man himself.

When Wes first moved into Brambleberry House, she had considered him the very last man in Cannon Beach she might come to trust, someone with whom she had nothing in common.

What an illuminating example of how very wrong first impressions could be. These past few weeks of coming to know him better—of seeing his gentleness with Theo, with his own daughter and with hers—had given her a picture of a kind man beneath the gruff, intimidating exterior.

She respected and admired him more than any other man she had met in a very long time.

What was she going to do about it?

As she reached her apartment, she let herself and Theo inside, where she took off the puppy's leash and harness. The dog rushed to his water bowl, and Jenna closed the door behind her, listening to the small, comforting noises of the apartment settling around her.

Nothing.

That was exactly what she planned to do about this attraction to Wes. They had kissed again and it had been amazing, but now she had to go back to her regular life and try to forget those few stirring moments in the garden had ever happened.

The idea depressed her, even though she knew she had no other option.

They were attracted to each other. She couldn't deny that. The heat they generated could have ignited a dozen beach fires.

Why not give in to it? They were both unattached adults. What would be the harm in finding a secluded spot in the garden, maybe the pergola or one of the padded benches in a dark corner, and surrendering to the attraction between them?

Because she would end up with a broken heart.

She was not a woman who could handle a casual fling. She had seen her mother's heart broken too many times by men who would move in and out of their lives.

She was a forever kind of woman. She knew that about herself and suspected it wouldn't take much for her to fall in love with Wes.

Then what?

Try as she might, she couldn't picture a future with Wes. She again couldn't imagine she could provide anything that a man like him might be looking for in a woman.

Someone adventurous. Audacious. Brave.

She wasn't any of those things. Eventually Wes would figure that out and grow tired of her.

She couldn't go through the pain of loving someone again and inevitably losing him.

Better to stop things now, before either of their hearts were involved. Before she could make a fool of herself over him and destroy a friendship she was coming to cherish.

Theo went to stand by the door of his crate, ready for bed. She opened it for him and watched him curl up on the soft blankets, then headed for her solitary bed.

Chapter Ten

Somehow, she and Wes managed to maintain a cordial relationship over the next week while she helped fill in the gaps of Brielle's care, between his work schedule and the girls' science camp schedule.

He was friendly enough when he would drop his daughter at Jenna's apartment in the morning, a half hour before she had to take the girls to camp.

He would chat with Jenna about her upcoming day and would ask questions of Addie about camp and what other activities she was doing that summer.

A few mornings when he had extra time, he even offered to take Theo outside to the garden so that Jenna could focus on finishing up breakfast and getting ready for her shift at the gift shop, on the days she worked.

In the evenings, the routine was reversed. He would come to pick up his daughter about an hour after camp finished for the day. He never lingered long but took time to chat a little about the day and their respective plans for the evening.

Despite her lingering tumult over the kisses they had shared— and the secret part of her that undeniably wanted more—she quite enjoyed the routine they had fallen into. She sensed he did as well.

Everything changed on the morning of the girls' last day of science camp.

The morning started like all the others. She and Addie both got up early to walk the dog on the beach as the morning mist hung heavy on the shore and the gulls swooped to scavenge for juicy treasure along the detritus left from high tide.

She wasn't quite sure what happened. One moment, they were enjoying the morning, the next, the dog stopped to sniff directly in front of Jenna and she got tangled in his leash.

She could feel herself topple and reached a hand out to brace herself. Under normal circumstances, she would have been fine, simply annoyed at her own clumsiness. She landed on soft sand, after all.

Something in the sand wasn't soft, though. She felt a slicing pain as her palm caught on something jagged buried in the sand. A piece of shell or driftwood, perhaps, or maybe even a shard of glass left by some unknown beach visitor.

She gasped at the pain and immediately rolled to her side, clutching her hand.

Addie looked down at her, wide-eyed. "What happened? Are you okay?"

"I'm fine," she lied.

She pulled her hand away and saw she had a nasty cut about four inches running right through her life line, between her right thumb and forefinger. "I'm afraid I'm bleeding, though," she admitted to her daughter.

She could only be glad she had been the one to fall and not Addie.

"Oh no! How did you cut yourself?"

"I'm not sure. Something sharp in the sand. I should find whatever it was so it doesn't hurt someone else."

"I can look."

"I'll do it," she said quickly, with visions of Addie being cut as well. "I don't want you to hurt yourself, too. Why don't you keep walking Theo down the beach a little more, and I'll dig around and see if I can figure out what it was."

Addie looked undecided but after a moment, her daughter obeyed. She and the dog headed away from Jenna a short distance.

Her hand was now bleeding copiously, which was one of the reasons she had sent Addie away. She didn't have anything with her to stop the bleeding so she grabbed a corner of her T-shirt and ripped, feeling a pang as she did.

This had been one of Ryan's T-shirts that she had packed away after he died. She wore them as sleep shirts and to work out.

She still had several of his shirts left, including three that she had sewn into pillows for Addie's room. Still, losing this one stung worse than her cut, like slicing one more thread between her and her past.

She quickly wrapped the strip of cloth around her hand, hoping to stop the worst of the bleeding, then dug through the deep sand there until she found the culprit, a shell from what looked like a Dungeness crab, with a broken, jagged edge.

She tossed it into one of the garbage cans set at intervals along the beach, then caught up with Addie.

"Mom, you need a real bandage," her daughter said, taking in the makeshift bandage that was also now covered in blood.

Jenna strongly suspected she needed stitches, but she didn't want to worry Addie. A trip to the doctor or urgent care clinic could wait until after she dropped off the girls at day camp. Meantime, she would do some rudimentary first aid back at their apartment to staunch the bleeding.

They reached the second floor landing to their apartment just as Wes came down the stairs from the third floor, chatting with Brielle.

He stopped on the stairs halfway to the landing and stared at her.

"Good Lord. What happened to you?"

He looked gorgeous, she couldn't help but notice, in worn

jeans, work boots and a T-shirt that stretched over his hard muscles.

She, on the other hand, looked like she had gone a few rounds with an angry badger. She had tried to hold her arm above her heart to slow the blood flow. As a result, blood had dripped through her makeshift bandage to streak down her arm.

"I'm fine. It's nothing. I stumbled while we were walking. When I reached out to catch myself, I landed on a broken shell with a sharp edge in the sand."

"That looks like it really hurt," Brielle exclaimed.

"It looks worse than it is."

"My mom didn't cry at all. She's tough."

Addie's admiring tone made Jenna feel about a thousand feet tall. She only hoped her daughter still looked up to her after she reached the difficult teenage years, just on the horizon.

"Let me take a look at it," Wes said, holding out a hand.

She didn't want to show him, though she wasn't sure if that was embarrassment at her own clumsiness or hesitation to have him touch her again, given the heat that flared between them at any given moment.

"You don't have time," she protested. "We're late returning from our walk. You'll be late for work. Don't worry about me. I'm fine."

"I have time for this," he said, in a tone that brooked no argument.

When her gaze met his, the implacable hardness there told her she had no choice. He intended to look at her hand. She should be grateful for his concern, not frustrated by his stubbornness.

With a resigned sigh, she unlocked her apartment and opened the door for all of them to follow her inside.

Theo, who had caused the whole disaster, trotted into the

house, planted himself on his haunches and grinned at the four of them, clearly delighted to have his favorite people all together.

"Addie, will you clean up the breakfast dishes and load the dishwasher?"

"Okay." Her daughter headed for the kitchen, Brielle right behind her.

"I'll help," her friend said.

Meanwhile, Wes pointed toward Addie's bathroom, the closest to the living room. "Let's start by rinsing it to get the sand and blood off so we can see what we're up against."

She followed him to the bathroom, wondering why she had never noticed how small the room was.

"I don't want to get blood all over you."

"By the end of the day, I usually have oil and brake fluid and any manner of other things all over me. This is nothing."

He turned on the water while he unwound the scrap of T-shirt from her palm. She winced as the fabric caught in her jagged wound.

"Sorry."

"It's not your fault I'm so clumsy. I still don't know quite how I tripped. I think I got tangled in the leash and caught myself before I could fall on Theo."

"Bad luck that you would land right on a broken shell."

"Yes. Out of the entire beach filled with soft, forgiving sand where I could have fallen, I had to choose that very spot."

She shook her head, trying at the same time to catch her breath as he gently held her hand this way and that under the stream of warm water.

He smelled so good. He was obviously just out of the shower and smelled like a combination of laundry soap and some outdoorsy kind of male shampoo.

He was warm, too. After their chilly walk along the beach,

she couldn't help wishing she could snuggle up against him to draw some of his heat back inside her.

"How bad is it, Dr. Calhoun?"

"I'm afraid you're going to need stitches. It's not long, but it's pretty deep. You said you landed on a broken shell? When was your last tetanus shot?"

She thought back to her most recent medical history and remembered getting one around the time that Ryan had died, when she had scraped herself on a nail trying to plant some flowers in the small fenced yard of their apartment.

"I should be good in that regard."

"Do you want me to take the girls to day camp and then run you to the urgent care clinic? I can call my bosses and let them know an emergency has come up."

She was very tempted to lean on him, to let him take over. It was very hard to ignore the allure of that broad chest, those strong shoulders.

She was tough, she reminded herself. She could handle this, even though her hand throbbed with pain, which was also giving her a headache.

"I should be all right. If you could just help me wrap it better, that would be really great. It's my right hand and I'm right-handed, so I don't think I will be able to do a very good job with my left hand."

"You got it."

Using her first-aid kit after she showed it to him, he applied antibacterial ointment with a gentleness that made her shiver.

She could only hope he didn't notice as he rooted through the kit to find the largest bandage she had.

"This should hold you for a little while, until you can have someone take a look. You should definitely take care of it sooner rather than later."

"Thank you."

Bending low over her hand, he applied the bandage to her

palm, pressing carefully around the edges to ensure the wound was protected as much as possible.

"I wish I could do more."

"You've done enough. I'll be fine. I'll call my primary care doctor right now and see if I can get in this morning to have Dr. Sanderson take a look."

"You see Eli Sanderson?"

"Yes. Do you know him?"

"I knew him in the military, only peripherally. But we have friends in common. He and his wife invited me to dinner when I first moved to town. They were very kind."

"Melissa actually lived here in Brambleberry House before I did. We've become friends through Rosa, who is her good friend."

"She's the one who convinced Rosa to rent me an apartment when I was looking."

"I'm glad she did," Jenna said.

His gaze met hers and the moment seemed to stretch between them, taut and fragile, like the thread of a spider's web, gleaming with morning dew.

Something sparked in his expression as he looked down at her, something hot and glittery that left her a little dizzy.

Maybe she had lost more blood than she thought, she told herself. Or maybe it was simply a result of being in such close proximity to Wes Calhoun.

He was the first to look away.

"That should do it. Are you certain you don't want me to take you to urgent care? I feel wrong leaving you in your hour of need."

"No. Definitely not. I'm fine. Thank you, though. You've been very kind."

"Right. That's what I've been," he said, his voice gruff.

She sensed he wanted to say more, but Addie and Brielle came to check on her and the moment was gone.

* * *

After she had been treated at Eli's office, Jenna returned to the house to let Theo out, then moved him to the fenced dog yard, placing his open crate in the shade under the covered porch, along with plenty of water and food.

When she was certain the puppy was settled and comfortable, she drove to the By-the-Wind gift shop for her noon shift.

The morning fog had blown away, as it usually did during the summer, leaving the day sunny and mild. She parked as close as she could manage. She would have been better off walking, judging by the number of vehicles clogging the downtown area.

The tourist season was in full force. From here, she could see the wide, long Cannon Beach stretching north for miles. It was dotted with umbrellas, bikes, swimmers and the occasional kite.

The crowds of visitors descending every summer could be a nuisance but so much of the Cannon Beach economy depended on them that she couldn't be too upset.

Crowds were a small price to pay for the sheer delight in living in such magnificent surroundings. And if the masses of people became too overwhelming, she could always take a drive down the coast and find an isolated beach somewhere or she could hike into the hills east of town and find a beautiful mountain river wending its way to the ocean.

That was the beauty of the Oregon Coast. It was long, vast and certainly not overpopulated.

She let herself into the employee entrance of the store just as Rosa was coming out.

"What is this?" her friend cried, looking aghast at her bandage. "What have you done to yourself?"

"It's nothing. Just a bit of bad luck. I fell on the beach this morning when I was walking with Theo and Addison and managed to land on a broken shell. I'm fine. Eli gave me only five stitches and some local anesthetic so I can't feel a thing right now."

"Oh, you poor thing. You must go home and rest your hand. I can work for you instead."

Jenna rolled her eyes at this very pregnant woman trying to be protective of her over a little scratch.

"Absolutely not. Please don't worry about me. The bandage is annoying but it should not stop me from doing anything."

"I am sorry this happened to you. Did Addie help you with your bandage?"

She held up her bandaged hand. "Dr. Sanderson and his staff get the credit for this one. But Wes helped me with the initial triage."

Rosa gave her a side glance. "Did he? I told you, he is a good man."

Jenna was beginning to agree. Whenever she remembered the tender way he cared for her injury, she felt warmth seep through her.

She did not tell her friend that Wes was not only a good man. He was definitely a good kisser.

"Do not worry about me," she said again to Rosa. "I'll be just fine. Go and put your feet up."

Rosa sighed. "Wyatt will probably come with his police car and drag me home if I don't rest. If not him, Carrie and Bella will do it."

Carrie was the sister of Rosa's husband and Bella was Carrie's daughter. Both of them adored Rosa and were even more protective of her than Jenna was.

"Good. You should listen to them. I'll see you later."

She hugged Rosa and hurried into the gift shop, grateful again for good friends.

Chapter Eleven

On his lunch hour, Wes decided to eat his brown-bag lunch while he walked three blocks downtown to find a birthday present for his sister, who lived in a little town in Idaho called Pine Gulch, on the west slope of the Tetons.

He had a single destination in mind, the gift shop owned by his landlady, Rosa. It was the logical choice, he told himself. By-the-Wind carried unique local products that represented the best artists and craftspeople in the area. His sister would love something handmade, especially something he had specifically picked for her.

As he walked toward the store, he reminded himself there was little chance he would bump into Jenna, though he knew she worked part-time at By-the-Wind during the summer.

Logic did nothing to stop the little buzz of anticipation as he made his way through town.

The sidewalks were busy, but it wasn't the kind of crowd he had been warned to expect in summer. Mostly families were browsing for beach toys or T-shirts or fudge.

He still could not believe he lived in this busy little beach community on the Oregon Coast, that he was working as a mechanic, of all things, and enjoying all of it.

Life had a funny way of taking a guy on adventures he never could have imagined.

Four years ago, he thought he had his life completely figured out. He had loved the hard work of making the security company a success. While his marriage definitely had its ups and downs, he was trying hard to make that a success as well.

He thought he would continue on that same path and eventually attain everything he wanted.

His life hadn't gone exactly as planned. Three years behind bars had a way of derailing an entire future.

Wes had always been a planner, goal oriented and ambitious. Now he tried to focus on the moment. The smell of ice-cream cones from the parlor he passed, the sound of children laughing as they watched someone making saltwater taffy at another shop, the hum of conversation between shoppers. All of it was underlined by the constant song of the sea, which gave him more comfort than he ever could have guessed.

When he finally reached By-the-Wind, he pushed open the door and immediately felt out of place.

Wes didn't consider himself sexist but this didn't really feel like the kind of store that catered to a guy like him. It was filled with scented candles, wind chimes, floral-patterned shopping bags and rows of handcrafted jewelry.

He was the only man in the store, he couldn't help but notice. A trio of older ladies were looking at carved lighthouse figures while a couple of teenagers spun a rotating rack of silver earrings.

What would his sister like here?

He had no idea. While he and Maggie had always been close as children, separated by only a few years, as adults, their paths had diverged. After his arrest and especially after his conviction, Wes had tried to build in more distance between them. Maggie's husband was a small-town lawyer with state political ambitions. He didn't need to be associated with someone who had been convicted on multiple felony charges.

Maggie had tried to stay in touch but he had discouraged contact. She hadn't given up, no matter how tough he made it on her.

He was scouring through some decorative ceramic vases when he saw Jenna emerge from a back room. She did an almost comical double take when she spotted him. He again felt large and ungainly in this store filled with delicate items.

"Hi." She smiled. "This is a surprise."

"For me, too. I wasn't expecting to see you. I figured even if you were scheduled to work, you would have taken time off because of your injury."

She held up her heavily bandaged hand. "Good news. They didn't have to amputate. I only needed a few stitches. Five, but who is counting?"

"Whew." He managed a smile. "Does it still hurt?"

"The local anesthetic they used to put in the stitches has worn off so it's throbbing a bit, but it's not too bad."

"Good. That's good."

Silence descended between them and he didn't want to do anything but stare at her. That wasn't creepy or anything, right?

Around Jenna, he experienced a strange paradox of emotions, both fierce awareness as well as an odd sort of peace.

"Was there something I could help you find?" she asked after a moment.

"Um. Yes. I'm looking for a birthday present for my sister."

"You have a sister?"

She seemed genuinely surprised, and he realized he hadn't mentioned his family much to her, other than to tell her about his father's death.

"Yes. Maggie is three years younger than I am. An artist and writer. She lives in Idaho with her husband and their two kids."

"Wow. Okay. Um, what are her tastes? Does she collect anything? You said she is an artist?"

"Yes. She paints. But I know she also collects pottery. I was looking at your vases here."

"They are very nice. Do you know what kind of pottery she collects?"

He felt stupid for his ignorance. Again, he wished he had not come, that he had simply picked out something for Maggie online.

Had his subconscious led him here, in the random hope that he might find himself in this very situation, speaking with the woman who fascinated him so much? He did not want to admit it, but the truth was becoming increasingly difficult to ignore.

Jenna Haynes was becoming a vital part of his life. He didn't want to think about how bereft he would feel when his daughter returned to her mother and stepfather's home and he had no more excuse to see Jenna at least twice a day.

He turned his attention back to the problem at hand, finding a gift for his sister. "To be honest, I am not at all sure what to get her. I don't know what she likes. Maggie and I haven't talked much for the past few years. Only a couple of times since I was arrested, actually."

"Why? Did she believe you were guilty?" she asked with a frown. He could almost see her mind working, possibly condemning his sister. He couldn't have that.

"I tried to keep Maggie and her family away from all the ugliness," he said quickly. "She had enough on her plate, with new twins and her husband opening his law practice. She didn't need to be dragged down by worry."

"You don't think she worried about you, whether you were in regular communication or not?"

"Probably," he admitted. In truth, he hadn't wanted the baby sister he adored to see what a mess his life had become.

"We've texted and emailed back and forth a few times since I was released. I was going to swing by and visit on my way to Oregon but it didn't quite work out."

She studied him and he had a feeling she saw right through his excuses and explanations.

"A birthday gift is a lovely way to reconnect," she finally said, her tone gentle. "Though perhaps the best thing you could give Maggie for her birthday would be a video call from her brother and niece so she can catch up on your life."

That was not a bad idea. Because his contact with the outside world had been limited while he had been incarcerated, he had lost the habit of remembering he could pick up the phone at any time now.

"Maybe I can do both. Send her a gift and also catch up over the phone."

She smiled. "That works. I can't help you with the phone call, but let's try to find something wonderful to send her. We have one section of pottery created by local artists. Would you like to take a look?"

"Definitely. I would love to give her something that represents the Oregon Coast."

He looked at the offerings on the shelves she indicated and was immediately drawn to a small, delicate bowl the same iridescent colors found on the inside of an abalone shell. It was even shaped a little like a shell.

"That is beautiful," he said, holding it up to admire the colors.

Her gaze softened. "That is by one of my favorite local artists. She is eighty years old, a real character who lives alone on an isolated stretch near Heceta Head and throws pots every day. You should meet her on one of her visits to town."

"I would like that," he said. He had never been one for art galleries or museums when he was younger but his time in prison had given him a true appreciation for those who could create beauty no matter their situation.

"This one works for me. That was easy. I might even make it back before my lunch hour is over."

"I can wrap it up for you. If you would like to pick out a birthday card while you're here and write a message, we can even ship for you. We have some nice original birthday cards as well as some all-occasion."

While it would certainly take a weight off him not to have to deal with the inconvenience of mailing, he suddenly caught sight of that glaring white bandage on her hand.

"I don't think you should be wrapping up anything right now, with your bum hand. Just slip it in a bag and I can take it home. Brie can help me deal with it tonight."

She made a face. "I appreciate your concern, Wes, but I'm really fine. I've already packaged things for other shoppers today and didn't drop a single thing. If I have trouble, some-one else here can handle that part of it."

She was a difficult woman to win an argument against.

"Thank you, I guess. Though I don't feel good about it."

She laughed. "Sorry about that."

He wanted to gaze at her for whatever time was left of his lunch hour but forced himself to head to the cards, where he finally found a lovely hand-painted card he knew Maggie would appreciate as much as the bowl.

Jenna handed him a pen from behind the counter and after a moment's reflection, he wrote a quick message wishing her the happiest of birthdays and expressing his love. It seemed inadequate but he couldn't think of anything else to say.

When he finished the card and slipped it into the envelope, he handed over his credit card and Jenna ran it through.

It sometimes struck him how amazing it was to be able to walk into a store and purchase whatever he wanted. For three years, he had been limited by the prison commissary and what friends on the outside could provide him.

All of his pre-arrest personal assets had been restored to him following the acquittal, along with a healthy settlement for wrongful prosecution. He had plenty of money right now. He couldn't work forever fixing motorcycles. He knew that, but he wasn't in any hurry to change the status quo.

After years of the grind to build his company, then the

stress and helplessness of the past three years, Wes found he enjoyed the work he was doing.

He liked taking something broken and repairing it to be as good as new…and sometimes better.

Maybe he would open his own shop somewhere, though probably not. He didn't feel right about going into competition with Paco and Carlos, after they had been so good to him.

"Thank you," Jenna said, handing him the receipt. "I'll try to get this wrapped up and shipped today. It should go out tomorrow at the latest. That's our guarantee. She should receive it within a week. Will that work?"

"It should. Her birthday isn't for a few more weeks. Thank you for your help."

"My pleasure."

He needed to return to work but he was loath to leave her.

"Why don't you let me take care of dinner for us and the girls tonight?" he said on impulse, gesturing to her hand. "It's the least I can do, after all you've done to help me out with Brie this week."

"It has really been no trouble," she protested.

"You keep saying that, but surely it's been a *little* trouble. You've got a sore hand and don't need to be rushing around tonight trying to fix dinner."

She gave a quick laugh that sounded prettier than any of the wind chimes in this charming little store ever could.

"You seem to have this idea that my hand has been grievously wounded. It's only a few stitches. I am really fine."

"Okay, let's take the hand completely out of it. For two weeks, you have stepped up to bail me out with my daughter. I would love the chance to repay you in some small way. Why don't we celebrate the last day of the girls' camp and my last day with Brielle full-time? We could explore one of the nearby state parks, if you have a favorite."

"Have you visited Oswald West State Park? It's just south

of town. It has lots of tide pools and trails through the forest that look like something out of *Lord of the Rings*. Addie loves it. It also has a picnic area close to the beach."

"I have not been there. That sounds perfect. The girls can show us everything they learned at camp and, bonus, Theo can get some exercise."

"That is actually not a bad idea," she said after a moment's thought. "It sounds really fun."

He felt a ridiculous sense of accomplishment. "Great. I'm done working today at four. I can pick up some picnic supplies. We can take my truck and load the back with whatever we might need."

"That sounds great. I'm off by three, in time to get the girls."

"Let's plan to leave about five. That will give us several hours before dark to enjoy the scenery."

"Perfect. We'll be ready."

He wanted to stay and talk to her more, but he had already taken too long and needed to return to the bike he was working on.

Besides that, the store had begun to fill with more customers, and he realized he had been completely monopolizing Jenna's time for the past fifteen minutes.

"Thanks again for your help. I'll see you this evening," he said.

"Great."

That buzz of anticipation carried him toward the door. Before he reached it, he spotted a few women with familiar features whom he knew he had seen around town before. He nodded to them but didn't miss the way the mouth of one of the women tightened. If she had been wearing long skirts, he had a feeling she would have brushed them out of his way with a dramatic sweep.

He wouldn't let it ruin his mood, he decided. Not when he had a fun evening ahead with Jenna and their respective daughters.

Chapter Twelve

As Wes made his way to the exit, Jenna released the breath she hadn't realized she had been holding and tried not to stare at his narrow hips or his broad shoulders in that snug T-shirt.

Seeing him in this setting, surrounded by lovely, fragile objects, only seemed to reinforce his contrasting masculinity.

She finished packaging up the lovely bowl for his sister, catching only bits and pieces of the conversation around her until she heard the word Brambleberry House.

Two women were looking at a collection of handmade jewelry close to the counter, local women she knew vaguely but who weren't close acquaintances.

Donna Martin was a former teacher with a reputation at the elementary school for having been rigid and cold to her students during her time there. She had retired before Jenna took a job at the school, and Jenna knew there were few students or parents who were sorry when she left.

She had always struck Jenna as being thoroughly unpleasant.

Her companion, Susan Lakewood, was tall, almost gaunt, a woman who volunteered at the library as well as managed a string of rental properties on the other side of town. When she wasn't in Donna's company, she could be quite pleasant.

The two had also apparently noticed how out of place Wes seemed in the store. It took Jenna a moment to realize they were talking about him.

"I don't know what Rosa was thinking, to let his type move into that house. Abigail would be rolling in her grave," Donna muttered.

"He has always been very nice in our few interactions."

"He's a criminal! I heard it on good authority that he hasn't even been out of prison four months. It's outrageous that someone like that is allowed to live in Cannon Beach at all, let alone in such a nice place as Brambleberry House."

"I don't know," Susan said in a timid sort of voice. "He seems polite enough when he comes into the library with his daughter. She likes to read the Magic Tree House books."

Donna made a derisive sound. "Doesn't matter how polite he is. You can't change the facts. He looks like a man who just got out of prison, doesn't he? I would be afraid to have him living anywhere close to me. Who knows what he did?"

Jenna frowned, her palm suddenly throbbing worse than ever with the itch to slap the woman, though she knew she never would.

She did not want to have any sort of confrontation with Donna, who had a reputation for being vindictive to anyone who crossed her. At the same time, she would not stand by and let the woman malign a good man who had done nothing wrong and didn't deserve her disdain.

Under normal circumstances, Jenna would never confront a customer at all, but somehow she sensed Rosa would back her a hundred percent if she were here.

"Can I help you two find something?" she asked loudly.

Susan, at least, had the decency to blush.

"We're just looking," she said quickly.

"Let me know if I can help," she said. Before she could move away to help someone else, she lowered her voice. "For the record, Wes Calhoun was wrongfully convicted and has been exonerated of all charges. He is a loving father and a hardworking employee who is trying to rebuild his life here in Cannon Beach so that he can be closer to his daughter. Don't you find that admirable? There are so many men out there who are only too willing to abandon their children after a divorce. I'm sure as a former educator, Donna, you saw evidence of that as well with your students. What a tough situation that can be on children."

"It's outrageous. Parents don't care about the harm they're doing to their children. All they care about is having what they want."

She let the woman ramble on for a few moments, then finally gave a polite smile.

"Yes. That's why it's so refreshing to see a man like Wes Calhoun, who is trying his best to be a positive influence in his child's life. Don't you agree?"

"Very refreshing," Susan said.

Donna still wore a sour frown. "He still looks like he just held up a bank somewhere."

"It's a good thing most people don't judge others wholly on their appearance but on their behavior, isn't it?"

She walked away before either woman could answer.

She was shaking a little but told herself it was simply a reaction to the pain shot wearing off.

"What was Donna going on about?" Carol Hardesty asked after the two women quickly bustled out of the store.

Jenna sighed, wishing she had handled things a different way. She would have liked to tell Donna she was a sanctimonious cow.

"Donna was bad-mouthing my neighbor. Wes Calhoun. I was gently trying to set her straight."

"Oooh. He's Lacey Summers's ex-husband, right?"

"That's right."

"Who would walk away from a guy like that?" Carol asked, shaking her head in disbelief. "I don't care if he was in prison. He's the sort of guy worth waiting for on the outside, you know?"

Yes. Jenna understood completely.

"He was innocent," she muttered. "He was cleared of all wrongdoing. That's what bugs me. It doesn't seem fair for people like Donna to treat him like some kind of criminal when he didn't do anything wrong."

"I wouldn't listen to anything she has to say. That woman is perpetually unhappy. She finds fault in everyone."

"It just bothers me. Wes is a wonderful father and a really good man."

Carol shrugged. "Here's the thing about Donna. If you don't fit the mold of what she considers acceptable, nothing else matters. You'll never measure up to her expectations. Some of us figured out a long time ago that it's not worth even trying."

Jenna knew Carol was right. What bothered her most about the encounter was that Jenna had been exactly like Donna. She had judged Wes as scary and intimidating when he first moved into Brambleberry House.

She cringed when she remembered that day he had jumped her car, when she had reacted to him out of fear and nerves.

Since then she had learned he was a kind man who made delicious pizza for his daughter, who loved his sister, who savored the smell of basil leaves and the Brambleberry House gardens after a rain.

And who kissed her until she forgot all the reasons why they weren't right for each other.

The girls were chattering with excitement when she picked them up after their last day of camp.

"That was the most fun *ever*," Brielle said as she slid into the back seat, her cheeks a little sunburned and her bucket hat hanging down her back.

"Yeah. It was so fun," Addie agreed. "I'm sad it's over. I wish we could go to science camp all summer long!"

"Wouldn't that be fun?" Jenna said. "But then you would miss soccer camp and art camp."

"I guess."

"How's your hand, Mrs. Haynes?" Brielle asked as Jenna turned her vehicle toward Brambleberry House. "Did you have to get a hundred stitches?"

"Not a hundred, no. Only five."

"Do you have to wear a cast?" Addie asked, peering around the seat to see.

"Only a bandage." She held up her right hand for the girls.

"I've never had stitches," Brielle said. "Does it hurt when the needle goes into your skin? I always thought it would be so weird."

"No. They give you a shot first that numbs your skin. You're right. It is a weird feeling. You can tell when they're tugging the stitches. But it wasn't bad."

"I'm really sorry you were hurt, Mom," Addie said. "Me and Brie can take care of Theo if you want. We can even take him out late tonight so you don't have to do it."

Her daughter's thoughtfulness touched her. "Thank you. I might need your help a little more than usual for the next few days."

"Maybe we can cook dinner tonight," Brielle suggested. "I know how to make nachos."

"Actually, your dad thought you might like to go on a picnic at the beach tonight for dinner, since it was your last day at camp today. Plus you'll be going back home tomorrow."

"Oh, that's right," Addie said, her voice disappointed.

"I totally forgot my mom and Ron were coming home tomorrow." Brielle seemed disappointed at the prospect of leaving Brambleberry House.

"It's not like you won't come back and will never see us again. You stay with your dad like every weekend," Addie reminded her.

Brielle's features brightened. "Oh yeah. We can totally hang out when I come stay with him."

For the remainder of the short drive, the girls chattered about their favorite part of science camp and what they planned to do the next week when they didn't have camp. When they pulled up to the house, the first thing Jenna saw was Wes's motorcycle. His daughter spied it as well.

"Dad's home from work already. Yay! Can we leave now for the picnic?"

"I'm afraid I will need some time to take care of Theo, change out of my work clothes and gather a few things," Jenna said, trying to ignore the little buzz of anticipation she felt at knowing she would be spending the evening with Wes and his daughter. "I'm sure your dad could use a little time as well."

They started for the house when the door opened and Wes walked out, arms loaded with blankets and lawn chairs.

Her little buzz became a full-on tremor.

"Oh. Hi. You're home," he said. His face seemed to light up when he spotted them. For his daughter, she told herself. Certainly not for her.

For a moment, she let her imagination wander, wondering what it might be like to have his hard features glow with welcome like that for her.

"There's my girl."

"Hi, Dad." Brielle launched herself at her father, who managed to set down the lawn chairs and blankets in time to catch her.

Jenna found the affection between the two of them sweetly touching, even as it made her ache a little for her fatherless child, who watched their joy-filled reunion with a little glint of envy in her expression.

How Wes must have missed his daughter during those three years he had been incarcerated. When children were young, even a few months' development could mean fundamental changes in maturity, communication and social skills. Jenna couldn't imagine how much Brielle had changed in the three years they were separated.

He lifted his gaze from his daughter to Jenna and something in his expression warmed her to her toes.

"Hi. I'm sorry I wasn't home half an hour earlier or I could have picked up the girls so you didn't have to."

"It's no problem. I was planning on it."

"How's your hand? Were you okay to drive?"

In truth, her hand was throbbing more now than it had since the initial injury but she didn't want to tell him, for fear he would suggest canceling the outing.

She didn't want to disappoint the girls. At least that's what she tried to tell herself was her motive for ignoring the pain.

"It's fine. I'm a little bit sore but not bad."

"Are you sure you're up for a picnic? If you're not, we can do it another day."

She shook her head. "We're all looking forward to it. Aren't we, girls?"

Brielle and Addie both nodded with enthusiasm.

"Give me a few moments and I'll be ready," she told him. "I have to change and take care of Theo."

"Take as long as you need."

The only trouble was, she had no idea how long it would take her to figure out how to protect her heart so she didn't completely fall for Wes Calhoun.

Chapter Thirteen

Could this really be his life or merely some delicious dream he didn't want to end?

Throughout the afternoon and evening Wes spent with Jenna and their respective daughters at the beautiful state park south of Cannon Beach, he had to stop more than once to soak in the moment.

It was a perfect summer evening, in company with his daughter, whom he loved more than anything else in the world, as well as the lovely Jenna Haynes and her daughter.

Only months earlier, he would have been standing in the chow line waiting for his bologna sandwich and pudding cup. If he was lucky.

Now he was sitting on a blanket a few dozen yards from the Pacific Ocean, watching the sky light up with color as the sun began its slow descent into the horizon.

The air was filled with the sound of the girls' laughter as a cute puppy with gangly legs loped around with enthusiasm, trying to catch the tennis ball they chucked between them.

Across from Wes on the blanket, watching the girls with a soft smile, was the warm, beautiful woman who was becoming increasingly important to him.

He wanted to bottle up this moment, to take it out when life felt hard or when he gave in to his occasional bouts of self-pity at all that had been taken from him by someone he had trusted.

"What a beautiful evening." Jenna gave a contented sort of sigh. "Thank you so much for suggesting this. It was exactly what I needed."

"Tough day? I mean, besides the stitches in your hand?"

She looked back at the girls. "Not really. It was busy, but no worse than usual for a Friday. I did have to deal with some… unpleasant customers, but I handled it the best way I could."

"That's always tough, isn't it? That was the hardest part for me of running a business. I tend to be impatient with people who are rude and demanding. It's hard not to want to respond in kind."

"What do you do?"

"Usually just try to remind myself that everybody has a bad day once in a while and I have no idea what they might be going through outside of this momentary interaction. Don't get me wrong. As you know probably too well, there are some garbage people in the world."

"Like your partner who set you up."

"He heads the list."

He didn't like thinking about Anthony Morris for even a moment longer than necessary.

"I doubt I'll ever be able to forgive him for trying to pin his crimes on me."

"And getting away with it for years," she pointed out.

"Right. But even with Tony, I try to remember that he is now behind bars, where he belongs, paying for what he did. I, on the other hand, am currently sitting on a spectacular beach watching the sunset with a beautiful woman."

He hadn't meant to add that part but had to admit he enjoyed seeing the wash of pink across her cheekbones.

She gazed at him for a long moment, then quickly looked away.

"Not so close to the water," she called to the girls, who

changed direction and returned to the blanket, with Theo leading the way.

The dog plopped onto the blanket, tongue panting.

"Oh. You're a thirsty guy, aren't you? That's what happens when you play so hard," Jenna said to the puppy.

Working around her injured hand, she opened her own water bottle and poured some into the dog's bowl they had brought. Theo lapped at it gratefully, which made the girls giggle.

"I'm thirsty, too," Brie declared. "Can I have another root beer?"

"I'm thirsty, too," Addie said.

"We have plenty of water but only one root beer left," he answered.

He had picked up a four-pack of craft root beer bottled by one of the local breweries. He and the girls each had enjoyed one but Jenna declared she was happy with water.

The girls studied the sole remaining bottle, clearly understanding the dilemma. Only one of them could have it. But which one?

"It's okay," Brielle said after a moment. "You have it."

Addie shook her head. "No. You have it."

"How about this," Jenna suggested. "You can share it. I can pour half the bottle into one of your empty water bottles."

"Good idea," Brie said, clearly thrilled with the solution.

"My water bottle is empty," Addie said, tipping it for the last drop to be sure.

"Why don't you let me do that?" Wes held out a hand to take the root beer bottle. "We don't want you to splash soda all over your bandages."

Jenna made a face but handed over the root beer bottle and Addie's water bottle.

Wes moved a few steps away from the blanket in case of fizzing and opened the bottle of root beer, carefully pouring out half into the water bottle.

As he returned to the blanket and handed the soda bottle to Brie and the pink water bottle to Addie, Wes couldn't help thinking about the time one of the guys in his block, a particularly nasty guy named Victor, had shivved a guy at lunch over a peanut butter cookie.

He remembered the scream and the blood and the shouting guards as if it happened that morning.

Would memories of that dark time always taint his future happiness? He didn't want it to. He wanted to be able to completely put it behind him, but he wasn't sure that would ever be possible.

He could not pretend it had never happened. Those three years were part of him, just like the time he had spent in the Army and the years of his childhood when he had lived on that breathtaking Colorado farm.

•He had to hope that eventually moments like these, pure and perfect, would overwhelm the darkness.

"Thank you for everything," Jenna said as the girls sipped at their respective root beers. "This was so fun going tide pooling with you girls and having you show us all the creatures you learned about at camp."

That had been one of Wes's favorite parts of the evening. Jenna had orders from the doctor to keep her hand dry, so Wes had set up a beach chair for her on the sand just above the surf. She watched, the dog at her side, while he and the girls scrambled carefully over the rocks looking at starfish, sea urchins and anemones of every color.

Addie and Brie used Wes's cell phone to snap pictures of what they found for Jenna, so she could enjoy the experience, too.

While he had set up their picnic dinner of fried chicken, pasta salad and kettle chips, Jenna had scrolled through the photos, asking the girls questions about their discoveries.

After dinner, the girls had begged to take a walk on one

of the lush trails around the state park. With the girls racing ahead, he and Jenna had walked together, chatting about places they had visited and bucket list destinations they would like to see.

Finally, they had returned here to watch the sunset.

"We should probably head back soon," Jenna told the girls as they finished their soda.

"I wish we could stay here all night," Addie said, lying back on the blanket and gazing up at the few pale stars beginning to appear.

"I'm afraid there's no camping allowed at this park," Jenna said. "But maybe one weekend this summer we could borrow a tent from Rosa and Wyatt and camp at one of the other places along the coast."

"Can we come?" Brie asked.

Wes gave an inward wince at his daughter's forwardness.

"That would be so fun!" Addie exclaimed. "Can we go camping together, Mom?"

That lovely pink rose on her cheeks as she sent Wes a quick look. "I'm not sure Rosa and Wyatt have a tent that would fit the four of us."

"We could bring our own tent!" Brie said. "You have one, don't you, Dad? If not, Mom and Ron do."

"I do have a tent. But maybe Jenna and Addie wanted to have their own trip together."

"It would be so fun to have you come, wouldn't it, Mom?"

Jenna lifted her gaze to his again. Heat surged between them. "Sure," she finally said. "We can probably make that work. We'll have to see."

He would love nothing more than spending a weekend camping with Jenna and their daughters. He had visions of talking by the fire until the early hours of the morning, gazing up at the stars, kissing her again until they were both shaking with need...

Wes sighed. He would be smarter to come up with excuses to stay away from Jenna, instead of letting his mind run wild, imagining mythical future outings together.

Though he didn't want this particular evening to end, he turned his energy toward loading up his pickup truck with all the things they had brought and making sure they carried away everything from their picnic site.

"Dad, can we stop and have gelato before we go home?" Brielle asked him when they were all finally loaded into the truck and he was about to drive out of the parking area.

His gaze met Jenna's and she shrugged. "Fine with me. I love gelato."

Wes pulled out onto the road back to Cannon Beach, feeling as if he had been handed a reprieve.

Maybe Jenna didn't want the evening to end, either.

After driving back to Cannon Beach, he parked down the street from the small storefront selling gelato in at least two dozen varieties, handmade on the premises.

He and Brielle had discovered the place shortly after he arrived in Cannon Beach, and stopping here occasionally had become something of a ritual for them.

The night was lovely and pleasant, not too warm and not cold enough for a jacket. The streets of downtown were bustling with visitors but the line at the gelato shop moved quickly.

After they ordered and received their gelato—chocolate chip for him and the girls and butter pecan for Jenna—they found an empty picnic table outside the shop and sat down, licking at their cones and people watching.

This was another moment he would store in his memory bank. The girls giggling about something, Theo lapping the ground of any drips from the cones, and Jenna pretty and soft in the lamplight as she tapped her sandal along with the live music coming out of the restaurant next door.

"This has been a perfect evening," she said as she worked to finish off the final few licks of her cone. "Thank you so much for suggesting it."

"Yeah," Addie said. "Thanks. It was really fun."

"Can we do it again the next time I come to stay with you?" Brielle asked him. "Maybe we could go to another beach and try tide pooling there."

"Sure."

He wasn't sure whether Jenna wanted to spend any more time with him, but Wes figured he could always take his daughter on his own.

Same for the camping trip. As much as he would enjoy going with Jenna and Addie, he and Brie could still have a great time, the two of them.

"Looks like somebody is pooped." Jenna gestured to Theo, who had plopped down at her feet and didn't look like he wanted to move.

"He's not the only one. I think I know two girls who are going to drop the moment they get home."

"I'm not tired," Addison insisted.

"Me neither," Brielle said.

"Well, Theo certainly is," Jenna answered.

"Because he's still a baby and babies sleep all the time," Brielle informed her. "That's what my mom says, anyway."

"They do sleep a lot," Jenna said. "All except Addie."

She smiled at her daughter. "You were up and down all night long and didn't sleep through the night until you were eight or nine months old. Your dad used to say you were afraid you were going to miss something. You were an early adopter of FOMO."

"What about me, Dad?"

Through his own choices, Wes had missed so much after Brie had been born, too busy trying to build the company. At least his time in prison had helped him realize that any success he earned professionally could be gone in an instant. This. This was the important thing. Family. Friends.

Love.

He didn't want to go there. Yes, he was developing feelings for Jenna but he certainly wasn't falling in love with her. That would be completely self-destructive of him.

"You are *still* afraid you're going to miss something," he said, focusing back on his daughter. "It's one of the things I love most about you."

She rolled her eyes at him. "I can't help it if all the good stuff happens after I go to bed!"

After they finished their gelato, he helped all three of them back into his pickup and drove the short distance back to Brambleberry House.

"Thank you again," Jenna said when he pulled into the driveway. "That was the most enjoyable evening I have had in a long time."

"Same for me," he admitted, his voice somewhat gruff.

"We can help you carry things back inside."

"I've got it. Don't worry."

"Okay. Well, um, have a good night."

He pushed down a hundred things he wanted to say. Especially *Can I carry you to my bed after the girls are asleep and keep you there all night long?*

"Thanks," he finally managed. "If you need help with Theo after Addie goes to sleep, let me know."

All evening, the girls had been taking turns holding the dog's leash so Jenna didn't have to risk reinjuring her wounded hand.

She nodded. "If I need help, I'll call. But I'm sure we'll be fine."

Before she headed toward the house, she shocked him one last time that day by reaching up and brushing her lips against his cheek.

It was all he could do not to turn his mouth to meet hers and devour her. Desire for her seemed to have become a steady beat through his veins.

"Good night," she murmured, then hurried into the house, leaving him to watch after her and ache.

Chapter Fourteen

She couldn't sleep.

Jenna opened one eye and glared at the clock on the night-stand. It was after 1:00 a.m. and she had been tossing and turning for an hour.

She was so tired but her mind couldn't seem to shut down. While she wasn't scheduled to work at the store the next day, Saturday, she had a packed agenda anyway. She and her friend Kim were cohosting the Brambleberry Book Group, consisting of twenty friends who gathered monthly, taking turns to be in charge.

She thought it would be fun to have dinner in the garden, shaded by the trees and the pergola. Kim was handling the meal, street tacos and taco salad catered by their favorite Mexican food place in town.

While Jenna was only baking a couple dozen cookies, she had plenty of other things to do. Cleaning off the lawn chairs. Setting up tables. Picking up the margarita mix.

She flipped her pillow over to the cool side, punched it with her good hand a few times for more fluff and rolled over.

She needed sleep so she could take on her chores the next day. But sleep still seemed a long way off. Instead, she couldn't seem to stop rehashing the evening spent with Wes and his daughter.

What was wrong with her?

She knew the answer to that, even before she asked it of herself.

She was lonely.

She wanted someone to hold her, to touch her, to cherish her and make her feel wanted.

And not any someone. She wanted Wes Calhoun.

Her mind kept replaying the hot, hungry look in his eyes when she had kissed his cheek several hours earlier.

He shared her attraction, which made it even harder for her to continue resisting him.

What was she going to do about Wes? She was developing feelings for the man, even though she knew anything between them was completely impossible.

Not feelings, she told herself. She couldn't be coming to care for him. They were friends. That was all.

Even as the thought popped into her mind, it rang hollow. Friends didn't make each other yearn. Friends didn't think about each other all the time. Friends didn't kiss each other until they were achy with need.

Wes made it so blasted hard to resist him. That evening with the girls had been magical. Even with her hand aching, she had loved spending time with him and his daughter. He had teased the girls, made them laugh, protected them.

Jenna sighed, turning over again before she finally sat up and pulled off her duvet. She had struggled so much with insomnia during the worst of Aaron's assault on her peace of mind that she was all too familiar with how it worked for her.

She likely had no chance of falling asleep anytime soon, not until she climbed out of bed and tried to do something else to distract herself and calm her mind for an hour or so.

Reading worked best for her, especially if it was something dry and uninteresting. While she focused on something else, all the worries keeping her awake either receded or sorted themselves out.

She had the perfect title in the living room, one of the rec-ommended reading texts left over from her master's program. She had only made it through about a third of the book, de-spite months of trying.

When she walked out to the kitchen, Theo greeted her with a tail thump inside his crate.

She could also take the dog out for a quick walk through the garden before she settled in to read. The flowers and shrubs laid out in the Brambleberry House landscaping never failed to soothe her, especially in the moonlight.

For a long time, all her instincts had told her to hide be-hind triple-locked doors and away from any open windows. Going outside by herself after dark would have been out of the question.

Maybe if she still lived in Utah, that might have been the case. As irrational as it might seem, she felt safe here in Can-non Beach.

Yes, bad things happened here. Bad things had happened to *her* here. Aaron had terrorized her and had physically hurt her dear friend and the wonderful Fiona.

Every time she remembered that awful time two summers ago, she felt a little nauseated and had to fight the urge to stay inside where she knew she would be safe.

All the more reason to go outside, she decided. She didn't want to be a person who cowered.

Without taking more time to think about it, she slid into her garden shoes, pulled a hoodie on over her pajama top and went to the dog's crate.

"I know you were all settled for the night, but would you like to go out one more time?"

Theo thumped his tail on the floor, which made her smile. What a joy the dog had been, even in only the short weeks he had been part of their family. She had almost forgotten what their life had been like without him.

Theo jumped from his crate and stretched in a good imitation of a yoga pose, then followed her eagerly out the door as she made her way quietly downstairs.

The house was hushed in these early hours of the morning. She didn't know whether Wes was asleep up on the third floor but the ground floor apartment was empty. The Andersons, the lovely older couple who lived there, were expected home the following week. The retired pair had gone on an extended trip through Europe, including a long cruise, and their weekly email updates filled Jenna with no small degree of envy.

Maybe she should take Addie on a cruise. She could plan it around fall break. They didn't have to go to Europe. Instead, they could stick close to home and take one of the cruises that traveled the Pacific coastline.

The idea was deeply appealing. Four or five days when she didn't have to make all the decisions in life, where someone else would feed them, entertain them, show them beautiful parts of the world.

Still, she couldn't ignore one inescapable truth.

If she was lonely in Cannon Beach, she was going to be every bit as lonely on a cruise, if not more so, surrounded by couples and families having fun together.

How would she ever meet someone new? Jenna wondered as she reached the bottom step. Her job as an elementary teacher didn't bring many unattached men into her life. She didn't socialize much, except with her female friends and other teachers. She would certainly never dare try a dating app again, though she knew several friends who swore by them and had found deep and lasting relationships that way.

Jenna sighed as she pushed open the exterior door to the front of the house.

She didn't want to meet a man, anyway.

Especially a man who wasn't Wes Calhoun.

She pushed away the thought, focusing instead on the fresh,

sweet night air, thick with the scent of roses and lavender. She inhaled deeply, feeling tension in her muscles instantly begin to ease.

This was her home. She didn't need to leave Brambleberry House, unless things grew too uncomfortable between her and Wes.

Yet another reason to try putting things back on a safer footing.

Theo lifted his leg on a tuft of grass, then followed after her as she walked through the garden toward the pergola overlooking the water. Jenna wanted to take one more look to see how many tables would fit in the small structure.

Before they reached it, Theo's tail began to wag and he gave a little yip of greeting, her first signs that she wasn't alone in the garden.

Inside the pergola, Wes wore a headlamp to light his task, which seemed to be tightening a screw on one of the wooden lawn chairs. Three other chairs were upside down, apparently waiting their turn.

He must have heard Theo's doggy greeting because he shifted in their direction, the headlamp aimed up at the sky like a beacon, forever guiding her toward him.

"What are you doing out here?" she asked when they approached.

"I noticed the chairs all felt a little wobbly so I thought it wouldn't hurt to reinforce them before one fell apart."

"In the dark, at one in the morning?"

"Is it that late? I hadn't noticed. What about you? What brings you out? I thought everybody was settled for the night. The house seemed quiet."

"I couldn't sleep so I got up to read for a bit. And as soon as I walked out into the living room, I realized Theo would see me and decide he needed to go out."

"It's a beautiful night, isn't it?"

She lifted her face up to the glitter of stars overhead, endless and lovely.

"It really is."

"Everybody told me to be prepared for gray skies and rain when I moved to Oregon. We've had a few of those, but it seems like we have far more sunny days than not."

"You came at a great time of year. Our winters can be cold and stormy."

"I'm looking forward to watching the storms roll in."

Jenna loved the drama of sitting in front of her bay window as the sea turned dark and frothy. "You might get your wish earlier than later," she told him. "A summer storm is supposed to hit tomorrow night. Tonight, I guess. Around ten or so. I just hope it holds off until later than that as I'm having my book club out here tomorrow evening."

"That sounds fun."

"What's not to love about it? Good friends talking about books, eating food and enjoying adult beverages."

He nodded to the overturned furniture in front of him. "Good thing I had a wild hare to fix the chairs, then. I would hate for one of your book club friends to sit down, only to have the whole thing fall apart."

"Yes. Great timing. Can I help you with anything here?"

"I'm nearly done. You could hold the flashlight for me, if you'd like. I've got the headlamp, but every time I turn my head, I can't see what I'm doing."

She picked up the flashlight he indicated, perched on one of the chairs he had apparently already tightened, and aimed it at the chair in front of him. Theo spent a moment sniffing around the pergola, then found a spot to curl up on atop one of the chair cushions.

A subtle intimacy seemed to curl around them, here in the quiet of the garden. Was this the reason she had been drawn outside? Had some part of her suspected he might be out here, the part of her that couldn't seem to stay away from this man?

She didn't want to think so.

"What time are you expecting Brielle's mom to return?"

"Their plane lands in Portland around noon, so a few hours after that."

"I'm sure Brie has missed her."

"They've talked on the phone nearly every day, but yeah. They're very close. Lacey is a great mom."

"That's good of you to say. I've heard other divorced parents who aren't nearly as complimentary of their exes."

He made a sound that was somewhere between a grunt and a sigh. "We're much better friends now than we ever were when we were married."

"Has it been hard for you, seeing Lacey go on with her life?" He must have loved her once, dreamed of a future with her.

This time the sound he made definitely sounded like a laugh. "Not one tiny bit. She deserves to be happy. Lacey had to carry a lot after I went to prison. She really stepped up. I can never repay her for that."

"How did you meet her?"

She wasn't only making conversation. She genuinely wanted to know, Jenna thought, as he turned that chair over and moved to work on another one. She followed with the flashlight, taking a seat on the chair he had just fixed.

"Friend of a friend. I was stationed in North Carolina and she came down from Michigan to visit a friend in the area, who happened to be dating one of my buddies. We went on a couple of double dates and then just sort of…fell into a relationship."

He was quiet, his muscles flexing as he tightened the screws on the underside of the chair. "She was desperate to escape a tough family life, and I was getting ready to head overseas after a transfer to Germany. We decided to tie the knot before I left so she could come with me. Not an uncommon story in the military."

"How long were you in Germany?"

While he worked, he talked about his military service and some of the experiences he'd had, not only there but during a short stint in the Middle East, protecting the base and being fired on by militants.

As they talked and she came to understand him a little, Jenna was aware of a grim realization.

She was doing a lousy job of resisting him.

In fact, quite the opposite.

She was falling for him.

The truth washed over her, and for an instant, she wobbled the flashlight in her shock. He looked over and she quickly corrected it.

Oh no. What had she done?

This wasn't simply an attraction. She was falling in love with him.

He definitely didn't feel the same way. Yes, he was attracted to her, but that was it. He had given her no indication that his feelings might run deeper.

Oh, what a mess.

They lived in the same house. Yes, they had different apartments, but it was impossible to avoid the other Brambleberry House tenants. How would she be able to live one floor below him? Could she possibly return to merely being friends when she was beginning to realize how very much more she wanted?

She didn't want to move out. She loved this house and so did Addie. But how could she stay here and keep her feelings to herself, when she saw him day after day and when their daughters were becoming such close friends?

"What's wrong?" he asked. She looked up to find him watching her, an expression of concern on his face.

She couldn't tell him any of the thoughts racing through her head. He wouldn't want to hear that his foolish neighbor was getting all kinds of inappropriate ideas about him.

She pasted on a smile, hoping the darkness would conceal her sudden distress. "Nothing. Everything's fine," she lied.

"Are you sure? You were frowning like you just spotted a skunk walking through the lilac bushes."

"Oh, I hope not! Don't you think Theo would alert us to any wandering creatures making their way through the yard?"

"Him?"

He pointed to the dog, curled up on the cushion and snoring softly.

She was grateful to turn the subject. "He's not turning into the greatest watchdog, is he? On the plus side, he's the most mellow dog ever and loves everybody. Not an aggressive bone in his body."

"I'm sure he still has enough protective instincts to watch out for you and Addie if the need arises. Dogs are amazing like that."

They talked about some of the dogs he had worked with in prison and the two great dogs he'd had when he was young, before his father died.

Jenna wasn't at all tired, though she knew she would pay the price next day. She would be lucky to stay awake until book club.

She knew she should go inside, to figure out what she was going to do next, but she couldn't seem to make herself move.

After she had been outside about a half hour, he set the last chair upright and took off his headlamp, switching it off. "There you go. That's the last one."

She handed him the flashlight. He aimed it downward, though didn't shut it off.

"Thank you for doing that. I'm sure my book club members will appreciate chairs that don't fall apart in the middle of dinner."

"Always a good thing, right?"

She managed a smile, and as he gazed down at her, sparkling awareness seemed to shiver to life between them.

Jenna wanted him to kiss her, even though she knew it would only leave her wanting more. She saw him swallow and had the most inappropriate urge to press her mouth to the strong column of his neck.

"I should…" She pointed to the house.

In the light cast from the flashlight, his expression seemed remote, hard. "Probably a good idea." His voice suddenly seemed abrupt and she wondered what she had done.

"Are you staying out a little longer?"

"Yeah."

"Are you sure? It has to be nearly two."

"I'll get there eventually."

Though she knew she needed to go inside, she was reluctant to leave him out here by himself.

They gazed at each other for a long moment as the night air seemed to sigh around them.

"Do you want to know the real reason I came out here?" he asked, his voice low and his features in shadow.

She shook her head, suddenly unable to find her voice.

"I had to do something physical to keep myself distracted from wanting something I can't have."

Her breath seemed to catch at the intensity of his words, the raw emotion there.

"What's that?" she finally asked, her voice barely above a whisper.

"I think you know, Jenna. You. You are what I want."

Heat rushed from her brain to pool in her belly, her thighs.

She swallowed, not sure how to answer him, finally settling on the truth.

"That's the reason I couldn't sleep, either. I keep remembering...kissing you."

He made a low sound, raw and hungry, and then the flashlight tumbled to the ground, pitching them into darkness as he reached for her.

When he kissed her, everything inside her seemed to sigh a welcome. She had wanted him to kiss her again for days. Forever, it seemed.

The reality was far better than any of her memories, and she was lost in the magic of his touch.

They kissed for a long time, tasting and exploring while the dog snored softly and the night breeze stirred the flowers around them.

She was only vaguely aware of Wes lowering down to one of the pergola chairs and pulling her with him onto his lap, where she seemed to fit perfectly. She felt a fleeting moment of gratitude that he had reinforced the chairs. How mortifying if one clattered apart underneath them.

The thought made her smile a little and he eased his mouth away.

"What's so funny?"

"I hope you knew what you were doing when you tightened the screws or we might be in for an unpleasant surprise."

His mouth lifted with a smile that left her breathless. "I wouldn't care. I would still want to kiss you amid the rubble of a dozen chairs."

She shivered at the intensity of his expression, the heat of him surrounding her.

"You're cold," he murmured.

She shook her head, though reality was beginning to push through the haze of desire.

What were they doing? What was *she* doing? A few more moments out here and she would have completely surrendered.

Though it was painfully hard, she slid off his lap. "I should never have come out here. I'm sorry. We...we can't do this."

He froze for a long second, heat and desire mixing with confusion in his gaze. "Why not?" he asked on a growl.

She released a long breath. "We both know where it would lead. Where would we go? Your apartment? We can't because Brielle is inside. My apartment? Addie."

He gazed at her, his breathing ragged.

"Even if the girls weren't inside, you know it wouldn't be a good idea," she said, hating herself for what she had to do.

"Right now, it feels like a damn good idea."

The fierce hunger in his voice thrummed through her.

He rose as well and in the darkness, she could only make out his profile. "You should know, this isn't just physical for me, though that's certainly a factor. I think about you all the time, Jenna. When I'm not with you, I want to be. When I *am* with you, I want to savor every second of it until I get the chance to spend time with you again."

A torrent of emotions poured through her at his words. Tenderness, joy, heat, need.

She wanted to lean into his words, to grab them and treasure them against her heart.

This seemed so very different from the love she and Ryan had shared. Their relationship had been like hot cocoa on a cold winter night. Warm, comforting, sustaining.

This thing between her and Wes was something else entirely.

More like cocoa with a heavy dash of hot sauce.

As much as she longed to consume every drop, a cold fear seemed to spread from her stomach outward, like frost blooms on the window.

She had fought so hard to be in a good place. Wes threatened to ruin all of that peace and calm.

She already had feelings for him. If she gave in to this heat between them, she would fall irrevocably in love and would end up bruised and broken.

But what if she didn't? a little voice whispered. What if they were able to work through all their differences and find happiness together?

It would be amazing. She had no doubt.

I think about you all the time, Jenna. When I'm not with you, I want to be. When I am *with you, I want to savor every second of it until I get the chance to spend time with you again.*

His words seemed seared into her heart. Was it possible he could be falling in love with her, too?

No. She couldn't believe it. His world was tattoos and motorcycles, while hers was book clubs and parent-teacher conferences. This heat would pass, like the storms that blew through Cannon Beach. After it was gone, what would they possibly have between them?

"I can't," she whispered, despising herself for giving in to the fear but unable to face the alternative.

"Because I've been in prison."

At his flat, emotionless tone, she stared at him, wishing she could see better in the darkness, could grab the flashlight from the ground and aim it at him so she could read his expression.

"No. That has nothing to do with it. Do you want the truth? Okay. I'm afraid, Wes. There it is. Four years ago, my husband died and left me devastated, then just as I was beginning to come back to life, I became tangled up with the wrong man and ended up in another version of hell. I'm finally beginning to figure things out again. I can't… I don't want to mess that up. Not for me and not for Addie."

"Why would this mess everything up?"

She sighed, moving away. "I love living here in Brambleberry House. So does Addie. I don't want to leave. But what if we give in to this heat between us and something goes wrong? How would I possibly be able to stay here?"

He was quiet for a long moment. When he spoke, his voice was low. "But what if everything between us goes *right*?"

His kisses certainly felt right to her. And she loved being with him and could spend all night talking to him out here in the pergola.

For a moment, she was tempted. So very tempted.

But she had ignored her instincts once with Aaron by going on a second date with him. She couldn't take that kind of risk again when she had so much at stake.

She didn't for a moment think Wes would hurt her intentionally. But she was already half in love with the man. If they gave in to this desire between them, how would she possibly protect what was left of her heart?

"I'm sorry," she said again. Despising herself, she grabbed a confused Theo and hurried back to the house.

After Jenna left so abruptly, Wes stayed in the pergola, staring at the night sky peeking through the open slat roof.

If this was love, he didn't want it. This ache in his chest, in his bones. In his heart.

He couldn't blame Jenna for not wanting to further explore the attraction between them and pursue a relationship.

How could he?

Wes wasn't exactly a prize. She had talked about her baggage, but he had so much he needed a damn cargo tanker to carry it all.

He sighed, frustrated all over again at the circumstances of his life that had led him here.

Would he change it if he could?

It was a stunning thought.

If he hadn't been arrested, he probably wouldn't be here in Cannon Beach, living upstairs from her.

He looked at the house, cold and dark now where it was usually so warm and filled with life.

She was right. How would they both be able to remain here, with these raw, unfulfilled emotions between them? He would find it excruciating to live one floor above her, to be so close to her but know she would remain forever out of reach.

Even now he wanted to march up those stairs, break down her door and pull her into his arms.

How could he stay here?

She had said she didn't want to move. He didn't want to leave Brambleberry House, either. The house was warm and comfortable, and the view and proximity to the water would be hard to beat somewhere else within his price range.

He would have an easier time moving, though. He had brought very little with him, and it would be simple enough to pack it up into his truck and find somewhere else to live.

It made the most sense. She had been here for years. This was her daughter's home. If they found the situation completely untenable, he would have to start looking for another place. He didn't know where he would go, only that he had to stay in town. He had been separated from Brie for long enough. He wouldn't do it again.

Would anywhere else along the coast be far enough to help him get over Jenna?

He wasn't sure.

What choice did he have? Whatever her reasons, she had made it clear she didn't want things to move forward.

His only option was to try like hell to put away his feelings, to focus on Brie and the future and rebuilding his life.

Chapter Fifteen

The encounter with Wes in the early hours haunted Jenna the rest of the day as she prepped for the book group meeting.

She had been looking forward to the meeting with her friends all week, but now she wasn't certain she would be able to get through it.

She was exhausted, for one thing, after returning to her house to toss and turn again in her bed until she had finally fallen into a fitful sleep.

She also wasn't in a cheerful mood. She had snapped at Addie when she complained about having to do her chores, then had to apologize. She explained that she was having a cranky morning and shouldn't have snapped...but that Addie still had to do her chores.

The rest of the day was busy as she cleaned her apartment, went to the grocery store and had Addie help her make cookies.

She didn't see Wes all day and tried to tell herself she was relieved, not disappointed.

Finally, an hour before the party, as she was covering the tables with linen cloths, she spotted his pickup truck pulling into its usual parking spot.

He climbed out, paused a moment as if trying to make up his mind, then approached her.

"Hi."

"Hello." She tried a smile, even as she felt a sharp pang of longing. "Did Brielle go back to her mom's?"

He nodded. "Yes. I took her there this afternoon. We went to a matinee this morning of a movie she's been wanting to see. Sort of our last hurrah together."

"It must have been tough to say goodbye."

"I won't say dropping her off with her mother becomes any easier with practice. But I'm slowly beginning to accept that I can see her anytime I want and she'll be here again in a week, not every few months when Lacey could arrange a prison visit."

"You're a good father, Wes."

He made a face as if he disagreed but didn't argue with her. "What time does your party start?"

She glanced at her watch. "Another hour. People should be arriving around seven. I've got a babysitter coming for Addie in about a half hour. Rosa's niece Bella is great with her and Rosa's stepson is coming to play, too."

He glanced out to sea, where she could see a rim of dark clouds on the horizon. "Forecasters are saying the storm should hold off until later. Maybe ten or eleven."

"We should be done by then."

"Good to know. I'll be sure to stay out of your way. I might take my bike for a drive down the coast."

She knew that was one of his outlets when he was particularly restless. Was she the cause of his current tumult? She didn't like thinking it.

"You don't have to stay away. In fact, you're welcome to join us at book group, if you'd like."

"I don't think I would quite fit in with your crowd."

She thought of her group, mostly women but a few men, too. "You might. We're open to everyone willing to read the featured book and offer insight."

He gestured to the tables and chairs. "Can I help you set things up? It can't be comfortable, with your injured hand."

She didn't want to feel beholden to him for even one more

thing, especially with these currents seething between them. But she had to admit she had been struggling all day to work around her stupid bandage.

"Would you mind carrying out some of the folding chairs from the shed? That would be very helpful."

"No problem. How many?"

"All of them. I think there are about a dozen there. That should give us enough, with the furniture you fixed last night."

As soon as she said the words, conjuring up memories that hadn't been far from her mind all day, her face felt hot. He gazed at her for a long moment, and she knew he was remembering their intense embrace as well.

"Sure. No problem."

He headed toward the shed at the bottom of the garden and returned with three chairs in each hand. He set them up, then returned to the shed for the rest, finishing in about two minutes when the job would have taken her at least ten.

He set them up where she indicated, at the folding tables she had already brought out with Addie's help.

"They're pretty dusty. I gather they haven't been used much lately."

She nodded. "When Rosa still lived here, she liked to have gatherings, but I'm afraid I'm not as social as she is. The Andersons do often have friends over to grill, but a few at a time, not enough that would require them to pull out the extra chairs."

"I can clean them off for you."

She started to protest that he didn't need to do that, then swallowed her words. She was running out of time and still needed to bring down a few more items for the party from her apartment. This was also a good test as to whether they could set aside their feelings and be friendly enough to both stay here at the house.

"I've got a few cleaning supplies stored under the serving table there."

He nodded and went to work without another word. For some reason, his simple thoughtfulness made her eyes burn with tears.

Wes was a good man. Any woman smart enough to build a relationship with him should consider herself very lucky.

She wanted to be that woman, suddenly, with a fierce intensity that brought a lump to her throat.

She swallowed it down quickly. "I've got to run upstairs for a few more things. Thank you so much for your help. I'll save you some cookies."

"This is the kind of thing friends do for each other, right?"

Was that a shadow of bitterness in his voice? She couldn't quite tell…and her daughter's excited shriek distracted her from trying to figure it out.

"Hi, Logan! You're here!"

She looked up to see Rosa walking toward them, along with Bella and Rosa's stepson, Logan, who had become fast friends with Addie when he and his father temporarily lived in Brambleberry House after a fire at their own home.

"Hi, Addie." Logan beamed at her. "Where's your dog? I can't wait to meet him! I wanted to bring Hank, but my dad said he should stay home since a book party might not be the best time to see if he and your new puppy get along."

"Theo likes everybody," Addie said. "Don't you, buddy?"

In answer, their new puppy licked at Logan, who giggled.

Rosa gave Wes a curious look as he continued wiping off the chairs. "I do hope you're joining us for book group."

"Not me. Sorry. I don't even know what book you're reading."

She told him and he shook his head. "Haven't read that one, thought I did read the author's last book."

"You should come next month," she said with a warm smile.

"By then, we'll have a new baby." Wyatt's teenage niece Bella beamed at Rosa.

"Are you sure you'll be okay with these three?" Jenna asked, pointing to the children and the dog, who were chasing each other around the part of the yard not currently set up with tables.

"We'll be great," Bella answered. "We'll go for a long walk on the beach and build sandcastles and tire everybody out, then come back and watch a movie. I can't wait to hang with them."

Bella was a sweet girl who looked enough like Rosa to be her sister.

Another car pulled in behind Rosa's. Kim, Jenna saw, with the food.

She hurried over to help carry the catering trays to the tables. By the time she returned to the pergola, Wes had disappeared.

"It was nice of Wes to help you set up for the party," Rosa said sometime later, after the book club gathering was in full swing.

Jenna knew she shouldn't feel this little pang in her heart just at the mention of his name. "Yes. He's been very kind."

"I wish he had stayed for the book group. He could have made more friends."

"Too bad he didn't," Kim said. "Maybe we can talk him into helping us move some tables or something later. All those muscles. *Mmm.*"

Jenna fought down a little spurt of annoyance with her friend, which she knew was completely unreasonable. Kim was extremely happily married and was only teasing about Wes. That didn't stop Jenna from feeling protective of him.

She had no right to feel that way. He wasn't hers. She had made sure of that.

She forced a smile. "I think Wes is making himself scarce on purpose tonight. He said doesn't want to get in the way of our fun."

"Are you talking about Wes Calhoun? I heard from Lacey that her ex was living here."

Jenna looked over at Erin Lawson, a yoga instructor who

always recommended motivational self-improvement books when it was her turn to host book group.

"Yes. He lives in the third-floor apartment," Jenna said, her tone guarded. "Do you know him?"

"Not personally, no." Erin looked at the house. "My friend Jewel is friends with Lacey and she told her about him. I just think you're really brave to live in this big house alone with an ex-con, especially with the Andersons still out of town."

Jenna frowned. "Wes is an excellent neighbor. And he was cleared of all charges."

Erin shrugged. "Innocent or not. Prison changes people. My sister's husband went away for a white-collar thing. He spent a year inside and came out a completely different man. And not in a good way, either. I just don't know if I could do it. I admire you."

Jenna had to bite down a sharp retort. First, she was the least brave woman she knew. Second, she had absolutely no reason to be afraid of Wes.

He would never hurt her. He would rather go back to prison than do that. She suddenly knew that with absolute conviction.

How horrible for him, that some people would always judge him for circumstances completely beyond his control.

She opened her mouth to say as much, but Erin had turned away to talk to someone else and the conversation turned away from Wes, much to her relief.

She tried to focus on the conversation and her friends instead of Wes, though she noted she was not the only woman who watched him when he came out of the house sometime later, started up his bike and rode off into the evening sun.

Chapter Sixteen

"That was a terrific book group," Kim said as she carried the last of the folding chairs back to the shed.

"It was fun, wasn't it?" Jenna said, smothering a yawn.

"And the best part is, we don't have to host it again for a whole year."

She smiled. "At least we made it through the book discussion before the storm hit."

"Barely." Kim gestured out to sea, where dark clouds gathered. Lightning arced over the water and she could hear the distant answering thunder.

"I'd better get home. Thanks for hosting. This was a lovely spot for the party."

Her friend hugged her and hurried to her car as the first few drops of rain hit.

Jenna carried the last few serving dishes into the house, worried about Wes. She had seen him leave the house and ride away on his bike during the first hour of the party and he had yet to return.

She hoped he wasn't caught out in the rain. She had heard raindrops could feel like tiny bullets to a motorcyclist.

Her hand throbbed as she made her way up the stairs to her apartment. She needed some ibuprofen and her bed.

She pushed open the door to her quiet apartment. Bella had left a half hour ago with Logan and Rosa, leaving Addie fast asleep in her bed. Jenna had checked on her fifteen minutes earlier when she had carried a load of items upstairs.

She spotted the empty crate as soon as she walked into the kitchen. Oh shoot. On that earlier trip up to the apartment, she had taken Theo back down with her to let him out for the night one last time and then got so busy talking with Kim and cleaning up the final debris from the party that she completely forgot him in the small fenced dog yard.

She made her way back down the stairs and out the back porch.

"Theo? Come on, bud."

She waited for the puppy to come bounding over to her. When he didn't, she frowned. "Theo? Come."

Still nothing.

The storm was moving closer, she saw. A flash of lightning illuminated the yard, revealing no sign of the dog.

She moved down the steps. Where could he be?

When she reached the back of the dog yard, which accessed the beach gate, everything inside her turned cold. The gate was ajar slightly, with just enough room for a puppy to squeeze through.

A few of her guests who lived close had opted to walk home via the beach. She could only guess that one of them must not have closed the gate completely.

Theo was gone.

A storm was coming, her daughter was alone in the house and their small, defenseless puppy was lost somewhere on the beach.

This was her fault. She should have checked to make sure the beach gate was closed before she ever let Theo out into the yard.

Anything could happen to him out there. She couldn't bear thinking about the hazards to a small puppy.

She had to find him, no matter if she had to search all night.

She turned and raced back into her apartment for her phone and a flashlight, tossing extra batteries in her pocket just in case, then hurried back downstairs.

Her fatigue, the ache in her hand and the ache in her heart were all forgotten for now as she focused on finding Theo.

After a long bike ride down to Pacific City and back, Wes hoped he might be tired enough to sleep.

Instead, his mind still raced, his heart still ached and now he was damp and cold from the rain that had caught him about fifteen miles from home.

The party was apparently over, he saw as he pulled into the driveway. The only other vehicles he could see were his pickup truck and Jenna's small SUV.

He looked up to the second floor, where he saw only a dim light on.

Just as he was climbing off his bike, the front door flung open and Jenna raced down the porch toward him wearing a raincoat and carrying a flashlight.

"Oh, thank heavens you're here," she said, her voice frantic. "I am so glad I heard your bike. I need your help."

"What's wrong?" he asked instantly, forgetting all about his wet clothing or the chill beginning to seep in.

"It's Theo. Somehow he wandered off through the beach gate." Her voice bordered on hysteria. "I'm just about to go look for him. Can you help me?"

"Of course." He didn't hesitate for a second. "I've got a flashlight and my headlamp in my pickup. Let me grab them."

He unlocked the truck and found the lights immediately. On impulse, he also threw in a couple of road flares. They might come in handy.

He shut the truck door as another flash of lightning rippled through the night, still distant but moving closer.

"What about Addie?" he asked suddenly. "You can't leave her for long. Why don't you stay with her and I'll go look."

She shook her head vigorously. "I called my friend Kim and she is on her way back to stay with Addie in case she wakes. She should be here in a few minutes. She knows the code to get in the house and I left my apartment unlocked. It's my fault. I should have been more careful and made sure the gate was shut after some of my guests left that way."

Ah. That explained how Theo had managed his escape.

"How long do you think he's been gone?"

"Maybe fifteen or twenty minutes. I don't think it can be longer than that."

A dog could move quickly in that amount of time.

As they hurried toward the beach, he wondered how they were supposed to spot a little tan-colored dog in the sand in the dark, in the middle of a storm.

He didn't want to be the voice of doom by raising the worry. Maybe the dog hadn't gone far. Maybe he would hear them calling him.

"I think we should split up," Jenna said, once they left Brambleberry House property. "Why don't you go north and I'll go south?"

He wasn't thrilled with the idea of separating from her, though it did make the most sense. They could cover twice the ground that way.

"Here. Take a flare. If you find him, light it so I know to come back. I should see it from far down the beach."

"Okay. And you'll do the same, right?"

In another flash of distant lightning, her features looked pale and frightened. He wanted to pull her against him, to keep her warm and safe from the storm, but he knew this wasn't the time for that.

"We'll find him, Jenna. I promise."

"I hope so. Addie has lost enough. She'll be devastated if something happens to him."

"We don't have long. As soon as that storm hits in earnest, we have to find shelter. Puppy or not. I'm sorry."

"I know."

"It's moving this way. We've maybe only got fifteen minutes before we'll have to head back. There's no safe shelter on the beach."

"Let's pray we find him soon then."

She raced toward the water, scanning the sand with the beam of her flashlight and calling the dog's name.

Still reluctant to leave her alone, he headed off in the opposite direction.

He had been looking for perhaps ten minutes. When he turned around, he could see her light still bobbing across the sand, though it was growing dimmer.

He called the dog but it was hard to hear anything with the waves beginning to crash and the wind blowing hard.

Lightning split the sky again, closer this time. In that instant of light, he thought he saw movement in the waves about ten yards from shore, a tiny dark head.

He thought at first it might be a seal or a sea turtle, then wondered if he had imagined it. He aimed his powerful flashlight in that direction. In a second flash of lightning, he realized it wasn't a sea creature, it was a small dog, swimming furiously for all he was worth toward shore and being tossed back again and again by the waves.

"I see him," he shouted, though he knew even as he did, she wouldn't be able to hear him.

Without another thought, he lit his flare, hoping she could see it, then kicked off his boots, yanked off his leather jacket and waded into the cold waters of the Pacific.

He had hoped he might be able to walk to the puppy, but the waves were too intense. They almost knocked him over twice.

Finally he dived over the next one as lightning illuminated the water and his path to the puppy. The thunder that followed only a few seconds later confirmed the storm was moving closer.

The puppy was tiring. He could tell. The next wave went over its head and it didn't pop up again for a long moment. With a fierce burst of energy, Wes swam the last few yards to the dog and scooped him under one arm, then began the journey back to shore.

When he was a few yards from shore, he stood up and fought his way through the waves to the sand as Jenna came running down the beach.

She gasped, trying to catch her breath. "Was he in the water? I saw your flare and then you jumped in and I was so scared. Did you find him? Is he...?"

He hadn't even had the chance to assess Theo's condition. He held the puppy up and felt vast relief when Theo gave a weak-sounding whine.

Jenna, her breath still coming harshly from her run down the beach, reached for Theo and hugged him tightly. "Oh, you poor thing. I'm so glad you're safe. Don't do that again. You scared me so much!"

The labradoodle licked her cheek and rested his wet head against her chest.

Wes couldn't help thinking he would like to do the same thing, just pull her into his arms and bask in her heat.

They couldn't stay here, though. Not with that storm moving ever closer.

He scooped up his boots and his jacket, not bothering to put them on now.

"We have to get back to the house. The lightning is too close."

"Are you okay? I can't believe you did that!"

"I'm fine," he said as they quickly raced back toward the house. "He wasn't that far out. I wouldn't have seen him if he'd been even a little farther out. I didn't think I would have to swim but the waves were stronger than I was expecting, which might be what happened to him. I can carry him. He's soaked, so he has to weigh twice as much as usual."

"I've got him," she said, racing along beside him.

The rain hit hard as they made it the final hundred yards to the Brambleberry House beach gate.

He opened it and together they ran to the back porch.

"Is he okay?" he asked.

"He seems to be." Jenna set the dog down. He sat on his haunches, looking far more alert in the glow from the porch light, but he didn't seem to want to leave her side.

"Wes, thank you," Jenna said as thunder rumbled just beyond the safety of the porch. "I don't know what I would have done if you hadn't been here. You have come to my rescue more times than I can count."

"I'm glad I made it back from my ride in time to help you."

"So am I. Oh, Wes. Thank you."

She wrapped her arms around him and he held her tightly. She was shaking, he realized.

"Let's get you inside. You're freezing."

She shook her head. "I'm a little cold but I'm not the one who went for a dip in the Pacific. I was so scared when you jumped into the water. Terrified. I have never felt so helpless. I could do nothing while you risked your life for my daughter's dog."

"He's a sweet little guy. I didn't want something to happen to him. Not if I could help."

She made a sound halfway between a laugh and a sob. "I can't believe you risked your life for a puppy. I'm so glad you did, but I feel sick when I think of all the things that could have happened to you. To both of you. An undertow. A rogue wave. Or a shark, for heaven's sake."

"Nothing happened," he said, his voice gruff. "I'm here. Just a little wet, but I was wet anyway from my ride."

"Thank you. I can never thank you enough."

When she placed her warm hands on either side of his face and pressed her mouth to his, she completely shattered him.

He closed his eyes and held himself still as she kissed him with a tenderness that made him yearn for more. Finally, he couldn't bear it another moment and he stepped away.

"You're killing me, Jenna. I can't do this anymore. There isn't enough pavement in Oregon for me to ride away how much I want to have you right here in my arms."

Without looking at her or waiting for an answer, he turned around and hurried into the house, already trying to figure out how soon he could move out so he could start the process of trying to get over her.

Jenna watched him go, her heart beating hard. She had been about to tell him she was falling in love with him. What might have happened if she had spoken sooner?

She hadn't. Once more, she had let her fear control her.

At her feet, the still-bedraggled puppy whimpered and she pushed away her angst to focus on his needs for now.

She carried him into the house, where Kim was waiting.

"You found him. Oh, I'm so glad. Where was he?"

"I didn't find him. Wes did. He somehow had gone into the water and then couldn't swim back out. Wes went in after him."

"Is he okay?"

She grabbed the microfiber towel she used to dry him and rubbed him vigorously. He was warm and alert, his eyes bright as he looked over at Kim. After a moment, the puppy wriggled to be let down, and Jenna set him on the floor again, where he trotted to his water bowl and drank it empty. Poor thing, surrounded by all that salt water he couldn't drink. There was a metaphor in that, she was fairly certain, but she couldn't put her finger on it.

She filled his bowl again, not caring that it meant she would have to take him out to do his business again in an hour.

After taking a few more sips, the puppy ate a little of his chow, then padded to his crate, where he curled up on the blankets and went immediately to sleep.

Kim, watching all of this, smiled. "Looks like he's fine. Exhausted, but fine."

"Thank you for coming back to stay with Addie."

"Glad to do it. I haven't even been here twenty minutes."

"Well, thank you. I had no idea how long it might take to find him."

"And you and Wes would have looked all night, wouldn't you?"

Jenna gave a little laugh. "Yes. Wes was going to make me stop if the lightning got too close, but as soon as the storm passed, we would have gone back out."

She knew she wouldn't have stopped looking and suddenly had no doubt that Wes would have been right there at her side.

He was a man she could count on. A man any woman could rely upon to help her through the storms of life. He would do anything for a woman he loved.

She closed her eyes as the realization filled her with a peaceful assurance. She wanted to be that woman, sharing troubles and joys and life with him.

The last of her fear, any lingering doubts, seemed to shrivel away. She wanted to be with Wes. The differences between them didn't matter. They had many more things in common.

"He's a good guy, isn't he?" Kim said, as if reading Jenna's thoughts.

"The very best," she answered.

"You should probably tell him you're in love with him. A guy deserves to know, don't you think? Especially after he risked his life for your dog."

"Yes. Probably." Jenna could feel her face heat.

"Want me to stay with Addie a little longer while you do? I can even stay all night, ahem, if necessary. I don't mind sleeping on the sofa."

Jenna could only shake her head. "Not necessary. I need to change into some dry clothes, then I'll go talk to him. Thank you again."

"Anytime. Though I hope your little buddy over there learns to stay put after his little adventure."

Kim let herself out while Jenna hurried to change into dry clothes. What did a woman wear when she was about to put her heart on the line? She had no idea, so she settled on a pair of yoga pants and a soft sweater that always gave her comfort.

After checking on her sleeping daughter and puppy, she opened her door, drawing on all her courage to make her way up the stairs to his apartment.

As she went, she thought she smelled flowers on the stairs. Was Abigail there, giving her strength? It was a comforting idea, though she still wasn't sure she was buying the whole ghost thing.

At his door, she lingered for a long moment. What if he was asleep already?

He wasn't. She was suddenly sure of it.

There isn't enough pavement in Oregon for me to ride away how much I want to have you right here in my arms.

She shivered, took a deep breath and knocked softly, then waited what felt like an eternity for him to open the door.

He had changed into dry clothes, too. Had possibly showered. His hair was damp and sticking up and he smelled clean and masculine and wonderful.

"Is something wrong?" he asked, his voice so remote she had to pause, some of her uncertainty fluttering back.

No. She wouldn't give in to it. This man had risked his life to save a puppy from drowning in the Pacific in the middle of a lightning storm.

She could certainly take a chance and tell him how she felt.

"Yes. Something is wrong," she murmured.

"What?"

"I need to tell you something. May I…come in?"

He appeared reluctant but finally opened the door further. She walked into the apartment, so different now than it had been when Rosa lived here. It was comfortable and clean, though fairly utilitarian and sparsely decorated. Rosa had taken all her personal things when she moved out to marry Wyatt.

Now that she was here, she didn't know where to start. Doubt began to creep back in but she firmly pushed it away and faced him.

"When my husband died, I told myself I was done with love. I didn't need or want the vulnerability and pain that went hand in hand with it. Then everything happened with Aaron, which only reinforced that relationships were far too messy."

She let out a breath and realized her hands were shaking. She curled them into fists and hoped he didn't notice.

"I told myself I was happy on my own. I had Addie and my students. A life here in Cannon Beach. I didn't need anything else."

She met his gaze but couldn't read anything in his features that looked as if they had been carved from a block of wood.

"And then you moved in and…everything changed. You kissed me. You made me feel cherished. You reminded me that I'm still a woman. A woman who…who apparently can still fall in love."

He gazed at her, still expressionless except for his eyes, which suddenly blazed with emotion.

"Are you?"

"In love? Yes. I'm afraid so. I didn't want to be, but you rode into my life and changed everything."

The last word barely emerged when he crossed the space

between them in a blink, pulled her tightly into his arms and kissed her with a humbling mix of ferocity and tenderness.

"Oh, Jenna," he said against her mouth a long moment later. "I love you. I think I have from the moment I moved in, when you were terrified of me."

"Not you," she assured him, kissing the corner of his mouth, arms around him as tightly as she could manage. "It was never you. It was the image of who I thought you were."

"An ex-con."

"A big, intimidating man who rode a motorcycle and had tattoos."

"I'm still that guy," he pointed out.

"No. You're so much more." She kissed him again, loving the feel of his arms around her and the knowledge that she was exactly where she wanted to be. Where she needed to be.

Where she belonged.

"You're so much more," she repeated. "You're a loving father. A loyal friend. A man willing to drop everything to come to the rescue of a fourteen-pound puppy."

She paused and kissed him again, her mouth slow and lingering. "And you're the man I love with all my heart."

He gave a low sound, picked her up as if she weighed nothing and carried her to the sofa.

"You are the most amazing woman I've ever known," he said, his voice low and rough. "We both know I don't deserve you, but I don't care. I swear to you, Jenna, that I will spend the rest of my life trying to be the man you need."

His mouth brushed hers with a tenderness and care that made her eyes burn.

"You already are," she whispered.

She loved this man deeply. This was right between them. No. Better than right. It was perfect.

* * * * *

A Beauty In The Beast

Michelle Lindo-Rice

MILLS & BOON

Michelle Lindo-Rice is an Emma Award winner and a Vivian Award finalist. She enjoys reading and crafting fiction across genres. Originally from Jamaica, West Indies, she has earned degrees from New York University, SUNY at Stony Brook, Teachers College at Columbia University and Argosy University, and has been an educator for over twenty years.

She also writes inspirational stories as Zoey Marie Jackson. You can reach her online at michellelindorice.com or on Facebook.

Dear Reader,

Thank you for choosing *A Beauty in the Beast*, a story that is dear to my heart. I have always been a fan of the fairy tale, so to be able to write this story for Harlequin Special Edition was a dream made reality. But of course, I had to put my own spin on it.

Both Eden and Mason had "beastly" behaviours that made them in need of a second chance. And what better way to get that than with a potential love interest? After past hurt, Eden curled into herself, like many of us do, but she was able to overcome her past fears with the help and support of her family and friends. Mason allowed fame to get to his head, but at his lowest point, he always had his family. I absolutely loved penning their redemptive arcs and experiencing how Eden and Mason's blossoming love for each other brought out their inner beauty.

You also get a bonus read in *The Ten-Day Bargain*, which answers the question, how can love for a couch lead to a love connection for two people? This story was such a fun, uplifting read and one that I hope leaves you with a smile on your face at the end.

I really hope you enjoy both these stories as much as I did. I would love to hear from you. Please consider joining my mailing list at www.michellelindorice.com.

Best,

Michelle

DEDICATION

For my son, Jordan Rice.
May you find the woman of your heart,
the one who will love you as you are
and who you will love freely in return.

Thank you to my editor, Gail,
Katixa, and the team at Harlequin
who support my vision, as well as my agent, Latoya,
and my sister, Sobi.

Chapter One

When Eden Tempest woke up that morning on the first day of May and heard nothing but birds chirping outside her window, she was all smiles. She wrapped her long tresses in a bun, slapped on sunscreen, donned a long-sleeved shirt, shorts, rain boots and a wide-brimmed hat before bounding down the stairs to eat a breakfast bar and gulp down a glass of orange juice. She grabbed her gardening tools and gloves.

"It's barely six a.m.," her grandmother Susan called out from her bedroom just behind the kitchen. "Where are you going?"

"The sun is finally out and I've got to go check on my rose-bushes," she yelled back.

"I'll be out in a few."

"Okay, Grams."

It sounded like her grandmother was still in bed, which wasn't like the energetic sixty-nine-year-old. Usually Grams would have had biscuits, gravy and eggs ready and would be getting started on dinner or heading out to the farmers market to purchase fresh produce. But Grams had spent most of the evening before cracking walnuts to make her famous black walnut cake. So, Eden suspected that task had tuckered out the older woman.

Eden ventured through the back door in the kitchen, the screen door swishing shut behind her. She stood still when she saw a family of deer munching by an overgrown thicket and bowed trees near the fence. A bee buzzed by her ear. She tilted her head and swatted at it, her movement causing the deer to flee into the woods nearby.

She tugged her hat low on her face and surveyed the one acre of land, surrounded by the iron fence bent like an elderly person with a hump. There was a dilapidated shed in the right corner, the slats gray and covered in moss, as well as an old gazebo where her grandmother used to host weddings or social gatherings for the town of Blue Hen, Delaware. She could still see the ladies and girls twirling in their bright summer dresses, and the men in casual wear milling about the yard, talking and laughing and eating from the spread on the table in the center of the yard. The last event had been thirteen years ago for Eden's sixteenth birthday. The day her life and her grandmother's changed…forever.

That's why she didn't celebrate birthdays.

Her eyes misted. She dipped her head and turned to look at the once-majestic two-story, seven-bedroom bed-and-breakfast, with the paint chipped and blackened with soot. The gutters needed cleaning and the vines had claimed a lot of the room. No wonder the people of Blue Hen called their house haunted, especially after… Nope. It was best for her psyche if she stopped thinking about it. It took some effort, but she shrugged off the gargantuan memories and stomped through high grass and weeds to the best-kept area in the backyard: her rose garden.

She inhaled, appreciating the smell of fresh rain and the heat of the sun. It had rained for three days and she feared her rosebushes had been overwatered. They weren't due to bloom until June, right on time for the yearly rose festival. Eden prided herself on having the most fragrant and beautiful roses in town. Every year, for the past ten years, her roses had won first prize at the Blue Hen Rose Fest and this year would be no different. Hopefully. If the rain hadn't caused irreparable damage.

Carefully, she lifted the bushes and squatted low to inspect the roots. There was no evidence of rotting, a common result of overwatering. Eden exhaled, her shoulders slumping. She steadied herself to keep from falling on her butt. Wearing tan-colored shorts might not have been the right choice, seeing as how the earth was damp and wet. Next, she checked the leaves to see if they had yellowed or were spotted. She saw nothing but green. *Yes!*

She stood and wiped her hands on her shorts before grab-bing the small bench she kept by the back door and started her pruning. She snipped and shaped and removed dead tissue; doting on her roses, ignoring the sun rays on her back and the sweat pouring from every crevice of her body. By the time she was finished, her boots and hands were covered in mud, three hours had passed and her skin was the shade of bronze.

She needed a tall, cold glass of water. And a shower.

Stepping back, Eden stood to take in the results of her labor, wiping her hands on her shorts. Beautiful. She pumped her fists. All this would be worth it when her grandmother came home with the first-prize trophy to put with the others on the mantel.

Speaking of her grandmother... Eden raced back into the house and tugged off her boots.

"Grams!" she yelled, but all was quiet. Her grandmother was nowhere about, and it was close to nine thirty. That was odd.

She washed her hands in one of the deep double sinks and helped herself to a tall glass of water then scuttled into her grandmother's room to find Grams nestled under the covers.

Eden heard a moan. "Are you all right?"

"My tummy hurts," Grams said, her body curled, her voice weak.

"Should I call Dr. Goodwin?" Eden crept closer. Her grand-mother's face was beaded with sweat.

"No, it was probably the ice cream I ate last night." Grams

was seriously lactose intolerant but that didn't stop her from indulging in the treat.

"Let me get you some tea," Eden offered, her heart beating fast in her chest. She couldn't remember when she had ever seen her grandmother bedridden. Grams must have eaten the entire pint. Unless it something more serious. Eden put on the kettle using the front burner that worked. The right one had stopped working about a year ago. The walls, painted buttercup yellow, the matching checkered curtains—slightly tattered—and the worn appliances could use an upgrade. Grams hadn't changed anything in close to fourteen years. It was like the house had been frozen in time since her parents' passing.

Opening the cupboard, Eden searched for a mug that wasn't chipped then dug into the drawer next to the stove for a spoon. She rifled through the different kinds of teas in a jar on the countertop—chamomile, Earl Grey, lemon—until she found a bag of ginger-and-honey. *Please let this solve whatever ails Grams.*

Eden lifted the lid of the cake stand where her grandmother stored freshly baked scones then placed one on a plate. Eden chose a large orange from the fruit basket on the tiled counter, her gaze falling on the oversize wall calendar and the big X on the date.

June 26. Her thirtieth birthday.

Her stomach knotted, and her hands shook as she cut into the orange and rested the slices on the plate. "It's just another day," she said, voice shaky. She drew deep, long breaths. "You'll be all right." Eden needed to make a tele-appointment with her therapist, who she used to see weekly until she had transitioned to an as-needed basis.

The kettle whistled and she poured the ginger-and-honey tea into the cup, the spoon making a light *clink* as she stirred. She gathered a wooden lap tray and placed the tea, the orange slices and some crackers on it, before making her way to the back room, rattling along the way and set it on the nightstand. Grams appeared to be sleeping. Eden touched her grandmother's forehead and gasped. Fever. Hot, roasting fever.

This was definitely not lactose intolerance.

She tried to shake Grams awake but the older woman was pretty lethargic. Panic raced through Eden's body. Her grandmother wouldn't approve but she called Dr. Goodwin from their landline since she didn't own a cell phone. What was the point? She never went anywhere. Eden did, however, have the most up-to-date computer. But that was because she needed it to teach her online courses for Blue Hen College. Eden taught English literature and composition courses to college freshmen and sophomores.

Twenty minutes later, she opened the front door, making sure to keep her neck semihidden, and the doctor went in to check on Grams. Eden used that time to shower, wash her hair and slip into a blue long-sleeved baby doll dress. She put on her hat and hurried down the stairs just in time to hear the bedroom door creak open.

In a flash, Eden was by his side. "Is Grams all right?"

He shook his head, his tone grim. "She's been doing too much. I'm putting her on bed rest for now."

Bed rest? "What's wrong?" she asked, wringing her hands.

"You'll have to talk with your grandmother about that," he said, marching toward the door.

"Wait," Eden called out. "Is it me? Did I somehow cause this?"

"No, my child. She's almost seventy. Some things happen with age. Talk to her."

"Okay, I will. I can't lose her," she whispered. "She's all I have."

Dr. Goodwin, the town physician, and the only one besides her grandmother who she trusted, gave Eden a look of compassion. "This house is too big for the both of you to manage by yourselves. You should think of hiring some help."

Eden stepped back and lifted a hand. She watched the exact moment his eyes took in her scars and shoved her hands in the pockets of her dress. "No one will want to work in the haunted house, and I—I can't be seen like this. I'm gossip fodder."

"Dear, there's more to you than what's on the outside," the doctor said. "There's a whole world out there for you to enjoy."

"I won't be ridiculed or be made into the town laughing-stock again." She shuddered, remembering how she had been taunted and teased when she had ventured into town after the fire.

"That was almost thirteen years ago. Things are different now. Even you're different," he urged. "You're not the same person you were all those nights ago. It's time you forgive yourself." Every time the doctor came to visit, he urged Eden to step out of her self-imposed cocoon. This house had become her haven since that fateful day. She never left, a prisoner of her past and fears.

"People don't change," she said, walking over to hold open the door. "And as for forgiving myself…" She shook her head, unable to continue from the heartache and guilt.

"Think about it. You don't want to end up alone, filled with regret for what you didn't do or should have done." After giving her a pat on her cheek, the doctor departed.

Eden trudged into the room to talk with her grandmother. Grams was now sitting up and sipping the tea. Grams's mother had been Chinese and her Jamaican father had been biracial, mixed with Black so Grams had inherited her mother's tiny frame and her father's olive color. Grams got a kick out people always trying to figure out her race. She would quip *I belong to the human race* every time they asked. Eden's mother had looked a lot like Grams while Eden had inherited her own father's height. Eden's father had been from Louisiana, and she had inherited his red curly hair, his cognac colored eyes and skin the color of sun-kissed sand. She felt like a giant next to Grams, standing at five-feet-eleven to Grams's five-feet-two. Grams would often say Eden had legs for days and beauty for a lifetime, which was why she had been crowned Junior Prom Queen at her high school. But that was history, a lifetime ago,

"Come sit here next to me, baby," Grams said, putting the cup down and patting the bed. Her long black hair hung to her shoulders and she looked frail.

Eden complied. "What's going on, Grams?" she asked, her lips quivering. "What aren't you telling me?"

"I'm not well. I…" She averted her eyes. "Dr. Goodwin ran some tests. We aren't sure what's wrong but I've got to take it easy."

"How long have you been feeling like this?" Eden asked, scooting close, inhaling the powder-and-lavender scent her grandmother always wore.

"I've known for a while but I didn't want to scare you." Grams wiped her eyes. "I've got a good amount of matured certificates of deposits and most of your parents' death bene-fits saved but I'm worried about how you're going to maintain this property long-term. I think it's time we consider selling this place so you can have those funds when I'm gone."

Eden touched her chest. "No. No. We can't sell. This has been in our family for decades. That's out of the question. Be-sides, I make good money teaching online."

"That's not enough to cover your living expenses. If you don't want to sell, then we've got to get the bed-and-breakfast going again. It would mean so much to me to restore this house as one of the best places to visit in town." Grams's voice wob-bled. "You don't know how much it hurts to have the neigh-borhood kids call this place haunted."

Every Halloween, they had their house egged or papered. Though her insides quaked at the thought of strangers traipsing through their home, Eden nodded. "After all you have done for me, how can I say no?" She gave a little laugh. "I just don't want to repulse the guests."

Her grandmother lifted the hat off Eden's face and ran her fingers down the scar leading from Eden's neck down to her left arm and hands. Eden sat still, clenching her jaw.

"You don't see what I see," Grams whispered. "You're beautiful, inside and out. I wish you would believe me when I tell you that."

Eden looked down at her hands and changed the subject. "The roses are going to be magnificent this year."

"They aren't the only thing that's magnificent. In time, my dear, I hope you'll truly see how valuable, how priceless you are." With a sigh, her grandmother drew Eden into her arms and kissed the top of her head. For someone who was burning up not too long ago, Grams felt cool. Odd. Maybe Dr. Goodwin had given her something. "Now let's get back to the house. We need to put an ad in the town paper, hire a handyman of sorts… Maybe you can make a flyer."

All she could do was nod, watching Grams's flashing eyes as she went on about her plans for the bed-and-breakfast. Eden didn't have the heart to tell her that no one would come. Because no one wanted to work for the girl they called the town monster.

Chapter Two

Even a beast deserved a second chance. But his producers didn't think so. His fans didn't think so. And his rumored married lover didn't think so, either.

Mason Powers sat the computer desk off the living-room area and read the email from his agent for the fourth time then bunched his fists. His television show, *Powers Property Rescue*, based in Columbus, Ohio, had been put on hiatus—which was code for canceled—while they worked out his severance pay.

The sad thing was, he was solely to blame.

He had let the fame and the fortune swell his head. Now he was hiding out from everyone at his agent's home in Blue Hen since the scandal broke. Who lived in Delaware? But he couldn't complain because no one, especially his estranged brother, wanted to have anything to do with him—and though Mason had good reason, he couldn't blame Max.

The chair scraped the floor when he stood and with every step the wood creaked. However, the plumbing and structure in the home was sound. Plus, all the appliances worked. He walked to the window. There was nothing but woods and cornfields for miles with the odd house here and there.

Ugh. He had only been there a week, but Mason had to get out and talk to someone. He couldn't stand his own company at the moment. All he had done was watch the video circling the internet of him giving one of the workers from his show a serious put-down before firing him. All because the man had selected the wrong tile for their home renovation. That's right. Mason admitted his behavior had been ghastly but that didn't mean someone should have photoshopped him into a fire-breathing dragon. The internet was ruthless. And he was a joke.

Before he was jobless, Mason was a sought-after home renovator, handling both the interior and exterior redesign, until he had been dubbed The Ogre of Ohio. His weekly show had been sitting pretty at the number three spot on cable television but had since plummeted into oblivion right along with his job prospects.

Everyone had left him.

Except for his agent, Lydia.

His supposed girlfriend had blocked him on social media and on her cell phone. Not that he minded. The media had made more of their relationship than what was true.

He stormed over to the table, stuck his cap on his head and grabbed the keys to his four-wheel drive pickup before starting up the engine. He backed out of the driveway with force, loving how the gravel spewed in his wake down the long driveway. *Whew.* Mason took a deep breath and decelerated once he was out on the main road, if one could call the narrow strip of pavement that. He remembered passing a deli and a department store a couple miles back and headed in that direction. Three miles later, all he saw was land. He must have made a wrong turn. Since there was no one else around, Mason decided to execute a U-turn. The minute he did that, he heard a loud *pop*.

Pop. Squish. Pop. Squish.

The sounds of his right front tire losing air.

Mason inched onto the curb and cut the engine. He dug into his jeans pocket for his cell phone but there was no service. Slamming a hand on the steering wheel, he shoved the door open with enough force that it swung on its hinges. Then he stomped over to investigate the damage before kicking the hubcap. There was a deep gash, which meant he was stuck here.

Clamping his jaw, he had no choice but to start walking. It was high noon and it was hot. His fury escalated with each step. A half mile down the road, he stopped by a rickety fence, bent low enough that he wondered why the owners hadn't just ripped it out. Then he looked at the house about an eighth of a mile from the gate. It was an odd shade of green. No. It looked like it might have been a light gray before all the moss and dried-up vines covered the house. And the lawn! The lawn had to be about eighteen inches high. If it weren't for the 1970s pickup in the yard, he would have thought the property had been abandoned. He wiped a hand on his jeans. It probably should be condemned and it was an echo of the desolation he felt.

The numbers on the mailbox said 345 and the street sign said Middle of Nowhere. This couldn't be real. Someone in this town had a ridiculous sense of humor.

Slowly, he made his way up the extended driveway, half-expecting a ghoul or some relative of the Addams Family to jump out at him. But he hoped they had a restroom, so he didn't have to whizz on the side of the road. The closer he got, the more he saw that needed fixing.

On the porch, there was a huge sign on a couch the color of lizard green that said Middle of Nowhere Bed-and-Breakfast. He rolled his eyes. *Really?*

Running up the three steps to the porch, Mason then pressed the doorbell several times before deciding to rap on the door. He cupped his face and peered into the window. Someone was in there. Someone hovered close.

"Hello? Can you please let me in?" he asked.

"Go—go away," a voice said from the other side of the door.

"We don't want your business and I've already found Jesus. He was never lost."

Mason cracked up. "I'm not selling anything. I broke down a couple miles back and I really have to use the bathroom. I rang the doorbell…"

"It doesn't work."

Figures. He was not surprised.

After a brief moment, the door cracked open and all he could see was a single suspicious eye trained on him. Mason lifted his hands. "Please, I don't have service around here and I need to get a new tire."

"Eden, let the poor man inside," another voice called out.

"Yes, Eden, please let me in," Mason echoed.

She opened the door and spun away before could get a good look at his rescuer. He stepped across the threshold and gasped. It was like he had stepped back in time. The furnishings and decorations were outdated. He would bet some of the art and decor was from the early eighties. He tilted his head. The foundation appeared to be secure but this place needed some serious TLC. It wasn't dirty. In fact, he could see the glasses sparkling in the wall unit nearby. It was that they were…dated. Definitely not antique, which would be considered chic.

This place needed an overhaul.

"Well, are you going to stand there gazing or are you going to go handle your business?"

Mason jumped. "I'm sorry. I was just taking it all in."

An older woman stood leaning against the wall and crooked her head. Her eyes shone and her smile seemed friendly. "Came to see the haunted house for yourself, huh?"

"What? I don't know what you mean." He shook his head. He had better get out of here. "Where is your restroom, please?"

She pointed to the left. "You can see your way out when you're done." With that she shuffled off in the opposite direction. The younger woman had also ventured off, though he felt eyes on him. She was probably lurking close by to make sure he didn't take anything. With a shrug, Mason walked down the narrow hallway and opened the first door he found. Luckily, it was a half bath smaller than a linen closet. He dipped his head, shut the door and clamped a hand over his mouth.

Pink. Frilly, pink curtains with a matching toilet seat cover. If he were on his show, he would be feigning outrage and ripping these off and tossing them out on the lawn.

He relieved himself and washed his hands before bending down to peer into the mirror made to accommodate someone of a much shorter stature. Goodness. This place needed…him. It could be magnificent.

Drying his hands with a paper towel placed on top of the toilet cistern, Mason then opened the door and returned to the living-room area. Wow. No one was around. They really were going to let a stranger roam their house at will. Unbothered. Unconcerned. Unheard of in this day and time.

"The exit is to your right," someone said from the staircase. Curious, Mason advanced and held onto the banister. "What are you doing?" Her voice sounded shaky, unsure.

"I just wanted to say thank you," he said. "I'm new here in town." He could see her shadow as she lurked by the turn. Talk about shy. Skittish.

He placed a foot on the step.

"Where are you going?" she asked, sounding fearful.

"Sorry." He took off his cap and ran his fingers through his damp coils. "Do you think I could have some water?"

A hand pointed in no specific direction. "Go help yourself in the kitchen. It's just past the living room. Have a scone. You must be hungry."

"All right, thank you." Mason followed her directions, feeling slightly uneasy. This has got to be the weirdest encounter he had ever had. And in his line of work—well, former line of work—Mason had met some folks with strange quirks. He entered the kitchen and saw three beautiful scones beckoning to him from under a glass cake stand.

His stomach growled. He hadn't eaten anything but a banana that morning. Mouth watering, Mason walked toward the counter. He felt like he was living a real-life version of a thriller film and the drawn blinds and dark interior added to the overall mystique. If he ate one of the desserts, would he pass out and wake up bound and gagged?

Then he chuckled. His imagination was putting in overtime. But it sort of felt like the place was enchanted. Mason took out his cell phone, relieved to see he had bars. He made a quick call to get a tow truck. Mason bit into one of the tastiest, fluffiest treats he had ever had. He groaned.

"Delicious, isn't it?"

Once again, he jumped, this time fumbling to keep the treat from falling to the floor. The elderly woman had returned. "Yes, very," he said, taking another bite. "I didn't hear you approach."

Her lips quirked. He suspected she quite enjoyed spooking him out. She picked up a leg. "It's the socks."

"Grams, you need to be in bed." From the corner of his eye, Mason saw a wide-brimmed hat and half of a body.

"Nonsense," Grams said, walking to the refrigerator. He noticed she was moving slow and was hunched over. "We have to entertain our visitor. Don't get much of them for the past thirteen years. Well, none, actually. Not since the fire." She took out a jug of lemonade and fetched a glass. Coming over to hand it to him, she said, "And such a handsome one at that. What's your name, sugar?"

"Mason," he said, mouth full of food. "Mason Powers."

"He's new in town," the younger woman added. Her voice was light, airy, melodic.

"Yes, I realize that," Grams said, all smiles. "You can call me Susan and my granddaughter's name is Eden." Then she grabbed her stomach and screeched as if she were in pain. "I'd better get back into bed. Come back soon, okay?"

He nodded. "I will, Ms. Susan." He sure as heck wouldn't.

The other woman scuttled over, keeping her head bent under that ginormous hat, and helped her grandmother out of the room. Finished with the snack, he took a taste of the most scrumptious, tart-yet-sweet-at-the-same-time lemonade he had ever had. De-li-cious.

Well, if this place was enchanted and he was stuck here for life, he would be happy with the food. Mason decided to grab another scone and leaned against the counter to savor the treat. His eyes fell on a small stack of letter-size posters. The words *Help Wanted* caught his attention. He picked it up.

It looked like they were seeking a contractor.

"What are you doing?" a voice boomed.

Startled, the paper fell from his hands to the floor. What was up with people sneaking up on him? It was the young lady who refused to give her name. "I see you're looking someone to restore your bed-and-breakfast back to its former glory," he said, quoting the words on the flyer.

She folded her hands. "And what's it to you?"

"Turns out, you're in luck. I'm well qualified, overqualified actually, but I'll take the job. I specialize in home makeovers." Mason doubted she had ever watched his show.

"You're hired," he heard Ms. Susan yell from the back room.

Eden rolled her eyes but didn't refute her grandmother. He could see that she wanted to though. Badly.

Mason popped the scone into his mouth, wiped his hands on his jeans and stuck out his hand. "I can start tomorrow."

She drew to her full height and whipped her hat off her head, her eyes glaring, challenging him. He was struck by her beauty and those incredible eyes. Then he saw the scar on her neck and his heart twisted. Mason wondered what had happened to her. He took a step toward her.

Eden lifted a hand, her eyes daring. "Are you sure you want to work here for the town's beast?"

Ah… He knew a thing about being a beast. But it was obvious: her scars were on the outside. His were deeper, darker. She stood, chest heaving, proud, defiant and…vulnerable. He reached out to touch her but before he made contact, she shirked away from him. She bent over to retrieve her hat, placing it just so, so that it hid her face and neck.

"I can start tomorrow," he repeated, gently. "Now I'm sure fate brought me here."

"Suit yourself. Stay out of my way," she snarled and stomped out of the room.

Oh but he had no intention of doing that. Mason intended to be in her way. Very much in her way.

Chapter Three

She had looked him up on his website. He was legit. And, she was guessing, expensive.

"We can't afford him, Grams. He's in the big leagues and won't be satisfied with the small-town life," she said to her grandmother the next morning as she stood by the doorjamb of Grams's bedroom with a huge amount of glee. That was her first argument. The second she wouldn't bring up unless she had to.

Eden didn't know what it was about the tall, lean man with skin the color of ebony, warm brown eyes, and those black, luscious coils that made her insides jump like grasshoppers. Um, she did know, using words like *luscious* to describe his hair. He was sexy, attractive, and the worst part was, he knew it.

No way could she chance that beautiful specimen looking at her with...with repulsion. That's why she planned on staying out of his way if Mason was about to be a fixture in their house. Having him there for hours on end meant she would have to quarantine in her room. The thought of that made her grit her teeth. Although she occupied the largest of the four suites on the second floor, she didn't relish not having free rein of the house.

"Let's hear him out first," Grams whispered, huddling further under her blanket. "I have money saved up for this." Eden shoved down her concerns for her grandmother's welfare. She had checked on Grams multiple times through the night until Grams had told her she was all right and to quit her fussing.

"I can put up the flyers tonight and see if we get someone else," Eden said instead, stepping inside. She wasn't about to go out when everyone was about and the thought of doing so caused her heart to hammer and her palms to sweat.

Grams pinned sharp eyes on Eden. "You said yourself no one would want to work here. I thought you would be relieved that we've found someone without trying. Someone who showed up on our doorstep at the right time." Then Grams's eyes went wide and she placed a hand over her mouth. "You like him?"

Eden backtracked. Leave it to her grandmother to pinpoint her real dilemma. "I—I— No, of course not. What's there to like?" His eyes, his smile, those hands, those lips.

"Oh, plenty. Plenty, my child. My eyes work just fine." Grams sat up and Eden clenched her fists to keep from helping.

"It's my body that has a mind of its own," she huffed, out of breath.

"Yes, I can see that." Eden inched her way inside, deciding not to continue that conversation track around Mason's good looks. Thankfully, her grandmother didn't either. Besides, if she had thought about him till the wee hours of the night, and if she took extra care with her clothing choice this morning, she would never admit it.

What she would talk about was the other disturbing news she had learned about their new contractor. She cleared her throat. "Grams, I think you need to know that Mason isn't as charming as he appears. He got fired from his television show because, and I quote, he is the Ogre of Ohio. He mistreated his employees and there's a clip of his bad behavior all over the internet."

"Pshaw. That's nothing but gossip. You should know better

than anyone that you can't believe everything you hear. How many lies have been told about us through town?"

Shame coursed through her. "But this is different. They have an actual video of his misbehaving."

Her grandmother raised a brow. "Everyone deserves a second chance, don't you agree?"

Yes, how she had yearned for one. How she had ached for her friends to treat her with kindness, instead of looking at her in horror. Eden knew that look on Grams's face. Nothing would change her mind. Eden lifted a hand. "All right. All right. I'll leave it alone, but I plan to keep my eyes on him."

"Yes, I think that's what you need to do," Grams said with a chuckle.

Eden rolled her eyes. "That's not what I—" She flashed a hand. "Ugh, forget it. Do you want me to make you some tea and bring you something to eat?" It was now close to six and she had to check on her roses but she needed to make sure Grams ate first. Eden would eat after she was finished in the garden. Then she would log online to meet with her freshman Composition classes to review before their final the following week.

Grams yawned. "No, I'm good. I just need some rest. I think chopping those walnuts the other day did me in." Um, that wouldn't cause a fever or her being bedridden but Eden wouldn't argue. "Ugh. I'm supposed to make some black walnut cakes for Doc and Kyle." Kyle worked for Vic's Grocers, the main supermarket in Blue Hen, as their delivery boy.

"I am going to order a couple bags of walnuts from Vic's, so you don't have to deal with those anymore."

The fact that Vic's was housed on a farm meant they often had a great supply of fresh fruit and veggies and Eden planned to get some watermelons, corn, and a couple bags of cherries. Corn was a must. No one had been happier than Eden when Vic's had finally caught up with the rest of the world and opened up for online shopping and delivery. Now Grams wouldn't have to drive all the way into town on her own, schlepping bags. Eden made sure to stay out of sight during the drop-off. But with Grams being sick, she would put in a request for Kyle to drop the bags and go. The young man would gladly comply as he tended to spray dust from speeding when he vacated their yard.

Grams closed her eyes. "All right. Whatever you think is best."

Those words gave her pause. Her Grams never gave in that easy. "Are you okay, Grams?"

"Yes," she said, nodding, her voice slightly weaker than it had been moments before. "Maybe I'll take you up on that tea after all."

"Sure thing." Eden rushed to prepare the brew, tugging her lower lip through her teeth. After getting her grandmother situated with breakfast and her antibiotics, Eden went outside. Surprisingly, the earth felt moist under her boots. Then she recalled the light pinging of raindrops she had heard while checking on Grams and sighed. If this rain kept up, the Rose Fest might not happen this year. She sloshed through the small puddles and squatted near the bush before letting out a gasp.

The leaves near the root of the bush had holes in them.

Rose slugs.

So much for the coffee grounds, and they were out of coffee beans. Eden rushed inside to get a spray bottle, water and vinegar. Seconds later, chest heaving, she realized there was no vinegar. She slapped her forehead. She had used the last of it the week before. She trounced up the stairs to see if she could add it to her online order, but it was too late. Dashing back down the steps, Eden eyed the truck keys on the key ring by the front door. She could borrow the keys and rush into town. It was early enough that her chances of seeing anyone were slim. Maybe she could order and get curbside delivery. Either way she needed to get moving before she had no leaves left.

Eden grabbed the keys between her hands and opened the front door, then froze. Her legs stayed rooted to the ground and her stomach felt hollow. She couldn't do it. She couldn't leave her self-imposed exile, not even for her beloved roses.

She shut the door and bunched her fists. She was going to spray them with the water hose and remove the slugs one by one if she had to. Eden hated touching the slick critters but what choice did she have? Swinging around, she stomped toward the back of the house. Just before she walked through the door, the house phone rang.

She scurried over to answer just in case it was the doctor calling. But it wasn't Dr. Goodwin's voice she heard. It was the one who made her stomach quiver.

"Hello, I was calling to see if you needed anything. I have to stop at the department store before coming there," Mason said. "You all live a good distance away, so I thought I'd ask."

She squinted at the phone, feeling suspicious for no reason at his impeccable timing, when this was of course a coincidence. It was on the tip of her tongue to tell Mason she didn't need anything and hang up, but her roses gave her pause. "Y-yes. I could use a bottle of vinegar, some baking soda and some coffee beans for my rose garden. I—I'll pay you back when you get here." Then with a quick thank you, she hung up the phone. Touching her chest, she drew deep breaths. Just talking to him had raised her heart rate. How was she going to survive having him around?

The phone rang again.

She fluttered her lashes. If that was him again…

It was the head of the English department, Dr. Loft. "Eden? We need to talk. One of your students, Naomi Bush, has lodged a complaint against you for biased grading. She says you gave her a lower grade over another student for the same assignment."

Biased grading? Eden gripped the phone before placing it closer to her ear. "I don't understand. I use a rubric for grading, and I go over all the expectations plus I offer extended office hours. Naomi never took me up on it. In fact, she has missed the last two classes." Sweat lined her brow. In her three years of working for them, she had never had any complaints. Anger whirled in her chest, but she couldn't let her temper get the best of her.

"I understand and I know how much you do for your students, but she is adamant that this is the case and is demanding a regrade. She is sending me both papers to look over to prove her case. Let's set a meeting for the three of us can discuss everything. How about you come in next week?"

Panic lined her stomach like rocks on the ocean. "C-can we set something up online instead?" That way Eden could go on camera and still hide in the shadows. She had the perfect vantage point in her room.

"I really think you should come in person, my dear."

"I—I…" She inhaled and raked her teeth across her bottom lip. "I have a lot going on here. Please can we meet online next week? I have a few days after the finals before I need to submit final grades so we can meet anytime after then."

There was a brief pause before Dr. Loft agreed. "I'll send you the login information. Look out for my email."

Relief curved her shoulders. "Great. I'll wait to hear from you."

"While I have you on the phone, I'd like for us to have a conversation on another matter," Dr. Loft said, raising Eden's anxiety levels all over again. But this time, she had an idea what this was about. The college had been pressuring her to accept a full tenure position but that would mean taking on face-to-face courses and she didn't do…in person. Though her therapist urged her to do so, constantly told her, she wasn't ready.

"Sure. We can talk after Naomi," she said, when Dr. Loft brought up that very issue.

"Okay. That will work. Look out for the invite."

Eden hung up the phone. Her eyes fell on one of the flyers advertising for the position and she curled her fists. She dipped her head to her chest. If her job forced her to come in person, she would have to quit. She didn't have the level of confidence to overcome the looks of disgust and the derision when the students saw her scars, learned her past. It looked like they were going to need Mason after all. And she hated needing anyone, having learned the only person she could depend on was herself…and Grams.

A small sliver of jealousy coursed through her. Mason had been called a beast, like she had been. But the difference was, he appeared to be…trying. He had grabbed this opportunity at a job. A do-over. While she was stuck here in the past.

No.

She was at a good place now in the present. It had taken her years to achieve this kind of…self-acceptance. She saw no reason to change that status quo. But it appeared as if she might not have a choice.

Chapter Four

Mason stalked down the aisle, the owner of the department store on his heels.

"Are you sure you know that you're going to the Middle of Nowhere?" Calvin asked. "No one goes out there unless they have to. Besides Doc and Vic's son, Kyle, nobody enters that property. It's creepy."

"I'm sure." Praying for patience, Mason pushed the cart with enough force to cause the wheels to rattle. The space was too small for them to be side by side, but Calvin sure was trying. Stopping midway, Mason raised his arm above the shorter man's head to grab crowbars, hammers, sledgehammers and other tools and such. His cart was already half-full. When he had been escorted off the set, Mason hadn't been able to take any of the tools with him, so he had to settle with what was in this store.

Although, one benefit was that he was supporting this local business.

"You know that place is haunted? Overrun with rodents and bug infestations."

Mason didn't bother to answer. Instead, he made his way to the next aisle to grab safety gear. It had been a minute since he had had to shop for his own tools and he was actually enjoying it, despite his undesired and unnecessary companion.

When he first entered the store, Calvin had been starstruck and Mason had obliged him with a few pictures, especially since Mason had needed to put up his own help wanted signs. All had been well until Mason had shared his intended destination. For the past ten minutes, Calvin had been determined to dissuade him from going back to the Middle of Nowhere Bed-and-Breakfast. But what the other man didn't know was Mason needed—and wanted—this job. He wasn't a man who liked to sit idle for days on end. That's how he had been for thirty-three years and he didn't see that changing, ever. Mason loved the long hours and seeing a house everyone believed should be demolished restored and made even better. Once he had gotten his tire mended, Mason had gone home to work on some preliminary sketches on his iPad to go over with Eden and Ms. Susan.

Thinking about Eden—something he had done too much of since he had met her—made him realize he didn't want to forget to get the items she requested. "Where can I find vinegar?" he asked the owner.

"On the other side of the store," Calvin replied. "By the cooking oil."

With a nod, Mason went to search for it, grabbing the coffee beans on the way. Another customer had called out to Calvin for assistance, for which Mason was more than grateful. He didn't want to hear any negative talk about Eden and Ms. Susan.

Not when they had given him a job. A fresh start.

For the first time in months, he had something else to do than troll social media to see what was being said about him. The brouhaha probably would have died down if his supposed girlfriend, Steffie, hadn't kept it going. As soon as the scandal broke, she had made sure to tout on social media that he had pursued her. Which was a lie but great fodder for her reality TV stint. The higher her ratings climbed, the more she added to the story. The more dirt she threw his way, the more innocent she appeared. Never mind that Mason hadn't known

Steffie was estranged from her husband when they met. Or that they'd never had an intimate relationship but were in the getting-to-know-you phase. And she neglected to mention that he had broken things off as soon as her spouse contacted him and asked Mason to kindly leave his wife alone. No one cared about the truth. Apparently, her husband didn't either, because the last he checked, they had reconciled. Well, good for them.

Lesson learned. Money brought out bad behavior.

He could definitely testify to that. That's why he hadn't refuted the rumors. Mason knew all too well how success was an aphrodisiac and how it came with a certain level of power that made one feel invulnerable, untouchable.

Until you weren't.

Briefly, he wondered if he should disclose the ghastly details of his show and firing to Eden and Ms. Susan. With his celebrity status, it would only be a matter of time before they found out from somebody in town. Although, they appeared to be somewhat reclusive… Naw. He would tell them. That's the man that he was. If they decided to fire him, he'd be disappointed, but he would understand.

After grabbing the box of baking soda, Mason made his way to the checkout line, avoiding eye contact with the other patrons. Seeing a cowboy hat on a rack near the register, Mason plopped it on his head and tugged it low.

Right as he finished paying for his goods, his agent, Lydia Silverstein, called.

"How goes it?" she asked, her voice husky from years of smoking. Even though she had quit that habit, Lydia tended to have a cigarette in her mouth. Said she loved the feel of it. There was a huge crack of thunder. The skies had darkened a bit.

"It's going. I got a job, actually," he said, surprised at the enthusiasm in his voice.

"Oh?" Lydia sounded intrigued. He supposed it was because he hadn't provided the usual dejected response. The cart cling-clanged the entire way to his truck.

"Yes, I'm renovating the town's supposed haunted mansion." He opened the bed of his pickup and began putting his purchases inside.

"Say what? Tell me more."

He chuckled. "Yeah, the owner of the department store swore he has seen at least ten ghosts on the property at Halloween." Then he gave her the rundown of how he had gotten lost, ended up on the property and left with employment.

"I love it." She cackled. "How about I see if I can string a crew together to record your shenanigans? I'm almost positive I could get this picked up. You could make a comeback. Plus, I don't know if you realize it, but your getting stranded up in a grand house in a deserted part of town screams *Beauty and the Beast* to me. Producers will eat this up."

The excitement in her voice was a siren, the thought of regaining his former television glory, a lure. He would be lying if he wasn't tempted. But then he pictured Ms. Susan's trusting face. And Eden's flash of daring when she had whipped off her hat and challenged him to see her as a beast. He thought about her scars and how she hid her beauty, her vulnerability. And those remarkable eyes. Eyes that had filled his sleep the night before. Nope. Mason couldn't exploit them like that, couldn't think of the hurt he could cause Eden by agreeing to this venture.

"Well?" Lydia asked. He could picture her tapping her pen, looking through her old-fashioned Rolodex and thinking of who she could call.

"I'll pass," he said.

"Has all that fresh air gotten to your head? Just a day or two ago you were all about clawing your way back to the top brick by brick if you had to. Your words, not mine. Remember?"

Mason tossed the hat in the back, slammed the door closed

and returned the cart to one of the designated areas. "Lydia, I'm not doing it. I haven't lost my ambition, I just hate... hurting people." The truth of his words grounded him. He had done enough wrong to his family, to his former employees and here was his chance to do something right. "We'll think of something else."

"Humph..."

He knew that tone. She wasn't going to drop this idea. "Lydia, I'm serious. Get me a new publicist and strategize."

"Got it." She disconnected the call but Mason wasn't bothered. Lydia was old enough to be his mother but she worked for him. Not the other way around.

Mason felt a plop hit his nose and looked upward. There was a gray streak across the horizon. Another plop hit his cheek and he bustled to his truck. He'd better get going to the Middle of Nowhere before the rain started. Not that it mattered with what he had planned for today. Today was all about going over his specs with Ms. Susan, hearing her vision, and then working out a timeline and budget. He was also going to have to hire someone to assist. He could use a crew of five but if others in the town shared Calvin's superstition, he couldn't see that happening.

More drops of rain on his windshield made him get a move on. He sent Ms. Susan a text.

On my way.

Fortunately, he was able to find his way back to the bed-and-breakfast without getting lost, using the tow truck driver's explicit directions. Just as he pulled up, the rain ceased and sunshine peeked through the clouds. To his left, he could see the rose bushes lined up in neat rows. Now he knew that had to be Eden's handiwork.

Mason rapped on the door, then picked up the bags and his iPad just as Ms. Susan answered his text message. Give me about twenty minutes. Eden will let you inside. His heart galloped in his chest and Mason knew that had nothing to do with the task at hand and everything to do with the young woman inside. She opened the door a crack, then stepped aside to let him in with a grunt for a greeting. Then she headed toward the kitchen.

He followed behind. "Where should I put the stuff you wanted?" he asked, hoping she would pin those gorgeous eyes on him. Mason wasn't sure why he was fascinated by her after one meeting when he could call a number of women who would be delighted if he showed any interest.

"On the counter is fine," she whispered, her voice barely above a decibel.

Then she sniffled.

After resting the bag on the counter, Mason went over to where she stood, with her back turned and her arms wrapped around her. "Are you all right?" She was once again dressed in a high collar blouse with long sleeves and a pair of tan shorts. He gave her toned, tanned legs an appreciative glance. And wouldn't he love to run his fingers through those strands. He had caught a glimpse of her hair before she stuffed it under her hat.

Mason sighed. This sudden infatuation had him feeling like he was nineteen instead of a man, fully grown. He should be able to control this attraction. Fortunately, Eden had no clue how fascinating he found her. He placed a tentative hand on her shoulder, expecting her to shrug him off. "What's wrong?" he asked, his hand tingling from contact. She tensed but she didn't rebuff him, although she had yet to answer. Dang it, if his heart didn't skip a little.

Then she faced him and wrung her fingers. The desolation etched on her face gave him pause. Bravely, he lifted her chin with his index finger. "What's got you all in your feelings?" To Mason, at that moment, she appeared as delicate, as lovely, as the roses she was trying to cultivate in her garden.

For a second, she leaned into his palm and he stood still, afraid to scare her off like a deer in the forest. Then she drew in a shaky breath and tilted her head away from him. "Don't touch me. You don't know me like that." Ah… here were the prickly thorns. She was probably upset with herself for showing any sign of weakness.

He lifted a hand. "I'm sorry. I just saw that you had been crying and I just wanted to help."

Her lips curled. "The only help I need from you is the kind you get paid to do." She jammed a hand in her pocket and pulled out a ten-dollar bill and thrust it toward him. "This should more than cover the cost of the items you picked up for me." She placed her tongue between her teeth and muttered a begrudging *thank you* before stalking over to the counter and digging into the bag. Then she reached for an empty spray bottle and poured vinegar inside before adding water.

Everything about her body language said she didn't want to be bothered with anyone—especially him. Normally, Mason would back off because he had a tankful of pride in his chest. But something compelled him to continue the conversation. "What are you going to do with them?" He went to stand by her side, all up in her space, loving the scent of apples and— he sniffed—champagne? Whatever that concoction was, it smelled heavenly. Too bad he couldn't say the same regarding the attitude of the woman wearing it.

"If you must know, I'm using this as a repellent for the rose slugs who decided to attack my rose bushes overnight. I was plucking away at them when the rain started pouring." She shook up her concoction and put on a pair of gardening gloves. "But this will zap them in no time." Her face held a wicked glee that made his lips quirk.

"Can I watch?" Mason asked.

Those cognac eyes slid his way. "Don't you have things to do?"

"Yes, but your grandmother texted that she needed twenty minutes, so…" He reached for his phone to show her the text message.

Eden pursed her lips. "I suppose I could use your help. The slugs are chomping away on my leaves." Then she went to get another spray bottle to make another bottle of repellant.

Mason was not a fan of the slimy creatures, but he wasn't about to make that known. Instead, he said, "I'm happy to go slugging with you."

She shook her head. "You can't resist, can you?" She did not sound amused.

"What?"

"Flirting? I've seen videos of you online with a woman on each arm." So, she had been checking him out. Interesting. He placed a hand on his chin. And was that a hint of jealousy he detected? But before he could mull on that or explain that had been a publicity stunt, Eden continued. "And, I see how you left Steffie Newman heartbroken." Her tone held contempt. "Going after a married woman is just…abhorrent. Beastly."

That stung. "You don't know me at all to judge me like that," Mason shot back through clenched teeth. "You have no right to pass judgment when you don't have all the facts." His chest heaved. Oh, he was in full spar-mode, but instead of a frosty comeback, she swung around, grabbed her hat and headed outside the kitchen, the screen door slamming behind her. Oh no, they weren't ending things like that. He grabbed the spray bottle and stormed after her.

She was spraying the slugs on the grass, having placed the baking soda on her stool. They were fat and green and squirmy.

"You owe me an apology," he said. She shrugged. Oh, so it was like that? Fine. He sought out slugs on the leaves and pumped twice.

"No!" she called out, coming over to touch his arm. "What

are you doing? You will damage the rosebush if you spray vinegar on it."

"How was I supposed to know that?" he snapped, feeling bad for possibly ruining her roses. "You didn't give me any directions." The spray bottle hung loosely in his arms.

Eden lifted her shoulders and took a deep breath. Then she addressed him in a somewhat friendlier tone. "You're right. I'm sorry. For judging you and for expecting you, an amateur, to know what to do with these pests. I should have given you instructions."

His brows rose. "What? Can you repeat that?" Mason made a show of taking out his cell phone to hit record. "I have to have this on playback."

She chuckled and gave his arm a playful shove. "I'm not that bad, am I?" Before he could respond, she stopped him. "Don't answer that." She exhaled and held out a hand. "Can we start over?" Eden asked. "I'm not used to handsome strangers all up in my space." His chest puffed. Handsome? But before he could bask in that compliment, she continued. "I received a tough phone call earlier and it put me on edge." She swallowed. "I'm sorry for taking it out on you."

"Apology accepted," he said, with a wave. "Yes, we can definitely start over." He held out a hand. "I'm Mason Powers, retired Ogre of Ohio. Pleased to meet you."

She giggled. Her laughter was like light and airy piano keys. "I'm Eden Tempest, Beast from the Middle of Nowhere. Happy to make your acquaintance." She slipped off her gardening gloves.

They shook hands and shared a smile.

Her hands felt small and delicate in his.

Gosh, she was beautiful when she sulked. But when she smiled like this, she was radiant. Breathtaking, actually. Mason's feet drew closer following his will. He saw her pupils narrow from newfound awareness. She fiddled with her collar and a red hue spread across her cheeks. If that wasn't the most adorable thing he had ever seen. A true sign of her innocence.

And an even bigger indication of why he should leave her alone.

Mason put some space between them, ruing the question in her eyes, particularly since he knew she would be insulted by his answer. Which was that he was afraid of corrupting her. He touched her curls, moving in the slight breeze. "Why did that phone call upset you?" he asked gently.

She licked her lips. "I don't want to talk about that now." Eden placed a hand on his chest then removed it quickly. "Do you?"

Nope. No. Not at all. His little beauty might be a minx in disguise. Oh what an intriguing discovery that would be if that were true. But he couldn't forget that she was indirectly his boss. Well, her grandmother was but he knew better than to muddle the waters.

His cell phone buzzed with another text from Ms. Susan. Can we do this tomorrow?

Sure, he texted back. I can email my plans if you'd like. Mason had spent a good number of hours working out the concrete details of all his recommendations for the interior and exterior as well as a projection of the costs and labor. It was an enormous feat, but she should be exultant with the end results.

Perfect. Ms. Susan included her email address.

Mason cleared this throat and glanced at Eden. "Seems like my schedule has opened up for the rest of the afternoon." He raised the bottle. "Should we get to spraying?"

"What? Argh." It took a beat but then her mouth formed an O and she cupped her cheeks. "Y-yes. The slugs." She scurried back over to the rosebushes, all business. "You can pluck them off the leaves and I will zap them with the vinegar."

"Erm. How about I zap and you pluck?" He suppressed a shudder before offering a logical excuse. "I don't have gloves."

She looked like she was about to call his bluff but then she pressed her lips together, like she was hiding a smile. "You got it." She sped off to tackle the bugs.

Watching her, Mason smiled. From her determined look, those slugs didn't stand a chance. He shoved his hands in his jeans pocket and chuckled. Though he hated the debacle that brought him here, he didn't have any regret making Eden's acquaintance. He admired her spunk and their spats were becoming a highlight in his day.

She looked up at him, shielding her eyes. "Get to work."

With a salute, he did just that. The task should have been tedious but with Eden by his side and their banter, Mason quite enjoyed it. Plus, they later shared a pizza pie and every now and again, their shoulders touched. She stiffened each time and Mason hoped she would grow less skittish with having him around.

When he pulled up to Lydia's place that night, his muscles were sore from bending over but he felt proud of his efforts and…grounded. Even Eden had praised him for rubbing shoulders with the common folk. Mason checked his cell phone and saw he had missed a call from Lydia. She had even texted him to give her a call.

He tossed the phone on the nightstand. He didn't want to talk shop tonight. Tomorrow. Tomorrow he would return her call. But tonight, he would go to sleep dreaming of a certain small-town girl.

Chapter Five

A week following the slug fiasco, Eden sat cross-legged on her bed and opened her laptop screen. Her roses appeared to be on track to bloom. Hope sprang in her chest about the Rose Fest. She pulled up her online meeting and entered the waiting room. Outside the sun was shining and the temperature was in the eighties but she had stayed in to grade student papers, wash her hair, paint her toes. A few seconds later, her therapist's face filled her screen. Ramona had a buzz cut and wore huge earrings which made her look more like an artist than a therapist.

"I was so glad to get your call," Ramona said once the perfunctory greetings were out the way. Her cheerful voice never failed to calm the quivers in Eden's stomach. "So, catch me up on what's been going on with you since we last met."

"I'm almost done with the spring semester at the university," Eden said. "I've enjoyed it so much, but I don't know if I'll be able to keep working there."

Ramona cocked her head. "What's going on?" For a brief second, Mason's face flashed before her. He had been working sixteen-hour shifts on one of the three master suites on the main floor. After their slug-removal adventure, Eden had kept out of his way, staying in her room and only coming out when he was gone. But she wasn't ready to talk about why she was avoiding the handsome contractor, so she broached her other main concern.

"A student accused me of biased grading," she began. Just saying the words made her fury kindle but she wasn't going to let that anger spread.

Ramona's brows rose. "Oh wow. That sounds serious."

She waved a hand. "I'm trying not to get upset or worry about it. I have enough evidence to support the grade she received. It's the in-person meeting that's making me feel like I'm going to break out in hives."

"Ah!" Ramona moved closer to the screen. "If you think about it, this is the opportunity we have been talking about. One of your goals for this year was to come out of your shell—make a friend or two."

Her heart palpitated. "I know but it's not as easy as I thought. The other day I needed to get some supplies and without thinking I grabbed the keys and started to head out. But I froze. I couldn't even walk through the door." She sniffled from the sudden tears and looked upward. "Like, why am I like this?"

"You are letting your past hold you back inside this house," the therapist said gently. "The guilt from losing your parents has imprisoned you and it's time you put it in its place and set yourself free. You made a mistake, Eden. You were a child, and very much human."

"No, what I did was monstrous. I don't get to have a second chance." She swallowed and wiped her face with the back of her hand. "My parents didn't, so why should I?"

Ramona cocked her head. "If you will excuse me, I am going to have a fierce conversation with you. I'm a mom and I can tell you there isn't a parent alive who would want their child burdened with this shame. I will take the liberty and speak for them and tell you that they have forgiven you. You need to do the same."

How she wished that were true. Eden sobbed. "I don't remember their voices," she admitted. "That's the worst part of all this. I wish I could hear my mother sing again and my father's laugh. I'd give…anything."

"Eden, I'm going to say something, and it might come across as real insensitive, but it has to be said." Ramona rubbed her nose and drew in a deep breath. Then she pinned Eden with a stern look. "You can't change what is. You can only change what will be. Your parents are gone and there is no bringing them back."

Eden reared back, her stomach muscles tight. "Wow. That's kind of harsh. Aren't therapists supposed to be sensitive?"

"But it's your reality and I can't tiptoe around the truth. It's called radical acceptance." Eden wished Ramona would lighten up a bit but her therapist was speaking her mind today. "You have to radically accept the things you don't like because you can't change them. You can fight and fight and try to make things different but there has to be acceptance as well. Now acceptance does not mean you agree with what happened but since you can't change it, you must learn to accept it." She pointed a finger at the screen. "Roll up your shirt and look at your scars."

Eden straightened at Ramona's tone. "I don't know—"

"Go ahead and do it."

She pulled up her sleeves.

"Those scars have been a part of you for thirteen years. It's time you embrace them and see them for what they are."

"What are they? Hideous markings?"

"No, child, they are your victory symbols of survival. You fought life and won."

She looked at the scars lining her neck through her arms and gulped. All she could see was the raging fire and her parents' still faces.

Ramona gave her some suggestions and strategies and at the end of their session, Eden gave a half-hearted promise to venture to the store before they met again. Of course, it was easy to do since Eden didn't intend to schedule another session anytime soon.

Eden trounced down the stairs to see her grandmother, who was up and about, in the kitchen. Grams's appetite had returned along with her cooking. Eden and Mason had eaten well the day before. Judging from the strong scent of cinnamon and vanilla, she would say her grandmother had baked cinnamon buns. Eden's go-to when she needed a pick-me-up. Sure enough, the buns were cooling on the counter.

The tears were immediate. "Grams, how do you always know?"

Grams shrugged. "Intuition." Her lips quirked. "Or it could be the fact that you've closeted yourself in your room because of a certain someone?" Eden looked outside the window to see that Mason's truck was gone. She buried the pierce of disappointment and continued her conversation.

"I was just talking to Ramona and she said some things that really shook me up."

Grams proceeded to ice the buns. "Oh?"

"Basically she said I should celebrate my scars, calling them victory symbols."

"I always knew that Ramona Giles was a smart one. I knew her when she was a little girl running after dandelions in our garden—well, when we had a garden—and she was precocious and full of life. And so caring. I completely agree with her advice."

Eden wrapped her arms about herself. "You know what else she said? She said Mom and Dad would have forgiven me and how I need to do the same."

"She's right, you know." Grams came over to hug her close. "You're too hard on yourself. And it's time for a mind shift. Change the way you view things." A door slammed, signaling Mason's return, and her grandmother gave her a pointed look. "And, you need to change your attitude about certain people."

Whatever. She stopped short of rolling her eyes. Grams wouldn't go for that. The door creaked and Mason strolled in holding a cardboard box with some containers.

"I brought Chinese for lunch. I ordered a little bit of everything." He sniffed then patted his stomach. "Is that cinnamon I smell? My mouth is already watering." Mason placed the food on the counter.

"Oh, thank you, Mason. How thoughtful. You spared us eating cinnamon buns for dinner," Grams said, reaching for spoons. *As if.* Grams would have whipped up some chili or Eden would have made grits and eggs. "Eden, you want to set the table?" she asked.

"In the dining room?" Eden knew her eyes were wide. They usually ate in their rooms or at the kitchen table. It had been, well, years, since they ate in that space but before she could process how she felt about it, Mason picked up their meal.

"Yes," Grams said with a soft smile.

"O-okay." Yet, Eden hesitated.

"Hang on, let me wipe down the table first," Grams said, grabbing a rag and furniture polish. She said to Mason, "You can get the place mats."

He placed the cardboard container down and picked up the cloth mats. The threading on the edges were frayed and old. She imagined Mason was used to much fancier table settings but he didn't seem to mind.

Eden reached upward to retrieve plates then gasped. She still had her sleeves rolled up. Her scars had been visible this entire time. Had Mason noticed? She bit her lower lip, hating how her eyes misted over. Of course he had. For a second panic coursed through her being and she was tempted to escape to her room, even while her voice within challenged her to be brave. And she wondered if her fear was more about her pride than of people's reactions.

But then he returned and came up behind her. "Eden, can I help you with anything?"

He was acting…normal. Yes, he had glimpsed the wounds to her neck, but the ones on her arms were much worse, a visual memory of the fire licking at her flesh while she attempted to get to her parents on the second floor.

"Eden?" He placed a hand on her shoulder and bent to look into her eyes.

A sob broke free.

"What is it?" he asked, enfolding her in his arms and drawing her close.

"Y-you didn't…" Oh goodness, she was a mess. And… rather dramatic. "You didn't look at me with scorn." She curved into him.

"Wh—" He touched her chin. "Eden, do you think me so…superficial that I would be repulsed by something that must have happened to you as a child?" The wonder in his tone showed he was genuinely surprised at her assumption.

Before she could answer, Grams called out to them to come and eat. She left her sleeves rolled up though she did decide to visit the half bath to wash her face and hands. She opened the door and drew in a sharp breath before looking around. Gone were the pinks and frills. He had replaced the toilet bowl, mounted a circular white ceramic bathroom sink and installed a gold brass waterfall faucet. She stepped onto the new woven marble tiles and turned on the faucet. Eden let it run for a few seconds, admiring the smooth fall, before remembering that Mason and Grams were probably waiting on her to eat.

She dried her hands, then caught up with Mason who was now entering the dining area. "That bathroom looks beyond amazing. It feels so spacious." She rubbed her hands together. "I can't wait to see the rest of your plans."

"Thank you. It took me longer than I anticipated but the end results were worth it." He puffed his chest. "Wait until you see what I have planned for the kitchen. That's next on my list. But I definitely need some help."

Seated at the head of the table, Grams smiled. "I see you finally enjoyed the fruits of Mason's labor."

"Yes. Oh, my goodness." She slipped in the chair to the left and addressed Mason. "I hope someone answers your ad for help soon. Although I doubt it."

Mason made sure to sit next to her. "Ms. Susan allowed me to post a picture of the bathroom so I might get some takers after that."

"I'll try to help if I can."

"Thanks, I might have to take you up on that." His arm grazed hers and she studied him from under her lashes to see if he was pretending to be unfazed by her scars. But no, he didn't appear to be thinking about any of that. Mason was too busy getting Grams to talk all about Eden's antics as a child. At times, she joined in the conversation, but mostly she reflected on her grandmother's words. She did need a mind shift. Sliding a glance Mason's way, she decided Mason might be willing to help her.

All she had to do was ask.

And that's how they ended up sitting in his pickup outside the flower shop the next morning. Her heart was pounding and her palms sweaty. Now all she had to do was get out of the truck, go inside the store and purchase a bag of fertilizer.

No big whoop.

Except…she knew the person behind the counter. Cadence Witherspoon.

A former best friend who had been especially mean and unkind after her parents' death and her first days back at school. The flower shop had large windows and she had spotted Cadence talking with a customer when they pulled up.

"I can't go in there," she whispered, pulling her hat further down her face.

When she explained why, Mason reminded her, "Sounds like that was years ago, Eden. When you were in high school? Haven't you changed since then?"

"Yes… I have." She gave Cadence a furtive glance and made a confession. "The thing is, we used to be friends." His eyes went wide. "But we were more like frenemies. Mean girls, together." She scoffed. "I don't know why I thought that there would be some loyalty between us."

"Ah… I see. But again, that is in the past. A lot could have happened between then and now. Besides, I'll be right here watching."

Eden squared her shoulders. "You're right. There's only way to find out." She gripped the door handle, pushed the door open and got out. Sweat lined her forehead but knowing Mason was observing everything gave her a small boost of confidence.

Just as she was entering, the customer was coming through the door, so she held the door open and held her breath. The lady barely spared her a glance and went on her way. *So far, so good.* She stepped inside, enjoying the cool blast of air. To her right was the checkout area which had various floral displays and a refrigerator that stored the cut bouquets. Cadence had her head lowered and was cutting a piece of baby blue ribbon for a bouquet she was putting together. To her left were different kinds of plants that needed to be in cooler temperatures as well as an assortment of teddy bears, vases and balloons.

"Welcome to Blue Hen's Garden and Flower Shop," Cadence called out, sounding cheery and welcoming. She had on a green-and-pink shirt which matched the decor of the store.

Eden grunted and sped up her footsteps, almost knocking into the greeting card stand. She headed straight toward the back where she could see a bags of mulch and fertilizer. There were also various kinds of repellants and other gardening supplies. By this time her heartbeat pounded in her ears. *You've got this.*

Ignoring the heat in that section, Eden scurried over and scooped the large bag in her arms then she dashed to check-out. She hoped Cadence would be too preoccupied to pay her any attention. But this was a small town. No one in Blue Hen could resist making small talk. As soon as she rested the bag on the counter, her chest rose and fell in rapid succession.

Cadence put aside her bouquet and gave Eden a wide smile. Eden watched the other woman's mouth drop. "Eden?" Eden froze, her eyes going wide like a deer caught in the road. Cadence narrowed her eyes and leaned forward. "It is you!" She placed a hand on her hip and smirked. "Well, well, well. I didn't know the Beast of Blue Hen would ever show her face in these parts."

Her tone might have been teasing but all Eden heard were the words *the Beast of Blue Hen*. All her confidence deflated. She was foolish to think Cadence would have changed. Spinning around, Eden stormed out of the flower shop, ignoring Cadence yelling, "Wait! Wait!"

Jumping in the vehicle, she ordered Mason to get them out of there, saying she would get the fertilizer online. No matter how much he prodded, Eden refused to tell him what happened. She kept her head trained outside the window and was out of the pickup before he even put the gear in the park. She darted up the stairs then retreated into her room, slamming the door behind her.

She dropped onto her bed. Only then did she allow the tears to fall. As she cried, Cadence's words haunted her. Her body shook as she poured out, her tears soaking her pillow. No matter how much time passed, the people here would only see her as a beast.

Eden would let Dr. Loft know this would be her final semester if they were transitioning to in-person classes, because she was never leaving this house again.

Chapter Six

Someone had finally answered his ad. That very morning at 7:00 a.m. Mason had hired Gabriel Sampson immediately, dispensing with the usual interview, and now Gabriel was on his way. Mason hadn't been so happy to receive a phone call in a long time. He couldn't renovate the house on his own and he needed strong hands. Over the past four days since the disaster at the flower shop, Eden had kept her distance. She stayed in her room, choosing to eat her meals there.

Ms. Susan had asked him to give Eden some time when he inquired about her. All he could do was nod, his chest tight. He missed her. It didn't make any sense because he didn't know her for long, but it was the truth, nonetheless. He liked talking to her and it wasn't like she had a cell phone so he could text her some cute emojis. And even if he could, he didn't dare climb those stairs and enter her private area.

Not seeing her didn't quell this obsession either. His eyes strained for a glimpse of her curls and his ears remained cocked for the sound of her footsteps. But nothing. Mason had no idea when she worked in her garden but it had to be at the crack of dawn because he hadn't spotted her out there and he arrived at six most days. But the rosebuds were about to bloom. Ms. Susan told him they would open in time for Rose Fest on June 20. Mason had already promised to help Ms. Susan carry them to the festival.

Now he stood on the front lawn, beside the huge dumpster he had rented, and waited for his new hire to arrive. Finally, an F-150 pulled in front of the gate. He watched the vehicle stall and prayed that Gabriel hadn't changed his mind. But then the truck turned and trekked slowly down the path, a trailer with various lawn equipment in tow.

Yes! Mason bunched his fists and walked up to the car to greet the other man. Gabriel got out and gave him a firm handshake. Gabe stood a good three inches above Mason's six-one frame, and he was brawny with his hair slicked back in a ponytail. If his former show producers saw Gabe, they would have snapped him up as a cast member.

Mason smiled. "You don't know how you made my day saying you were willing to start today."

"I recently got laid off my landscaping job and I've been doing odd jobs here and there but I can't go long without a solid paycheck, so I decided it wouldn't hurt to answer your ad." Gabe, as he preferred to be called, surveyed the yard and the house. "This here is a major undertaking. I do also have experience in construction, and I've dabbled a little bit in everything, so I can do whatever you need."

"That's good to hear," he said, patting Gabe on the back. "Let me show you what I have done so far." He led Gabe inside, noting how Gabe hesitated before stepping inside the home. Ms. Susan had gone into town to run errands and pick up groceries and Eden, of course, was in her suite.

"I was a teen the last time I came here," Gabe said, his eyes sweeping the kitchen. "Eden used to throw the best parties."

"You know her?"

"Yeah. Not sure she would remember me, though." He chuckled. "I was the class nerd. She used to tease me mercilessly back then."

He defended Eden in her absence. "Oh, really? The woman

I know now is really sweet." Well, sort of. Mason led him to the bathroom to take a look.

Gabe stopped. "I do remember her being super smart and helping me out in my computer class." Ducking into the half bath, he whistled. "You did a bang-up job in here."

Mason's chest puffed. "Yes, I got rid of a closet to widen it a little." He pulled up his phone to show Gabe the before-and-after pictures.

"Whoa. The transformation is beyond impressive."

And he had done it all himself. "I'm almost finished with the two master suites down here, but I need to lift up the carpeting and replace some of the flooring. The house is in pretty good shape structurally."

Gabe tapped the wall in different places and then nodded. "Seems like it. That makes your job a little easier."

"I do want to give the kitchen an overhaul. But I'll save that for right before the living and dining areas."

Mason then proceeded to show Gabe his plans. The other man's face lit up. "You have great vision." Then he gave Mason a somber look. "I'm sorry that you lost your television show."

All he could do was nod. "I deserved it."

Gabe cackled. "Well, every now and again, a man's britches get too tight, and he makes a move and splits his pants. It's humbling. You know what I mean?"

Mason straightened. Did he ever. Gabe was obviously someone who spoke his mind. Mason liked that, especially since it was the truth. He had gotten swellheaded and lorded his power over his employees. "I suppose you're right."

"I know I am." Gabe pierced him with a penetrating gaze. "A real man learns from his mistakes and doesn't repeat them."

Hearing the slight warning in Gabe's tone, Mason dipped his head. "Oh, I have learned, and I have every intention of mending my ways."

"Great. Then we will work well together." Without pausing

for air, Gabe launched into giving ideas toward the renovation that were sound but cost-effective. Evidently, Gabe was also more than a landscaper, but Mason wouldn't pry. By the end of the day, Gabe had helped him with the flooring, cut the lawn, and was now hacking away at the vines on the house, leaving the area with Eden's rosebushes alone.

At one point, Mason saw the curtains shift on the upper floor and he figured that Eden had peeked out to make sure her flowers remained unscathed. But when he waved, she had skirted away out of sight, the curtains falling back into place.

Ms. Susan came tearing down the driveway. He rushed to help her take the groceries into the house, performing introductions. Gabe came to lend a hand as well, introducing himself to Ms. Susan.

She waved him off and tilted her head back to look at Gabe. "I know who you are, Gabriel Sampson, even though you've lost the thick glasses and fixed that gap between your teeth."

"I'm glad you didn't see me when I was twelve." Mason snorted at that visual image. "Or when I recall myself trying to rock the cornrows." He placed the bags on the counter.

Gabe laughed, putting the rest of the groceries on the counter also. Mason admired how good-natured the younger man appeared to be. "Ms. Susan, I'm glad you're restoring the bed-and-breakfast. I do remember you baked the best pies in town." He rubbed his tummy and licked his lips.

Ms. Susan blushed. "Stop now with all that. Your mother would throw a fit if she heard you say that but I do seem to remember you showing up here—"

"Every Wednesday," Gabe said. "Those were the good old days." Gabe looked over at Mason. "This was the hangout place for us as teens. Not much else to do in town back then besides the movies and bowling. So, we would come out here and kick back, go fishing and play volleyball. Plus, there were always visitors on this end—and occasionally some pretty houseguests our age. But, always, always there was food."

Ms. Susan smiled. "I hope to bring that all back and then some."

"Fishing?" Mason asked.

"Yeah, it's about a five-minute walk from here," Ms. Susan said, "But it's hard to see with all the thicket."

"All that will be gone in a few days," Gabe said, sounding confident.

Mason's brows rose. "That's a lot of trees to trim and weeds to bring down."

"I've got it." Gabe placed a hand to his chin. "Say, I had a small crew I had to release because I couldn't pay them their worth. I can give them a call and see if anybody else would be interested?"

"That would be wonderful," Mason said, and provided an offer of generous compensation.

Ms. Susan beamed. "Tell them there will be food. Lots of food."

"I sure will." Gabe held up a hand. "I'll see you all tomorrow." He left, with his phone cupped to his ear, presumably making his first call.

Mason pointed upward. "Is she going to show her face?" he asked, referring to Eden.

"Give her time," Ms. Susan said, unpacking the groceries. "The other night was a huge deal but if I know my granddaughter, it's a minor setback. She's more ready than she realizes to move on." She gave him a look that could best be described as calculating. "She just needs incentive."

"Humph. Like your playing sick?" He began helping her put items away, taking note of how she had to use a step stool at times. Hmmm…maybe he would tweak his design a bit to make reaching her goods accessible.

Ms. Susan's mouth dropped, and she couldn't meet his eyes. "I have no idea what you're talking about."

"Don't think I didn't notice you made a quick recovery," he said challengingly.

Ms. Susan's shoulders drooped. "What gave me away?" She gave the hallway a furtive glance, probably to see if Eden lurked in the shadows.

"Lucky guess." He shrugged, before adding, "Let's say my stint in reality television has given me an eye to spot the dramatic." He cracked up. "Honestly, I am relieved you are okay, though I wasn't completely sure until you confirmed it just now."

She placed a hand on her hip. "Goodness, you have a good poker face. But yes, I know that's the only way I would get Eden to agree to all of this. She turns thirty on June 26 and I wanted to throw a party here, invite the whole town. I won't be here forever, and I need to know she isn't alone. I had to do something." She spread her hands and gave him a sly look. "And, if I'm not mistaken, she might have found a beau."

He slid his gaze from hers. "I like her. She's remarkable. Unlike anyone I've ever met. But…"

"But what?" she challenged.

"She's too good for me," he confessed.

"Pshaw!" She waved a hand. "That's pure baloney."

This conversation reminded him that he had never told Ms. Susan about his past. "I was fired from my previous job because I was horrible to my staff." He took off his hat and held it in his hands. "I'm not the man you think I am."

"I know all that already. I've seen the video and I hit the delete button." She wiped her apron. "I'm a pretty good judge of character and you're all right by me."

Wow. This was the second time today someone had spoken sincere words of faith about his character. He hadn't expected such grace. Mason swallowed. He hadn't known how important second chances were to him until today. He was beginning to like himself, see himself through their eyes, becoming the man they saw.

"Thank you for that, Ms. Susan," he whispered, somewhat overcome with emotion. He wished his own family would say the same. He knew he had to reach out, fix that.

Ms. Susan asked him to get a couple of glasses and a pitcher while she started cutting lemons. He went to help her with squeezing lemons, after he had washed his hands. She added sugar, ice cubes and water and gave the contents a good stir. Then she poured some into both their glasses before putting the rest away in the refrigerator.

He took a few gulps. "Oh, this is good." Then he asked, "So...you wouldn't mind if I asked Eden out?" His pulse rate escalated, and hope flickered in his chest. He took a huge gulp to cover his sudden nervousness.

Ms. Susan rolled her eyes. "Of course not. My granddaughter needs what you young folks call a hookup."

He spit some of the juice out of his mouth. "Are you asking me to—to..." He lifted his hands and shook his head. "Um, Ms. Susan, I'm sorry. I can't have this conversation with you. But Eden doesn't strike me as a smash-and-dash kind of girl. Not that I'm looking for that kind of girl..." He mopped his brow and decided to stop talking.

She pulled her lips into her mouth like she was trying hard not to grin. "I'm just messing with you... Sort of." She picked up her glass, her eyes filled with mischief. "I'll see you tomorrow. Lock yourself out."

Mason finished his drink and washed his glass. Then he went through the door, his steps light as he got into his pickup. He put on some jazz music and whistled along until he was back at Lydia's house. If Gabe's crew started tomorrow, he would be able to get most of the bedrooms finished in about two days. The new furnishings and materials were scheduled to arrive early the next morning.

Trudging up the front steps, Mason couldn't wait to get into the shower. His back ached and his muscles felt tight. He yawned. He sure was going to sleep good tonight. He entered the home and flipped the switch. But nothing happened.

He groaned. The electricity was out and he was covered in darkness. That's when he looked around the neighborhood and saw that the entire area was pitch black. He had been too preoccupied to notice. Mason rubbed his eyes. Maybe a power line went down or something. But whatever it was, it might be hours before the power returned. *Sigh*. It was going to be a long night.

Chapter Seven

Mason was moving in. Mason was *moving* in. Mason was moving *in*. Into her home. Into her space. Ugh. And Grams's firm expression said there was nothing she could do about it.

"I get that you want to help, but he's a distraction I don't need," Eden wailed the next morning. She had been sitting by her computer desk, finalizing the syllabus for the summer course—if she still had a job after today—when Grams came into her room and told her about Mason's plight.

"The power on that side of town will be out for about a week or more due to a power-line issue at the main plant. He had no place to go and we have more than enough room here," Grams said, coming farther into the room to stand by her desk, unmoved by her theatrics. "Both inns are full and I can't have him sleeping in his car like he did last night. Or worse, leaving." *Shoot.* She hadn't considered that. Eden didn't want him *gone* gone. Before she could respond, Grams continued. "Plus, need I remind you that this used to be a functioning bed-and-breakfast? I ran this place with an assistant for years before you moved in."

She swallowed. "I know, Grams. If it wasn't for me, you would still be in business." Guilt felt like bile in her stomach.

"Nonsense, child. I have no regrets." Grams made sure to meet her eyes. "Did you hear me? I have no regrets." Grams had given up the business after Eden's parents' death. Eden had been inconsolable and the first time she ventured back to school, her supposed friends had mocked her behind her back, calling her everything from a beast to a ghoul, while she stood in the bathroom stall, overhearing every word. She avoided them after that, refusing to speak or eat until she became gaunt and thin, collapsing one day on the high school soccer field. That's when Grams pulled her out of school, put her in therapy and allowed her to attend classes online.

Eden gave a jerky nod. "I'm just not mentally prepared to deal with visitors right now." And by visitors, she meant him.

"When have you ever been?" Grams asked wryly. "You'll adapt." She gave Eden's arm a gentle squeeze. "He's what you young girls call *eye candy.*"

Eden definitely agreed with that. It took considerable effort for her to ignore those abs, those taut muscles when she spied on him working outside. But to know he was directly below her, in bed, taking a shower… it was too much. *Whew.* She was feeling warm just thinking about it.

"He's really messing with my equilibrium right now," Eden confessed, running her fingers through her hair. "I'm supposed to be meeting with my student and Dr. Loft this afternoon and I don't need the extra stress." Having him here made her ache for things she shouldn't be wanting—like the feel of a man's arms about her; his lips on hers. It was odd but until he came around, she didn't realize how siloed she was. How sequestered. Sheltered.

Grams patted her shoulder. "You might find that you rather like having Mason here. He's great company and quite charming. You can't avoid the man forever," she teased. Well, Eden had planned on it. Then Grams said, "Whatever happened in the flower shop wasn't his fault."

Eden sighed. "I know. I just hate that he was there to witness my mortification. I was a wreck when I came out of the store. The main reason I've been avoiding him is that I am straight-up embarrassed."

"What happened, by the way?" Grams prodded in a gentle tone.

"You remember Cadence? Well, she works in the flower shop. When I went to purchase the fertilizer, she made a nasty comment about me being a beast or something like that. I stormed out of there and I could hear her calling me back but I wasn't going to stay there and have her continue her vitriol."

Grams eyes flashed. "I've a good mind to go down there and give her a thorough tongue-lashing. Cadence is too old for this level of insensitivity. I'm surprised, actually. She's always been sweet to me when I go in." She wagged a finger. "Well, Cadence just lost a customer. I'll drive over to the next town before I step foot in that shop again."

"No, Grams," Eden protested. "I don't need you doing all that. I'm grown and I shouldn't need my grandmother coming to my defense." She sighed and touched her bare arm before walking over to look at herself in the mirror. After working on her plants, Eden had showered and slipped into a sleeveless tank dress as the weather outside would be close to ninety-five degrees. "These scars aren't going anywhere and I've been doing a lot of thinking in here these past few days. Maybe it's time I take both your and Ramona's advice and change my point of view." Her chin wobbled. "I'm closeting myself inside this house, a prisoner of my own making, and..." She gulped. "I hate it. I'm—I'm lonely. I want to make friends and laugh and meet people my age. And..." She sniffled, unable to say the words.

Grams came to stand next to her and gave her hand a squeeze. They stood side by side eyeing each other's reflection. Her eyes were wet. "Fall in love?"

Touching her stomach, she nodded. "But who's going to want me like this?"

Leaning into her, Grams whispered, "Oh, my dear. I want you to have the kind of love I had with your grandfather. That your parents had. A man worthy of you won't be turned off by your victory wounds. He won't place value on superficial things. He'll treasure you. Worship you." She closed her eyes. "There's nothing like being loved by a man who loves you. And, that's what I want for you." She rested her head on Eden's arm and said not too subtly, "Mason's been looking out for you and asking about you, every day."

Eden turned to face her grandmother and spoke her biggest fear. "What if I repulse him?"

"Impossible." Grams rested a hand on Eden's cheek. "Listen, the world has two kinds of people—those who care and those who don't. We have to share this planet with them but we don't have to live with them. You don't have to take them into your circle. But don't throw the baby out with the bathwater, child."

"What do you mean?"

"Don't let the opinions of people who mean you no good shape your life, your path." She jabbed a finger in Eden's chest. "Take that power from them. You don't have to let them into your circle. You decide. At least if things don't go as you hoped, it was based on your choices."

"Oh, Grams, I love you. I have the best grandmother in the world." Eden snatched her grandmother into a tight embrace. "You are so right."

Grams kissed her cheek. "You are a rosebud and it's time for you to bloom." She pointed to the bookshelf laden with romance novels. "It's time you stop reading them—well, not stop—but take a break from reading romances and actually start living one of your own." She fanned herself. "'Cause honey, you don't know what you're missing."

With a chuckle, Eden gathered her courage, reached for her sweater on the back of her chair then paused. Squaring her shoulders, she scrambled down the stairs to greet the man who occupied her thoughts more often than she would ever admit.

She found him stretched across the bed, shirtless, in a pair of worn blue jeans, his hands tucked behind his head, looking up at the ceiling. A black duffel bag was in the corner and various toiletries sprinkled across the huge chest in the room. The room had been done over in a blue-gray scheme. Eden watched him with her arms wrapped about her, intense hunger swirling on her insides—and it wasn't for food. Although she needed to eat.

He picked up his head and spotted her. His eyes went wide before he sprang off the bed. "Eden, you're here." The wonderment and joy in his voice boosted her confidence. Mason came to stand in front of her with all his male fineness and she had to struggle to keep from dropping her eyes to his chest. Her hands itched to touch his smooth skin and to see if those muscles were as firm as they looked. "Do you want to sit with me a little?" he asked, tentatively reaching for her hand.

All she could do was nod. Because a sudden onset of nerves made her remain frozen in place. Mason steepled his fingers through hers. Quick tears dimmed her eyes. She placed a hand to her chest. This was the first time in thirteen years she had held a man's hand.

"Are you okay?" he asked.

"Yes," she whispered. "I'm more than fine." She cleared her throat. "Just having a moment and snapping a picture in my mind." She was going to replay this action over and over tonight. Her heart soared. They sat side by side on his bed. She looked down at their conjoined hands and fought to hold her smile. "I'm sorry if I've been avoiding you."

"It's all good. You're here now." He shifted his weight, so he was closer to her. Searing heat crackled at the spot where their thighs met.

"I've never had sex before," she blurted out.

Mason's jaw dropped. "Okay… Talk about a conversation shift." He raised a brow. "And, you're telling me this because?"

"I thought you should know that because I'm attracted to you. I tried to fight it but since I learned you're going to be right under me, it's all I can think about. What is it like to have you under me?" Eden was very aware that she was rambling but her mouth was like a waterspout and she couldn't stop talking. "I've read all about the act but having never engaged in it before, I'm unsure of what to expect and if it is as good as I've read about." Then she plopped back on the bed, folded her arms and waited.

He placed a hand to her lips and gave her a tender smile, before trailing a finger to her neck. Scooping his arm under hers, he pulled her back into a sitting position. Eden closed her eyes and puckered her lips…but nothing happened. She popped an eye open to see a small grin on his face, and for a moment wondered if he had been staring at her scars. But when she glanced at him, his eyes—those eyes reflected a hunger that made her squirm. With eagerness.

Mason peered at her for several moments before saying, "First, I'm honored you have chosen me. Second, I'm not going to give a girl her first experience with her grandmother right upstairs—no matter how soundproof this room is. And third, before I make love to you—and believe me, I will—I would like to take you out on a date. On a real date. Out of this house." He lowered his voice to a growl. "I want to get to know Eden Tempest inside and out."

Goodness. She squeezed her knees together. Those words held sexual promise that made her body quiver. "Okay," she breathed out. "How about later tonight? Let's go into town for ice cream. Small steps."

Mason nodded. "You sure? I was going to start with us going on walks and working our way up slowly to venturing back into town."

"Nope. At the rate you're talking about, it will be ages before we make it to the bedroom."

Throwing back his head, Mason laughed. "Eden, I am going to enjoy you."

Eden was glad she had followed her instincts and visited with him. She jumped off the bed and gave him a wink and a wave. "Later."

Chapter Eight

Gabe had been good on his word. Four days after Gabe started, he had recruited more helpers and there were now seven of them. Seven men working in various parts of the main level of the bed-and-breakfast to bring the property back to magnificence. But besides their vehicles, there were two other cars he didn't recognize. Ms. Susan must have visitors.

It was now mid-May. Mason stood outside reviewing the before-and-after shots he had recorded through every part of their labor. He also took daily pictures of Eden's rose garden.

His heart rejoiced that the bed-and-breakfast would be ready before Eden's birthday in about five weeks.

Ms. Susan had already started ordering decorations and had begun preparing handwritten invitations. Since Eden loved historical novels from the Regency era, she was planning a tea party where everyone would dress from that era. Ms. Susan disclosed that Eden loved magenta and she was searching for garb to complement that color. The old him would have scoffed at this idea but Ms. Susan's and Eden's relationship was pure and sweet and warmed his heart. Which is why he had called his brother, Max, when they broke for lunch. Max hadn't answered so he had left a message, pleading with his brother to return the call.

After Eden left his room, he had hurriedly dressed before the men arrived. When the electricity went out, Mason discovered all the lodging in a twenty-five-mile radius had been booked. So, he had spent the night in his car and his lower back pain and sore neck made him ask Ms. Susan for housing suggestions. Mason hadn't expected her to open her home. So fast. So willingly. But that was Ms. Susan. That's why he was willing to do all he could to help her. Including supplement her budget to pay for these workers.

Mason hadn't accepted a salary for himself, having only charged Ms. Susan for labor. Ms. Susan had asked to see the books, but he assured her that the funds were okay.

His cell phone rang. It was Lydia. He slapped his forehead. Had he returned his agent's call that day? He didn't think so. And he needed to tell her that he had moved out of her home. Mason quickly answered. Gabe and one of the men came out toting some rotted drywall to toss in the dumpster.

"Hey, I have the most exciting news!" she boomed. "Someone posted a couple of photos from your current project and your fans are eating it up. They are demanding your return."

"Who?" he bellowed, his chest heaving. "Who posted the pics? Because I know I sure didn't." The only person besides Ms. Susan he had shown them to was Gabe. Gabe who was out of a job. Desperate, even? Desperate enough to take advantage of Ms. Susan and Eden? Maybe. Mason slid his glance the other man's way and told himself not to presume. Ask.

"Who knows, but that random posting got you the *in* you needed. The producers plan to come out there with a film crew to stream and they are ready to put up some serious bank if you agree."

Mason almost dropped the phone. "What do you mean they are making plans? I didn't give consent."

"Well, I sort of did on your behalf."

He blinked. "You had no right to do that. That is beyond your scope as my agent." Gabe gestured to him. They were getting ready to rewire the plumbing for one of the bathrooms upstairs and he needed to provide oversight. "I've got to go but I'll call you back. In the meantime, please contact them and let them know I'm not interested."

"But—"

"This isn't up for discussion." He drew deep breaths and changed the topic. "There was a power outage in your neighborhood last night so I moved out of your house."

"Oh? I didn't receive any notifications about it... Where are you staying?"

"Here." He lifted a finger to gesture to Gabe that he was on his way and began walking back inside the house.

"Here where?" Then he heard a sharp intake of air. "You're staying at the haunted house?" She cackled. "This gets better and better. Please say you'll reconsider. Your moving into the house provides better access and even better footage."

"No."

"Fine. Have it your way."

"Great, I hope this is the end of it." Lydia could be tenacious when she wanted something or envisioned something for him. It was what made her a great agent but sometimes not so good a listener. He rushed back inside the house to assist the men.

Ms. Susan stood in the kitchen with two women flanking her sides. They had an assortment of veggies and he saw beef ribs dripping with barbecue sauce and blackened salmon. He could see the steam. And the smell. *Mmm.* The smell made his stomach growl. He sniffed the air and swallowed. "All right now. It looks like some good home cooking in here." The women tittered. "Let me go get the men."

"And Eden," Ms. Susan called out.

He headed upstairs and called out to the guys in the other wing before jogging down to Eden's suite. In the middle of the landing was a small sitting area that had a couch, a coffee table and a small bookshelf holding books and games. He could envision guests using this area to entertain and made a mental note to find more comfortable furnishings that had a pop of color. He continued until he stood outside Eden's room.

Dang it if he's knees didn't wobble. Mason pressed his ear to the wood. He didn't hear even a peep. He rapped on the door, his heart doing a weird sort of flutter.

She opened the door a crack and peered through. "Mason?" She opened the crack wider and stood close to him, propping one leg up on the doorjamb behind her. The tank dress rose high on those tanned legs and his mouth watered now for a different reason.

"Lunch is ready," he said.

She bit back a smile. "Those words are coming off a bit flirty."

He stepped back, his eyes raking her body from head to toe. "Can you blame me? Look at all I'm dealing with here."

Eden's face flushed with pleasure. "Whatever. Tell Grams I'll be down in a minute. I just wanted to prep some things before my call this afternoon."

"Call?"

"Yes, I have to meet with the department chair for the university and a student. I'll tell you all about it later on our date." She blew him a kiss and sashayed back inside her room.

He took the stairs two at a time, anticipation flaring in his chest for their date later. With such good food coming from the kitchen here, Mason thought a trip to the beach to enjoy the sunset would be a good idea. He wanted to hear all about her meeting, anything she had to say really, and he wanted to tell her about the television show offer and the photo someone had shared. The last thing he wanted was for Eden or Ms. Susan to learn about that mishap from anybody but him.

Mason planned to ask Gabe if he had sent the photo.

The men were already huddled around the table, helping themselves to all that food. The dining table could comfortably hold twelve, so there was room enough for everyone.

The men were already seated on one end with Ms. Susan at the head, her two friends, whom she introduced as Mona and Pearl, next to her. Mason piled his plate with a sample of everything, then took a seat at the other end, making sure to save a seat next to him for Eden.

There was an air of congeniality and a lot of clinking and scraping of utensils from the men getting their grub on.

"We had another table like this one, but it got damaged," Ms. Susan said. "I'll have to get another one before we re-open." The excitement in her voice was palpable.

"I can build you a new set," Gabe offered, then bit into one of the ribs.

"You're a carpenter as well?" Mason asked. "Why am I not surprised?"

"That's right. Your daddy used to own a furniture store be-fore he…" Ms. Susan didn't finish that thought but everybody at the table nodded then shook their heads.

"This is some good food here," one of the men said, dig-ging in.

Mason supposed that's what it was like being in a small town. Everyone knew everything there was to know about a person. He didn't feel comfortable asking especially since Gabe's face was now centered on his plate. Mason had his own daddy issues so he could respect someone not wanting to talk about theirs.

But what he couldn't respect was someone out for personal gain. He asked for everyone's attention. "I got a call from my agent that someone posted pictures of my gig here and it's going viral."

The room went silent.

"It wasn't me," someone said loudly.

"Me neither."

The men went right back to their meal. Unbothered.

Except for Gabe, who pushed his plate aside. "Why would you even fix your mouth to ask us that?"

"Easy now," Ms. Susan said, putting a hand up.

"Because I didn't send it… How else would it have…" He trailed off, hating to see the hurt mingled with disgust on Gabe's face. "Hey, listen, I had to ask, man."

Gabe stood and bunched his fists. "I thought we were friends. I don't betray my friends. And you good people." Was he though? Good people didn't put others on the spot like that.

Friends? He couldn't tell the last time someone had called him that. But he supposed making enemies and friends came easy in a small town. Mason stood down, walking around the table to talk to the other man. "I'm sorry, bro. I had to ask, you know what I'm saying? I couldn't walk around wondering because I was feeling some type of way when I heard somebody sold me out. Nevertheless, I should have pulled you to the side."

"I'm feeling some sort of way being accused, especially in front of a roomful of people," Gabe said. Then he relaxed his shoulders. "But I do understand. We good, man." The chair scraped as he moved to stand and they hugged it out.

"You good with us, man," another man chimed.

"Good, so we can get back to packing our stomachs because we have work to do,"

The men took their seats. He didn't know who did it but it felt good to settle the squabble instead of letting it fester until he lost his temper. That's what had happened before. The worker had shown up to work late four days in a row—his pet peeve—and then had been on his cell phone when he should have been working. Instead of talking to him about it, Mason had let it pile up until it overflowed. Mason wasn't trying to operate that way anymore.

That's when Eden trounced inside and gave a shy wave. He noticed she had thrown on a sweater over her dress and he rued missing another chance to see those curves. But, if everything went as it should, he would be seeing a lot more of her soon.

Mason took in the interested gazes of all the men in the room but Eden kept her eyes on him. She gave him a bright smile and came to claim her spot. His chest puffed. The men got the message and returned their focus to their food and to each other. Conversation buzzed around them. Ms. Susan was in her element serving everyone.

Eden helped herself to a small portion of salmon and veggies.

"Is that all you're going to have?" he asked under his breath.

"I didn't want to ruin my appetite for later since I wasn't sure where we were going."

He might as well tell her. "I was thinking ice cream by the beach?" Saying it aloud sounded corny. He hoped she didn't get the impression that he didn't think she was worth a five-star date. Or worse, that he had money issues since the loss of his show and couldn't afford it. To cover his embarrassment, he bit into his food.

But to his surprise, she smiled. "I would like that. I haven't been to the beach in years. We could catch a good sunset, listen to the waves and I'll make sure to bring my book with me."

He frowned. "You're bringing a book on our date?" What did that say about his expectations as a conversationalist?

"Good point. I wasn't thinking. The last time I went on a date it was with my mom schlepping us back and forth. I'm rusty." She giggled, then heaped more food on her plate. "Oh snap, I'll have to get a swimsuit."

Ooh, all those curves. All kinds of salacious images raced through his mind. Maybe he needed to take his own book. The Bible. Because Mason didn't know how he was going to keep his hands off her. He gave her the side-eye. Maybe that was her diabolical intention.

And, oh, was he looking forward to it.

Chapter Nine

When Eden entered the online meeting that afternoon, she was surprised to see that her former student, Naomi, and Dr. Loft were already deep in conversation, sharing a laugh.

A measure of unease crawled up her spine at their interaction, but she would not jump to any conclusions nor get upset. She placed a friendly smile on her face and greeted the other two women.

Dr. Loft cleared her throat. "I'm glad you could make it, Professor Tempest." Then she signaled to Naomi to present her concern. Eden folded her lips into her mouth and counted to three.

"I had a lot going on at home and I have to work two jobs but I didn't want to drop the course. I know I missed the last two classes and the review, but I felt confident I could bring my grades up with the research paper. I followed the rubric and made sure I made all the requirements. When I got my paper back, I got a C. I just happened to mention this to another student who received a B and he let me look over his paper and gave me permission to share. We had almost the same things. So, I feel Professor Tempest was being unfair to me because I talk out against a lot of things in class, and she always cut me off."

Eden wiped her brow. "I have no issues with healthy debates. In fact, I encourage it, but I also have course material to cover so I exercise proper time management." She refused to offer any defense about her grading practices and to give credence to Naomi's assumptions. Eden would wait to hear what Dr. Loft had to say.

"I have had a chance to review Professor Tempest's rubric and both of your papers." Eden stomach muscles tensed. "And, Naomi, I find that your concerns are unfounded." The head of the department cleared her throat. "I believe your grade was much more than generous than I personally would have given. The paper was riddled with errors, and you neglected to follow the Chicago Manual of Style when turning in the paper. I won't discuss the other student's paper with you since he is not on the call, but I will say, I concur with both grades assigned."

The tightness in Eden's chest eased.

"Oh… I didn't realize…" Naomi leaned back into her chair. "Are you going to lower my grade?" The cockiness had been replaced by fear.

"No. But I will offer you some advice. Communication is key. If you are unable to attend a session or complete a task, you need to communicate ahead of time, as soon as possible," Eden said.

Naomi gave a nod, thanked her and then left.

Once it was just the two of them, Dr. Loft switched gears. "Great. Now that we have that settled, let's talk about your plans for the fall. We would like to move all our composition classes to in person. We have found that the students make better gains with face-to-face instruction. Our upperclassmen seem to do well with either model, but our freshman classes need that support." She pushed the rim of her glasses up the bridge of her nose. "We want you to take over the bulk of the freshman classes because the student evaluations show that the students love you. They love how you break the content down to them and also prepare them to write college-level papers in their classes moving forward."

Eden's throat constricted. "I'm glad to hear that the students enjoy having me as their instructor, but…" She licked her lips. "If you're moving the freshman classes in person, I would love if you would consider having me teach the sophomore courses?"

The professor released a long plume of air. "I'll talk it through with the dean today and get back to you tomorrow."

"O-okay, thank you." Eden mopped her brow. "I'll remain hopeful until I hear from you."

"Don't get your hopes up," she warned before shaking her head. "You're a perfect fit with the freshman class." Then they ended the meeting. Though she was glad Dr. Loft had been somewhat agreeable with her proposition, Eden didn't feel at ease.

She stood and walked over to the mirror. She slipped off her sweater, then slipped her tank dress over her head and cradled her hands under her breasts. Turning, she took a good look at her scars. Because she had sustained fourth-degree burns, she had lost muscle and tendons in her arms and neck. Restorative surgery had only done so much. So, this was how she would leave the earth. The question was, how long was she going to allow them to dictate her life?

Maybe she should face her fears and teach the in-person courses.

Today when she had went to lunch, none of men at the table had focused on her wounds. Instead, she had seen curiosity in some of the men's eyes about her. The flattering kind of curiosity. It had been a minute since she'd had all eyes on her and though it felt good, she cared most what Mason thought. Watching the banked hunger in his eyes gave her the courage to sit with everyone for lunch. And sitting next to him, knowing he had saved her a seat, made her feel like she was sixteen again.

She inhaled and ran her hands down the side of her body. Closing her eyes, she wondered what it would feel like if it were Mason's hands instead. She moaned, before a realization stopped her cold. If she and Mason got together, he would see her naked.

Flaws and all.

Eden swallowed.

There was a rap on her door. Eden slipped on her dress and opened her door. Her eyes grew wide when she saw who stood outside.

"Your grandmother told me to come right up," Cadence said, her eyes beseeching and…kind? Eden gave her the once over, noting her shorts and T-shirt over a blemish-free skin. Her sandals were cute though.

"What are you doing here?" Eden croaked out, coming outside of her room and closing the door behind her. Simultaneously, she wondered why Grams would allow the very woman who called her a beast to enter their house, much less venture up into her private space. You best believe she was going to get that question answered after she got rid of Cadence.

Cadence couldn't look her in the eyes. "After what happened the other day, I had to come see you. I know you have a lot going on with the renovation right now—it's looking good—but I couldn't go one more night and not try to settle things." She pointed toward the sitting area. "Can we sit and talk for a minute?"

Eden gave a nod before trailing behind the other woman. She could hear the clamor below, signaling the men were back at work. She sat at the end of the couch and wrapped her arms about her, her stomach tense. Cadence clasped her hands in her lap.

For a beat, there was an awkward silence before Cadence chuckled. "Remember how we used to sit in here and sneak popcorn late at night while watching horror movies?"

"Yes…" Eden stood. "I'm sorry, but I can't do this. I don't think you came here to take a trip down memory lane after thirteen years and I can't go there with you. Like everything is all cool between us after the…after the fire." Just uttering the word *fire* made Eden's chest tighten. She took short, raspy breaths. "I think you should leave."

Cadence got to her feet. "I—I don't know where to start." Her lower lip quivered before she cleared her throat and met Eden's gaze. Eden was shocked to see Cadence had tears in her eyes. "Actually, I do know." Stepping close, she reached her hand out to touch Eden's arm. The first thing Eden felt was the warmth.

She hated how she welcomed that feeling. That human touch.

The second thing Eden realized was that Cadence didn't have a look of repulsion, though her fingers were almost touching Eden's warped skin.

She hated how her eyes grew slick from that knowledge.

"We were friends, once," Cadence whispered, giving Eden's arm a squeeze. "Real friends. And when you got…injured… I turned on you. I was mean and harsh." She sniffled and wiped her eyes with the back of her hands. "I was horrible."

"Yes, you were. But what made it worse was how you turned everyone else against me. Teasing me. Ruthlessly," she said, hiccupping, averting her eyes. Waves of humiliation at the memory washed over her. Plump tears trekked down her face but Eden didn't care. Cadence's presence had pierced the sore of the past and now the excretion was seeping out. It wasn't pretty but very necessary if she wanted healing.

"Yes, I know," Cadence sobbed. "When you dropped out of school, so many days I wanted to come and say sorry, but I… I was too ashamed to face you."

"Really?" Eden asked, bitterly. "How ashamed were you the other day when I came into your store?"

Cadence removed her hand off Eden's arm and covered her mouth with her hand. "When you walked through that door, my heart was happy to see you. You see, for years I couldn't face myself in the mirror. I couldn't face the person who had done such abominable things in high school. I blamed myself for your self-imposed isolation but then you strutted in, your head held high, so confident…and I cracked that insensitive joke." She held out a hand. "In a weird way, I wanted to bring up the subject so I could segue into my apology." She sighed. "But as soon as the words left my mouth and I saw how crushed you were, I knew I had done the wrong thing." She sniffled again. "I called after you, but you were too upset to hear me out. Understandably so. Please know that was not my intention."

Eden's heart responded to the sincerity in Cadence's tone. She went with her gut and released all the hurt that had festered on the inside.

"My grandmother raised me right, so I'll accept your explanation, but I want it known that your rationale makes no sense to me. We're not teenagers anymore." Eden shrugged. "A simply apology was the way to go."

"I see that now," Cadence said, sounding grateful. "I'm sorry. I'm sorry. I'm sorry." Then she fell apart. Sank into the couch and sobbed until Eden had to get her a glass of water and a handful of tissues. "Thanks," she said, her eyes and nose reddened. Cadence ran a hand through her long black hair that rested a little above her butt. "I must look a hot mess but I don't care. I was glad I had the courage to come out here and face you."

Wiping her face, Eden didn't voice that she thought Cadence looked beautiful.

"I'm glad, too," Eden replied, realizing she uttered the truth. Then she asked a question to satisfy her curiosity. "I was shocked to see you in the flower shop. If I remember right, I thought you had big plans to go to LA and become the reincarnated Meryl Streep."

Cadence's cheeks reddened. "Well, yes, but plans change. Circumstances change. Like most of our class, I went away to college but…life happened. Something you know more than most." She opened her mouth like she was about to say more before she shook her head. Eden didn't push. They weren't cool like that. "I started working part time the flower shop, but I am mostly in the back or doing deliveries. Two of the workers were graduating so I worked out front a few days."

When they were girls, leaving for Los Angeles to pursue an acting career was all Cadence spoke about, especially when they watched *The Devil Wears Prada*, which they had seen at least twenty times. So, it had to be something major why Cadence returned to Blue Hen.

"You had a birthday, recently," Eden recalled, rubbing her chin. Though she was out of practice, she marveled at how at ease she was engaging in small talk. Small steps.

"Yes, on the eighth," Cadence said, smiling. "I turned thirty last week. I know yours is coming up on the twenty-sixth."

"You remembered?"

"Of course. Hard to forget when our parents would throw us parties in the middle of the month because—"

"That was the only fair thing to do," they said in unison before sharing a laugh.

Cadence grew serious. "Just when I got my big break, my parents were in a serious car accident and I left LA and came back home to take care of them. To be close. I have never been so scared in my life." She gave Eden a quick glance. "I know you understand."

"Yes. Yes, I do." Her breath hitched. Even though Cadence had been terrible, Eden wouldn't wish that kind of loss on anyone. "But at least your parents survived."

"Yes." Cadence breathed out and then shuddered. "For a while, I believed it was karma."

Eden furrowed her brows. "I don't know about all that." Cadence was really hard on herself but who was Eden to argue that point? She had plenty of guilt to take her into more than one lifetime.

"Guilt will make you view things from a whole different perspective." She looked down at her hands.

Looking at her watch, Eden was surprised to see that it was close to 5:00 p.m. She had a date to get ready for. She jumped to her feet. "Cadence, thank you for coming by. For settling things between us."

Cadence shifted from one foot to the next. "I hope we can get together again."

Suddenly, she wasn't ready for their time to conclude just yet. It had been nice to talk with someone her age. Someone who knew her. "I have a—a, um, I have something I have to do. But if you have five minutes, I'll take you out to my rose garden?"

"I'd love to see it," Cadence said, grinning. "I'm entering the Blue Hen Rose Festival this year and I can't wait to beat you."

"I'll be there to see you lose," Eden countered.

The other woman's eyes went wide. "You're coming?"

"Y-yes," she said, wiping her hands on her dress. Then she straightened and said, "I will be there this year."

Cadence mouth stretched into a wide smile. "Let the games begin."

Chapter Ten

Mason's lips twitched. Since Eden and Cadence had come outside to peek at her rosebushes, Gabe had been behaving like a roebuck. He was prancing—yes, prancing around the women—lifting this or that, yakking up a storm, but the funny thing was they weren't paying him any mind.

Well, more specifically, Cadence. The other woman had tried to shoo him away like he was a nuisance but Gabe wasn't having it. Even when Mason called him over to discuss his landscaping plans for the exterior, Gabe wouldn't budge.

As for him, his eyes remained trained on Eden, his heart warming at seeing her interact with her former friend.

But man, did he rag on Gabe when Cadence finally left. "Dude, you were going hard over there. Did you get her number?"

Gabe shook his head. "Not yet. But I will."

Mason cracked up. "I thought everybody knew everybody in this small town. I'm surprised you don't have those digits already."

Scuffing his boot on the freshly paved driveway, Gabe averted his gaze. "I dated her friend for a couple weeks back in the day and that's why Cadence won't give me a chance. Small-town people have a long memory."

"Whoa. That's…" Mason busted out into laughter. Gabe's face turned stony and he tried to compose himself. It was just seeing the antics of this huge man for a woman who barely stood five feet tall was unexpected. "I don't know what to say, man. Maybe she'll change her mind in time. But if not, I'm sure you won't have a problem choosing from your share of single women in this town." Then he patted Gabe on the shoulder. "By the look on your face, I can tell you only want this particular woman."

His face transformed into a smile. "I'm going to win her over too. Just watch me." The crew came outside, all packed and ready to head home.

"That was some good work today, guys," Mason called out. "We start on the upstairs tomorrow." They gave him a friendly wave and went on their way. It was now close to 5:00 p.m. Mason jogged into the house and surveyed the completed rooms on the opposite end of the house from his master suite. One of the bedrooms had been done in shades of brown and gold and the other, which belonged to Ms. Susan, had purple and cream hues. She had gone out with her friends so that they could get the work done.

Ms. Susan was excited with his idea of giving each room a theme, but she hadn't yet made a decision for each suite.

His cell vibrated, and he pulled his phone out of his pocket and took a look. *Whoa.* It was his brother Maxim. "Hey, Max. I'm glad you called me back." His heart squeezed. It had been a good five years since he had heard his younger brother's voice.

"I almost didn't," Max said, his deep voice a rumble. "But I didn't want you reading about this online because there've been a few reporters hanging around since you got fired from that show."

"What's going on?"

"Dad's sick and according to the doctors there is no cure. It's his kidneys. They gave him six months unless he gets a donor. You know I can't give him one because of my renal agenesis. But if I could I would do it in a heartbeat," Max choked out. "And he's way down on the list and I feel it's because of his past alcoholism, though they say otherwise."

Six months. Wow. Mason felt sucker punched. When he was a child, his father, Alton, had seemed invincible, so hearing news of his demise jarred him. He rocked back on his heels, striving to remain aloof, composed, though his heart grieved for Max. "Thanks for letting me know. If you need anything please reach out."

"If we need anything? If we *need* anything?" Max huffed, his voice raising. "You know what you need to do. You need to make peace with Dad. Forgiveness goes a long way. For once in your life put your own selfish needs aside and think of Dad. Think of me." The line went dead after that. Mason had to get ready for his date and this call had definitely pierced his enthusiasm. However, he didn't want to cancel his plans with Eden. If he did, she might think it had to do with her. Truthfully, after hearing the news about his father, he needed to be around her right now.

So, he pushed all these conflicting emotions aside, put a basket of goodies and an oversized blanket inside his pickup and then rushed inside to get ready.

When he met Eden by the stairs dressed in a blue shirt, dark blue jeans and blue Timbs for their date, she must have seen something on his face and asked if everything was all right. Eyeing her yellow sundress with the upper body fitted then flaring off at the waist, he nodded, then gave her hand a squeeze. Just that act grounded him.

Mason forced a smile on his face, and they made small talk about the beautiful weather, but Max's words lingered, and he grew quiet with his thoughts. The day Mason turned twenty was the day he left Virginia and he had vowed never to return. He had been generous with his resources but kept his distance, except visiting once a year. But even that ended after his epic falling-out with his father. It had been a volcanic eruption caused by pent-up resentment for most of his life.

Mason's only regret had been leaving Max behind.

A regret that stayed with him to this very day.

Eden dug into her bag for her book and that shook him back into the present. "You really brought reading material for our date? Have you no faith in my ability to keep you entertained?" he teased. He didn't mention that he had seen her white sweater—her crutch—tucked inside as well. Mason hoped he could convince her to leave it inside the vehicle.

She smiled. "Don't take it personal. You've got to understand that books have been my stalwart companions the past thirteen years. I can depend on them. They give me hours of pleasure and they don't laugh at me, or make me feel less than. Books are equal opportunity friends."

"I'm just messing with you," Mason said. "I also love books. My bookshelves at home have the usual renovating and design books but…" He hesitated before dropping his voice to a whisper. "I'm a closet women's fiction reader. Also romance."

She placed a hand over her mouth. "Come again? What do you mean, you're a closet women's fiction reader?"

Mason's face felt hot. "It all started out because of my hormones. Now you won't see these books on my shelves though. You'll see the Harlan Coben, Michael Connelly, James Patterson in my collection. I read the women's fiction and romances on my Kindle or I borrow them from my library."

She raised her brows. "I find this utterly fascinating." Her voice dropped. "And a major turn-on."

"Well, I didn't have the kind of relationship with my father where I could talk to him about girls and dating and… sex. And, I was curious. In high school, I would see all these girls hiding romances between their textbooks, their faces bright and red from whatever they were reading. And then it dawned on me that I could learn about the opposite sex by reading romances. And, let me tell you, those love scenes taught me some stuff."

Eden laughed. Boy, did he love that sound. He must get her to do more of that. "What did you learn?"

"I'll show you soon enough. But let's just say, I've never had any complaints." He slid a quick glance her way, satisfied to see the interest in her eyes. The curiosity. The anticipation.

"Who have you read?" she asked.

"*An American Marriage, Miss Pearly's Girls*…who else?" He drummed his fingers on the steering wheel. "Oh yeah, I read *Lessons in Chemistry* and I just bought *Yellowface*. Basically, if there is buzz about a book, I'm going to read it."

"Wow," she said, "I'm impressed. Mason Powers, you have managed to surprise me. I'm floored. I've read all of those books. I feel like you're talking my love language here."

"As far as romances, I do love me some Emily Henry and Tessa Bailey. But my props go out to LaQuette and Naima Simone. Those ladies know how to write a love scene. They break it down for a brother."

Eden covered her mouth and laughed until her shoulders shook. "You are hilarious. Until recently, I haven't been into romances since I was a teen. It was hard for me to read about people falling in love when I…" She trailed off and looked out the window. "I didn't want to read about something that I didn't ever see happening for me. I also didn't want to be in heat and have no outlet."

"You deserve to be loved and even more." Mason gripped the wheel. His heart hurt thinking of a young Eden grappling with loneliness and the fear that she would remain unloved for the rest of her life. But he couldn't resist adding, "You know they do have toys that could have helped you with your sexual frustration."

Since they were stopped at a light, he peered over at her face which had taken on a rosy hue.

"Ah… Oh… Well, I didn't think about that."

"I can't wait to show you what you've been missing."

"I can't wait either." She tilted her head. "I just started reading some hot romances and so I do have some ideas I want to try out."

The air in the car grew hot and tight as tension rose between them. Mason debated pulling over to the side of the road and satisfying this craving, the potent desire coursing through him. He had read that scene in a romance where the couple got wild on the hood of the car and since then that had become a fantasy, but there was no way he going there with Eden.

At least not yet. He smiled. He was going to relish awakening her inner freak.

Eden must have been watching him. "What put that smile on your face?" she asked.

Nope. He was so not telling her his actual thoughts. Instead, he said, "I was thinking about ice cream." The navigator backed him up by saying he needed to make a turn. "I'm taking us to a creamery I saw that had rave reviews."

That launched a new discussion about ice cream, how it was made, and their favorite flavors. A topic that lasted until they arrived at their destination. He opened her door and helped her out, then they went to purchase their ice creams.

There were a few families out, but they were the last customers of the day. He noticed that Eden received a few curious glances but other than that, no one addressed her wounds. Which was fantastic.

Once they had ordered—he, a double scoop of butter pecan, and she, a single scoop of chocolate chip, they decided to follow one of the trails on the farm. While they enjoyed their treats, Mason reached out to hold her hand. He laced his fingers through hers and turned to make conversation. But at that very moment, she took a lick of her ice-cream cone. And he stopped walking.

Entranced.

She looked delectable and there was nothing more he wanted to do than sample that ice cream right off her tongue.

Chapter Eleven

Dang, his hand was heavy. Eden needed to clench and un-clench her fingers a bit but she also wanted to savor the warm feeling coursing through her insides. She was holding hands with Mason.

But she needed to give her hand a rest. Just for a few seconds. And she had thought of the perfect way to distract him. Eden saw how he was looking at her eat her ice-cream cone and a mischievous voice told her to play that up. Since they were alone on the trail, she circled her tongue around the tip of the ice cream, chuckling when she heard Mason's groan.

He released her hand—thank goodness—and snaked his arm around her waist, drawing her close into that broad chest. Much better. "Can I have some?" Mason asked with a low growl. By then, he had already devoured his cone.

She raised a brow. "Some of what?"

"Your ice cream." His breath smelled like butter pecan but she detected a scent of sandalwood and spice which reduced her insides to jelly.

Eden purposely ate another mouthful. She was learning she was quite the tease. A bead of sweat lined his brow. "Nervous?" she asked.

"I want to kiss you so bad." The desperate tone in his confession made her feel sexy and wanton.

"Then kiss me," she breathed out, her chest rising and fall

as desire coursed through her. A new kind of frustration was building within, and she needed relief.

"This wasn't how I planned this."

"The best things in life aren't planned."

Mason stepped forward, walking her backward until her back was against a tree. The branches hung low enough to hide them from view. He trailed small kisses behind her ear and she arched her neck to give him access, her hands gripping his back.

Then he kissed her.

And she lost her breath, her balance and her ice-cream cone. He kissed her until she had no air left, squeezing every drop of passion out of her, giving all of himself.

And it was not enough.

As soon as he pulled apart, she grabbed his head and planted her lips to his. Eden lost track of time. All she knew was that when they finally pulled apart, the sun had started to set.

"Let's get to the beach." Mason took her hand, and they ran toward the car, laughing like they were teenagers.

A few minutes later, he parked in a secluded area and retrieved the basket and blanket.

"Oh, you came prepared," Eden said.

"I want tonight to be perfect."

"It already is," she whispered, savoring the taste of him on her lips. She had had her first grown-up kiss and it had been marvelous, exceeding her imagination. Eden didn't know if there was any romance novel that could accurately describe the rightfulness of being in the arms of someone who you clicked with. The sense of belonging.

And that's how it felt when Mason held her close.

He declined her offer to help but set up a romantic spot, sprinkling rose petals and pulling out candle jars, wine glasses, sparkling cider and a charcuterie board. He had ice packs that kept everything chilled. "Wow, you thought of everything." She touched her chest. "Thank you."

"I'm glad you're happy." He snuggled her close to him, her back against his chest and together they watched the sun lower on the horizon, painting streaks of oranges, blues and purples. Oh, there was nothing like it. They ate and kissed and just basked in the moment of being together. Then Mason lit the candles, the scent of cinnamon and apples wafting in the air. A light breeze added to the tender atmosphere.

Mason snapped a few pictures of them and also the sunset on his cell phone. Then he offered to send her the pictures.

"I don't have a cell phone," she said, flicking away some of the sand on her dress. "I never had the need for one." *Until now.*

"I know. We have to remedy that," he said. "I'll email them to you for now, but I want to be able to text my girlfriend some naughty messages." He waggled his brows.

Girlfriend? Her heart did a weird flip-flop. How smooth, how easy that rolled off his tongue. She supposed at their age, it was just understood. Eden didn't want to appear naive by asking, especially since her brain kept zinging on *girlfriend.* She was somebody's *girlfriend.* Specifically, Mason's *girl-friend.* Her inner girl shouted, *Whee!*

"I'll get one tomorrow," she said, trying to sound unaffected by the fact that suddenly, she had a *boyfriend.* She took her *boyfriend's* hands and placed them into her lap, before covering his hands with her smaller ones. They spoon-fed each other between lots of long kisses, her favorite moment when Mason cupped her breasts. She took off her dress to reveal her black bikini—one she had ordered for same-day delivery from Amazon—then held up the blanket so he could change into his colorful trunks. They frolicked by the water, chasing each other and just having fun. The best thing, besides their make-out sessions, was the laughter.

Spent, they returned to recoup on the blanket. As far as first dates went, this was an 11/10. "So, I don't want to ruin our good mood but right before we left the house, you seemed… preoccupied, like something was on your mind. I'm not trying to be nosy but I'm concerned." She played with the hem of her dress. "Did you want to talk about it?"

"I will if you tell me about your meeting."

She touched his cheek. "I guess we're both curious about each other… You've got a deal."

Mason leaned back onto the blanket and looked up at the sky. "I learned today from my brother that my father is dying, and it shook me up a bit. I didn't expect it to as my father engaged in certain lifestyle choices—he was an alcoholic, a heavy smoker and…he was verbally and physically abusive. I had a tough childhood and once I hit twenty, I was out of there. I have only been back a few times."

She stretched out next to him. "I'm so sorry to hear that." This time she reached to hold his hand but she didn't steeple their fingers together. "When are you planning to go see him?" She felt a pang at the thought of him leaving but family was important.

"I'm not," he said, moving onto his side so that he faced her, propping a hand under his head.

"What do you mean you're not?" she blurted out. "I'm sorry, I shouldn't have said that."

"No, it's cool. Your question is only natural. That would be what's expected if I grew up in a normal family." He sat up, as if restless.

She held out a hand and he tugged her to a sitting position. Placing a hand on his arm, she said softly, "Tell me."

"My father worked in a factory and my mother passed when me and my brother were too young to understand fully what that meant. I was seven and Maxim was two and my dad was shattered. Shattered to the point where he started drinking. He drank around the clock, and it started the very night we buried her. Once everyone had left, he sent us to bed, but

I wanted to check on him. Now, when he wasn't drunk, my dad was amazing but when he was, he was mean. He was vicious and I got the brunt of it. Of course, in time, he lost his job and we lost everything."

She heard the venom in his tone and wrapped an arm around his waist. He leaned into her. "You sure you want to hear this?"

Eden nodded. "I want to know everything about you."

He made circles in the sand with his finger. "The only reason we had a roof over our heads was because the house had been paid for by my mother's parents and they had passed it down to my mother. But other than that, I had to cook and clean and take care of Maxim and myself."

"That's a lot of responsibility for a child," she said. "What about your church? Or family? Wasn't there anyone you could call?"

"No, I didn't dare. I knew early on that what happened in our house, stayed in our house." His tone grew bitter. "If I dared open my mouth, my father would backhand me. The only great thing was that Alton Powers never laid a hand on Maxim." Mason reached over to take a sip of sparkling cider. "Maybe it was because he looked like Mom, I don't know, but that was a relief. When I finally got the courage to leave, I wanted to take Maxim with me, but I had scraped enough for only one bus ticket. And I knew he would be okay." He drained the glass. "Turns out that Dad got sober once I was out of the house. Maxim was fifteen and started getting into some trouble and my father got his act together. For him."

Eden could hear the hurt in Mason's voice and she wished she had the right words to comfort him. She gave him a light kiss instead, which he seemed to welcome.

"But all's well that ends well, I guess. Maxim is now a chef at a five-star restaurant and well, you see how I turned out." He stared out at the ocean. "My brother wants me to go home and mend fences with my father and I admit that when I see you with your grandmother, it makes me tempted to reach out." His lips curled. "But the last time I did that, it did not go well."

"What happened?" She reached for a cheese cube. It was slightly hardened from being exposed to the air but still delicious.

"I was turning thirty and there's something about hitting that milestone that makes you reflect on your life and make changes."

"I get that. I'm turning thirty in a couple weeks and that's all I can think about."

"Yeah, so you get it." He continued. "So, I got on a plane but as I look back, I realize I didn't go back with reconciliation in mind. I was too angry. I was all about confrontation. I was all about making him pay for all the hurt he'd caused. I wanted to battle the demons of the past, not settle them." He shook his head. "Well, that was a bad idea. My father refused to fight with me and Maxim got in my face. Me and my brother got into it real bad. You see, he had a different childhood, a different dad than I did and he wasn't going to sit back and see his father get disrespected. Which though I understood, didn't make it hurt any less."

"But you are allowed to feel how you feel," Eden said, defending him. She knew a thing or two about being angry with your past—only most of her anger was directed at herself.

"Maxim doesn't see it that way." He scoffed, "I don't get how the same man could be two distinctly different people." Then he shook his shoulders like he was shaking off the past. He patted her leg. "But enough about me. Please tell me you had a childhood that was all roses and everything nice." Mason began packing up the basket.

"I thought you wanted to hear about my meeting," she teased, helping him fold the blanket. Or rather, stalled. Her past wasn't all that pleasant, but she found she wanted to open up to Mason the way he had to her.

"That too. But I'm curious as to how you ended up a beautiful girl in a castle." They began walking back to his pickup, her hand in his.

"You're being tactful…you want to know about the fire. I'll tell you on the ride home." Feeling a slight chill, Eden took out her sweater and slipped it over her shoulders. She had shocked herself with how at ease with her body she had been. Maybe it was because of Mason's eyeing her like she was a delectable French treat or maybe it was because the beach was deserted? Eden didn't know for sure, but she did know she had had a beyond amazing time. She told Mason as much when they arrived at his truck.

"I'm so glad you did. This is the best first date I have ever had." Her heart preened at that. Mason was a man of experience, and she wouldn't obsess with wondering if he was just being nice, she was going to take that compliment at face value and squeal on the inside.

He opened the passenger door and helped her up by squeezing her bottom. It would be close to midnight before they made it home. Mason jogged around the front of the truck and slammed the door.

"I'm going to need a good shower once we're back," he commented as the vehicle roared to life.

"Maybe we can shower together," she suggested.

"That's a pretty bold suggestion. Daring even. The shy miss of a few weeks ago is fading," he teased.

She grinned. "I don't believe in half stepping anything I do."

"Well, all right then. I can check to see if the power is back yet at Lydia's place. I was so comfortable with you and Ms. Susan; I didn't even think to check. I don't want to wear out my welcome."

"Nonsense. You don't have to move back there. You're staying with us for as long as you'd like." Forever. For an eternity. Her heart sang.

"Thanks, but I prefer a more intimate setting for our first time."

"The true heart of a romantic." She rolled the window down, enjoying the wind in her hair and the smell of the sea.

"Blame it on the adult novels." He glanced her way before turning back to the road. "How about I book us this weekend at the Bellmore Inn & Spa on Rehoboth Beach? We can enjoy a quiet stroll on the boardwalk and check out the shops on that end."

"Oh, someone has been doing their research. I'd like that a lot."

He backed out of the parking space. "Consider it a date. Now let's get back to my question."

She drew quiet, her shoulders curving. "About the fire…"

"Yes."

"All right." Eden feared she might lose her boyfriend of a few hours when she was done but she knew she needed to be authentic if she wanted to have a real relationship. Though her heart thundered in her chest, she opened her mouth and began.

Chapter Twelve

Mason heard the slight tremor in Eden's voice and tension squeezed his gut.

Maybe asking her about the fire had been poor judgment on his part but this was a life-changing occurrence and he wanted to know everything about her. The absolute high and, in this case, the extreme low. Still, maybe he shouldn't have pushed and should have waited for her to share whenever she was ready.

"You don't have to talk about it if it's going to cause you serious emotional trauma," he offered, giving their joined hands a squeeze.

"No, no. I—I do want to share. I want to open up to you. I just…it's difficult." Eden cleared her throat. "I am an only child and my parents doted on me. They had battled infertility and miscarriages, so I was a miracle baby."

"I bet you were cute as a button," he couldn't resist adding. "I can just imagine you had a head full of curls with those remarkable eyes. Your parents must have been putty in your fists."

"Probably." She laughed. "I don't know if I would call myself cute with that wrinkly face, but I guess Grams and my mom and dad would agree. I had tons of pictures…before." She straightened, removing her hand from his, and wrapped her arms about her. Mason didn't think she noticed doing so but that indicated to him how stressed she might feel. He pulled over into a parking lot and cut the engine so he could give her his undivided attention.

"So, I guess you could say I had an ideal childhood. This small town is like a village so I had many aunts and uncles and friends. Lots of friends. We all played together, went to each other's houses. You could walk the streets at midnight and be safe—not that I was allowed to. Just saying. It wasn't until high school that there's a great divide—the in-crowd and the others." She scoffed. "Of course, I was in the in-crowd and I let it get to my head. I was ghastly to anybody who wasn't in our little crew. Cadence was the designated leader of the pack. We were smart but we were bored. A boredom that led to trouble."

"What kind of trouble?" Mason asked. "Trouble is relative depending on where you're from."

She lifted her shoulders. "We would skip school, get rides to the beach, sneak a sip of wine here and there."

Mason cracked up. "Sounds like normal teenage stuff to me."

"Well, you couldn't tell our little clique nothing. We thought we were so cool. A few days before my sixteenth birthday, Cadence snuck a pack of cigarettes from her father's pants pocket and we decided to try them."

"Oh no…" Dread set in. He hoped she wasn't about to say what he thought she was.

"My mom caught me smoking behind the bed-and-break-fast and gave me a stern talking-to and I promised not to do it anymore. But back then the voices of my peers held more weight." She fiddled with her skirt. "If only I had listened…"

Mason could hear the regret in her voice. Man, she caused the fire that took her parents' lives. He couldn't comprehend the guilt. "Listen, I get the gist. You don't have to continue."

She faced him, her eyes glistening. "I've got to finish. Please." She wet her lips and continued. "The day of my birthday party, Cadence decided to bring us a pack of smokes so we could party right. So the two of us and a couple of guys went into my bedroom and we started to smoke. We had candles lit and the windows open and our parents were chatting and hamming it with each other so we weren't worried about getting caught. I remember inhaling and my chest getting so tight that I coughed and coughed so hard that Cadence ran to get me water. I kept puffing away though. Then my mother called up the stairs for me to come down to cut the cake.

"I squished the cigarette on a paper plate," she said, her lips quivering. "I'm pretty sure I did. I even checked to see that it was out and I went downstairs. Right as we sang 'Happy Birthday' someone yelled, 'Fire,' and pandemonium ensued."

"That was an accident," Mason said.

Tears spilled down Eden's face and she shook her head, seemingly caught up in her tale. He wasn't even sure she had heard his defense. "My parents rushed upstairs while everyone else ran out in the yard. I stayed rooted in disbelief, waiting for them to come back down. But the fire caught on quickly, and I heard a loud bang, like the roof had caved in and I rushed up the stairs into the smoke, screaming and calling for them. I called and called but I heard nothing. But the fire was raging at that point, and it was so black and foggy that I think I fell and passed out."

The faraway look in her eyes told him that Eden was back there, seeing everything all over again. Mason drew her into his arms and rocked her back and forth.

She sniffled. "The next thing I know, I was being awakened in the hospital. And that's when I heard the news." She swallowed. "My parents hadn't made it out and some of the ceiling fell on me, giving me these." She lifted her arms. "These are reminders that because of me my parents are dead. If—if I hadn't—" She hiccuped. "Every time I look at them, I remember what I did."

He drew back so she could see his face. "You didn't intend for this to happen. You can't keep blaming yourself. Your parents didn't have to go upstairs. They should have run outside the house."

"The firefighters said they found vestiges of my photo albums, my baby shoes and other memorabilia that my mother was trying to save." Holding her face in her hands, she sobbed and sobbed, as if this had happened yesterday instead of thirteen years ago.

Goodness. That had to cut her to the core knowing that. Mason snatched her close. "They wouldn't want you blaming yourself. I know that."

"That's what Grams says. That's what my therapist says. But my heart says differently." She raised her tearstained face toward him. "Their lives being cut short is strictly because of my rebellion and the very friends I tried to impress turned on me. Treated me like a pariah. That's what hurt the most. I learned too late the true value of my family. I don't even have a proper picture of my parents and me as a teenager. Grams had some but a lot of them are blurred and the professional ones that were on the wall...destroyed. All I have is the one on the staircase that is damaged, but it was a favorite of mine."

"You still have Grams," he said, aching, acutely aware of her loneliness. He wanted to add that she also had him, but it was too soon for that. Plus, he didn't know how long he would be in town, and he had no clue what would happen with their relationship then. But that was a think for another day.

"Yes, it was Grams who got me into planting the roses. They saved me. Before caring for my roses, I didn't do much. Actually, I did nothing."

Mason reached into the glove box to retrieve some napkins he had saved from ordering takeout and gently wiped her face. "You and Cadence seemed to have made up."

"Yeah, she apologized and life is too short to hold on to anger. I know all too well how you can be here one day and gone the next." The knowledge of how she knew that ripped his heart. She gripped the crumbled napkin.

"How long did it take you to rebuild the bed-and-breakfast?" he asked.

She squinted. "We didn't rebuild… I'm not following."

"You said the bed-and-breakfast burned down, so I thought…"

"No. No. We lived behind the bed-and-breakfast in a two-story house."

"Oh, I see," he said. "I would have never known."

Her next words shook him to the core. "Yes, they tore down the entire infrastructure. I would stare at the empty plot for days on end. I stopped eating and communicating. I would just sit in the chair and relive my personal nightmare, every single day."

"Oh, Eden. That was no way to live."

"I know that now. I would have wasted away but Grams dragged me outside and made me start planting. She said a rose's bloom was a sign of a new beginning and that I needed one. So, each morning, we devoted time to tending to the roses on the same plot of land where my house used to be."

It took a minute for him to process her words. Mason drew in a sharp breath. "Your rose garden used to be your home?" Dang it, if his eyes didn't get moist after that. His chest expanded and he placed a hand over his chest. "Your grandmother deserves a medal. She is brilliant and one of a kind."

"I agree." She smiled. "Grams chose roses because she said every year, by my birthday, the roses would be in bloom. A reminder of my parents' love for me. And she was right. I have seen them bloom for the past ten years and every time I win the Blue Hen Rose Festival, I know it's because of my parents. I do it for them. And this year, for the first time, I hope to claim that reward in person."

Mason nodded. He was just the person to help her do it.

Chapter Thirteen

Eden awakened before her five-thirty alarm and stretched. She hadn't gotten home until close to 2:00 a.m. but her body was conditioned to arise at that time. She yawned. Once she was finished with her roses, she would catch a nap. But she had to get to them. The sun peeked over the horizon and she could tell from the mugginess in the air it was going to be a scorcher. She took care of her morning rituals, making sure to apply a generous amount of sunscreen, then dragged on a pair of shorts, a tank top and her hat before shoving her feet into a pair of boots. If she closed her eyes, she could go right back to sleep. But she wanted first prize. Mind on her motivation, Eden bounded down the stairs and stopped short.

Mason.

"What are you doing up?" she asked, her voice sounding groggy from unuse. He was dressed in similar garb, only while she felt like she had been run over by a horse-and-buggy, he appeared rested and camera ready. *Really?*

That fine man gave her a searing kiss that made her toes curl. Oh, she was wide-awake now. "I want to help you with your rose garden. Plus, I get the pleasure of your company all to myself." He walked in step with her toward the kitchen. "Unless… I'm intruding on your quiet time." He paused. "I didn't think about that."

"No, I'm glad for your company. Nothing speeds up work

like conversation." Eden strolled toward the kitchen. Grams was already up and working on breakfast. Her grandmother was dressed in a pair of white capris and a colorful top and she had washed and blown out her hair. She was the picture of great health, which made Eden's heart glad. "Something tells me you're making your famous biscuits and omelets this morning," Eden said, eyeing the eggs, veggies, chicken strips and batter.

"You would be correct," Grams said.

"Do you need my help?" Mason asked.

"No, no. You two go on ahead with your plans."

"All right. I'm outside if you need me. Don't overdo it." Ever since Grams got sick, Eden still kept a watchful eye. Her grandmother had looked great the day before she fell terribly ill. Not that Grams was having it.

"Pshaw. I'm fine." Grams shooed them out but not before she and Mason exchanged meaningful glances.

Eden wondered what that was about but her desire to get to her plants exceeded her curiosity. She pushed open the back door and drew in a deep breath. From where she stood, she could already smell the fragrance from the roses, and they hadn't even bloomed yet. She grinned and then addressed Mason. "Let's get to work."

They sat side by side in her rose garden while she taught him how to prune and weed and take care of pesky critters while they yakked away. He about his time on the show and she dished on her job situation. "Dr. Loft should be reaching out today to let me know what's going on…" Eden lifted her hat. "I was thinking of telling her I changed my mind, you know. I really like the freshman classes and I feel I connect with the students. But what if I freeze up?"

Mason wiped his brow. "Eden Tempest, you're the bravest person I know. I think there would be an adjustment, but you have a great support system around you. I believe you'll be just fine. And I think you'll like it."

His optimism pumped up her confidence. "All right. I think I'll do it. I'll email as soon as we're done." She jutted her chin his way. "And what about you?"

He gave her a wary look. "What about me?"

"Your father? Your brother? You've got stuff to settle."

"I think it's best I leave that door closed. I'll send my brother some money." He stomped across the yard to grab a fresh bag of fertilizer delivered the day before. He obviously didn't want to talk about reconciliation, and she knew from experience it wasn't easy. She had had to accept her grandmother's forgiveness and Eden was just now beginning to truly forgive herself. She was a constant work in progress, and she wanted the same for Mason.

When he returned, she gently pressed on. "I lost my parents at a young age and there isn't a day that goes by that I don't think of them. Not a single one that I don't live with this enormous regret. I'd give anything to hear their voices, have them fuss at me. Anything but this silence."

"I get that but you had a loving family. My case was different." He hunched his shoulders and his voice was stern. She had to try a different approach.

Grabbing his arm, she asked, "If the TV station reached out and offered you another chance, wouldn't you take it?"

Mason didn't meet her eyes. "Um, they did offer me something but I turned them down. For now. My agent is on the lookout for other possibilities."

"Oh? I didn't know that." A hollow feeling formed in her gut. "So, you're leaving soon." Of course he would be. He belonged in front of the camera, thrived on the public attention. Eden had watched some of his past shows and Mason was way too talented to hide out in a small town. However, she steeled herself. He was here now, and she was going to cherish all that he had to give her. Then when the time came, she would let him go without a fuss. Eden had known loss before, she would be fine. She hoped. 'Cause just the thought felt like someone was grating her heart.

But she had her rose garden to remind her that life would go on, and in time, she would thrive again.

"I'm here now, with you," he said softly. "And this is where I want to be." He splayed his hand toward the house. "Being in the limelight, you lose a part of yourself. You become more concerned with what your viewers think, what your producers think, that you forget your first love." He lips quirked. "I am loving every moment of this makeover—and I'm not just talking about the B and B."

Her heart soared but she couldn't abandon the conversation around his family just yet. "Have you thought about your brother?"

"What about him?"

"Have you considered that maybe Maxim needs this? His big brother left him to deal with an alcoholic, abusive parent. What kind of trauma do you think he endured? He had to carry that weight on his own, while you pursued your own interests."

Mason placed a hand over his chest. "I did the right thing. Dad never hurt him physically and I did send Max money, like I said. He was well-provided for."

"Money isn't everything. I've never touched my parents' life insurance, and a huge part of that was because of guilt. Grams saved her insurance money from losing the property—I think that's what she's using to fix up the bed-and-breakfast. I worked hard and got a grant to attend college. That insurance money would have made my life easier but I always saw it as stained from the horror of their death."

Mason lifted her chin with his index finger. "It's all about perspective. That money is evidence that your parents loved you enough to secure your future."

She gave him a tender kiss. "I'm going to guess that that's how you were showing your brother your love. But he might see it differently. He's losing the father he loves and he could use your emotional support." She enfolded her arms about him and rested her head against his chest. "Sometimes, a hug is priceless," she choked out, her chin wobbling "What I wouldn't pay to feel my parents' embrace again. I'm discovering that physical touch and quality time are my love languages. Yours might be giving gifts but it doesn't mean your brother feels the same about those monetary favors."

He stiffened. "I think I've been taking my brother for granted, and I didn't realize—until you said it—that he's losing a father who was great to him." Mason's voice was a pleasant low rumble in her ear. "I can't tell you the last time Max and I hugged." He rested a hand on her back. "You're right. I didn't think about the power of human contact. I was so busy thinking about myself and my ordeal that I didn't see that he might just need to see me."

"Go see him then," Eden suggested, tilting her head back. "Now, I'm not an expert but the thing about building bridges is that once you start building one, it might give you the momentum to build another."

"I don't want to desert the crew," he said, rubbing her back. "And I most definitely don't want to leave you."

To her surprise, her lips formed the words "I'll come with you, if you want."

He drew back, his hands on her shoulders. "You would do that? For me?"

Eden swallowed, her heart rate escalating. "Yes. I care about you. I won't lie though. The mere thought of venturing among strangers scares me. Going to the rose festival among people who know me is already terrifying, but I want to be there for you."

"You're right. Some things are priceless. We can make a

date of it. If we leave this afternoon, we can have a date night in Virginia. Then we go visit with my family tomorrow before driving back to Blue Hen."

Her brows rose. "An overnight trip..."

His eyes alighted with promise. "Yes, I will reserve our rooms or...one room. It's up to you."

"Make it one." She stood on tiptoes and kissed him long and deep. "I'll let Grams know."

Mason exhaled. "Okay, when Gabe comes, I'll run through what he needs to do until we get back tomorrow." His voice cracked with emotion. "Eden, you make it easy for a man to fall in love with you, if he were so inclined." Mason kissed her with passion, and she was too swept away to mull on what those words signified. It wasn't until she had spoken to Grams that Eden considered his words. Mason had told her clearly that he wasn't about to fall in love with her, or anyone, so she had better not hope for more.

Problem was, she suspected she was already halfway there. She stole a glance his way. But what did she know? She lacked experience and this could be a serious case of infatuation. Still, her gut feared it could be the start of something deeper. Something more.

Chapter Fourteen

Mason knew a tired man working on fumes and sheer will when he saw one. And that was Gabe. Oh, he was doing the work, but the energy level told the truth. Gabe had been crawling up and down the staircase like he had bad knees since he arrived twenty minutes ago.

Mason couldn't have an accident occurring because a man was exhausted or hungover. He pulled Gabe outside to talk before the rest of the crew arrived. "What's going on with you? You good?" The sun was beating on his back but he didn't want to chance anyone overhearing their conversation.

"Yeah. I just had a really good night," Gabe said, waggling his brows. His eyes had dark circles but they were shining. "It's been a long while. I'll get a cup of coffee."

"Really? You had me thinking you were... I didn't know what to think." Mason was glad he had asked instead of jumping to conclusions like he would have done in the past. He hid a smile. "I'm glad you got lucky. I don't want your silly behind getting injured so make sure you eat and get a couple strong cups in you."

"Ms. Susan's got biscuits warming in the oven and she's working on a fresh batch of chicken fajita omelets." Gabe rubbed his tummy. "I can't wait to dig in. I need to replenish because I had quite a workout last night."

"Wait. What?" Normally, Mason wouldn't pry because he valued his own privacy.

"Yeah a pretty lady needed some company minus the conversation and I was happy to oblige. We're seeing each other again tonight."

"Oh, all right… I'm glad you could be of service." Mason cleared his throat. "I'm going to need you to rest up tonight because I have to go out of town, and I need my best man in charge."

Gabe puffed his chest. "I'm on it. What's going on?"

"I have to go see my father. He isn't doing well."

"Oh, I'm sorry to hear that, bro. Keep your head up and if you need anything, reach out." The genuine concern on Gabe's face gave Mason pause. The other man wasn't just speaking the words, he meant them. Gabe opened his arms, and they shared a brief but awkward hug. It made him feel cared for. Like he had someone besides himself. Eden's words about physical contact came back to him. He was now eager to see his brother.

"Thank you, friend. I'll keep you posted," Mason said. "Since we won't be here, today might be a good day to work on Eden's room."

"So, Eden's going with you?" Gabe stretched the words out, grinning from ear to ear. "You two an item?"

"Yes, she's coming for moral support."

Gabe's face said, *Oh, is that what you're calling it?* But his words were, "I'm glad she'll be there with you. Let me go see if Ms. Susan's got any caramel cappuccino to give me a boost." Then he jogged back inside the house.

Just then a delivery truck pulled up by the gate and a driver in shorts and a T-shirt jumped out with a box. "Oh, good. My package is here," Mason said. The young man started the trek up the driveway. Mason made a note to talk to Ms. Susan about a potential redesign of the driveway. Mason decided to meet the delivery driver halfway, his long strides eating up the length of the path.

After signing for his package, Mason went inside the house, appreciating the cool temperature. Working inside during the mornings had been Gabe's suggestion and a really good one. Any work on the exterior—and there wasn't much left—was just some landscaping around the premises, and of course, the driveway redesign if Ms. Susan agreed.

Mason sniffed. "Those smell amazing." His stomach grumbled.

"Come on and have one," Ms. Susan said, her face beaming. Mason had a hard time believing she was Eden's grandmother. Now that she was "well" again, Ms. Susan looked at least two decades younger than she must be based on sheer mathematics of having a grandchild who was almost thirty.

"How is the surprise birthday party coming?" he asked, since Eden wasn't lurking about.

"Everything is going according to plan," Ms. Susan whispered. "I told Eden we're doing a grand reopening on that day, so she won't be surprised to see the party truck and all the tables and chairs being set up on the lawn. I also took your advice and decided to have it catered. Momma D's has some of the best barbecue on this side of the Delaware and we're planning for a good three hundred people to turn out."

"I didn't know there were that many people in this town," Mason teased. He was so glad Ms. Susan hadn't taken on everything herself like she had originally planned.

"Whatever." She rolled her eyes.

He sat on one of the stools behind the counter. "I wanted to ask how you would feel if we added paving to the driveway so that we had circular parking. We could put a fountain in the middle and expand the gate, so delivery trucks could get in and out without having to back in."

She tapped her chin. "I like that. It sounds regal and we do have the land space." Her eyes narrowed. "Will we encroach on Eden's garden? We can't take an inch away from it."

"I know what it symbolizes. That won't happen."

"Awesome. Then go for it."

"Great. I'll work out the numbers and get back to you."

Ms. Susan waved a hand. "Just do it. I trust you."

His shoulders lifted at her words. "Consider it done."

The door creaked and the crew came in just in time for breakfast, as was their pattern since they had arrived. Ms. Susan directed them to wash their hands and they all began laying out the meal in the dining hall. Mason loved seeing the diminutive Ms. Susan commandeering the men, who were more than happy to oblige. One in particular seemed to be a bit chummy but Mason gave him a quelling glare and the other man backed off.

Ms. Susan must have seen their interaction because she sashayed over to him. "I can take care of myself, young man. Been doing it before you were born." He dipped his head and she went to take her usual spot. Gabe strolled in with Eden behind.

His breath caught. She was dressed in a pair of blue shorts, sandals and a yellow shirt, the color of a sunflower. The smile she gave him would melt an icicle. Eden came to sit with him and waited until after Ms. Susan said grace before spilling out, "I just spoke with Dr. Loft, and I told her that I decided to take the position. I didn't expect to feel excited. Thank you for the pep talk."

Mason wished he could kiss her, really kiss her right there, but he didn't want to embarrass her. So he settled for giving her a kiss on the cheek. "I'll give you a proper kiss later," he whispered in her ear. She blushed, the rosy hue spreading across her skin. Tonight, he would see how far that blush went. He exhaled and focused on helping himself to one of the biscuits.

The flaky goodness tasted like heaven in his mouth. "Ms. Susan, you put your *whole* foot in these biscuits. You need to box these and sell them. You would make a fortune. Say the word and I'll make it happen."

"Hush, now. Those are only for family and guests at the bed-and-breakfast," Ms. Susan tittered.

He tapped his head. "I understand. But if you change your mind, I'm here. Just saying."

Ms. Susan pointed to his plate. "Go on now and eat. You have a long journey ahead and I don't want you buying none of that processed food. I'm packing you and Eden a basket."

"Grams, you don't have to do all that," Eden said. "I can do it."

"I've got it." Ms. Susan's warning tone told them arguing with her would be a waste of time, so he didn't bother. Besides, Eden had bitten into her omelet and all that cheese greasing her lips proved to be a scintillating distraction. If she had her phone—

Oh yes. That reminded him. Mason excused himself and returned to the kitchen to retrieve the package he had placed on the counter earlier. He turned around and bumped into Eden. He had to grip the box to keep it from falling out of his hands.

"I came to get that proper kiss you promised me," she said, her arms circling his waist.

Mason took in those full lips and helped himself to a full serving. She kissed him with abandon, like they were alone, instead of in a kitchen where anyone could enter. And Mason returned kiss for kiss, not caring who they gave a show for. A few minutes later, he ended the kiss. Reluctantly. "We'd better get back in there. Our food is getting cold."

She shrugged. "I'll use a microwave."

He remembered he was holding the package and handed it to her.

"What's this?" she asked.

"Open it and see."

"You don't have to buy me anything," she said, opening the

box and taking out the small package inside. Then she gasped. "You bought me a phone?"

"Yes." He smiled, then kissed her on the mouth that had popped open, which gave him access into that beautiful cavern. He explored further, gathering her close to his chest and grinding his hips against hers. This time when they both pulled away, they were out of breath.

"You got me all weak-kneed. How am I supposed to walk in there?" Mason scooped her into his arms, and she squealed, kicking her legs. "Put me down, you silly man. I was just joking."

Mason kept walking until they were close to the dining hall. Then he put her to stand and took in her wild hair and reddened lips. "You look like you've been thoroughly kissed," he said, leaving her standing there wide-eyed while he strutted inside and returned to his meal.

It took a minute or two before Eden reentered, looking more composed. She picked up her fork and cut into the rest of her omelet before leaning over to him. "I'm going to make you pay for that later."

"I'm looking forward to it," he shot back, loving their banter. He had a feeling she was going to be all that and then some in the bedroom and he couldn't wait to find out how right he was. Though he didn't like the reason he was driving to Virginia, Mason liked the person who was accompanying him. He liked her a whole lot. Probably too much if he were being honest. But he wouldn't worry about that now. Mason would focus on enjoying Eden and giving her the most pleasurable experience he could, tonight.

Then tomorrow, tomorrow, he would face the man who gave him the most painful memories of his life.

Chapter Fifteen

To prepare for her date that night, Eden gathered her courage and entered the beauty salon and spa. She had reached out to Cadence for beauty tips and the other woman had suggested they get makeovers together.

Cadence had then made them ten o'clock appointments, an hour before the salon actually opened. Grams had dropped her off since Cadence had offered to give her a ride home when they were finished.

She waved at her friend and scurried over to sit next to her. "Thank you for the hookup." There were sounds in the back of the spa and she assumed that was the owner getting ready. She heard the footsteps and saw the shadow before the person turned the corner.

"Raine?" Eden squealed, jumping to her feet. "I didn't know you owned the salon. When did you come back into town?" Raine was a military kid and had been with them in middle school before her father got deployed to Germany. Raine had left at the end of their freshman year of high school. They had tried to stay in touch but lost contact after a while.

Raine came forward with her arms open, a full-figured beauty with sparkling brown eyes. She had on an apron with a scissors and comb embroidered on the front over a pair of black jeans and a purple shirt. Her hair and nails were on point. "I've been back the last two years and Cadence and I reconnected."

"Wow." That was all Eden could say while her brain caught up with the fact that the old crew was now reunited.

"I wanted to come see you, but I heard what happened and I didn't want to intrude," Raine said.

"It's okay. I was curled into myself for a while so I don't think I would have welcomed any reconciliation. But I'm working on that." She reached over to take Cadence's hand and pulled her to her feet.

Then the three women hugged it out. There was some laughter, some tears but much healing. Her soul rejoiced. Time had passed, things were said and done, but life had brought them back together and she was appreciative of that.

Eden then put herself into Raine's care and got herself waxed and plucked and prodded right along with Cadence. When they left, she felt like a new woman. Literally and figuratively.

"Now, let's get you some lingerie for your night with Mason."

Eden lowered her lashes. "Good idea." She had already packed her cotton panties and T-shirt bras but now she giggled. "I want to knock his socks off when he sees me."

Cadence's luxury vehicle purred to life. "I know just the place to go." They then spent the next hour shopping for just the right outfit. She found a fuchsia two-piece ensemble that made her feel sexy and desirable. The top half was a lacy apron with a cage back detail. The matching thong had bows in the back.

"Thank you for your help, Cadence," she said, once they were parked outside the bed-and-breakfast. "You definitely understood the assignment." She giggled. "Mason won't know what to do with himself when he sees me in this."

"I'm pretty sure you're right. You are so welcome." She reached over to hold Eden's hand. "Thank you for giving me a second chance." Her voice broke with emotion.

When Eden turned and looked at Cadence, she was surprised to see that the other woman had tears in her eyes. "No more talk about second chances," Eden said. "The past is the past and all we can do is keep pressing forward."

Cadence wiped her face. "Okay, I'm just happy with our friendship." Eden gripped the door handle to exit the vehicle when she heard Cadence mumble, "Things will work out as they should. I've got to believe that."

Pausing, Eden asked, "Are you okay?"

For a second Cadence looked like she was about to say something but then she shook her head. "I'm fine. I don't want anything sullying your time away with Mason. Have a great time."

"Okay." Eden didn't want to push. They were still in the reconnecting stage of their friendship and she didn't want to intrude by demanding Cadence tell her what was wrong. She pulled out her cell phone and waved it. "You have my number, so reach out if you need."

"I will." Cadence pressed the start button and Eden got out. She stood and watched as Cadence backed her way down the path. There was something weighing the other woman down and it made Eden concerned. But all she could do was be there when Cadence was ready to talk. Cadence had shared that she and Gabe were in an entanglement of sorts. Nothing serious. Maybe she should tell Mason about it. Then she quashed that idea.

No. She couldn't blab about something she didn't know. That would be a violation of the unwritten friendship code.

Her cell phone rang so loudly that it echoed. She turned down the volume and tapped on the screen a few times until it answered. She hadn't yet fully mastered the touch screen, but Cadence had shown her how to text at least. She was eager to try all that out on Mason.

"Are you ready?" he asked. "I'd like us to get on the road in the next five minutes."

"Yes. I just have to get my overnight bag." She dashed up the stairs and exchanged her drab underwear for the lingerie. Eden also dropped in the new perfume and makeup she had purchased from Raine. However, she did leave a comfortable pair of lace undies for the next day.

Before she left, she went to check in on her grandmother. Grams sat in her new white rocking chair with her knitting needles in hand and her cheaters on. "I don't feel right leaving you out here all alone."

Her grandmother placed her handiwork aside. "I've got my shotgun in my nightstand but I'm pretty sure I won't need it. Plus, Mason arranged for Gabe to spend the night here and you know no one's getting through Mr. Beefy Abs."

"Really, Grams? Mr. Beefy Abs?" Eden chuckled, heading farther in the room. "Please don't tell me you've called him that to his face."

"I did more than that. I also said it behind his back."

Eden busted out laughing. "Grams, you must have been a trip back in your heyday."

Grams peered over her cheaters. "My lips are sealed." Then she gave Eden a tender look. "I'm so happy to see you out with friends and just enjoying life. That's all I ever wanted. To see my grandbaby happy again. Your parents weren't all I lost that day."

She rushed over and gave her grandmother a hug before slipping onto the mat and resting her head in her grandmother's lap. "I'm so glad I have you. So glad." The tears came fast.

"There now." Her grandmother patted her on the back. "We've come a long way and there's some ways to go, but at least we're taking steps. That's what matters."

Eden wiped her face and stood, then kissed her grandmother's soft cheek. "I'll text you once we're in Virginia."

"Okay. Now get going."

Mason stood by the door. "Gabe should be here within the hour," he said to the older woman, who opened her arms. Mason took tentative steps before bending over to give her a hug.

"Take care of my baby girl and no speeding," she said.

Eden heard a muffled "I will" before Mason pulled away. He held out a hand toward Eden. With joined hands they left for Virginia. Mason told her it would be one straight path down the US 13 for almost the entire trip to Virginia Beach. He had made reservations at The Cavalier, an oceanfront luxury suite with views of the Atlantic Ocean. Then he gave her a pair of sunglasses before slapping a pair on along with a baseball cap.

Mason tuned the radio to some old jams and she settled back to read her book. They drove in companionable silence until he pulled into a gas station to fill the tank. Eden excused herself to use the restroom and when she came out, he was surrounded by fans, taking selfies and signing a few autographs.

She stopped short. She had forgotten he was a celebrity.

No wonder he had given her the shades. His "cover-up" hadn't stopped him from being recognized. She lowered her head so her hair shielded her face and slipped into the passenger side. The last thing she wanted was to end up with her face all over the internet or in a gossip mag as his current fling.

"Sorry about that," he said once they were on their way.

"We're in such a cocoon out in Blue Hen that I forgot that you have a very recognizable face."

"Being in the spotlight means you sacrifice your privacy. Sometimes people forget you're human. That you need space. You always have to be on. You always have to be nice. This is the trade-off for me being financially secure. You are at the public's whim. You don't get to have a bad day."

"That doesn't sound like fun," Eden said.

"As with any career, there are pluses and minuses. But if

you're not careful, it can consume you and you can lose touch with yourself, become someone you never dreamed of becoming." He tapped her on the shoulder. "So, when do your classes start?"

She understood his need for a conversation shift and followed along. "Technically, I begin mid-August since the fall semester begins the last Monday in August. But of course, I'll start prepping way before then. My accepting the position means I'll get a pay hike."

"What about your grandmother's bed-and-breakfast? I thought you would be the one running it."

"No, Grams will still be in charge for now. When I'm not working, I'll assist and learn the ropes. Teaching is my passion though. I feel such joy when I see my students get excited about learning and when I see them put skills I've taught them into practice."

"Wow. You should see how your face is beaming right now." He smiled. "Before coming to Blue Hen, I had lost my passion. But working on Ms. Susan's property has revived my love for what I do. I enjoy working with my hands. It fulfills me. If I ever have the opportunity to do a show again, I would definitely be getting my hands dirty instead of giving orders from the sidelines."

She heard the wistfulness in his voice. It sounded like Mason wanted to be back on the air. "But what if it doesn't happen? What if you're never given that second chance?"

"I can't consider that possibility," he said. "The idea of a second chance is what keeps me going."

"And when that happens, where does that leave us?" she asked.

"We'll figure it out. Find a happy medium between both our worlds." He sounded so confident that she didn't want to ruin the mood with the truth. She couldn't see becoming a part of his world. She couldn't leave her rose garden. She could only savor what they had now and enjoy the ride for as long as it lasts.

Eden looked over at his profile from under her lashes. He was rapping along to a song from way back in the day, spitting out the rhymes and verses like a pro. She could see she surprised him by rapping out the next verse.

"Hey, what you know about that, girl?" he said, eyeing her with admiration.

Chapter Sixteen

Mason couldn't recall a time he had been this nervous. His hand shook while using the key card to enter the Presidential Suite.

Luckily, Eden appeared too awestruck to notice, gaping at the plush surroundings and the view. But the focal point was the king-size bed. It was close to 10:00 p.m. and they had already grabbed dinner. He had asked for a late checkout and had arranged to meet his brother for lunch at his father's house the next day.

Eden placed her overnight bag on the deep red bedroom bench at the edge of the bed. The curtains and headboard were the same luxurious color. He dropped his bag next to hers and moved to close the curtains.

If it were any other woman, he would have already had her out of her clothes. But this was Eden. All innocent yet sweet and naughty at the same time. He didn't want to mess up her first experience.

She fiddled with her shirt, and he put on the television because after nonstop conversation the last three to four hours, he now couldn't think of anything to say. This was so anti-hero-like. He wasn't accomplishing any romance fantasies standing there all awkward and shy.

So he sat.

Great, now he was sitting all awkward and shy. Good grief.

He snuck a glance her way. Unlike him, she seemed calm and assured.

Eden picked up her bag. "I'm going to take a shower. I'll be right back." As soon as the door clicked, he sprung to his feet and called the front desk. A few minutes later, the staff arrived with flowers and rose petals and chocolates. He went to work on setting up a romance-worthy scene. They had also added vanilla-scented candles which he placed in a couple areas of the room. Mason stepped back to view his handiwork and smiled. He didn't know why he hadn't thought of this before. The staff could have had it ready before they checked in.

Oh well. No point in backpedaling now. He could hear Eden humming off-key and grinned. Mason loved hearing her special sounds. He would discover more of them real soon.

When Eden opened the door, the scent of jasmine and something else filled his nostrils. Whatever it was, it was intoxicating. She had donned one of the white hotel robes and Mason wanted to investigate the bare shoulder but he consoled himself with giving her a quick peck on the cheek. Then he headed into the shower. The heat level and the force of the spray on his back had him lingering a little longer than he normally would. He turned off the spigot, then grabbed one of the generously long towels off the rack and dried his upper body, and then wrapped it around his waist. He quickly brushed his teeth, applied deodorant and tiny sprays of his cologne. Mason exited the bathroom, his eyes searching for Eden.

His mouth dropped open. He had found her all right.

All glorious five-feet-eleven inches of her was stretched out across the bed, with one leg propped up and an arm behind her head. She was dressed in a frilly sheer top and a barely there panty, the ultimate definition of seduction. But that color. That pinkish-purple color popped against her skin.

Mason feasted on that visual image, pulling his bottom lip into his mouth.

Then she turned over and he lost his breath for a second. *Whew.*

"You look… Wow." Dropping the towel to the floor, Mason moved to the foot of the bed and grabbed her feet, pulling her to the edge of the bed. "I am going to sample every part of your body, front and back."

Her eyes darkened, the orbs the color of honeyed liqueur, and she gave herself over to him. And he loved on her. Then when her body was ready, he led her on the age-old path to a scorching climax.

Drenched with sweat and their body perfume, Mason drew her close, cuddling her against him. Sometime during the wee hours of the morning, he awakened to her returning all the pleasurable favors he had bestowed on her. And this time, their joining was furious, frenzied, the resulting orgasm shattering him in a thousand brilliant pieces.

Aww, this woman, this gem he had found in the middle of nowhere was his sexual fantasy come alive. He didn't think he would ever get enough of her.

In her arms, he rested.

Then when dawn loomed, slithers of sunlight coming through the curtains, he awakened and watched her in repose. She had a small smile on her face and he hoped he was a part of the reason for that. Mason allowed his hands to roam her beautiful sun-kissed body before running his fingers through her soft curls. Then he took her gently, their consummation in sync with the sunrise.

In due time, she pinned those cognac orbs on him, and they fed on the last two pieces of chocolates. "This isn't going to hold me," she purred in his ear. "I'm going to need serious sustenance after experiencing the best night of my life."

"I'm happy to hear that." He kissed her forehead. "We're

getting room service with a little bit of everything. You'll be well replenished before we leave."

"Let's take a bath together," she said, curling into him, like they had been doing it for years.

Mason kissed her lips and went to get the water ready. He poured in the bath salts and rose petals, making sure the temperature was on the hotter side. After testing the heat level with his toe, Mason got into the tub, and called for her join him.

She came into the bathroom, tall and proud, holding a pink loofah, and without an ounce of shyness, used the restroom before slipping underneath the bubbles. Using Eden's loofah, he gently washed her.

Eden dunked her entire body under the water before popping out and whipping her hair back, mermaid style. He cracked up. "Come here, my little siren." Spooning her against him, at her urging, he entered her, his mind filled with amazement at the number of times he was going to come.

Their breakfast came and they assuaged their hunger, ravenous after all their encounters from the night before. Once they were full, they jumped into the shower, dressed and departed for his father's house which was fifteen minutes away. Reaching over to take her hand, Mason said, "I'm so glad you're here with me. Are you sore?" He had tried to be gentle but a few times she had egged him on past the point of reason.

"I'm glad too. For obvious reasons," she teased. "And I'm a little sore but that's to be expected, considering…but I'm not in pain. It's all good. No worries."

His shoulders relaxed. "I've never taken a girl home," he confessed.

Her brows rose. "Never?"

"Nope. But you're all kinds of special and most of all, a true friend." He kissed the back of her hand. "I'm going to apologize in advance for anything that might go down once I'm at my father's house."

"There's no need to apologize. All will go the way it's supposed to go."

"That sounds like something Ms. Susan would say."

Eden chuckled. "That's because she did."

Chapter Seventeen

Hearing about Mason's terrible childhood, Eden didn't know why she had visualized the house to match. But they pulled into a well-paved driveway of a sprawling home in a cul-de-sac. When they exited his pickup, the lush perennial gardens caught her eyes. "Those are quite lovely." Mason then told her that the five-bedroom, three-bathroom property included a sunroom, an in-ground swimming pool and an oasis in the backyard. Mason even added that they had recently installed solar panels.

"This seems like a nice place to grow up," she said.

Mason gave her a somber look. "On the outside."

"What did your father do?" she asked.

"When he was sober, he was into real estate. Lots of rich clientele who wanted to purchase property on Virginia Beach."

"Ah, I see."

Taking her hand, Mason led Eden toward the door and rang the doorbell. His hand tightened around hers when the door swung open.

A brown-skinned man with curly hair and light brown eyes, about an inch shorter than Mason, opened the door. Without hesitation, Mason went into his brother's arms. Lots of rocking and back-patting ensued before the brothers pulled apart.

"Bro, it's good to see you here," Maxim said, before turning his gaze on Eden. "And you must be the girlfriend I've heard so much about."

He told his brother about her? "I'm hoping he said good things." Eden extended her hand and smiled.

"He said you had a great sense of humor and I see why." Maxim gently swatted her hand away and gave her a quick hug. Then he invited them inside. They passed through the large sunroom, her eyes taking in a large family picture of two young boys—she figured must be Mason and Maxim—and their parents.

He continued until they were in the dining area but because it was a large, open-concept space, she had a clear view of another family picture on the mantel. Maxim looked a lot like their mother. The woman was standing next to a younger version of Alton, who looked a lot like Mason. Mason and his father shared a strong resemblance, giving Eden a clear picture of what Mason would like in a few years.

She sat next to Mason while Maxim dressed the table. The spread from a five-star chef was picture worthy and by the look of it, he had gone all out. She snapped pictures of balsamic–brown sugar lamb chops, pumpkin risotto, white truffle mac and cheese, crispy potatoes and grilled asparagus.

"Wow, this is quite the feast," Eden said.

"Now you see why my son is in high demand," a new voice said from behind.

Eden spun in her seat as Mason stood, his face stoic. She got to her feet and scooted beside him.

"I'll go get the rolls out of the oven." Maxim departed for the kitchen.

Alton Powers did not look like his diagnosis. Eden had expected to see him frail and bent but he was sprightly and energetic. Alton was shorter than both his sons and was closer to her height.

"Hello, Dad," Mason said, looping his arm through hers. "This is my girlfriend, Eden."

Alton came over to clasp her hand in his briefly. "It's a pleasure to meet you."

"You have a lovely home."

He looked like he would give his son a hug, but Mason's demeanor didn't invite physical contact. Alton rolled back on his heels and dipped his head to his chest before addressing Mason. "You look well."

"Considering I got booted off my own show?" Mason scoffed.

His father gave him a quelling look. "More like I'm proud of you rising above through all this turmoil. Learning and doing better."

"Dad, let's eat before the food gets cold," Maxim said, holding some rolls in his hand.

They all took their seats and Alton led them in prayer, thanking God for bringing Mason home and then blessing the food.

Eden found Mason's father and brother positively darling. She was now rooting for Mason and his family to reconcile, but judging by the brooding expression on Mason's face, she would say that was unlikely to happen during this visit. But good food and full stomachs softened the chill in the room and the brothers entertained Eden by sharing escapades from their childhood.

Alton didn't eat more than a spoonful of his serving of pumpkin risotto, and she could see the corresponding worry etched on Maxim's face.

"You should take Eden on a tour," Maxim said after they were finished with their meal. He had already provided Eden and Mason with to-go containers. Eden had packed an extra one for her grandmother and at Maxim's prodding, Mason would take a tray for Gabe and the rest of the crew.

"Yes, show her your room," Alton said with a charming smile.

"You mean where I spent most of my time licking my

wounds," Mason shot back, acid in his tone. Eden slid him a warning glance, but he clamped his jaw.

Maxim looked at him with thunder in his eyes. "You don't let up, do you?"

"Do you want me to pretend that my life was like roses? Well, it wasn't," Mason replied.

"I do expect you to treat our guest with courtesy," his father said with steel in his voice. Both Mason and Maxim straightened.

"Yes, sir," Mason said, getting to his feet before eyeing her with tenderness. "Let's check out the gardens. I do think you'll like them."

Eden stood as well and followed him out the room. As soon as they were out of earshot, she rounded on Mason. "What was that about in there? Did you forget your purpose in coming?"

He spoke through gritted teeth. "I hugged my brother."

"Yes, but you're behaving abominably. It's embarrassing. Not to mention childish."

He cut his eyes at her. "I'm sorry if I'm an embarrassment to you."

"Nope. Not to me. You're an embarrassment to yourself. I get that your father hurt you and it's okay to be an angry about that, because I'm certainly not excusing any abusive behavior of any kind. But if you want a second chance, you've got to be willing to give others a second chance." She placed a hand on her hip. "Has your father ever apologized?"

"He's sent letters and has called and left messages but like I told you, I'm not interested in reconciliation."

"I see. But you're clearly not interested that you're hurting your brother in the process. You were here to be a source of comfort to him, but right now, you're causing him distress."

His shoulders slumped. "That's not my intention." His voice dropping to a whisper. "I'm making a muck of things."

"Until you deal with the anger you have toward your father,

you're going to keep lashing out at the wrong people. People like your brother or those who work for you. How does that make you any different from your father? He abused his authority and you're doing the same."

"So, you think I'm a beast. An ogre." He folded his arms.

"No, I see the beauty within you," she said. "I see the generous man helping my grandmother, working without pay. Yes, we know that's what you're doing," she added when his brows rose. "I see your patience toward me when I was afraid to venture out, and your gentleness when you made love to me. That's what I see. And I wish you would give your family the chance to see the man I'm getting to know. The man I'm trying hard not to fall for."

Mason's mouth hung open. "Did you just say what I think you're saying?" All the anger appeared to have seeped out of him.

"Your ears work, correct?" She rolled her eyes. "But your behavior today has given me pause. I'm determined not to fall for your disguise. You are showing me another side to you that I never imagined."

She brushed past him, intending to return to finish the visit with his family but he took her arm. "I'm sorry I'm not the man you think I am. The truth is, I'm not deserving of love, especially not your love. I can't accept that and I can't give it. I'm incapable because I ruin everything I touch. This anger simmers within and it builds and builds until it boils over." He placed a hand under her chin. "What if it boils over and burns you? I could never bear the thought of causing you pain."

Her eyes flew to his. "I'm not the least bit concerned about that happening because I know the man that you are. The problem is, you don't know it. And you're more than capable of loving and accepting love, if you're willing to do the work. I can recommend my therapist, if you'd like. I'm glad to be your friend, your sounding board, but you need someone with the level of expertise to truly help."

"I thought I could pretend that everything was all right and make my brother happy." His lowered his head to his chest. "Maybe we should just go home. I'll take her contact information."

"Nope. You need to make this right. Your father and brother have been wonderful. I can't say the same for you. But I would like to be able to say that before we leave."

He took her through the house after that, delighting her with his stories. When they approached his bedroom, he tensed up right before he opened the door before admitting, "This is the first time I am actually coming in here since I have left home. I usually get a hotel or sleep on the couch."

"Wow," Eden said.

When they got inside, he gasped. It was the typical room you would expect to see for a young man—posters of his music icons, trophies from playing various sports—but one wall was almost a shrine in Mason's honor. There were framed news articles of his television show and his awards. All the current news about him was there on display.

"I can't believe my brother did all this…" His voice held amazement and his face depicted shock. Eden could see Mason was bowled over. His eyes misted. "You're so right, Eden. I do need to set things right with Maxim."

"All I see is love on this wall," she choked out, overcome.

They rejoined his family, who were now sitting in the living area having a hushed conversation, which ended when Eden and Mason returned.

Mason went over to his brother and snatched him into a tight hug. "I saw the wall in my room. I can't believe you did that. It really touched my heart."

Maxim smiled. "Thanks, but I didn't do that."

Eden watched when the realization of who did hit Mason

in the chest. His lower lip quivered, and he turned to face his father. She dropped into the chair, the scene playing out before her like a movie. And this was one she really wanted to see.

Chapter Eighteen

"I'm proud of you, son," Alton said, spreading his arms wide.

For a beat, Mason froze. How he had longed to hear those words as a youth. His heart cracked. That longing hadn't changed as an adult. He just realized that. He looked back at his brother just to make sure he wasn't about to play himself and that his father was talking to him. Maxim was standing there, a goofy grin on his face. Then Mason met Eden's eyes and she was smiling and nodding, as if saying *Yes, he's talking to you.*

Mason turned to face his father, who still had his arms open. "I'm sorry I didn't say that enough to you when you were growing up. I wanted to but the grief of losing your mother was bigger than me and I took that out on you. A child. If I could rewind the past…" Alton shuddered. "I had to hit rock bottom before I joined AA and get into counseling before I lost another son," he choked out.

He heard a sharp intake of breath and realized it came from him. "I—I don't understand."

Maxim walked over to place a hand on his shoulder. "I hated being the middleman between you and Dad. And though Dad was good to me, he was a functional drunk. He would leave in the mornings, slap on the happy face for his clients and then come home and drink himself in a stupor. After I graduated college, I told him I was leaving, and I planned to be done with both of you."

"That's when I knew I had to change. My heart already had a gaping hole when you left but I could live with that because I knew I deserved your contempt. I accepted that you would hate me forever for failing you as a father. And you should."

Goose bumps popped up on Mason's arms. He was more like his father than he realized. Just a few minutes ago, he had pretty much said the same thing—different words, same meaning—that he was undeserving of love. Slaking his eyes over at Eden, he figured she was thinking the same thing because she was sniffling and dabbing at her eyes.

His father wasn't done talking. "But I had been good to Maxim and now even he wanted to leave." Alton pointed to his chest. "That's what told me I was the problem. I was the common denominator."

"But you went into therapy. You got the help you needed," Maxim said, his chest puffed. "And our relationship is better and stronger than it was before. I just wish—" He stopped. "I don't want to ruin the little bit of progress by saying what I want."

"I can fill in the blanks," Mason said with a smile, giving his brother yet another hug. Eden was onto something with that physical contact. Once you started, it was kind of hard to stop. Not that he wanted to. Mason looked at Alton, really looked at him for the first time. All he saw was love, genuine love, reflected in those depths.

Alton lowered his arms. "Even if you hate me forever, I want to advise you to deal with your anger. I don't want you losing time with loved ones the way I did. Don't repeat the same mistake I did."

Wow. His dad sounded like…a father. Mason's eyes blurred and he took a small step and another before falling into his father's arms. "I'll get help too, Dad." He couldn't quite say *I love you* yet, but maybe in time he could? It was worth exploring... He registered a flash of light, and he pulled back to glance behind him.

"Sorry, I had to record this moment to make sure it's not a figment of my imagination," Maxim said, sheepish. "I don't know when I might see this again."

"I did, too," Eden said, her voice sounding stuffy from crying. "You need a keepsake."

A keepsake. That's right. His father was dying. Mason wobbled on his feet. His father's strong grip steadied him. "It's all right, son. I'm ready to go."

Tears streamed down Mason's face as fresh realization hit. "I don't think I am ready for you to go." His chest rose and fell. The words *I'll be your donor* were right there, stuck in his throat, but Mason refused to utter them. He didn't want to go off raw emotion—though losing his father was emotional—but he wanted to make sure he really meant them, and he wouldn't resent doing this in the future.

For the next hour, Mason, his brother and his father talked. Talked without any ill will between them. He had Eden beside him, his hand resting on her thigh. Eden joined in at times, but she also pulled out her Kindle and read, content to allow them to connect as a family. She would have probably gone out to the gardens if he hadn't squeezed her thigh to keep her from leaving.

For some reason, Mason needed her with him. He didn't know what that meant but it was yet another topic worth exploring when he entered counseling.

When they walked out the door of his childhood home, Mason felt light and...happy. He looked over at Eden. This woman had a lot to do with this cheesy grin on his face.

"I had a lovely time," she said.

"I had an enlightening time," he replied. Standing in the driveway, Mason drew her close and kissed the top of her head. He kissed her forehead, her cheeks, behind her ear, her neck and finally, finally, those precious lips. Lips that belonged to a woman who wasn't afraid to speak her mind, to tell him the truth, to say she could fall for him.

And just like that, his eyes popped open and joy filled his chest. Mason stepped back and grinned. Eden's brows furrowed. "What is it?"

Mason placed a finger over his mouth. "It's nothing. I'm just happy, that's all." Well, it was something but he couldn't tell her just yet. He wasn't just happy. He was in love with the woman standing before him. He would laugh but he didn't want Eden wondering if he was okay. Because you don't know how many times in the romance novel where the hero gets slapped with that knowledge that Mason had said, *Yeah, right*, but here he was experiencing the same thing, and yeah, he was now a believer. And yeah, he got why, everyone loved happy endings. 'Cause, shoot, it was bubbling over and threatening to spill.

Mason opened the passenger door, humming under his breath, and settled her inside the pickup before getting in. Excitement thrummed within. He pulled up his playlist and played happy songs. Eden gave him the side-eye. "You're in a good mood."

"I am. I am. And it's because of you."

She cracked up. If only she knew how true that was.

"You're infectious when you're like this," she said while singing along. If only that were true, and she could "catch" some of this love he had, but she pretty much told him she wasn't trying to fall for him. But that's okay, he would work on changing her mind.

If Mason was going to be the hero in this romance that was his life, he was going to show Eden Tempest how much he loved her in a big way, and he was going to get his happy ending. Because that's what he did for a living. Made things happen.

Chapter Nineteen

"**W**hat on earth did you do to that man?" Grams asked, pointing at Mason through the kitchen window as she packed away the kitchen goods into boxes. There were about ten men now working on the property if Eden's count was correct. All the clanging and banging was leading to some wonderful makeovers. The kitchen was among the last rooms to get renovated as Mason and the crew planned to start the next day, which was June 7. He was in their yard adding perennial plants to the perimeter of the property and singing at the top of his lungs. "Since you all returned from Virginia Beach, what's it been? Two weeks? He has been humming and singing, and so happy my teeth hurt."

"It's been sixteen days, but who's counting?" Eden giggled as she used the town's old newspapers to wrap the plates. "I don't know what I did, but he has been over-the-top affectionate. Every morning, he waits by the stairs for me, and we go outside to work on the roses. He's been leaving me little gifts everywhere—in the garden, in my bathroom, in my laptop bag—I don't even know when or how he's doing that."

"That the power of the P," Grams said. "That man is sprung wide open."

It took a moment for that to sink in and Eden placed a hand over her mouth. She was sure her cheeks were warm, although they were enjoying quite a robust sex life. She sealed one box with packing tape. "Grams, I can't believe you said that."

Grams rested a hand to her chest. "To clarify, by *P* I meant pheromones."

Eden snorted. *Yeah, right.* The mischief in Grams' eyes told the truth.

Grams's shoulders shook. "Reminds me of your grandfather when he used to come calling for me at my parents' house. He was at my house from sunrise to sunset. It got to the point where my mother said, *Why don't you put this girl on your head and carry her around with you everywhere you go?*" She shook her head. "And you know that man sure did try. I remember kicking and screaming for him to put me down."

"That's hilarious. I love it." Eden loved when her grandmother recounted her and Pop's love story. It wasn't the first she had heard this, but it never failed to make her feel good. Eden's parents had experienced the same kind of loving relationship. It was too bad she wouldn't. She enjoyed Mason's presence, but she wasn't about to tip over into love. The heartache of loving and losing was too real, too crushing. Especially since losing her parents had been her fault. Being with her might cost him her life.

Now rationally, she knew that kind of thinking wasn't true but her heart was afraid to leap, afraid to hope, afraid to accept love.

"His improved disposition probably has to do with the counseling he's been getting."

"Hmm…if that's what you think," Grams replied, with heavy sarcasm. Since Grams finished packing her box, Eden sealed that carton as well and wrote the appropriate label on the top, including the word *fragile*.

The women stood arm in arm and surveyed the area that had been their refuge for much laughter and tears. "In a couple days or so, we will have a brand-new kitchen from top to bottom. Mason has some solid plans. I'm excited but sad about it at the same time," Grams said.

Eden's heart squeezed. "This was the kitchen Mom and Dad knew."

Grams patted her hand. "And this will be the kitchen Mason designs and where you will make new memories. Hopefully, with him."

For a second, Eden allowed herself to imagine the idyllic image of her and Mason and a little girl, a blend of them, sitting at the kitchenette making turkey treats or coloring eggs or decorating gingerbread houses. How wonderful would that be if she took a chance and told him how she felt, only to learn he reciprocated those feelings. But Mason was leaving soon to return to the limelight and she couldn't picture herself anywhere but this small town. So, what was the point? She cared about him enough not to put him in that position to choose.

Ugh, this man had her teeter-tottering all over the place.

The man of her thoughts came inside beaming and swooped her in his arms. "Eden, you've got to see this."

"I can walk on my own two feet," she protested, hearing Grams's cackle behind her. Her grandmother was eating this up.

"Look," he said, placing her at the far end of her rose garden. She inhaled. A single bud had formed, its petals tightly closed, and it was marvelous to see. "It's almost bloom time," she whispered.

"Yes, the festival is in fourteen days."

She scurried into action. "I've got to water them." Mason ran to get the hose.

"They are going to be magnificent," Grams proclaimed, clapping her hands.

Eden could only nod, dabbing at her eyes. Seeing the wonder of the rosebuds open in bloom never got tiring. She could hardly wait. It was a culmination of all her efforts and her yearly reminder of the continuation of life after tragedy. Even those of one's doing. She looked over at Mason, who was now watering the roses and whistling, his eyes bright and filled with hope and her heart expanded.

Maybe after the rose festival, she would have an open and honest conversation with Mason. Suddenly, a splash of water hit the side of her face. And another.

"No! Mason, stop!" she squealed, lifting her hands. Grams took off for the house, moving with speed and dexterity.

Immediately, he stopped and she grabbed the hose from him before proceeding to drench him from head to toe. A fun game of tag ensued coupled with laughter and dirt. He circled the rose garden and came in low toward her, tackling her to the ground, making sure to twist his body and take the brunt of the fall. Thus, she was on top of him and they were laughing like children.

"We're too grown for this," she said, tapping his nose. Something else tapped her midriff and she rolled her eyes. "Really? You're as randy as a jackrabbit."

"Only for you," he said, lifting his head to kiss her. A kiss she gladly returned, the sun beaming down on them. Since they were by the rosebushes, she didn't think her grandmother could see what they were up to. Mason trailed kisses down her neck. "What do you say we take this inside?"

"I need to finish giving the roses a good watering." She sure was tempted though.

He wagged his brows. "Funny, cause that's what I want to do with your garden."

Chuckling, she gave him a gentle shove and stood, holding out her hand. He got to his feet, brushing the mud off his pants. "I've got to shower," Mason said, wiping at the grime. "These wet clothes are uncomfortable."

"Me too. I've got dirt in places I didn't know I had."

"We can shower together to save water," Mason suggested.

"Oh, is that what we're doing?" They joined hands and went inside his suite. It was several hours before she closed his bedroom door, leaving Mason to talk with his physician. He had told her about being tested as a donor for his father and wanted to make sure he was able to do so before telling his family. Since Eden had been spending so much time in Mason's room, she had left clothes in the closet and had pretty much taken over his sock drawer with her undies. Her toiletries were lined up right along with his on the huge chest. She had donned a floral sundress and planned to let her hair air-dry after putting in a curl activator.

Eden went into the kitchen and opened the refrigerator in search of a snack. Seeing a bag of cherry plums, she took three and washed them before taking a bite. Grams had left a note that she had gone into town and would bring back dinner.

Right as Eden bit into one of the plums, there was a rap on the kitchen door.

It was Cadence. Her eyes looked red and puffy, like she had been crying.

"Come in," Eden said invitingly and led her over to the kitchen table to have a seat. "We packed up the kitchen, but I can offer you bottled water?"

Cadence followed her but declined to sit. "No. No. I don't need anything." Fresh tears plopped down her face. "I... I don't know how to tell you this but it's going to eat away at me for the rest of my life if I don't."

For some reason, Eden felt a sense of foreboding. But she couldn't think of any reason to feel that way. They had only just reconnected so she had no clue what this could be about. But Cadence appeared visibly upset, on the verge of falling apart. "What's going on, Cadence?"

"Now that I'm here, I don't know if I can do this." Her chin wobbled, her knuckles turned white gripping her purse. "Give me a minute." She paced across the length of the kitchen, mumbling to herself.

Seeing her in such distress, Eden rushed over and stilled Cadence's movements, holding onto both her arms. "Whatever it is, it can't be that bad. Just spill it out. We will figure it out. We will handle it together."

Cadence wiped her face and sniffled. "You'll hate me."

"Okay, now you're putting me on edge and if I'm going to freak out, I should at least know why." Slouching her shoulders, Cadence walked over to the table and sat, face away from Eden, her body shaking hard enough to rattle the table. "I'm the one who started the fire." Those whispered words threatened to destroy Eden's very soul but she was positive she hadn't heard right.

Eden leaned forward. "I'm sorry. I must have heard you wrong. What did you say?"

Cadence pinned her with a gaze of desolation and repeated, "I started the fire. It was me."

"No! No! You're mistaken." Eden jumped to her feet and rounded on the other woman. "Why would you come here and utter such lies?"

Cadence rushed over to her. "I'm not lying. We were up in your room smoking ciggies, remember? But then you went downstairs to cut your cake. I—I went into the bathroom to finish off my smoke. But I was messing around with the lighter and, I don't even know how, the curtains caught fire. It spread like wildfire. I tried dousing everything with water until I finally had to scream out *Fire!* I screamed, *Fire, Fire*, and raced outside the house." She started to sob in earnest. "I didn't expect your parents would rush up the stairs and get trapped. And I didn't expect you would…go after them."

"All this time…" Eden's knees buckled. She would have fallen if Cadence hadn't caught her. She struggled to catch her breath, inhaling and exhaling but she couldn't get enough air.

Cadence bent before her, urging her breath in, breath in, until she calmed somewhat. As soon as she could, Eden lashed out, "All this time I thought I was the one who…" She grabbed her midriff. "How could you make me believe that about myself?" Before Cadence could answer, another memory sliced her to the core and her mouth dropped. "How could you tease me and taunt me, calling me a beast when it was your fault?"

"I—I was a kid myself. I wasn't thinking," Cadence said, wringing her hands.

Rage built and just seeing Cadence's face stoked her anger. "I can't believe you did that. You aren't a friend. You're the one who's actually a monster," she screamed.

"Please, I am so sorry for hurting you," Cadence said, grabbing onto Eden's hand.

"Get out," she commanded through gritted teeth.

Cadence pleaded, "These past few years hasn't been easy for me."

"And you think they have been for me?" Eden held up her hands. "Look at what your careless actions did to my body. This isn't about starting the fire. This is about your allowing me to take the blame and then calling yourself a friend." Her chest rose and fell. "I suggest you get to stepping."

"No, Eden, please. We have been working on our friendship and I can't lose that. Please. I'm sorry." Cadence covered her face in her hands.

"Your apologies are too late and they can't bring my mom and dad back. Get out! Get out before I call the police and don't you dare come back here again. If I see your face, I won't be responsible for my actions."

Mason came bounding into the kitchen just as Cadence flew through the back door. "Are you all right?"

All she could do was shake her head. Eden crumpled to the floor. The tears flowed then, her body wracked with sorrow. Mason scooped her up and cradled her in his arms. She burrowed into him, welcoming the comfort his strong arms provided. He sank onto the living room couch, remained silent and allowed her to cry until she was spent. By then, Grams had returned and when she regained her composure, Eden told them what Cadence had confessed.

Mason was understandably upset, but Grams… Grams shocked her. "Poor girl. To carry that lie for thirteen years was too big a burden for anyone."

Eden rubbed her temples. "How can you have an ounce of compassion after what I just told you?"

"Maybe you should consider pressing charges," Mason added. "I wonder if there is a statute of limitations on arson."

"Yeah. I think that's a good idea," Eden said. "I can do some research. Or we can call the sheriff in the morning. He would know."

"Let's leave the past in the past," Grams replied, sounding weary. "Nothing that is said or done will bring my children back. They need to keep resting in peace."

Eyeing her grandmother's ashen face, Eden didn't know if Grams would survive that kind of ordeal. "Fine, Grams. I'll do as you ask, but I don't want to see Cadence's lying face ever again."

"That will be kind of hard to do, dear," Grams said. "I just hired her to run the bed-and-breakfast."

Chapter Twenty

When his phone rang at 6:00 a.m. the morning of June 10, Mason knew it could only be one person calling.

Lydia.

Gripping the fitted sheet, he groaned and decided to let the call go to voicemail. Again. After Ms. Susan dropped that bombshell, Eden had stormed upstairs into her room. Mason had texted her to see if she wanted to talk but she responded that she would see him tomorrow. So that meant he was sleeping alone. Something he had done for most of thirty-three years. Something he didn't want to do as long as he was here with Eden.

As a result, he hadn't slept well the night before and talking with Lydia wouldn't improve his disposition. Still, he couldn't avoid his agent much longer but—ugh, she was calling again. Reaching over to the nightstand, he grabbed his cell phone and answered the call.

"Thank goodness, you finally answered," she said, worry in her voice. "I thought something happened to you."

Hearing the genuine concern, Mason sat up. "I'm sorry. I didn't mean to freak you out but I had some personal things going on that I had to take care of." He then shared about his reunion with his family.

"Oh, Mason. I'm so happy for you. That would have been a great special to record," she said, giving a shaky laugh. "I'm just joking—" they both knew she wasn't, though "—but don't add years to my life like that again. If I didn't get you today, I was going to be calling nearby hospitals." She cleared her throat. "I know the Blue Hen Rose Festival is coming up on the twentieth, and I wanted to check in to see if you wanted me to send a crew out there. Just to talk with you. Maybe get a few snapshots of you with the members of the community."

"I told you already how I felt about that."

"Yes, but the pictures you've been posting have generated a lot of interest. You're gaining positive attention and doubling your followers."

"Say what?" With a start Mason realized that he hadn't been on social media in a while. There was a time when he monitored his feed after every single post, every interaction, to see what everyone else was saying, to see what they thought about him. Scrolling took up a lot of his time. He frowned. Now he realized that their opinions no longer outweighed his opinion of himself.

Mason liked who he was here in Blue Hen. He liked his friends here—Gabe and Ms. Susan. And he loved, loved, loved Eden Tempest. He just had to find the right time and the best way to tell her. He was pretty sure she knew how he felt but it was important to actually say the words. Give her the fairytale reveal she deserved. The usual chocolates and flowers felt…mundane. He believed in bringing it home, going big.

"Are you there?" Lydia asked, breaking into his thoughts.

"Oh yes." He retrieved his laptop from the other side of the bed—a poor substitute for a bed partner—and pulled up his socials. Sure enough, Lydia was right. There were more pictures of him working on the house, smiling and looking as good as he felt. His brows furrowed. "Who's doing this?" He swung his legs off the bed and sprang to his feet, pacing the length of the room.

"It's not you?" Lydia asked.

"No. It isn't."

"Well, whoever it is, tell them your agent said thank you."

He rubbed his head. "This isn't humorous at all. I hope it's not a stalker." When he first started out, Mason had attracted the attention of a real zealous fan. At first, he had found the woman annoying but harmless. Until he woke up one night to see her standing by the foot of his bed. Mason had had to call 911 and keep her entertained until the cops arrived. The thought of someone harming Eden or Ms. Susan gave him pause.

In the short space of time, he had come to love these women.

"I don't think you need to worry about that," Lydia said. "What are the odds of that happening twice?"

"It's not unlikely…"

"I live near that town. I doubt it. Everybody's good people. They look out for each other."

"Really? Lydia, drop the clueless act. You're not naive about the realities of being a celebrity. You just want me to agree to filming. Plus, people move in and out of towns all the time."

Mason wondered if he should tell Lydia his discovery. If he didn't, she might keep pressing to have him do a show. "Um, so, I met a wonderful woman. And she isn't one for the spotlight so we're in the early stages—well, I'm crazy about her—and I don't want to mess this up."

"Wow." Judging by the genuine shock in Lydia's voice, his declaration had caught her by surprise. But this was Lydia, so of course her next question was, "Have you told her how you feel?"

"No. Not yet. I've never said those words to a woman and it might sound corny but I want the moment to be big for her. For the both of us."

"What's bigger than television?" Lydia shot back. "The whole world tuning in to have you put yourself out there, declare your love for the woman of your heart." Okay, so Mason had had no idea that Lydia was such a romantic. She continued; her voice dreamy. "Just thinking about it warms my heart. Love is the biggest comeback of all and your fans would eat this up."

Mason rubbed his chin. "It would be nice to record it. But not for television. I'm thinking more as a personal memento."

"I suppose I understand your need to keep this private. Sentimental," Lydia said. "I tell you what, how about I send a crew down there to get your special moment on film? It will be for your eyes only. And your lady friend's, of course. But if you ever change your mind, we have it on video."

"That could work." His heart pounded. "What if she rejects me?"

"What if she rejects you?" Linda sputtered. "Are you serious? I doubt that very much."

He smiled at his agent's loyalty. "It can happen."

"Don't put that in the atmosphere. Positive vibes only. I'm glad to do this for you. I'll get in touch with your old camera crew and get them to Blue Hen in time for the Rose Festival."

"All right." The line went dead. Anticipation rose in Mason's chest. Especially when he thought of the perfect gift for his beauty. He got dressed quickly and went upstairs to retrieve what he needed, slip it into a bag, then hurried down into the kitchen. Every time he strolled by the finished product, Mason felt a mixture of amazement and pride. The kitchen had been done in all white with sleek accents and pops of color. He had chosen apple green and burnt orange as potholders or kitchen towels. All the appliances were also sleek and white, but his favorite—and Ms. Susan's—was the oversize transparent refrigerator.

Right now, Ms. Susan was using her new marble countertop with a cutting board embedded into it to roll out some dough. "Where are you off to so early?" she asked.

"I've got to get into town to run an errand so I can get back here before the men get here." They were in the planning stages for the living and dining areas and once those were complete, the house would be ready for Eden's birthday party.

Ms. Susan gave him a wide smile. "You have transformed my home into a magazine-worthy showpiece. I've almost finished checking off my to-do list for her party." She trembled with excitement. "I can't wait to see her face."

"I'm eager to see that too. Especially since she has no idea what you have planned." He was bursting to tell Ms. Susan his intentions but he wanted her to be equally bowled over. Her authentic reaction would make for good filming.

Ms. Susan began cutting the dough into small squares. "What are you making?" he asked to distract himself from blabbing.

"Some soda bread to go with the grits and eggs."

His stomach grumbled. "Well, I'll be sure to keep my appetite. I shouldn't be gone long."

"Did you see Eden this morning? She hasn't been down to look about the roses." There was slight worry in her eyes.

"No. I haven't. But I can give the roses a good water. Most are beginning to open and it smells amazing out there. I think Eden has more than enough from what's already there to make her designs."

"Might seem like it, but she is going to need extra in case they don't hold up. These are natural flowers and way more delicate than imitation ones."

"That makes sense."

A thought hit his mind and he gave Ms. Susan a side-glance. "Say, you wouldn't happen to know who is posting pictures of me on the internet, would you?"

She avoided his gaze and basted the dough with butter. "No. No. I don't have any idea," she squeaked out, her pitch at least two octaves higher than before. "But I'm sure whoever did must have their reasons. I don't know—maybe they want others to see you how they see you. I don't know but I wouldn't worry about it too much." She opened the oven and put the dough inside before putting the timer on.

"All right. If you think so." He bit back a smile.

Ms. Susan now stirred her pot of grits, still not meeting his eyes. "You'd best get going."

He glanced at the clock. "Okay. See you soon." He went over to kiss her on the cheek and then he was out the door. All the way there and back Mason kept grinning like a hyena. This was going to be an event to remember.

Chapter Twenty-One

Eden couldn't recall the last time she and Grams had been at odds. But she couldn't agree with Grams's decision to hire Cadence, which was why she was staying upstairs no matter how much her stomach growled. Boy, those sure were some delicious smells coming from the kitchen. Sitting at her desk, she rubbed her tummy. Grams wasn't playing fair. She knew how much Eden loved her grits.

A chat around a bowl of grits could solve anything was one of Grams's mottos. She rolled her eyes. Well, not this time. Cadence worked at the flower shop and drove a fancy car. She didn't need to be in Eden's face. But Grams had only offered a cryptic *Not everything is as it seems* then clammed up. Whatever.

Just then her cell buzzed. It was Mason.

Want me to bring you some food?

Yes. Pls.

Be right up.

Thx. Luv U.

Eden opened up her laptop and clicked on the meeting link that would connect her with Ramona. She had been meaning to connect with her therapist after their last frank discussion.

Eden thought she had done tremendous progress and couldn't wait to share that with Ramona. She also needed to talk about these dueling feelings of elation at dating Mason versus the outrage of Cadence's betrayal.

Grams had taught her to practice forgiveness but overlooking Cadence's actions was asking a bit too much. Ramona's smiling face popped up on the screen at the same time that Mason was knocking on her door.

Lifting a finger, she told Ramona, "I'll be just one moment," turned off her camera and microphone then proceeded to open the door. Holding a tray in one hand, Mason used the other to circle her waist then kiss her with the kind of abandon that tempted her to shove him on the bed and try sexual healing.

Breaking the kiss, she took deep breaths and thanked him for the food, which he now rested on the table, before letting him know she was on a video chat with Ramona.

"Oh, okay. I kind of wanted to ask you about…" He paused, then shrugged. "Never mind. Another time. I understand. I'll leave you to it then." He sounded mildly disappointed. "I have a meeting with her later today as well." Throwing her a kiss, he backed out of the room.

"So, how are things going?" Ramona asked once Eden was back on the line.

"I've been seeing someone," she said, giggling when she saw Ramona's eyes go wide. "I'm trying to keep it super casual but I think he's a great guy." And gorgeous. And helpful. And kind. And thoughtful.

"Whoa. Talk about putting yourself out there. I'm happy for you."

"Thanks, I'm happy for me too." She swiveled in her chair. "And I've decided to teach on campus this coming fall."

Ramona moved closer to the screen. "Okay, who are you and what you done with my client?"

Eden laughed. "It's still me. Thanks to you and Grams—"

and Mason "—I found the courage to put myself out there and when I did, it wasn't as bad as I thought. It wasn't as scary as I imagined. And it was…freeing. I'm actually looking forward to working with the students this fall. I'm going on campus later today to talk with Dr. Loft about their freshman program."

"Look at you." Ramona clapped her hands. "My heart is overflowing for you. I'm proud of you."

Eden leaned in. "So, now that I've gotten the good stuff out of the way. I have something I really need to talk to you about." Her breath hitched. "I'm struggling to navigate through this one."

"What's going on?" Ramona asked.

She then filled Ramona in on Cadence's admission, her grandmother's decision to hire Cadence and how she and Grams were now at odds. "Just when I thought I was at peace and at a good place, Cadence drops all this on me, and I feel betrayed. But on the other hand, I feel like an enormous weight has been lifted off my shoulders knowing I didn't directly cause my parents' deaths."

Ramona exhaled. "Let's talk through that for a minute. Your grandmother forgave you for starting the fire that killed her only child. Why are you surprised she would do the same for Cadence? You guys were sixteen."

Eden didn't have an answer for that. She folded her arms. "Cadence lied to me. That's what I'm most upset about. Made me shoulder the blame when it was her all along." Resentment swept through her body. And hurt. Lots of hurt.

"Yes, that was a horrible thing to do. But what do you think should be done now, thirteen years later?"

"I don't care if it's fifty years later." She slammed a fist on the table. "I want Grams to be upset on my behalf, not offer Cadence a job. All this has just made me miss my parents even more. It stirred up the grief I thought I had finally put to bed for good and then all this happens…" Her voice cracked.

Ramona nodded. "If I know Ms. Susan, she has her reasons." She cocked her head. "Maybe this is her way of coping with her loss. Who knows. But when it comes to death, you will never get to zero. Your parents' deaths will always affect you, though it might vary in intensity. You're always going to have moments of sadness that will come and go." She paused for a beat. "We can't undo the past."

Tears pooled in Eden's eyes. "She hurt me."

"Yes, but for your own healing, you've got to forgive her. Maybe that's what Ms. Susan is doing."

She blinked, allowing the tears to fall. "I don't think I want Cadence to suffer. It was an accident." She touched her chest. "I just wish it didn't feel like my chest was on fire."

"Like you said, your grief is all stirred up right now. Things will settle soon. You just have to go through the process."

As usual, Ramona had given her sound advice. She just wasn't sure she was ready to take it. She couldn't look at Grams without a sour feeling forming in her stomach. So, she went to seek out Mason, but he was working and she didn't want to disturb him.

Eden took a moment to study him. He was standing with his iPad in hand with Gabe and the others forming a semi-circle around him. Whatever he was saying had them animated. Mason was a natural leader and what he had done to the B and B was spectacular. Seeing him eased some of the turmoil raging in her gut and she didn't know why. Warm sensations flooded through her body. Her shoulders slackened and she smiled.

And just like that. She knew.

There was no denying how she felt for this man.

She had found the best aid for grief. Love. The question was, what was the aid for love? Because loving him would be akin to confining an orca to a tiny tank. Mason would constantly yearn for deeper, wider waters and it would pain her to see him limited. Turning, she walked toward Grams's truck to head down to the college. The best thing she could do for Mason was enjoy him while he was here and not stand in his way when it was time for him to leave.

For that reason, Eden would keep what was in her heart to herself. To tell him she loved him might make him feel obligated to stay. And he might end up hating her, resenting her because of it. And that would be a hurt from which she might never recover.

Chapter Twenty-Two

Luv U.

Ugh. Don't read too much into it. Eden could be one of those super casual people who used the L-word for everything. *I love those shoes. I love eggs.* But what if she meant she *loved loved* him and he hadn't replied?

Mason had gone into his room right after lunch on the pretext of using the bathroom. But really it was to reread and analyze this text message until he could decide on his next step.

Pulling up his phone, he read the text message one more time, pacing the length of his room. He rubbed his eyes and decided he was reading way too much into two little words. If she meant more, she would have added a heart emoji or something.

Luv U. Luv U. Luv U. Luv U. Luv U. Luv U. Luv U. Luv U. Luv U.

Ugh. He was officially obsessing. He scrolled through his contacts and tapped on Maxim's phone number. If anyone could answer this question, it would be his brother. Maxim answered and Mason poured out his confusion.

"I just don't know what that means. And how should I answer?" He slipped into the armchair in the corner of his room and waited.

His brother paused for a beat, nodding, his brows furrowed, his lips bunched tight.

"Is everything all right on that end?" Mason finally asked, suddenly realizing he hadn't even inquired about their father. "Is Dad okay? I wanted to tell you that I am looking into being a donor. I have an appointment scheduled for the first week in July."

Maxim shook his head. "Dad is just fine. It's... It's just that..." Then Maxim squinted, his shoulders shaking hard before he busted into laughter. "Yo, If you could only see your face right now." He covered his mouth with his hand and broke into more laughter. "Tell me why that is the funniest thing I ever heard. I was trying to be sensitive but I can't hold it."

Drawing in a deep breath, Mason demanded, "Quit cackling like a hyena and answer me though."

That only made Maxim laugh even more. "You sound like you're fifteen years old." He placed the phone to stand somewhere, bent over, gripping his sides. Mason would have hung up if he didn't need his brother's advice. Then he slapped his forehead. He could have asked Gabe. But in his defense, he wasn't used to having real friends in a long time.

"This is my heart we're talking about. I've never been in love before." Mason said. Those words sobered Maxim.

"Dang, bro. You really are in love." He cleared his throat. "I don't think she was making a declaration but maybe she's testing the waters, so to speak. Maybe Eden wants to see how you react when she says *Luv U* and then she plans on slipping in the real *I love you* later."

Mason placed a hand to his chin. "Like she wants to see if it's going to scare me off or something."

"Could be, bro." He shrugged. "I don't know. I don't have any experience with love and I don't plan to get caught in that web. If you are looking for me, I'll be swimming in the sea, no strings, no attachments."

Maxim's words succeeded in making Mason focus on something other than himself. "Maxim, I'll admit that falling in love got me a little twisted but there's nothing like it. I feel like I am soaring. Everything is brighter, more beautiful. It's like you're walking around with a ray of sunshine in your chest."

"Whoa." Maxim's brows rose. "That sounds dope." Then he shrugged. "Nope. Still not doing it. The reason why they say *fall in love* is because it's a free fall to certain death." He chuckled. "That's a good one. I'll have to remember that."

"Is it because I left you?" Mason asked, saddened. "Or because Dad is now leaving you? Not everyone who loves you will leave, bro. I'm still here."

Maxim's eyes went wide before they filled with skepticism. "You sound like a therapist. But you're way off base…"

Mason wasn't too convinced but that wasn't a battle he had to win today. "When that time comes, allow yourself to fall, to take a chance." He had a sharp intake of breath and stood. "That's it. Thanks, bro." Renewed energy surged through him. "I'm going to interpret those words the way that I want to and take a chance. Maybe in addition to declaring how I feel at the rose festival, I'll ask her to marry me." As soon as he spoke the words, he felt…settled. A wedding proposal was the ultimate step in the happy-ever-after.

"Wait, what? How did you get to marriage out of a simple *Luv U* text? You need to slow your roll, bro."

But he wasn't about to be deterred. Mason was a man of action. "I admit, it might seem over-the-top, but I'm sure of how I feel. If she thinks those two words are going to send me running back to Ohio, then she has another think coming. I've got to run out to the jewelers."

"You need to run and make another appointment with your therapist," Maxim joked.

Mason froze. "Oh, shoot. I actually have a meeting with Ramona today." He looked at his watch. "But if I leave now, I could make it if I don't dawdle."

Suddenly, he heard his father's voice. "Go for it. I'm rooting for you." Mason didn't realize his father had been in earshot. Maxim handed his father the phone. "This is how I felt with your mother. She was the only love of my life."

"Thanks, Dad," he yelled back, pumping his fists.

"Let's take a road trip," his father said to Maxim. "I need to see how this plays out and I want to cheer for you on the sidelines." He bunched his fists and yelled, "Go big, son."

Dang it, if he didn't get a little misty-eyed. "It would mean a lot to have my family share this moment with me. No matter the outcome."

"It's settled then. See you at the festival."

Mason dashed out of the house and raced to town, his heart light. Thanks to Eden, he now had a relationship with his family again. It felt good knowing they would drive four hours to support him. The old him would have rejected their offer. But this new and improved Mason knew having them there would boost his confidence and also be the firm grip he needed if this didn't work out how he hoped.

Ramona's words came back to him. *Through the trauma, we can find the beauty, we just have to search for it.* Well, that's what he had down. He had found his beauty and he didn't want to ever let her go. For a split second, doubt entered his mind. What if Eden didn't love him in return? But he pushed that out with *What if she did?* He turned into the parking lot of the strip mall. There was only one way to find out and the by the end of the day of the festival, he would find out.

Chapter Twenty-Three

The sun painted gorgeous strokes across the sky when Mason, Eden and Ms. Susan headed to the Blue Hen Rose Festival. The fragrance from the roses stacked in the rear of the pickup filled his nostrils and he kept the windows down so they could enjoy the benefits of a rare eighty-degree day in a summer month.

In contrast to the loveliness of the surroundings, there was a distinct chill in the air with Eden and Ms. Susan still at odds. No matter how Eden pressed, her grandmother refused to explain why she had given Cadence a job. Eden had spent the past few nights in her room and though he had tossed and turned—having gotten used to her presence beside him—Mason had respected her space. However, it troubled him seeing Eden so upset.

But if ever there was a picture of unbothered, it was Ms. Susan.

Dressed in a pair of black jeans, a blue shirt with an embroidered blue hen and a pair of comfortable walking shoes, Ms. Susan sat up front with him and chattered on like a magpie. "You are going to enjoy yourself, Mason," she said. "Not only are there roses, but we have a barbecue contest and our annual pie contest. It's a great day for our town." She patted the oval glass carrier in her lap. "I'm definitely beating Ruthie this year with this recipe."

"It smells good, I can tell you that," Mason said, following the directions on the navigation system. They were now about five minutes away from the fairgrounds. He pointed. "They have a Ferris wheel?"

"Oh yes, plus there's a carousel and a dunk tank. Last year, we had clowns. But they scared the babies, so we're not doing that this year." She twisted in her seat to address Eden. "You used to be afraid of them too. Remember that?"

"Yes," she replied. A one-word answer. No further elaboration. Ms. Susan shrugged, her face serene. Mason eyed Eden through the rearview mirror but she kept her gaze firmly out the window. *Boy.* He wiped his brow. He hoped her mood lifted before his big declaration.

Following the directions of the flaggers, he pulled into a parking spot near the entrance. There were only a handful of cars. Eden jumped out of the pickup before he turned off the engine. He heard the truck bed open and sighed. This was going to be a long day unless Eden and her grandmother resolved things between them.

Ms. Susan tapped his arm. "Don't worry yourself. We'll be like peanut butter and jelly soon."

Chuckling at her analogy, Mason went around the vehicle to hold onto the pie while Ms. Susan exited. "Thank you. Do you need help with the roses?" she asked Eden.

"No. I've got it."

"Suit yourself," Ms. Susan breezily replied. "Mason, I'm heading out to get a good spot for my pie." She gave him a quick wave and took off with her pie in hand.

Heading to where Eden stood placing roses on the cart they had carried, he snatched her flush against him, spooning her from behind. "I've missed you," he whispered in her ear. He used his nose to play with the blue hen earrings dangling near her neck. "You're looking real cute today." She was wearing a T-shirt that said Queen of the Blue Hen Rose Festival with a pair of white shorts and a tiara made of—no surprise—

roses and blue hens. This was her first time wearing one of the shirts she had won and her crown, which had warmed his heart when she told him.

"Thank you." She turned to face him and hugged him tight. "I've just had a lot on my mind as you know. I'll come see you later tonight. I promise."

"I'll hold you to that," he said, giving her a light squeeze and a quick kiss. She tasted so good, he had to get another taste. And another.

"Mason, we've got to go set up," she said between kisses. "I want to get a good location with enough room for my special design and we have to complete before judging at noon."

More cars were pulling in and he could hear the slight panic in her tone. Mason reluctantly pulled away. "I just needed my fix. I think I'm getting addicted to you. Two days and it's like I'm experiencing withdrawal symptoms." She rolled her eyes. "I know it's corny, but it's true," he said.

Together, they continued filling the cart. Eden planned to do a mosaic butterfly using roses of different colors, signifying her personal freedom. Her plans were dope, meaningful and he had gotten emotional seeing them.

"Aww." She placed a hand on his chest. "What a nice thing to say."

"Not so nice to feel."

"You're a big boy. You can handle it," she teased. They began making their way to the grounds, the cart rattling along the pavement. So many roses lined the path—though Eden told him those were fake, including the huge awning at the entrance.

"They look so real," he proclaimed once they had arrived at their designated spot.

"They were all handmade by the ladies of our town," she explained, keeping in step with him. "I couldn't wait to turn eight so I could start making my own. Each year, we add to it, replacing the old ones with new." A family of four passed them. The young girl's dress was made to look like petals, and the little boy had on a green outfit, resembling a stalk. Some families had matching shirts with roses, some with blue hens. He felt underdressed with his T-shirt and jeans until Eden gave him a cap stitched with the town's blue hen.

"Wow. This festival is a big deal." And, very characteristic of a small town. Quite honestly, he had never seen anything like it.

"It's the event of the year," Eden replied, her hands deftly prepping her roses. She stopped to show him how she wanted him to strip the thorns and then wire the roses.

"So, what do the men do?" he asked once they had began setting up the roses on her display.

"Generally, they make the vines, the wire hooks, the stalks and assemble the lighting. Or, some help with the roses. Stuff like that. Wait until you see these roses at night. There's nothing like it." She pointed to her wired butterfly-shaped stand. "Grams had this made for me a couple months ago." He could see the mini lights behind the display.

Beside them, a young woman and a couple other girls put up a wired stand that was shaped like a hen, and they had tons of blue roses and other flowers. Boy, this town sure was proud of its blue hen.

Pointing over at them, he said, "I thought you could only use roses."

"According to the rules, you can supplement with other flowers but the rose has to be the star." Her chest puffed. "Thank goodness, I've never had to supplement except for the usual greens and baby's breath."

He heard her sharp intake of breath and followed her gaze. Cadence was there, right along with Gabe, putting up her design right across from them. He couldn't tell from the wiring but it looked like words. Their bodies blocked him from seeing fully but Eden redirected his attention.

She spoke through gritted teeth. "I didn't see her name on the entrants list, so she must have registered at the last minute. And now she's right in front of me when there are so many other places she could go," Eden said, hurt in her voice, her eyes misty. "It's like she's rubbing it in my face what she did."

Mason cupped her face with his hands. "Don't allow her to distract you off your path." She met his gaze, pinning those cognac eyes on his. "Take deep breaths and focus. You've won the past five years and you will claim that crown again."

"You're right." Grabbing his head, Eden gave him a deep kiss in front of the whole town before squaring her shoulders, then whispered, "Let's get to work." A half hour into their task, she asked, "How is your father doing?"

"He's stable. For now," Mason said, hooking a rose onto the wire. They were one-third of the way finished. His fingers cramped up on him and he opened and closed his hands. "I've set the appointment to get on the donor's list." Maxim had texted that they would arrive within the hour. Good thing too because as each hour went by, nervousness wrapped itself like a vine around his heart.

"That's good to hear. Have you told your dad yet?"

"No, I don't want to get his hopes up until I'm sure it's a done deal." Just then a young teen approached to take a selfie and request his autograph. Mason posed with him before obliging a few others.

"You are wonderful." She gave him a quick kiss on the lips, her eyes warm.

Her praise gave him a shot of confidence. Eden wouldn't look at him that way if she didn't care about him. Caring can grow to love. All will be good. A half hour before noon, they finished her design. Stepping back, Mason said, "This is exquisite."

She beamed. "Thank you." They shared a kiss. "Having you here made it fun."

That's when Mason looked over at Cadence's stand. Both she and Gabe gestured at him to have Eden turned around. He placed a hand on her shoulders and twisted her around. Eden gasped, before covering her mouth. Cadence and Gabe's display featured the words *I'm Sorry.* He could feel her shoulders shake as she dissolved into fresh tears.

"Let it go, honey," he encouraged, patting her back. "Let it go."

She nodded against his chest. Cadence came over to where Eden was and the two friends embraced. "I know I don't deserve it, but I could use a second chance."

With a nod, Eden said, "I forgive you." She gave Mason a look of tenderness. "I've got too much good happening in my life to keep wading in the past."

To Mason, that was his cue.

From the corner of his eye, Mason saw his crew approaching and his brother and father were a few feet behind. Once they were close, he signaled for them to start recording. Then he took Eden's hand.

Cadence must have caught on what was about to occur because she uttered a quick *We'll catch up later* and scampered out of the way. The townspeople began to gather around. He could feel their excitement and that made his heart gallop in his chest.

"Eden," he began, breathy, nervous. "Since I met you, everything in my life is better."

She nodded, her lashes wet from crying. "I feel the same about you."

"I've never felt this way about anyone before." He moved his gaze away from her to nod at his brother and father, who held up their phones. Come to think of it, there were quite a few people holding up their phones. He spotted Ms. Susan grinning and she signaled to him to continue. And wait, was that Lydia he saw munching on an ice-cream cone?

Meanwhile, Eden faced the crowd. "What the—" She glanced at him with doe eyes. "What's going on?"

Mason spun her around, then gave her a searing kiss. There was a lot of hooting and hollering, which would make for good memories. He couldn't wait to see the tape. Tearing his lips off hers, he said, "I want you to know in front of the entire town, that I love you, Eden Tempest. You are the ultimate woman of my fairy tale."

Her eyes shone. "I love you, too."

The crowd broke into applause. Someone started chanting, "Kiss, Kiss, Kiss," and soon the throng joined in.

Mason and Eden were happy to oblige. His chest puffed at her smiling face. Squaring his shoulders, Mason dropped to his knees. Lowering his head, he reached into his jeans pocket. The crowd stilled to a hush.

"Um, Mason… What are you doing? Is that a camera crew?" she growled out.

"Yes. I'll explain later. Hang on, my love." He dug into his pocket and pulled out the small velvet box. Everyone cheered. Ms. Susan hovered close with Lydia standing beside her. His father wiped his eyes.

"What are you doing?" Eden whispered again. His mind registered that she sounded more frantic than excited, but he pushed on.

With a broad grin, Mason held up the ring and looked at her. He expected to see her smiling. Maybe even crying, overcome with emotion. What he didn't expect to see was the thunderous expression on her face, which brought his marriage request to a grinding halt.

Chapter Twenty-Four

Was he seriously about to propose?

That indicated permanence.

Forever.

Eden was ready for happy-for-now. Not ever after. Mason had read way too many romances to think she would marry him. That would mean leaving the town. Leaving her life. She wasn't cut out for the celebrity life.

Even now, knowing the cameras were on her made her antsy and self-conscious. Why would he put her on blast like this? And how did he expect her to live in the land of the perfect face, booty and hips when she was scarred. She could feel her face burn with mortification. She could feel the crowd's ears cocked listening to their every word but she had to stop him.

"Get up," she urged. Awkwardly, Mason rose to his feet, the box in hand. She eyed it like it was a viper and commanded, "Put that away."

He began to shove it in his pocket but then stopped. "I can't do that." He placed his hands on her shoulders. "I love you and it would be my honor if you would be my wife. For me, marriage is the ultimate indicator of my love. I want to spend the rest of my life with you. Forever." He touched her face and smiled. "I don't want to spend another day without you by my side."

Dropping back to his knees, he opened the box. A large solitaire glistened in the sun and the crowd oohed and aahed.

Then he boomed out, "Eden Tempest, will you marry me?" Oh, why did he have to ruin their fling by asking for something permanent?

She placed a hand on her hip. "Is everything a show for you?"

"No, you don't understand. That's for—"

"And where are we spending our days?" she interrupted.

He stepped back. "Huh? What do you mean?" He then beckoned the camera to stop rolling. The crowd began to thin. In that moment, she was grateful for the people of Blue Hen. They knew when to give someone space.

"Where do you see us living in your version of the fairy tale?" she asked when it was just her, Mason and family.

"Well, I—uh—I figure you would live with me." He ran a hand across his scalp. "I have everything you need right there in Ohio."

"Goes to show you don't know me, Mason Powers. You don't know me at all. And that's why I can't marry you." Afraid of falling apart in front of everyone, she dashed off, moving as fast as her feet would take her. She just made it out of the parking lot when she heard a honk behind her. If that was Mason... Cadence pulled up beside her.

"Need a ride?" the other woman asked.

Sweat poured off her from all that adrenaline and she needed to cool down. Plus, she had run off leaving her purse behind. So she didn't have her house keys or her cell phone. With a nod, Eden got inside Cadence's car. "I don't want to talk about what just transpired," she said, slamming the door shut.

"Okay, I hear you. You don't want to talk about the brave man who just poured his heart out to you in front of the whole town. You don't want to talk about how you shot him down, leaving him crushed and dejected. You don't want to talk about how this is about you feeling scared, like you don't deserve to be loved."

Eden gave her a cutting glance.

"Noted." Lifting a hand, Cadence pumped up the air-conditioning and pressed the gas. "Do you want me to give you a ride home?" she offered, her tone gentle.

"N-no. I can't go back there yet. I…just…need…a…minute." Eden broke into heavy sobs. Her heart felt like it was ripping open and that shouldn't be happening. Not when she had done the right thing. The best thing for the both of them.

After driving for a few minutes, Cadence turned into a strip mall and parked. The stores were closed today because everyone was at the rose festival. The area looked as desolate as she felt, which led to fresh tears.

"Why are you crying if you felt turning him down was the best move?" Cadence prodded.

"Because I didn't expect my heart to feel like someone took an axe to it." She slouched over, her pulse rhythm shaky. "Please tell me I did the right thing." From her peripheral view, Cadence reached behind her and grabbed a bottled water before handing it to Eden. Unscrewing the cap, she guzzled down half of the contents. "Thanks."

"Now to answer your question… Three years ago, I met a man who swept me off my feet. With his southern drawl, cowboy hat and boots, Thad was hard to resist. He was an imaginative lover though a bit possessive, which I didn't like at all. But when he proposed, I said yes, without a care in the world."

Eden took off her seat belt then curved her body to give Cadence her complete attention.

"We moved to this sprawling ranch in Texas. He told me I would never have to work a day in my life again. Now, you know I grew up in a house where I had to get a part-time job at fourteen cleaning houses with my mom. So, imagine how appealing that was for me. I quit my senior year of college, feeding on Thad's bull. As soon as I entered that house, I got a bad vibe but I ignored it."

Cadence picked at an imaginary piece of lint on her blouse. "The first month was marvelous. I was living in newlywed bliss. He even gifted me this car," she said, patting the seat. "Then one night, I was taking a bath, and something caught my eye. I had to get a step stool but what I saw made goose bumps pop up on my flesh. It was a camera. I quickly realized Thad had one in every room, watching my every move."

Eden gasped.

"Yes, girl. That wasn't pretty. I felt like I was a cast member in a psychotic thriller movie. But I confronted Thad. To my surprise, he didn't bother denying any of it. It was like he was proud of what he had done. When I tried to leave—" she straightened "—he backhanded me."

"Say what?"

"Now you know after that, all I could think about was how he could keep me a prisoner inside his home. As soon as he went to bed that night, I jumped into the car he gave me and hightailed it back to Delaware."

Eden ran a hand through her damp curls. "Where is he now?"

"Same place in Texas, right where I left him. Except he's six feet under."

"Did you…?" Eden trailed off, disgusted for thinking Cadence capable of violence. But still. This was sounding like a thriller so she couldn't rule it out.

Cadence slapped Eden's wrist. "No, girl. The very night I left, someone who Thad owed money to broke into the house and shot him. Now, you know I would have been a chief suspect if it weren't for those doggone cameras." Eden's mouth dropped open for a beat before they started laughing uncontrollably.

When they calmed down, Eden said, "I don't get how that correlates to my situation though. In fact, you seem to be saying the same thing I'm saying."

"The first lesson of the story is that you have to follow your gut. Trust your instincts. If I had listened to my intuition, I wouldn't have dropped out of school. I wouldn't have married Thad and I wouldn't have quit school. Ms. Susan gave me that job so I could quit the flower shop, complete the internship and finish my hospitality degree." That's why Grams had hired Cadence. It all made sense now. It also explained how Cadence was driving this luxury car.

Eden reached over to give Cadence a hug. "I'm glad you got out before it was too late."

"That's the second lesson." Cadence gave her an expectant look but Eden wasn't getting it. "Let me spell it out for you then. Your gut is telling you everything you need to know about Mason. You just have to search deep and listen. And, if you're wrong, trust yourself to know you'll get out of a bad situation." Then she quirked her lips. "Or, at the very least, you'll get a sweet ride out of it. And I mean that in every sense of the word."

"Wow." Eden relaxed against the seat and exhaled. "You went through a lot."

"Mmm-hmm. But now imagine, just imagine, if Thad was wonderful and my gut agreed. I would still be in Texas. Still married. Still happy. And you know what, I would have deserved it. Because every woman deserves to love herself and be loved by a good man."

Several beats went by, the only sound Cadence drumming her fingers on the steering wheel. Eden sank into the seat. "I messed up, didn't I?"

"Yep."

"I can't keep living in fear."

"Nope."

"I deserve to be loved."

"Right."

"I have a gut. I can trust it."

"I agree."

Eden put on her seat belt and tapped her right foot like she was pressing on the gas. "How fast can this thing go?"

Chapter Twenty-Five

Everybody meant well. Mason knew that. But if one more person came up to pat him on the back, he was going to…what? Scream? He sighed. He was going to accept the thoughtful gesture for what it was.

At Ms. Susan's request, Mason had stayed for the judging. Actually, she had guilt-tripped him into staying, saying she would need a ride home. He had kept his head up. His brother and father had left to check into Blue Hen's only hotel. Mason would go hang with them later. And then his personal pity party could begin.

Ms. Susan had gone to check on her pie. Once again, Eden had won first place. And, once again, because of him this time, she had missed hearing her name called. Cadence, who had disappeared as well, had come in second and people had started posing with her sign.

Lydia and the crew had already departed but not before she told him that the execs had okayed a new reality show for him where he would travel to small towns and renovate bed-and-breakfasts and that his name was trending on social media with the hashtag #ManCrushMason. Apparently, all these women were posting that they accepted his proposal. And even a few men. A Photoshop guru had already redone the video inserting other celebrities. Everyone was making light of what was the most humiliating act of his life, but he knew that came with his career.

For some reason, people didn't picture a celebrity feeling the same things they did. Like right now, he felt like he had been mauled by a tiger, but people still wanted autographs. He stretched his lips into a semblance of a smile but on the inside, he mulled on Eden's questions.

What had he expected? Eden loved being in a small town. And so did Mason. But he hadn't thought about that when he proposed. His vision was that they would return to his home in Ohio. Then today, when Lydia gave him the news about the series offer, he had skipped on the inside and even a little on the outside.

Meanwhile, Eden had just accepted an offer to teach. Expecting her to give that up was plain...selfish. He could see that now.

He massaged his temples. Happy-ever-after was complicated.

Just then, he spotted Eden running to where he stood. She was probably coming back to see how she had placed and if he cared for her at all, the wisest thing he could do was get out of there. You know what? What he could do was give Ms. Susan the keys to his pickup and ask his brother to come pick him up. He'd sort out getting his belongings shipped to him later. He fired off a text to Max then raced to where Ms. Susan was, claiming her prize. He thought he heard Eden calling his name but he wasn't sure. Probably wishful thinking. He was pretty sure he was the last person she wanted to see right now. If ever again.

He handed Ms. Susan the keys and kept moving. The throng slowed his progress as he had to worm his way past the Ferris wheel queue and then avoid tripping into the barbecue line. A toddler crossed his path which brought him to a screeching halt.

The little boy was crying *Mama* at the top of his lungs. Mason had to pick him up. Panting, Mason looked in all directions, expecting to encounter the worried glances of the tot's parents but he didn't see anyone. "Hush, now," he said, as the youngster was now kicking his legs and trying to wriggle out of Mason's arms.

Seeing that he had attracted speculative glances, Mason bellowed out, "Does anyone know this little boy? He's lost his parents."

Everyone shook their heads. "I thought this was a small town," he mumbled, deciding he would hunt for the sheriff.

That's when he felt a hand snatch his arm in a grip that could best be described as lethal. Holding the toddler against him, Mason stared into the anxious eyes of a beautiful woman.

"My baby. My baby. Thank goodness you found him." She scooped the boy out of his arms, laughing and crying at the same time. She spread kisses across her son's cheek before explaining, "I had to use the bathroom and went into the stall, but while I was going, this little one crawls under the door and leaves. I've never been so scared in all my life."

"It's all right. He's safe. You're safe." He tried to leave but the woman wouldn't let go of his hand. She kept thanking him and offering him money, which he refused. But she finally loosened her grip and her son's wails had reduced to sniffles.

Then someone tapped him from behind and once again he found his arm snatched. "Thank goodness, I found you." Eden curled over like she was catching her breath. "I haven't run that fast since I tried out for the track team in high school." Then she registered his companion and her mouth dropped open. "Raine? I didn't know you were here."

Cadence strolled up with Gabe in tow.

"Hey, Eden," Raine said, rocking the baby who now had his head on her chest. He had stuck his finger in his mouth and was now studying Mason from under his lashes.

"You have a son?" Eden said. "I didn't know... You never said."

"He is the cutest," Cadence said.

Raine dipped her head. "Yes, I returned home single and pregnant, to my parents' regret, but my hair salon is doing well, and my mom watches Rocky when I work." She cocked her head at Mason. "He's a handful as this man can attest."

"This is Mason," Eden said, pointedly.

"Oh… Mason." Raine gave him the once-over. Mason watched some kind of silent communication pass between the women. Like they had been talking about him. He rocked back on his heels. This was the perfect opportunity for him to leave but now Eden had a hold on him. Seeing Max scanning the crowd, Mason waved with his free arm. His brother jogged over.

"Hey, I parked by the entrance, so we should get go—" Max stopped midsentence as if mesmerized. His brother scanned Raine's ring finger and seeing nothing there, extended his hand toward her. "Hello, I'm this ugly man's much better looking brother, Max."

Raine batted her lashes and gave him her name.

The two struck up a conversation. Really? Max was supposed to be his escape ride. But even after Mason reminded him about possibly getting a ticket, Max had kept right on talking and flirting. And, Raine had been all with it, the baby now asleep in her arms.

"Gabe, do you think I could hitch a ride with you?" Mason asked.

"No," Eden said, her tone pleading, as if she didn't want him riding with anyone else. But after earlier today, Mason wasn't making any assumptions.

"I gave Ms. Susan the keys, if that's why you're looking for me." He pinned his eyes on Gabe.

"I'm uh—I'm not going out that way," Gabe sputtered out, obviously not about to challenge what Eden said.

Eden led him out of earshot. "Can we talk?" she asked, her

voice warm, like she hadn't run like she was being chased to get away from him within the past hour or so.

Mason's brows furrowed. "I'm sorry but am I missing something here?"

"Yes. I mean, no." She released a long plume of air. "I shouldn't have bolted like that. I was wrong. I made a mistake and I'm going to need you to ask me again."

"Wait, what?" Eden had rattled on so fast that he couldn't be sure he had heard what he just heard.

"I said, I'm going to need you to ask me again."

"You want me to get down on my knees a second time in this dirt and ask you to marry me?"

"Yes." She wrung her fingers.

"What about all the concerns you mentioned earlier?" He made a show of peering at his watch. "Nothing has changed in the hour or so that you've turned me down."

"Yes," she breathed out, raising her voice. "Something has changed since you asked me to marry you." Those words made the others around them grow silent. He felt all eyes on them. "My perspective has changed. I want to be with you, and we will work everything else out." She placed a hand on her hip. "Now, unless you've fallen out of love with me in the past hour, are you getting down on one knee or do I have to?"

"Get it done, bro," Max bellowed out.

"Go for it," Gabe yelled.

Another crowd converged. Seeing she had begun to lower herself, Mason lifted a hand. "I've got this. I swear if you make me humiliate myself…" he mumbled under his breath then pulled out the box and got to his knees, noting how this time his hands shook. "Eden, I love you with all my heart. Will you do me the honor of becoming my wife?"

"Yes, yes, I will." She dashed over to him and lunged into his arms. The applause around them was thunderous but couldn't outdo the racing of his heart.

He opened the ring box and slipped the ring on her finger. It was slightly too big. Mason froze. Not one fairy tale ended with where the heroine's ring didn't fit.

But Eden wasn't concerned. Curling her fingers, she cupped his head and smiled. "It's okay. We'll have it sized. Nothing's going to spoil our happy-ever-after." And with a grin, she sealed that promise with a kiss worthy of a fairy-tale ending.

Epilogue

While the guests waltzed on the makeshift dance floor outside the bed-and-breakfast, Eden snuck Mason inside his suite. "This was the best birthday ever. I can't believe Grams managed to surprise me. But now I want to end the night in your arms." She shimmied out of her blue chiffon dress.

"Were you really surprised?" Mason asked.

"Yes, most definitely." He raised a brow. "Okay, maybe I caught a clue when you and Grams would go silent every time that I entered the room." The last week had been a whirlwind and the happiest she had ever been in her life. "Thanks to the both of you, I celebrated my first birthday in fourteen years. I was shocked to see so many people show up."

"The townspeople of Blue Hen love you, Eden."

"Yes. It was either that, or they came for the free food." There was a barbecue station, an Italian station, a dessert station and even a hibachi station. The chef had performed tricks making the crowd break out into applause.

Her engagement ring sparkled in the sliver of moonlight peeking through the curtains. "I'm going to miss this place."

"We don't have to leave," Mason said, kissing the back of her hand. "I haven't signed my contract yet."

She started working on the buttons of his dress shirt. "No, no. I won't change my mind. Dr. Loft has already found my replacement and I'm excited at the idea of exploring different small towns with you and making the wishes of other bed-and-breakfast owners come true. Besides, Cadence has already moved into my bedroom, so I don't have to worry about Grams being alone."

"Okay, but just know you can change your mind at any time."

"I'm not. I am going to enjoy making love to you in all fifty states and the provinces." She pushed him onto the bed. "Our first stop will be Virginia and I've already found us great housing."

"I've got my surgery scheduled for next month so it makes sense to start there. That way we can keep an eye on Dad while he recovers." He gave her a long kiss, his hands roaming her body. "Thank you so much for suggesting it."

"The thing about forever is that when you're with the person you love for life, you can be flexible. What works today might not work tomorrow but if we're navigating together, wherever we end up is where we were meant to go."

"I like the sound of that."

And that was the last thing they uttered for a long time.

* * * * *

Keep reading for the bonus novella
THE TEN-DAY BARGAIN
by Michelle Lindo-Rice

The Ten-Day Bargain

Michelle Lindo-Rice

MILLS & BOON

Chapter One

Four thousand nine hundred and ninety-five dollars.

Yep. She had read the price tag correctly. That wasn't a typo or a misplaced zero. That was legit the cost of this particular one-of-a-kind couch in Elmer's Furniture Shop. Oh, there were cheaper ones, but it was like the owner had thought of her, Tia Powell, when he'd designed this one. Just by looking at it, she could feel the love that had shaped every angle, every curve. It was cerulean blue, handcrafted and extended into a right chaise lounge. She reached over and rubbed the material with her hand. It was soft, plush and velvety. Her bum would love every minute on this couch. If it weren't for the fact that Elmer had posted a sign saying No Sitting, she would have tried it out.

She rolled back on her heels. That's it. She was buying it. She had just enough on her credit card if she could haggle him down a bit.

Yes, it was over her budget and she would have to eat fried bologna sandwiches for months, but they were her favorite, so eating those sandwiches on this couch would make it all worth it. Speaking of which, she dug into her oversized purse for one of the two sandwiches she had made that morning for her lunch. Her grumbling stomach didn't care that this was still breakfast time. Unwrapping the foil, she took a big bite, a dollop of mustard seeping out of the sandwich onto her white sundress with hibiscus flowers. It was mid-May and the temperature had been in the upper nineties since the beginning of the month. On hot days like this one, sundresses were her preferred attire, and the nearby thrift stores kept her closet well-stocked. She dabbed at the spot.

A lock of her reddish-brown hair fell across her face, landing on her nose. Blowing at it, Tia wished she had tied it back with a scrunchie. Holding the sandwich between her teeth, she moved the wayward curl with the back of her arm.

Ugh. Great, now she had mustard on her nose. She shrugged and reached into her bag for the foil paper. Carefully wrapping her sandwich, Tia wiped her face. Then she made her way to the counter.

She rested a hand on the counter. "Hey, Elmer. I'm here to buy that couch."

He knew which one as Tia had asked about it every time she'd visited the store. The stout Amish man gave her a nod. "It's been six months and one day. The owner hasn't claimed it, so it's yours to purchase."

"Whew. Great. But I'll need a discount as it is used."

"No one has sat in that couch since I made it," he argued.

"It doesn't matter. It is being resold, so that means it's used."

Pushing his glasses up the bridge of his nose, Elmer gave her a look, which she returned. Tia was fully prepared to haggle until he budged.

"I'll take ten percent off," he conceded.

"You can do better than that. No one else but me wants it." She didn't know how true that was but resisted pumping her fists when Elmer shrugged.

"Fine, I'll do twenty percent, *Englischer*. But that's as low as I can go and make a profit."

Perfect. Four dollars under her credit-card limit and so worth the dip in her credit score. Thank goodness Delaware didn't have sales tax. Once she had sold a few pieces of her furniture, she would be able to pay off the balance.

"Awesome—thank you so much." She gave a sweet smile and handed over her credit card. Now, some would think it was irresponsible, but Tia didn't mind taking a risk or, in this case, rewarding herself.

Tia was the proud owner of a furniture-restoration business, Tia's Hidden Gems. After apprenticing under one of the best restorers and crafters in New York, she had moved back home to Delaware to be close to her parents. Clint and Sallie Powell had allowed her to use their three-car garage while she grew her clientele. She had built a great platform of twenty thousand followers on TikTok and her YouTube followers had grown exponentially, so she was going to celebrate by purchasing herself something new. And unusual. Now, if only she would get paid what her male counterparts did, then that would be an added benefit.

"Do you offer delivery?" she asked.

"*Jah*, it's free. I'll have my son get it to you."

Her shoulders sagged. This was all working out. Further proof she was meant to have this couch. Just as Elmer swiped her card, the bell at the entrance of the door jingled. She inhaled, waiting for the approval to go through.

"I'll go see if Joseph is able to load it into his truck for you," he said.

A man entered and rushed over, waving a small piece of paper. "Excuse me, I've got to get to court, but I'm hoping you can help me." He came to stand next to her in front of the window, a waft of sandalwood teasing her nostrils, but with the sun angled just so, she could only make out smooth brown skin, a strong jawline and pursed lips. She couldn't tell his age, but he appeared to be a few years older than her thirty-two years and was dressed in a white shirt and fitted black suit. Not that she was looking.

"I'll be right with you," Elmer said, lifting a hand, then he gave her a smile.

"I've only got a few minutes," the man said.

She rolled her eyes and shifted her body weight so he would have to step back and wait his turn. "Thank you so much, Elmer."

"I'm Judge Maddox Fisher, and I'm here to arrange delivery on the couch for Governor Evangeline Fisher," he continued, taking a quick peek at his wristwatch, a bulky, expensive contraption that she recognized as the Invicta Carbon Hawk. She knew this because her father had one like it.

He tapped his fingers on the desk expectant of an immediate response. He must not have lived in Delaware long or he would've known that the Amish didn't rush for anyone. They lived a simple life.

"I'll go see about the delivery and I'll be right back with your receipt," Elmer said to her, then gave the gentleman a nod before exiting through the back door.

"You might want to come back when you're not in a rush, Judge Maddox." She chuckled and took out her sandwich.

He responded in a polite *mind your business* tone. "Thank you for your suggestion, but I'll be in court all day." He turned to face her, giving her a full-on of his features. He had beautifully arched brows, a well-shaped moustache and a light dimple in his right cheek. She bit into her sandwich to do something besides ogle his fineness while she thought of what else she could say to make conversation. This was her way. Wherever she went, Tia made small talk—in the grocery line, at the bank, etcetera. Her parents told her she had been that way since she'd been a toddler.

She thought she saw interest spark in his eyes and broke eye contact, then leaned against the corner to chew her food. He followed her lead, scooting close to her. Their shoulders touched. She felt a tingle before she pulled away.

"So, what are you here to pick up, Maddox?" she asked to fill the quiet.

He hesitated for a second, like he was debating if she were worth the time it took for him to answer, but then he took off his jacket. She enjoyed the display of muscles under the formfitting white shirt. He unfolded a piece of paper from his jacket and handed it to her.

She gasped and touched her chest, her sandwich leaving a smear. "This is my couch."

"No, it can't be your couch. This was commissioned by my mother, but then she fell sick."

Tia eyed the date of purchase. Six months. Her stomach clenched. "Well, it's mine now. I bought it right before you came inside, and this wasn't a light decision. In fact, this one's right up there with my quitting medical school. I spent months, *months*, waiting and watching, and now one hundred and eighty-one days later, I get to claim it. Fair and square." She snapped her fingers. "In fact, if the couch could talk, it would back me up."

They squared off, while she took another bite of her sandwich.

"What does that even mean?" he asked, shaking his head. "And you quit medical school?"

"I withdrew from the program because I found out I liked taking things that people see as garbage and giving them a second chance." When she saw him squint, she explained, "I restore furniture and occasionally I create original pieces." Then, pointing to the couch, she said, "And I also collect unusual furnishings like this one. You don't see many couches shaped like that with that color. When my sunflower couch dry-rotted and broke apart, I didn't know if I would find another couch that spoke to my heart. So, yes, that couch can vouch for me. In fact, we should let the couch decide." She ran her fingers through her hair. "For every couch, there is a right-ful owner, a direct match, and I'm the yang to this couch's yin."

He chuckled. "That doesn't make any sense. But that doesn't matter. You can't buy it because it already has a home. In my mother's house. Well, mine now," he said, eyes pinned to the mustard on her chest. Her puckered nipples couldn't discern if he was looking at the spot or her chest. This so was not the day to go braless, but in her defense, she had no idea she would meet the first man in three years she was attracted to. A man who wanted her couch.

Tia cleared her throat. "I just did, Maddox." She was en-joying saying his name way too much.

"Since you seem to know my name, what's yours?" he asked.

"It's Tia."

Hearing a door slam behind them, both Tia and the wannabe couch-snatcher spun around.

Her sandwich grazed his shirt, leaving a comet-path streak on his white shirt. Tia placed a hand over her mouth, the paper falling to the floor. "I'm so sorry. I didn't mean to—"

"I don't believe this," Maddox huffed, dabbing at his shirt, spreading the stain further.

"I can pay to have it dry-cleaned," she offered, patting at his chest with her bare hands. She registered his firm pectorals and drew in a shaky breath. "I don't suppose this is helping."

"Nope. The damage is already done." He put on his jacket. "I'll have to go to court like this."

"I'm sorry again." She took the last bite of her sandwich and rolled her eyes. "Do you have to mention going to court every five minutes? And who introduces themselves as a judge?" She rolled her eyes. "That's so pretentious and braggy braggy. Is that all you are?"

"Braggy bra—" He shook his head. "Never mind. I don't think I want to figure out what you mean."

Elmer looked between them before addressing her. "Good

news—Joseph can do it now. He's unloading the back of his truck and giving the cab a good clean out before delivering it." He then handed her the receipt.

"He needs to take it to my place since I'm the rightful owner," Maddox interjected, reaching down to pick up his receipt. "My mother paid close to five thousand for an original design." Maddox jabbed the counter with his index finger. "You selling it is unethical."

Elmer's face reddened and he folded his arms. "You leave my store now, sir."

"You just insulted the Amish?" Tia placed a hand over her mouth. "They are the most honest people I know. I can't believe your gall. That couch has been sitting here for six months, and no one claimed it. Yet you breeze in here putting on airs and degrading the owner. Look at the date. This is six months and one day. He honored his policy. You should have done the same. What gives you the right to do that, and why should we listen to a word you say?"

Maddox's held up a hand. "My mother died. Keeping this couch was her dying wish."

Chapter Two

Okay, saying the couch was his mother's dying wish was a bit dramatic, but Maddox wasn't used to losing. And Evangeline had asked him to pick it up for her a month before she'd died but he had...forgotten.

This task had been a low priority while settling his mother's estate. As she had been the former governor of Delaware, that had been a vast undertaking. Trying to shoulder that with his natural grief made it monumental.

"I'm sorry for your loss," Tia whispered before tucking generous plum-colored lips into her mouth. The fire in Tia's eyes waned, and the light brown orbs filled with sympathy, fanning his guilt. But then he thought about his ruined shirt and stiffened. He would have to go to court with this stain since his spare shirt was in the cleaner's. His mother was gone, but he could almost hear her scolding him for his lack of preparedness.

He cocked his ear. Her authoritative voice was now a whisper, an echo, a sound he couldn't quite catch. He felt the piercing quiet of her absence before dipping his chin to his chest. This couch was Evangeline's last demand—um, request. He needed to honor that, even though it was a ghastly color and unlike anything his mother had ever owned. Maybe her decision to have this built was proof of the aggressive brain tumor which had ravaged her mind and left the once-commanding woman debilitated with pain.

By mutual consent, they walked toward the chaise lounge with Elmer in tow. Maddox studied it from his lashes. He would spruce it up with coordinated pillows.

"You know what, you did have first dibs on the couch," Tia said, interrupting his thoughts, disappointment etched in her tone. "I assume you can repay me for the funds."

Elmer nodded. "Okay, I'll let Joseph know to send it over to your place."

She tucked her purse under her arm. "Do you want my Zelle? Or email, so you can PayPal me?" She rattled off her phone number.

"I'll pay you back," Elmer said before Maddox could respond.

Maddox held up a hand. "No, your policy was fair. I'm sorry for insulting your integrity. I'll buy it from Tia. That's the right thing to do."

"Deduct the cost of the dry cleaning and we'll be even," she said.

He was about to agree to her terms when he realized he wasn't ready part ways with her as yet. She was like a splash of color on his mother's to-do list. And it had been a lengthy one. His mother had been fond of them. Evangeline had even left a list of five potential suitors who would make him a good wife. Imagine that—his mother had named names…dictating his life, his actions, even from the grave. And Maddox had been prepared to check these women out, but then he'd entered this shop and Tia had torn into him, her hair a fiery halo against the rays of the sun. And she had given him a shock, a jolt. Right along with the freckles dotting her olive skin, that pert nose and those succulent lips.

Then she had opened her mouth. She'd ripped into him—calling him pretentious, defending the Amish man and yelling at him to do what was right. Well, that had been CPR to his mundane existence. And her quitting medical school? How brave. How defiant. That part of his nature had been eradicated when he'd been seventeen, a rebellious teen, hiding a smoke in the bathroom on an aircraft—an act that had been sensationalized across social media that his mother had quashed right along with his mutiny. Since then, Maddox had stayed on the straight and narrow, doing all his mother had asked so he could rise above his past and keep from blighting the Fisher name.

Yet here Tia was challenging his status quo. It was refreshing and, truth be told, a turn-on. Maddox wanted to be in her presence a little longer. His mother would not have liked her at all. Too spirited, she would say. Evangeline would tell him he needed a woman whose family lineage went back to John Lewis or Ketanji Brown Jackson. One who dressed well, spoke well, who had pedigree. Not someone who boasted about dropping out of medical school. Not someone who turned her nose up at him and asked, *Is that all you are?* The answer to that question burrowed its way into his complacency, unsettling him. It was a question that brought to surface a dissatisfaction he had been feeling for months but couldn't put a name on. His mother's death had made it real to him how life was like a flower—shining bright one day and wilted on the next.

So when Tia moved toward the door, he couldn't see her depart. Not just yet. "Why don't we share it instead? The couch, I mean. And instead of paying me back for the dry cleaning, I'd—I'd love a taste of your bologna sandwich," he blurted out, his heart hammering while he waited for her to respond.

That delicious mouth of hers formed an O. "Wh-what do you mean?"

At that point, Elmer flailed his hands. "*Englischers!* I'll leave you both to figure it out." Another patron entered the shop, and Elmer went to talk to him.

"You said yourself that we should let the couch decide," Maddox continued. He strung a plan together on the spot.

"Yeah. You can have it for ten days and then I'll have it for ten days. Then after that, we'll decide."

A lot could happen in twenty days.

"That is…ridiculous."

He averted his gaze to cover his embarrassment, his disappointment and rubbed his chin. "You're right. It was an outlandish suggestion. I understand." Then he looked at his watch. "I've got to get going."

"Yes, yes." She giggled, cupping her hands. "Hear ye, hear ye. The not-so-honorable Judge Maddox Fisher is on his way to court."

He jutted his jaw. "You don't know me well enough to jest with me. Actually, you don't me at all." He stomped toward the door.

"You don't know me either," she said. He paused and cocked his ears. "I'm sorry to make fun of you, but it was too easy to resist." Maddox turned around, and she lowered her lashes. "That suggestion is the kind of ridiculousness I live for. I'm not about to turn down my chance to rest my bottom on those luscious seat cushions." He swallowed at that visual image. "Now, how will we move the couch back and forth between us?"

"I'll hire movers," Maddox said.

"Great, then that's settled." Tia stuck out her hand. "Here's to the first ten days, and I'll make you the best fried bologna sandwich of your life for lunch today to seal the deal."

"That sounds like a plan."

They joined hands. Electricity shot from his body to hers, and they released hands, both taking a step back. Neither acknowledged what they'd both felt.

Maddox gave a small laugh to break the awareness, deciding not to mention that he'd never had a fried bologna sandwich. Well, not that he remembered. His mother had done her best to develop a sophisticated palate. He hadn't grown up eating hot dogs or munching on potato chips. Maddox had had charcuterie boards filled with imported cheeses and fresh fruit. Evangeline had dined in the finest restaurants and hired chefs to prepare their meals. His mouth was ready to try something new.

And by something new, he didn't mean just the sandwich.

"Let's sweeten the deal. Bring your sandwich, and if I like it…how about a kiss instead to seal the deal?" he tossed out. His heart thumped. Now where had that come from?

Her eyes went wide. But of course, she was quick with the comeback. "You're saying if you like my bologna sandwich, I have to kiss you. Make that make sense?" She didn't pause a beat. "Your ego is off the charts."

"No, this isn't about my ego. I'm saying if I like what you give me, I get to kiss you, the most remarkable woman I have met in a long time."

She gasped. Tia must have no idea just how desirable, how beautiful she was. She puckered those luscious lips before she looked down at her feet. His compliment had thrown her off. "I guess…" Her cheeks reddened. She sounded breathy, unsure, but she hadn't turned him down and her eyes had a new curiosity.

"So, I'll see you later?" He held his breath. At her shy nod, he exhaled. "Awesome. I just need your address."

Tia wagged a finger, her eyes alight with mischief. "Nope. Not giving it to you. I'm pretty sure you can find me if you need to, *Judge*."

Chapter Three

Of course he was going to find her. He had to. That was his thought as he stood in the courthouse, waiting by the elevator. Though their encounter had been brief, Tia's fiery, carefree spirit had stirred something within him that he hadn't felt in a long time. Excitement. Talk about a strong first impression. Maddox was used to dating women so polished that every word they spoke had intent and everything about them was carefully planned, down to their wardrobe and hairdo. Tia didn't appear to be like anything like that. She seemed like a grab-and-go, off-the-rack kind of girl, which intrigued him. He had watched her jump into her pickup and noted the name of her business and email address. She would be easy to locate, though she needed her phone number painted on or a QR code.

After a quick internet search, Maddox had secured the address for Tia's Hidden Gems. It appeared to be in a residential area not too far from the courthouse. Perfect.

Wait a minute… That might not be her home address. He snapped his fingers. Elmer! He would know Tia's address since the couch would be delivered that day. Maddox called the shop owner, hoping Elmer would give him Tia's location, especially if he offered to cover the costs for the delivery.

Turned out Elmer didn't mind and was a romantic, saying he knew Maddox and Tia might have made a love connection.

He didn't have to pay delivery fees, but Elmer was grateful Maddox would be there to help his son with lifting the couch.

He slid his phone into his pocket and tucked his jacket close, conscious of the mustard stain. A mother and her teenaged son came to stand beside him. Maddox gave a nod in greeting, making sure to avoid eye contact, having learned early on not to engage with potential defendants in one of his cases. But of course, he couldn't control what he heard.

"You couldn't make it through the final weeks of school without causing me grief. A few months of doing what you supposed to, and you would be graduating this fall. But no. Where are we? In court." Her voice rose. "I had to take time off from my job because you decide to be a wannabe drug dealer selling vapes in school."

Maddox froze. Something about this mother's tone caused him to flashback to himself as a teen. His mother had given him a severe tongue lashing behind the scenes for smoking on that plane. By the time she'd been finished, he had been crushed and in tears. Maddox had never done anything to displease her again. And Evangeline had never let him forget what he had done.

The teen cleared his throat.

"I'm sorry, Mama," he whispered. "I was trying to come up with the cash to pay for my prom tickets."

"By doing something illegal, Jefferson?" she ground out. "Spare me the act. At the rate you are going, you gonna end up behind bars just like your no-good daddy. Looking just like him too. Right now, I don't want to see your face."

The young man face drooped at those words, his blond hair hanging on his shoulders. Despite the boy's wrongdoing, Maddox felt his heart squeeze. No one should hear degrading words about their father. Not when you shared some of the same physical and personality traits. Even if what the mother had said about the boy's father was true, she should keep those thoughts to herself. Who knew the potential lifelong damage she was inflicting on the young man's psyche, his heart. Maddox was pretty sure this mother meant nothing but good things for her child, but this was so not the way. Correct him, yes. Degrade him, no.

Maddox clenched his jaw to keep from saying something. This wasn't his concern, he reminded herself. His mother had been tough on him, and look at how good he had turned out. But she hadn't bad-talked his daddy though. If anything, Evangeline had felt Maddox would never live up to Ashton's legacy. Or hers. That was why she had steered him away from social work—by refusing to pay his tuition—and encouraged him to go into law. Once he'd passed the bar, Maddox had worked for a few years as a public defender before he earned this promotion as a judge. What rankled was that many believed he was here because of good old-fashioned nepotism and not because he had earned it. Yes, as governor, his mother had nominated him but he had been confirmed by the senate because of his merit.

The elevator came and creaked open.

Maddox gestured for the two to enter before him.

The woman stomped inside, her brows knitted, her chest heaving, while her son had his chin dipped to his chest. They pressed the third floor, which was the same destination as Maddox. He held the door open as others got into the car.

He spared them a sideways glance, making eye contact with the youth. For the second time that day, emotions slammed his heart. Those brown eyes were filled with a bleakness that made Maddox want to…help.

The elevator dinged. They were at the second floor. Most exited.

The woman wasn't done. "Word is we have the Iron Fist of the courts as our judge, so you're doomed." Her voice trembled.

Maddox stiffened. He was the Iron Fist, a nickname bestowed on him because he tended to give the maximum sentences for those found guilty. When a reporter had asked him to comment on his moniker, he had quipped, *If you do the crime, get ready to do the time*. His mother had been tickled by it, loving the write-up in the local paper. Seeing her proud of him for once had egged him on, and he had adopted the cloak of the Iron Fist with honor.

The elevator whooshed open. He hadn't even realized they were at his destination.

"He's going to toss my baby in jail." Now the mother grabbed her son close, his head towered over hers. Her body racked with tears as she sobbed openly against his chest. Maddox could see her love and her fear. They shuffled out the elevator with Maddox behind them.

That was it. He wasn't about be late again. Ever. By the time he'd arrived, there had been no empty spaces in parking lot behind the courthouse, so he'd had to park in the front of the building. If he hadn't been behind schedule, he wouldn't be witnessing or hearing any of this.

All of a sudden, Tia's words from earlier echoed in his mind. *Is that all you are?* Maddox entered his chambers and donned his robe while his mind churned. *Was* that all he was…an Iron Fist? He shrugged. Whatever. What did Tia know? Maddox had a job to do. His reputation made sentencing easier for him. He didn't have to agonize over what was fair. He just executed judgment, reducing the defendants to a case number.

When they were very much human. With parents and loved ones who cared about them. But he blocked it out because… Maddox paused as realization dawned. All his actions had been about him so he didn't have to care. Because caring would make his decisions infinitely harder, gut churning at midnight, wondering if he'd done the right thing.

He touched his chest, remembering that underneath this

robe of justice was a stained shirt, an imperfection none would see. But just because they couldn't see it didn't mean it wasn't there. The stain that made us maintain our humanity, to keep from casting the first stone, and—dang. He was getting too deep with this analogy. If he continued, he wouldn't be able to do his job today.

His *j-o-b*. That had to be his focus. *You are the Iron Fist.*

Maddox squared his shoulders and walked into the hushed courtroom, his long strides sure. He steeled himself against searching the crowd for the mother and son, his eyes falling on the cup of pens on his desk. He blinked before scooting the cup close to him, the scraping sound made louder by the microphone on his desk. Nine pens—blue, black, pink and three yellow highlighters. He took a moment to arrange them by color, returned the cup twelve inches from his gavel, then signaled for his first case to be called.

For the next few hours, Maddox stayed true to his persona. In fact, he was even more swift with his rulings. The quicker the verdict, the faster he could get out of here. For today the robe felt like bricks on his shoulders, his conscience. He couldn't wait until they broke for lunch.

During a short recess, he sent Tia a text. Having a phonographic memory, he remembered her phone number from when she had recited it earlier.

Hello, Tia. This is Maddox. My mouth's ready for some of your bologna.

The minute he hit Send, Maddox regretted penning such a flirty message. She might think he was only interested in a hookup. There was no way he could unsend the message because he saw the read receipt. He held his breath. It was a couple of agonizing seconds until his cell vibrated.

I hope you can handle it.

All right. All right. All right. He exhaled. She was giving as good as she got. He could get with that. The bailiff was about to call the final case before lunch. So, he sent her another quick text and put his phone away, though there was nothing he could do about the silly grin on his face.

However, when the court clerk called the docket for the next case. Jefferson Monroe. His smile dissipated. This had to the mother and son he had overheard earlier.

Sure enough, the mother and son from earlier stood. The woman wiped her face, her sniffles loud in the otherwise quiet room. Maddox could see the young man shivering. Maddox's heart went out to Jefferson, who kept his eyes lowered to his feet.

Maddox beckoned to the attorneys to approach, told them the situation, then recused himself. He reassigned the hearing to Xiang Li, a fellow judge and his best friend, who could hear the case the same day. Knowing Xi, he might exact a hefty fine and move on. But Maddox couldn't shake the image of the young man from his thoughts.

Tia's question plagued his mind.

The mother's words plagued his mind.

The desolation on the teen's face plagued his mind.

All he could see was himself at that age—a little lost but not a bad kid. And Tia's slogan on her pickup, *Making New Beginnings from Old Roots*, took on a new meaning. He could give this boy a new beginning, a second chance. Yes, it was the same old story for many young men with fathers behind bars, but Jefferson didn't need to end up in the same destination. And he could help… Before he could second guess himself, he sent Xi a text.

Give that Jefferson kid community service with me instead of a fine.

Who is this? And what have you done with the Iron Fist?

Ha ha. Twenty hours. Every day after school for two hours. His time starts tomorrow.

Sounds good to me.

Doubt whether he had done the right thing raced through his mind. But his heart felt light. He had done something out of his norm but very much a part of his true character, and it felt good. Real good. At lunch, Maddox dashed out the court-house. He had no idea what he was going to do with Jefferson when he showed up tomorrow, but Maddox was resourceful—he would think of something.

Because this was a small city, he wouldn't be surprised if this verdict made the papers. However, that was the least of his concern. He had a date to catch, and he had no intentions of being late.

Chapter Four

If she could stop cheesing, maybe the owner of the high-end furniture shop would take her seriously. At least that was what Tia told herself while trying to talk Fred, the owner, into paying her what she was due. After she'd left Elmer's store, she had driven to her first of three stops to sell the lamp, the chest and the coffee table she had spent hours refurbishing. She had repurposed these finds into exquisite pieces, and this lamp was worth more than the two hundred dollars Fred was offering. But she couldn't stop the grin pulling her lips wide, especially thinking about that kiss. So though Fred was low-balling her, as always, it did nothing to damper her good mood.

Because she had met a man.

A bit stuffy. Suit and tie. But that preposterous deal of switching out the couch had increased his placement on the desirability scale. Judge Handsome was sitting at a seven.

"I'll head on down to the other store," she said. "Send my TikTok followers to Joyce's instead." Tia maintained eye contact, hoping he didn't call her bluff. She needed this sale.

He chewed on his tobacco leaves before saying, "Two fifty. That's my final offer."

See now. She should take her lamp and leave. Wait to see what Joyce had to offer. Or at best, demand more. But then she thought about the couch she had just purchased and the fact that Joyce was out of town. It was close to the middle of the month, and her credit card payment was due soon. So, she rolled back on her heels and dipped her head. Fred gave her a look of smug satisfaction. She gritted her teeth, knowing she should not have backed down.

And that was what she told Charlie Knox, her best friend since middle school and her assistant, when they met up in the garage about an hour later.

"But yet you always do," Charlie said, blowing a tendril of her hair off her forehead. She was applying a coat of dark blue paint with white trimming on a shelf Tia had found in a yard sale. "That lamp would easily sell for a thousand dollars in New York. You owe yourself an apology."

"What?"

Charlie paused and raised a brow. "Yes, for taking less than you deserve."

Tia exhaled. "A sale is still a sale. At least that's what I tell myself."

Charlie returned to her painting. "No, no sale is better than accepting peanuts when you should be getting almonds. Actually, make those hazelnuts."

Tia bit back a smile. "That's a weird analogy, but I know you mean well for me." She went to inspect Charlie's work.

"You know what I'm trying to say." She did, however, believe her friend was biased although Charlie would say she was just proud. Charlie bumped Tia's shoulder with her arm. "You are the bomb-dot-com at what you do. You worked under the best in New York, and your skills are off the charts. But unless you take a stand, you'll never be compensated as you should be. I bet if you were a man, you would get more."

All Tia could do was nod. There was no denying the truth in Charlie's statement. She had been there and seen Fred plunk down dollars on subpar work all because the other dude was a golf partner.

She went over to her pickup truck—admiring her freshly

painted *Tia's Hidden Gems*, her slogan, *Making New Beginnings from Old Roots*, and her eagle logo—and took out an end table she had found on the side of the road. It was a light brown color and had some water damage, but she envisioned a chic bar cart. Maybe she could put that for sale online. Charlie had started up a website, and they had begun receiving orders. Just last night she'd received a huge request to restore some Italian pieces dating back to the early 1900s, adding her own personal flair. The owner, Lorenzo Romano, was willing to pay her some serious bucks to restore them and planned to have them on display at a local museum in Maryland. The event was three months away. That meant a lot of late nights and the potential for even more business.

Tia had asked for twenty-four hours to respond. When she told Charlie, her friend's eyes went wide.

"That's a no-brainer. I don't get the hesitation," Charlie said, surveying her finished product with a sigh of satisfaction.

Standing at opposite ends, Tia and Charlie hoisted the shelf onto a dolly and rolled it to the back of the garage. Then they lifted and placed it a few inches from the wall. "For one thing, space. Space is an issue," she huffed. And for another, she wasn't sure she could meet his expectations for such a big task where she had all creative control. She had to choose the fabric, the paint and the design. All of that. She turned and swept her hands across the open space. In one corner of the garage, there were boxes with paints and tools of various sizes. In the other corner was her woodcutting table and even more tools and paints.

Charlie placed a hand on her hip. "I so agree. But you could easily solve that problem if you put a down payment on the storefront and start up the DIY classes I've been telling you about. I know your training videos on TikTok have been a hit, but doing something in-person is a great way to connect with the community—your direct purchasers."

"I knew you were going to mention that," Tia said, picturing the large space that had been up for rent for a good six months. "I keep telling you that I'm not…ready."

"What you mean is, you're scared."

"Not scared…exactly." She pulled on the hem of her sundress. She had been so sure she'd wanted to be a doctor, and look how that had turned out. If she failed at her business in this small city, everyone would know. It might even make front-page news. And she would be crushed.

"Then if you aren't scared, why are you hedging?"

She averted her eyes and changed the topic. "Um. I… I bought the couch." She could feel her face warm even more under the hot sun because she knew that Charlie was going to disagree with her decision.

"How could you?" Charlie asked. "You can't afford that."

"I can if I stay here." Tia walked over by the AC vent to cool down. She had an idea of what her friend would say next.

"When your parents allowed you to use this space, it was agreed that it would be for a maximum of two years. Now it's going on three years, and you're comfortable." Charlie lifted her chin. "Frankly, you're taking advantage of them."

"Wh-what?"

Charlie wagged a finger. "Don't go acting like you're shocked about what I'm saying. Your mom and dad had you later in life, and you are the *a-p-p-l-e* of their lives. There's nothing you want that they don't give you. And that is the truth on Mary had a little lamb."

Despite her friend's serious tone, Tia snorted. "I can't believe you repeated that line from the nursery rhyme with a straight face."

"Whatever, it was a meme and everything," Charlie quipped. "You get the point."

"I do." She sighed. "And you're right. The last thing I want to do is usurp my parents' kindness. They are the best—"

"But you are spoilt, with a *t*, girl. You need to move out of this space so your folks can park their cars in here."

Guilt tugged at her heart. Clint and Sallie had had her in their midforties after trying for several years. Charlie was right. They gave her anything she desired if they could. And to herself she could admit that she did take them for granted. As a child, they had supported her every whimsy—ballet, swimming, guitar, gymnastics, cheer. She had been pretty good at them, but the minute she'd failed to master something, she'd quit. With ballet, she couldn't jeté the highest, so she'd stopped. With swimming, she couldn't master the breast stroke, she'd stopped. With cheer, she hadn't made the first round, she'd stopped... Her life had a distinct pattern.

As did her relationships. She bit her lower lip. The few men she had dated (yes, she was picky) had all found her too... intense. Like she'd been trying too hard to please them instead of just being herself. But she was past being someone she was not. The next man she met had to accept her just as she was.

"I should not have bought the couch."

"Well, to be fair, you needed a new couch. The one you rescued from the trash was beyond repair."

Tia smiled. Even when she was chewing her out, her friend was loyal. She lived in a one-bedroom apartment above a pizza store in downtown Dover, and the owner had put out a worn-out leather couch for trash day. Of course Tia had rescued it. But nothing she did took out the smell of grease, onion and garlic from the fabric.

"But I didn't need to get that particular one." No matter how perfect, how spectacularly it would fit in her apartment. She loved collecting unusual things—her coffee table was a puzzle top and her toilet-bowl cleaner was a gigantic cherry— and her friends and family helped her habit.

"Yep." Charlie plopped into a chair and wiped her brow. "I know why you did it though. That couch is the perfect complement with the rest of your—" she cleared her throat "—unique decor." Reaching into her jeans rear pocket, she pulled out her phone. "I'm about to order lunch. What do you want?"

"Not sure yet. I might be doing something else for lunch."

"Oh?"

She smoothed her dress. "I'll just say that couch is the reason why I might have a lunch date. That is if the judge figures out my address."

Charlie leaned forward, her eyes bright. "Date?"

"Well, yes. Sort of." She could feel her face warm.

"Why didn't you start off the convo with that? I can't believe you had us chatting up about business when this is so much juicier."

Tia bit back a smile. "I met him when I went to purchase the couch. He's a cutie. Came off a little cocky at first, dropping that he's a judge, but he is actually the first owner of the couch." She explained about Maddox's mom's last wish and told how they'd ended up setting up a date. "But he seems like he has a good sense of humor."

"That's a must for anyone who stands a chance of being with you."

"I can't be in a relationship right now. I have to focus on getting this store off the ground. You know that." Even as she said the words, her heart protested. Her work was not comfort at night.

"Yes, but you can relax and have fun."

The image of her new acquaintance teased her mind. "That is what I'm aiming to do." Although there was nothing relaxing about the way her heart was beating. She wanted to see him again.

Charlie rubbed her hands together. "I can't wait to meet this guy. What's his name? I want to look him up."

"Maddox Fisher."

Charlie's mouth popped open. "Wait, Maddox Fisher as in *the former governor of Delaware's son* Maddox Fisher? Oh snap. He is beyond fine and a definite upgrade from anyone you've dated before. I'm pretty sure I've seen photos of him with the POTUS on the White House lawn."

"Yep. The one and the same."

"All right, all right. I see you, I see you. You doing big things." Charlie rubbed her chin. "Maybe we can go on double dates if he's good rubbing shoulders with the common folks."

"Whoa." Tia lifted a hand. "Talk about too much, too soon. I'm making him a fried bologna sandwich since I ruined his shirt with mustard."

Charlie's brows rose. "Pray tell."

Tia's cell buzzed before she could. There was a text from a number that wasn't in her contacts.

Hello, Tia. This is Maddox. My mouth's ready for some of your bologna.

Dang. That sounded suggestive, made her remember it had over a year since she had been kissed. Or held. Or anything else. Partly by choice, partly because she hadn't met anyone who captured her interest. She was quick with the comeback.

I hope you can handle it.

Only one way to find out. See you in thirty.

When she read that, Tia placed a hand over her mouth and stepped back. "Oh my goodness. He found me. He found me." Seeing Charlie's puzzled expression, Tia quickly filled her friend in. "I told him since he was this big fancy judge, he shouldn't have a problem locating me, and he did."

"Girl, stop. You didn't! This is beyond romantic. This could be your frog," Charlie said, referencing their all-time favorite movie, *The Princess and the Frog*. Unlike many other girls who sought their prince, Tia and Charlie had been all about finding their frog. Because the frog had to have serious game for the girl to even put her lips on him in the first place.

"Have you seen him? That man is no frog. He's too regal to be content sitting on somebody's lily pad. Maddox is most definitely a prince, but I'm nobody's princess, so this is far from romantic." But it very much was, and her inner girl was jumping up and down. She glanced at her watch and squealed. "I've got to go. I don't want him to beat me home."

"Yes, 'cause you're, like, five minutes away from the court-house," Charlie said. "I wish I could be a fly in your hair when he sees that you live above a pizza shop."

She patted her curls on instinct. "Whatever. Pretty sure he puts his pants on one leg at a time like the rest of us." Tia refused to be intimidated by their difference in socioeconomic status. "Besides, I love my apartment and I'm close to everything."

"Well, I'm impressed. Look at you, all calm and secure. I'd be a bumbling mess if it were me. But then again, you're used to hanging with the fancy folks in Manhattan, so I guess it's all good."

Tia just nodded. Charlie usually rambled her way full circle in a conversation. With a wave, Tia hopped into her pickup and dashed toward downtown Dover, her hands gripping the wheel. Her parents had balked at the neighborhood, even offering to buy her a condo or a small house, but she had declined. They already did a lot for her, and it felt good to do this for herself by herself. There was a lot behind the store designated for residents, and she wanted to be there to direct Maddox to park in that area instead of in front of the pizza store.

Right as she pulled into the parking place, Elmer called to say that his son was on his way with the couch. Talk about perfect timing. She was going to enjoy her lunch with Maddox on that very couch.

It just so happened that both Maddox and the truck arrived at the same time. Once she showed them where to park, Tia went up the flight of stairs in the rear of the building to enter her apartment. Along the wall hung some of the paintings she and Charlie had done at the local sip and paint. She took a moment to steady one of the canvases at the top of the steps. Standing at the landing, Tia glanced into the small kitchen on the left, relieved she had washed her dishes before leaving that morning. When she was working on a piece, she neglected her chores—which was pretty much often, since she hated doing the mundane tasks. Tia had redone the countertops with butcher-block wood, then stained them an espresso color, which popped against the white cabinets. She had left the bread out along with the condiments when she'd made her sandwich that morning.

Tia then gave the bathroom next door a quick check. She quickly brushed her teeth—because you never know—and lit a lemon-scented candle before scurrying down the hallway. She closed her bedroom door on the right before traipsing down the hall and into the large common area that served as both her dining and living space. She then opened the blinds on all four of the huge windows for some natural light inside and gave her coffee table a quick dusting. By then, Maddox and the other man entered holding the couch.

"Where do you want it?" Maddox asked, not sounding winded or even the slightest out of breath. Impressive. He was now a solid eight.

"Against the wall should be fine," she said, handing Elmer's son a generous tip. "Thank you." With a nod, he bounded down the stairs leaving Tia and Maddox alone. She had never brought a man into this space. And Maddox made her tiny apartment feel like she was inside a sardine can.

They both faced each other and chuckled awkwardly. Beneath them, they could hear the clamor of the utensils, the strong smell of coal-fired pizza, but they stood eyeing each other. Tia clasped her hands in front of her, her heart rate spiking while she tried to think of what to say next. There was a magnetic pull between them that drew her in. She stepped toward him before she realized what she was about to do and broke eye contact.

"Welcome to my place," she said to fill the quiet, the underlying tension.

Maddox looked around her living area. She had some old records and an antique turntable stacked into a corner and some paints and other gadgets in another. She wasn't the neatest, but she was clean.

"You have a nice, cozy spot."

"Yeah. It's not the Ritz, but it does have pizazz." It occurred to Tia that Maddox might've been nervous too, but she dismissed it. He was used to being around society's elite. There was no way he was experiencing the slightest unease around little old her. Her heart, on the other hand, hammered in her chest. She smoothed her sundress to discreetly wipe her sweaty palms and gestured to the couch. "Do you want to sit?"

"Okay."

"Hang on—let me put my touch on this." Grabbing the stack of colorful pillows off the floor, she arranged them on the couch and stood back to admire her handiwork.

Maddox sat, then sighed. "I've got to say this couch is comfy."

She rushed over, plopped next to him and squirmed. "I agree. It does feel nice on my butt." Too late she realized how that might seem like she was bringing attention to her derriere. She felt her cheeks flame and covered her mouth. "I'm sorry. I didn't mean to—"

"It's quite all right." His hand reached over to touch her

face, and he scooted close. Her eyes dropped to his lips, and desire stoked, catching her off guard. He opened his mouth to ask, "Do you think we could…?"

She leaned closer. His masculine scent teased her nostrils. "Could what?" she asked, her breath shaky. If he was trying to kiss her, then he was going to be disappointed because her answer would be no. *Liar.* Okay, but that was all she would allow. Nothing more. The fact that she had to have this internal pep talk told Tia she really liked this guy.

"Um, do you think we could eat?" he asked. Then his stomach rumbled loud. "I didn't have time to make my breakfast smoothie and…you talked about this fried bologna sandwich. Plus the pizza from downstairs is really making me hungry."

She blinked, processing his words, before jumping to her feet. "Oh, yes, of course—I was caught up with…with the couch. Let me go get started because I imagine you've got get back to court, or whatever you do." She skittered toward the kitchen, swallowing her disappointment. Oh, goodness—that was so embarrassing.

Tia retrieved her grill pan and turned on the stove before giving her hands a quick wash and slipping on a pair of clear plastic gloves. She worked with chemicals all the time and didn't want to risk any contamination on her food. Then she poured a small bit of olive oil and took the beef bologna out of the fridge along with lettuce, tomato, cheddar cheese, mustard and mayonnaise. She placed slits in the three slices of bologna before putting them in the pan, finding the sound of the sizzle satisfying. Her mind strayed to the man in the other room. Maddox must've thought she was thirsty, sitting there ogling him like that. She'd promised the man lunch, nothing more. She had no business thinking about kisses. But to be fair, Maddox was the one who suggested the lip-locking in the first place… *If* he liked her bologna sandwich.

She licked her lips then frowned. Dang, they felt dry and

chapped. Like she could grate cheese on them. Her color must have come off when she'd brushed her teeth, and being in the sun hadn't helped. As soon as she was done, she was going to rub on some Vaseline.

Tia had just retrieved two plates from the cupboard when a shadow fell by the entrance.

"Do you need any help?" Maddox asked. "I followed my nose in here."

"Um, sure." She couldn't meet his eyes. "You can wash the tomato and slice it. The lettuce is already prewashed." He washed his hands, then did as she'd asked while she spread a dollop of mayo on two slices of bread and mustard on the other two slices of bread. She then flipped the bologna slices. They had a nice black sear, and her mouth watered. With him in the small kitchen, they couldn't work without their bodies touching. An arm brush here or a hip bump there and her senses were on overdrive. She was sweating, and it wasn't just from the heat.

"So does today count as the first day?" She told Maddox to place lettuce and tomato on the bread slices that had the mayo.

"Yeah, that's fine. I'm pretty confident that the couch will choose me, so it's all good."

"Oh, you got jokes." He chuckled, while doing as she asked.

"I'm laughing but very serious. You see how nicely it fits in this space." Tia ripped a slice of paper towel to lay the bologna on it to drain the excess oil before putting three more slices in the pan. Then she assembled his sandwich, adding the cheese before cutting the sandwich in half. "Voilà!"

"This looks so good," he said.

"It will taste even better if you eat it on the couch." Maddox gave her a look of skepticism. She flipped her bologna, her mouth now watering for a bite. "Grab yourself a bottle of water from the fridge and head on out there."

He took out two bottles of water. Aww. How thoughtful. That warmed her heart. No. Not her heart. It was just a thoughtful gesture.

"I don't know about eating this on that couch. I can't chance the couch getting ruined," he said.

With a wave of the hand, she shooed him out of the kitchen. "Live a little. It will be all right."

Chapter Five

It was definitely not all right with him. Eating should be done around a dining table, not on a five-thousand-dollar couch. But he didn't want to come off as arrogant, and according to Tia, he needed to live a little.

Maddox perched at the edge of the couch, holding his plate close to his mouth, and took a careful bite. Tia had no such qualms. She came next to him, her plate in her lap, and there was mayo all over her lips and chin. Plus new mustard stains on her dress. Maddox bit back a smile. He had no idea how she ate so messily. He was halfway finished with his sandwich and had remained unscathed.

"I've got to admit this tastes way better than it looks." He wiped his mouth with a piece of paper towel. Then he placed his plate on top of a coffee table that had puzzle pieces on the inside, careful not the touch the flower planters shaped like Chinese takeout boxes. "The mustard gives it just the right kick. I could easily eat another of these."

"I told you. Making these are my specialty. I can make you another if you'd like." She bit into her sandwich.

"No, I'm good. I don't want to get too full and fall asleep on the bench later."

She giggled. "Have you ever done that?"

"No."

"Pity. That would have been interesting. I'll have to come visit your courtroom."

"I don't know about that. You would be a distraction, and I have to stay focused in court."

She raised a brow. "Now I definitely have to come."

A small piece of bologna fell onto her chest. Really? "You sure you don't want us to eat at the table?" Sweat beaded his forehead at the thought of her messing up the couch. And more of her dress. Why wear white if you're dabbling in paint and sandwiches? Before leaving the courthouse, Maddox had stopped to wash out the mustard stain out of his shirt. It was faded and had left his shirt wrinkled, and that imperfection bothered him. If it weren't for the fact that he was eager to see Tia, Maddox would have gone home to change.

"Nope. I'm good." She wiped her chest, scooping the bit of food with her paper towel. Then she gave him a sheepish grin.

"You missed a spot," he whispered, reaching over to wipe her chin. His finger grazed her mouth and a different hunger sparked. He wanted to feel those lips against his. Her eyes were shuttered, so he had no idea what she was thinking or if she was experiencing what he was, but all he knew was he was very aware of this woman. When they had been in close proximity in the kitchen, Maddox had relished every accidental skin-on-skin contact. Even now, sitting close to her made him feel energized.

He couldn't be the only one. "You feel it too, don't you?" he whispered, his voice deepening.

She nodded. Maddox was glad she didn't deny it, didn't play coy. She touched his chin and cocked her head. "Is it weird that I feel so comfortable with someone I just met?" Then she splayed her hand across his chest. "Like I just have to make physical contact. I want to touch you." She snorted. "Maybe it's the couch. Maybe it has some mystical powers and entranced us."

He was sure she could feel his racing heart under her palm.

This attraction was sudden and forceful. "I don't think it's the couch. I think it's us."

"Yeah, but if it weren't for the couch, we wouldn't have met. Sorry—I make jokes when I'm nervous…or ridiculously attracted to men I've just met."

He met her eyes. "How many times has this happened to you?"

She cleared her throat before pinning him with those earnest brown eyes. "You're the first."

Maddox touched her curls. "It's a first for me too." He leaned toward her, lifting her chin with his index finger. "If it's all right with you, I'd like to kiss you."

"Go ahead. You might be my frog." She tilted her head back.

Did she call him a frog? If he wasn't mistaken, weren't girls all about finding a prince? Maddox asked her about it, and she said the frog had more game than the prince or something like that. He wrapped his arms about her and placed his lips to hers, intending to be gentle. After all, they were very much strangers and he didn't want to scare her. But the minute their lips touched, she released the most tantalizing moan and cupped his head, her grip tight. Maddox was happy to oblige by deepening the kiss.

The next thing he knew, she had straddled him, taking charge. She peppered his neck with kisses and ground her hips into his. This was no kitten. She was a she-cat, claiming her territory, hungry to be fed, and he basked in this discovery. Heat coursed through his body as red-hot fire ignited between them. He was more than happy to indulge her. Their mouths dueled, and he delighted in her lack of restraint, her energy. He fought the urge to ravage her, to touch and discover every secret part of her.

Tia growled and sucked on his neck. He groaned. "Yes, yes," he urged. Whew. Talk about intense.

Wait. If she kept sucking, she might give him a love bite. He couldn't go back to court with a hickey on his neck. How would it look if the Iron Fist had a red splotch in court? Maddox pushed on her shoulders lightly. She ceased instantly and looked at him.

"Sorry—I got carried away. This is so not like me. I don't even know who I am right now." She averted her gaze and slid off his lap. If she felt evidence of his desire, she didn't acknowledge it.

"No. No, don't apologize." He released a long breath. "I just need a minute to compose myself." Man, was he sorry he had to go back to court. He closed his eyes and tried to think of wet paint, an iceberg, anything that would cool his ardor so he could return to work with a clear head.

Her curls were now matted to her forehead. She wiped her face. Then she gasped. "Oh, my goodness, I don't know what came over me just now." She covered her face with her hands, her eyes on his. "What must you think of me? We just met and…"

"And I was right there with you. A willing participant. And the only thoughts I have are that I love your boldness and your fire."

"Yeah, but if you hadn't stopped me, I would have gone all the way."

Her honesty was a massive turn-on. He lifted a hand. "Okay, you have got to stop talking, or I won't be able to function the rest of my shift. As it is, I don't know how I'm going to be able to concentrate on my cases."

"For real?" she asked, hopeful. "So, it's not just me? I'm not a prude, but I'm also not the kind of girl that gets this… expressive on a first date." She mumbled. "At least not normally."

Date? That was what this was? Well, they had shared a meal together, the very definition of a date. So, yes, technically this was very much a date. "No. This is very much a 'we' thing and quite new for me." He glanced at his watch. "I have to get going, but can I call you later?"

She gave a shy nod and pulled her sundress over her knees. "If you want to."

"Of course—you think I'm going to let this couch forget about me?"

As he intended, she smiled and perked up before saying, "Listen, if I'm being honest, I'm not looking for anything long term. I have too much going on with my business to get it to thriving to devote to the demands of a relationship. Honestly, I'm not good at them, so I don't even want to try. My friend says it's because I suffer from perfectionism. Who knows?" She sidled into his space and placed a hand on his rib cage. "But I wouldn't mind exploring more of this physical attraction between us if you're game." She nibbled his ear. "I think you'll find what I'm offering mutually satisfying until it fizzles out."

"Wait. Just so I'm clear. You're offering me a short-term, no-strings affair?"

"Yep, my only caveat is that we're exclusive. I'm not into bed-hopping. As a matter of fact, if you agree, we can end when the couch is with its rightful owner."

This was one of the best days he had had since his mother's passing. Maddox was more than happy to date her for a short period. He could get this attraction out of his system and then give one of the women on his mother's list consideration. This was a win-win. He would be happy, extremely happy, and he would also fulfill his mother's expectations. "Deal. I can get with that."

"Great. Let the good times begin."

The thought that anything that sounded too good to be true probably was came to him, but Maddox dismissed it. This was a rational transaction between two consenting adults, and he was looking forward to seeing how this all played out. No matter who got the couch—and he was sure it was going to be him—his body was going to thank him. He had better stock up on protection. Maddox had a feeling he was going to need it. Lots of it.

Chapter Six

The next day when she wasn't caught up in a haze of desire, Tia regretted her spontaneous proposition. Maddox had texted that he was on his way, bringing lunch, and here she was by the window facing the parking lot, fretting over her rash decision. She wasn't a *love 'em and leave 'em* sort of gal. In fact, she was the very opposite. Her last boyfriend had called her intense, breaking up with her via an inbox message. All because she'd tried to be the girl that she'd thought he wanted, when, as Charlie had pointed out, she should be herself.

Well, that was how she had been with Maddox. Herself. And apparently the true her offered herself on a platter like she was fish and chips, without requiring any commitment.

But in her defense, look at him. *Look at him.* The man was a slice of cinnamon bun with white icing and pecans sprinkled on it. No, he wasn't a slice. He was the whole bun, and she couldn't wait to sink her teeth into him.

Whoa. She had to get a handle of this fascination. Tia had spent the entire night tossing and turning, thinking about Maddox, craving his touch and more of his kisses. She didn't understand how something so new could be so potent, consuming every bit of her brain space. While she worked on filming the couch to post to her social media account, she thought about him. While she sanded a piece of wood, she thought about him.

You know what, this was too much. Maybe she should call

him and cancel. But maybe yesterday was a fluke, and today when she saw him, things would be normal, even-keeled. She might see a flaw—maybe he had bad breath, stained teeth, or…something that would make him more normal, less other-worldly and temper this attraction a notch. Then they would share a laugh, go their separate ways and he would decide to let her have the couch as a good gesture.

His sleek car entered the parking lot and parked next to her pickup. She watched as the door opened and he got out. He shook his leg, adjusting himself, and she was a goner. Maddox reached into the back to lift out a brown paper bag. Her heart was now pitter-pattering in her chest, and she wanted to check out that package, see what was in his lunch box—and she wasn't talking about food.

She took a moment to spot-check her sunburnt-orange dress—no food stains this time—and then went downstairs to unlock the door. The first thing he did when he saw her was snatch her close and kiss her until her toes curled. Literally.

"I've been waiting to do that all day," he said, shutting the door behind him.

Unsure how to respond to that, particularly since she felt the same, Tia spun around to head up the stairs with him in tow, acutely aware that he was right behind her. Maddox had dressed in a similar outfit as yesterday, except the shirt was the color of peridot, and it looked brand-new. Like Tiana's dress? As in, *The Princess and the Frog*? No. No, she was reading too much into the color of a shirt. That color choice had to be a coincidence.

Unless he was silently communicating that he was her frog? Naw. She was being too fanciful.

Once they were settled around the table, at Maddox's insistence, she exclaimed when she saw what he had brought for them to eat.

"Caviar? On a random weekday?"

"Yes. The owner was gracious enough to box it and have it delivered it from Rehoboth Beach."

She leaned back into her chair. "So you mean to tell me somebody brought this to you from one hour away?"

He nodded. "It was nothing. The owner and my mother go way back. He knew her before she became governor. He used to send my mother specialty dishes all the time." He helped himself to a serving. "Even though they don't open until late evening, he was happy to send this my way."

"You know that's not normal, right?"

"It is for me" was the simple response. He motioned for her to try the caviar with crème fraîche and toast points.

Her first taste of the delicacy was as she'd expected—fishy. But it was mild, fresh and had a buttery taste. "Not bad," she said. Then after she had helped herself to another serving, she lifted her shoulders. "Definitely can't beat my bologna sandwich though."

Maddox quirked those fine lips of his. "I can say your bologna sandwich is classic."

"Sometimes I air fry them or add potato chips to the sandwich. There's nothing like it."

He cackled. "What else do you make?"

"My pastrami sandwich will make you sing soprano, and I add a cranberry sauce to my turkey sandwich that will make you think you are floating on clouds."

"You know, I once heard that self-praise is no recommendation." His eyes were teasing, but his tone held just a sliver of disbelief that got Tia excited.

She raised a brow. "Is that a challenge?"

He wiped his mouth. "I guess it is."

"Hmm…" She tapped her chin. "Let's do a friendly wager. On most days, there are a group of boys playing ball by the park. I imagine they get real hungry. How about we each make or bring them lunch and we let the kids decide whose is best?"

His eyes lit up. "I like the way your mind works. You got the synapses in my brain popping. What's the prize for the winner?"

She grinned. It was nice to know he had a competitive spirit. "How about the winner gets the couch?"

"We already set the parameters for the couch. You get an A for effort though."

"All right. You can't blame a girl for trying." She shrugged. "I'll think of something else, unless you come up with something."

"Oh, I already know what I would want."

Something about his suggestive tone made Tia very interested in hearing what he wanted. She opened her mouth to ask when her cell phone buzzed. It was the client who wanted her to restore the Italian pieces. She had promised to give Mr. Romano an answer today. Tia decided to let the call go to voicemail. She would email him later. Immediately after that call, she received another. This time it was Fred. Thinking about her recent sale, she accepted the call. Since she was eating, Tia put the phone on speaker.

"Hey, Tia. I got someone here who wanted a pair of lamps. Something original. They liked the one you designed, but I already sold that this morning." He lowered his voice. "Made a good profit too."

Hmm… Interesting. So he'd lowballed her, then turned around and made good money off her work. Tia felt like telling him she didn't have anything that would suit him. But she needed to maintain a good working relationship with her vendors and remain professional. Plus this was money. She noticed Maddox had also finished his meal and was now gathering the refuse, including hers, and mouthed a thank-you.

"I actually do have a pair that I found and refurbished. I can send you a pic."

"Yes, I'll hold."

From Fred's conspiratorial tone, Tia surmised he was set

to make some serious bucks. Muting the call, she addressed Maddox, who had returned with a cloth to wipe down the table. "Sorry about this. I shouldn't be too long."

"No worries. Handle your business. I can wait." His low baritone made her insides rumble. He returned to sit across from her, but now their knees touched. Tia searched through her photos and sent Fred a couple choices. She could see Maddox looking at her pictures, his eyes going wide.

"Okay, I'll present these to her and be in touch," Fred said, ending the call.

She placed her phone on the table and looked at Maddox. "Thanks for understanding."

"Not a problem," Maddox said. "You are so talented." He gave her a pointed look. "You could just refurbish another couch and give me this one."

"Hey. Hey. Good one. As an artist, I believe in supporting other talented people, like the Amish. So, I plan on keeping that couch."

"Like you said, I had to try."

They shared a laugh. She enjoyed their smooth conversation, their banter. But then thinking of Fred, she sighed. "Hopefully Fred will pay me what I'm worth this time."

"This time?" A brow arched. "What do you mean?"

She told him about the lamp, what he'd paid versus what it was worth. "And I've got receipts." She showed Maddox similar projects and how much they went for in New York.

His mouth hung open. "Wow. You probably should have walked instead of accepting. What he gave you was insulting."

"I know. I know. My best friend, Charlie, said the same thing. But I feel like since my business is fairly new and I'm establishing my rep, I can't demand more."

"Humph. I doubt it has anything to do with that." He glanced at his watch before rapping his fingers on the table. "Do you have those lamps that you showed him here?"

She nodded. "As a matter of fact, I do. I finished working on the stain last night to make sure both lamps were an exact match in hue."

"How about we try an experiment. I could be wrong, but let's see what he offers me if I went in with them."

"But I just sent these same pics to him."

"Okay, give me something else, then. Let's see what he says."

She pulled on her lower lip. "All right. I have a centerpiece that I redesigned. Let's see what happens."

"Great. I believe this has everything to do with your being a woman. I could be wrong, but let's see what he says."

Just then Fred sent her a text message: I'll give you $600 for the pair.

Turning her phone so Maddox could see, she fumed. "I spent at least thirty hours working on those lamps. What he wants to give me works out to be about two dollars an hour. Not that six hundred dollars isn't a decent offer, but he is going to sell them for at least four times that much."

"Agreed." Maddox jumped to his feet and held out a hand. "I don't have to be back in court until later this afternoon, so let's go down there and see what he says to me."

Tia boxed up the lamps and gathered her purse. She hoped Maddox was wrong about Fred. Because she was going to be all up in that man's face if Maddox was right. In the meantime, she would sit back and admire those pectoral muscles on full display as Maddox entered the store.

Chapter Seven

Maddox held his head high when he entered Fred's establishment carrying the box with Tia's centerpiece. Tia was waiting in the car while he executed his plan. He looked around, appreciating the high-end pieces that appeared to be one of a kind. He noted there were three customers inside milling about, and judging by their mannerisms and apparel, they could afford whatever Fred demanded.

A man, he assumed to be Fred, was behind the counter ringing up a purchase. Maddox saw him pick up the phone and look at it several times. Probably waiting on Tia's response. Maddox pretended interest in some of the pieces but stayed close enough that he could get a feel for the man in question.

He eyed a lamp boasting a Sold sticker and went to investigate. There was a tiny sticker price of twelve hundred and fifty dollars. If this was anything like Tia's lamp, that man had made a thousand dollars. Anger boiled. He hated knowing Fred was taking advantage of Tia like this.

Then he heard Fred tell a woman standing to the side, "That will be eighteen hundred apiece. The artist studied in New York under the best, and her work is guaranteed."

Maddox tensed. Fred sounded like he was talking about Tia.

"Wonderful. I'm happy to wait."

Maddox curled his lips. So, Fred was going to make at least six times what he was paying Tia, all the while bragging on her skills.

Fred lifted a hand. "I should have an answer for you in a few minutes. She is supposed to text me back so you can get a look at the lamps in person."

"All right. I'll go take another look at that imported mirror in the back room in the meantime."

Once the woman had ventured off, Maddox approached and placed the box on the table. "Hello. I'm new to the area." He gave Fred a fake name. "I wanted to show you a sample of my goods. If you like what I have, maybe we can do business together."

Fred shook his hand. "I'm always looking for new people to work with. I have a select clientele who shop here weekly, searching for something that catches their eye."

"I believe you'll like what I have."

Maddox took out the centerpiece created out of pine cones and placed it on the table. Fred's eyes went round. He picked it up. "This is exquisite," he said. "You have a gift. A gift I think my clients will pay good money for." Fred sounded enthusiastic. "I'm pretty sure I can sell this." Placing the centerpiece down, he said, "How about I give you eight hundred dollars?"

Eight hundred dollars for pine cones? Wow. Maddox covered his shock at the offer and added steel in his tone. "I think you can do better."

At that very convenient moment, the same woman approached, and when she saw the centerpiece, she exclaimed, "Frederique, I simply must have that. I am going to a housewarming, and I know Cecilia would drool over that piece of art."

Fred mopped his brow. "All right, I'll see what I can do. If you'll allow me to finish with this gentleman, I'll work out a price with you."

"One thousand dollars," Fred said, through gritted teeth. Maddox tapped his fingers on the table. He wasn't sure if he should press for more. But his moment of hesitation worked in his favor. "Fine, I'll add another hundred, but I can't do anymore as I need to make a profit. It costs money to keep my clients happy."

"Done." Within minutes, Maddox left the store with the cash in his pocket and Fred's business card.

As soon as he was back in his car, Maddox filled her in, telling her all that had transpired. She squealed at the cash. "I can't believe you got that much for that piece." Then she sat further in her seat and touched her chest. "So, it is because I'm a woman that he did this."

"Um, well, I don't know if this proves that without a reasonable doubt, but it does show your designs are worth more than you think. So, request more."

"You sound so lawyerly," Tia said. She grabbed his cheeks and smacked his lips. Her spontaneous action made his lips tingle. "Thank you! This experiment was a success," she continued. "I'll be right back." She directed him to pop the trunk and hopped out of the vehicle. Then, tucking the boxes containing the lamps under her arms, she marched inside the building.

Maddox wanted to go in with her, but he figured if Tia wanted him to tag along she would have asked. While he waited, he pulled up his schedule. He had his next case at 2:30 p.m., so he had to get back to court. Jefferson was supposed to show up for his first day of community hours. Maddox found he anticipated seeing the young man more than he did his court cases.

Within minutes, Tia was coming back out the door, practically skipping. Her face shone and she held up a stack of bills. "Twenty-four hundred dollars. I just made a bucket of cash, and it's all thanks to you."

"No, no, it's your work. You were just compensated as you should be."

"Yes, it is," she whispered. Her voice hitched.

"Now, I've got to admit, I don't get how someone would plunk down that amount of cash on pine cones."

"Well, it makes sense when you think about how I had to search for perfect matches every day for about seven months. Each pine cone had to be of similar height and size. Then, I had to clean them, shape them, hand paint each one before creating the centerpiece. That was my fourth attempt to create the vision I had in my mind. That was no easy feat."

"Wow. You were still undercharged."

She nodded. "Exactly." Then she shifted the topic. "Maybe I'll use this money to pay down on my own storefront. Then I won't need a middleman."

"You don't have a storefront?" Maddox asked. Before she could respond he said, "Oh, you must be selling online, correct?"

"No, I'm in my parents' garage. I have a huge TikTok following, but I don't sell what I make online. I give free tips and classes to show others how to do what I do."

"Say what?" Maddox shook his head. "You need to stop doing that pronto. You are throwing away the potential to earn money. If you record the classes and charged a nominal fee, you would have a win-win situation."

"Okay, have you been talking to Charlie?" She laughed. "This exercise today shows me that you are both right." She waved the cash. "This is great incentive for me to get on it starting later today."

"I'm glad to be of help." Maddox left the lot to return to Tia's apartment.

"Thank you, Maddox. I'm glad I met you. So glad."

Her raw, sincere sentiment warmed his heart. It was good to be with a woman who spoke how she felt without filter. That made him do the same. "You are so welcome. It feels like longer than a day that I've known you. I couldn't stop thinking about you last night."

"Me neither. It might be too soon to say this, but this short friendship will be good for me. As well as the benefits. Because to be clear, that's the kind of friends we will be. Just let's get to date three first, 'cause a girl can't be too easy."

He cracked up. "Understood. I'm looking forward to said benefits, and there is no rush on that. I like being in your company. And yes, I do believe this friendship will be good for me as well. No matter how long it lasts." He was willing to bet it would be past the timeline they established because though it had only been about thirty hours or so, he knew he would always be up to kicking it with her, even without the sex. Maddox had never done that before—just be friends with a woman. Not that he wasn't about to indulge in the benefits because, um, she was fine as ever. But unlike other women of the past, they were already engaging in meaningful conversation. Something about her made it easy to share of himself.

Maddox pulled in front of her building. They got out and stood in front of the pizza store. He had exactly twenty minutes to get to the court, but he had to share this with her. "I've got to tell you, when you asked me whether being a judge was all I was, that question stayed with me. I did something in court I had never done before. I offered to help mentor a young man who deserved a hefty fine, and that makes me excited to get to work today. More excited than I've been in a long time."

Her eyes teared up. "Wow. You have a chance to impact people's lives, make a real difference. I'm glad my question was a catalyst for that."

"Yes, it was."

She wrinkled her nose. "It feels like we're becoming actual friends. Do we want to murky that by getting physical?"

"Girl, speak for yourself," Maddox said, swooping her into his arms and kissing her, releasing all the banked passion. When he was done, he saw her eyes had darkened.

"I guess that answers my question," she said, breath shaky.

"I definitely need more of this." She bunched his shirt with her fist. "How about you come over later?"

"How about you come to my place instead? We can have a late dinner. That will be our third date."

"I like the way you think."

Her voice was deep and sultry. He couldn't wait to hear how she sounded when he made her come. He bet she was a screamer, and he couldn't wait to see if he was right.

Chapter Eight

Sweet, delicious agony. The man had made love to her with a single-minded precision that had made her bellow at the top of her lungs.

After she'd enjoyed a light dinner of filet mignon and a tossed salad, Maddox had kissed her senseless before taking her upstairs to his bedroom. He had showered and changed into a green shirt (also looked new) and a pair of khakis. She hadn't gotten to ask about his choice of garment. She hadn't even gotten to ask if Jefferson had shown up and how the community service had gone. Not even under oath could Tia recall if Maddox had eaten actual food because he had been too busy feasting on her. So, by the time his lips had trailed her entire body, undressing her along the way, she had been begging, begging him to give her release. She had never acted so wanton in her life. *Dang.* And here she was, thirsty for more.

Now she lay twisted in the sheets, her body convulsing with pleasure while Maddox prepped her body for a second release, and she was just letting him do this thing. She had sweated out the silk press she had spent hours getting ready for their date, and Tia lamented not wearing the fancy Victoria's Secret undies instead of toting them in her bag. But in her defense, the men she had been with before had been more...reserved. Not Maddox. He was like a bull and she, his matador. She had guzzled down an entire bottle of water in between sessions.

If she were a *kiss and tell* type, she would have *plllleenttty* to tell Charlie. But baby, she had to savor this one, keep it to herself. Because when they were done, she was going to turn up her kinky meter, try out a few new things. They were going to need shades to face each other tomorrow morning. For sure.

But neither would have regrets.

"You ready, princess?" he asked.

"Yes," she squealed, squeezing her toes together. She was losing control, and his chortle told her he was enjoying making her squirm. "I'm a get you back," she huffed out. "As soon as…I…can…think. It's…on."

"I welcome it," he said, sheathing himself with protection. And once he was done making her scream in botched Spanish—who knew those lessons in college would come in handy—she made good on her word. She took charge and made the brother sing. Yep. She sure had.

Now he drank his water while sweat dripped off his body. She folded her lips inside her mouth to keep from gloating and went down the stairs to warm the meat, placing a double portion of salad on his plate. Because after their lovemaking session, he was in need of serious sustenance.

Tia returned to his bedroom and eyed the fine Adonis, white silk sheets around his hips.

He balked when he saw her overloaded plate. "I should get out of bed. I don't want to mess up the linens."

"Then eat carefully," she advised before handing it to him. Then she said cheekily, "I'm ravenous myself." While he ate, she loved on him, giving him a love mark in a place that only the two of them could see before she straddled him and led them both to a final release.

Afterward, they rested side by side and just talked. Talked about their childhoods. Their experiences. Their fears. He told her all about his experience on the airplane, losing his father and feeling like a failure at meeting his mother's demands.

She told him about her wonderful parents, who spoiled her and gave her everything, which made her afraid to truly go out on her own. She hugged him, he hugged her, then she made him a grilled-cheese-and-tomato sandwich, and they played Bananagrams in bed while they talked some more. The conversation flowed from one subject to the next with ease until Maddox looked out the window. He gasped.

"The sun is almost out. I can't believe it. I haven't bleached like that in years." He placed a hand to his forehead. "I won't be able to stay awake in court today."

Tia yawned and stretched. "Then take a day off."

"A day off?" he repeated, brows furrowed.

"Yes… Let's get some sleep, and then we can do the lunch challenge by the park." Her eyes began to flutter closed. Sleep was like a Mack Truck over her eyes.

"But… I have never called off. I have a schedule that I follow."

Say what now? Her eyes popped open, and she turned to face him. "Never? You've never played hooky?"

"No. I keep my commitments."

She gave him a playful shove, then dipped her hand lower to explore what was beneath the sheets. "Well, it's time you changed that. Just call off. They will find a replacement."

"A replacement?" He brushed a wayward curl off her face.

She kissed his chest. "You do know you're replaceable, right? The court will still run if you don't show up."

"I know that… But… I work from nine to seven every day. It's my routine." He rubbed his chin. "Jefferson told me he was going to be at football practice, so that's covered. And I was only going to be in session for a half day. I suppose I could get someone to stand in. I've done it for many others…"

"You are thinking too hard about this." She cracked up. "Just do it."

"All right." He swung his legs off the bed and sat up, his

back to her, and reached for his phone. She missed him—yes, she knew how that made her seem when he was mere feet away—so she hugged him from behind. Tia listened in as he placed the call.

Maddox fumbled through the words. Wow. He really had never done this before. The thought that he would do this for her made her feel…special. "Okay, email me the instructions. I'll put in my leave request online." Once he was off the phone, Maddox went for his laptop and put in his hours.

Then they wrapped their arms around each other and fell asleep. Tia's last coherent thought was that she could stay like this forever…

"Well, I guess it's safe to say that this contest was a tie. Because these kids tore into your sandwiches and devoured everything off my charcuterie boards." Maddox folded his arms and leaned against the iron fence of the park.

They had slept until close to three o'clock that day. Tia had jumped up, and after a quick shower and change at her place, they had returned to Maddox's house since he had ordered all the condiments they would need and he had a much larger counter space. He had showered and changed into a light green tank and black basketball shorts. Okay, unless, green was his favorite color, she figured Maddox had bought those shirts after she'd told him she was waiting to kiss a frog. Maybe that was his way of showing her he was her frog. But since she wanted to be sure, Tia would wait to see what he wore the next time she saw him.

His kitchen had everything and then some for what she would need, even though his pantry and refrigerator were about bare. She had to admit that he had her beat on presentation, but the boys had raved about how great her turkey sandwiches tasted. She felt extra good because the cranberry relish had been a hit.

Now they worked together to bag the empty wrappers, plastic bottles and scrape the remnants off the boards.

She patted her stomach, her blue sundress swaying in the tiny hint of breeze. "I have to agree. This was a wash. Not only was turkey the best, but I had to sample everything off your boards twice." She went to sit by the picnic table and jutted her chin toward the boys, who were back at playing basketball. "But those kids were happy as all get out when we showed up with this food."

Maddox tied the trash bag and placed it in the receptacle. "Yeah, I heard a few of them saying they hadn't known what they were going to eat for dinner, so this was a blessing." He sat next to her and gave her a playful nudge. "Thank you for convincing me to play hooky today. I'm having fun."

Tia nudged him back. "The day is still young. How about we catch a movie together?"

"I'm game, but I say we stay in and curl up on that couch. We haven't visited her today."

"Oh, so the couch is a her?"

"Yep. Look at all those smooth curves. Elmer had to be thinking about his wife when he made that."

Tia scrunched her nose. "I guess… I like that plan." He had the bigger television screen though. She almost suggested they pack the couch in her pickup and haul it over to his place. Almost. But she had seven more days before it was his turn, and she couldn't give that up.

"I'll drop you off and then go grab our meal." He leaned over to give her an impromptu kiss on the cheek.

Well, she could do one better. Tia pressed her lips to his. The moment they made contact, their tongues engaged in a tango and neither appeared to want it to end. It was the whistling behind them that brought them to their senses.

"Let's skip dinner and go try out that couch," she whispered into his ear.

"You think that couch can hold up? We can be, ah, quite vigorous in our lovemaking." He looked around as if worried about being overheard, which made her smile. He was cute when he was self-conscious.

"It will be fine."

"As a matter of fact, I think we should go to my place. I don't want the owners of the pizza shop hearing all that ruckus."

"We can be quiet. It's all good."

Chapter Nine

As he pushed his legs into his jeans later that night, Maddox grinned when he heard Tia snoring behind him. She looked so cute curled up on the couch with her little nose in the air and her mouth puckered open. He retrieved a blanket from her linen closet and covered her with it, tucking it around the sides.

Tia had been so wrong. They had been so loud that the owners had had to tap on the ceiling and yell for them to calm down. Her inner she-cat had emerged and had lapped on him while leaving scratch marks on his back. That was going to hurt so good come morning, and he was there for all of it.

He slipped his cell phone into his pocket and tiptoed down the stairs to let himself out, locking the door behind him. There was a light shower and he dashed to his car, avoiding mini puddles on the gravel in the lot.

He felt the emptiness surround his heart like a heavy fog.

Once he was in his car and heading back to that huge, vacuous house, Maddox admitted he hadn't wanted to leave. It was like he had left a core part of him back in that apartment above the pizza shop. Whoa. He slammed on the brakes, and a car honked behind him. His heart pounded, his hands felt clammy and he broke out into a sweat. Had he fallen in love with this woman? He pressed on the gas and kept going while he contemplated that question. He couldn't be in love. It had only been days—days since they met. It was unreal that he would even be debating this possibility. Who in their right mind fell in love after three measly days?

That was unheard of.

Unless the switch to his heart had tripped the very moment he'd seen her. Maddox slammed the steering wheel with his fist. No, no, no. This couldn't be happening. Not now. Not when Tia wanted a no-strings affair.

Although if his father were to be believed, Ashton had fallen for Evangeline upon first sight. Oh no. Was this some rare genetic curse? Like father, like son? His dad had died when he'd been a teen, and that had been one of the few times that he had seen his mother heartbroken. But she had pulled herself together and continued her race to become governor. While Maddox had tried to handle his grief by sneaking a ciggy in the airplane restroom.

If he were a smoker, he would take a draw right now because his nerves were shot. But his mother had hated the habit. It was the one vice of his father's that she hadn't been able to convince Ashton to give up.

Entering into his home, Maddox eyed the mail his housekeeper had placed on the console table in the foyer. There were the usual bills that he had automatically deducted from his account and also an official embossed invitation to the HBCU Week Awards Gala held in June. This was an annual celebration of historically black colleges and universities held in Wilmington that helped young people attend college. Last year, they had raised 343,000 dollars, and Maddox planned to donate a large sum on his mother's behalf. Maddox had already registered for the event, and that the time he had intended to take one of the women from his mother's list. But now there was only one person he would want by his side, and he wasn't sure if they would even be an item still by then.

Dang it. His chest tightened.

His cell vibrated. It was a text from Tia.

You left? (sad face emoji) You want me to come over?

Yes, he did. Maddox heart raced. How was he going to act the same around her when he had messed up like this? He fired off a quick response.

I'm pretty tired. I won't be good company.

We can just snuggle.

Good grief, she was making this hard for him. But he needed tonight to process before he faced her again. So as much as he wanted to, Maddox wrote: I'll catch up with you tomorrow.

Then he waited several tense seconds while the bubbles floated across his screen. But all she said was Okay.

Great. Now he felt like an ogre for blowing her off, which led to a restless night and an even worse day in court. Tia hadn't texted either, which he understood. He would've done the same if it appeared as if someone was giving him the cold shoulder. When Jefferson arrived for his community service, he must have picked up on Maddox's grumpy mood. Maddox had arranged for the young man to shred some old files, and the teen had given him a furtive glance before scurrying off.

Maddox tried to do his job with his new mindset of being a more caring judge, but it was easier to be the Iron Fist when his mind was otherwise occupied.

This falling-in-love thing gnawed at him. He even googled several variations of *Can you fall in love after one day? What is the success rate of love at first sight? Is there such a thing as love at first sight?* during his lunch hour. On and on he researched, and the answers were pretty much the same.

It depends.

That was it. Also if the experts were to be believed, the

odds of two people feeling the same level of emotion at the same time were rare. One usually had to play catch-up. The question was, could Tia fall for him in time? Which led him to look up *How to get someone to fall in love with you.* That sounded pathetic, but he had no experience with love and how else was he going to find out what to do? A quick scan of different answers and suggestions made Maddox conclude there was no rushing love. One couldn't force it either.

He sighed. Until Tia caught up—and he hoped she would—he was stuck with this torture all on his own. When he left court that evening, it had been twenty-four hours since their last encounter, and Maddox missed her so bad, his heart hurt. He was absolutely miserable.

His cell phone alert went off. It was the restaurant in Rehoboth letting him know that his reservation had been approved. Maddox slapped his forehead. He had put it in the day before his revelatory feelings. However, it gave him a good excuse to contact Tia. Maddox got into his car and sent her a text, praying she would answer, though that was more than he deserved after ghosting her all day.

Hello. How's the couch doing?

A few seconds later he saw a picture of the couch hit his inbox, followed by, She's still standing. Relief seeped through his body. Tia had answered. She wasn't mad that he had blown her off yesterday. But then a thought occurred. Of course she wouldn't be upset. Tia was carefree. For her, this attraction between them was exclusive fun that would eventually run its course.

Not so for him. Especially not if he took after his father. Evangeline had been the only love of Ashton's life, which meant Maddox was doomed. But he had to see her. He sent another message.

Can I see you today? His stomach muscles tensed. A part of him wished Tia would snap off at him for not reaching out.

Sure! XOXO, she texted. How agreeable she was being. He hated it.

Gritting his teeth, he asked, Hungry?

Yes.

How about I take you out to dinner?

Cool.

Battling fluctuating emotions of happiness while feeling bummed at this one-sided love, Maddox stopped at home to take a quicker shower, dressing in a lime-green dress shirt and slacks before driving to Tia's apartment. His stomach felt like rocks lined its inside, and he wasn't sure if he would be able to eat. But the minute she opened the car door and he saw her face, his nerves settled, his insides calmed. She was dressed in a black cocktail dress and kitten heels. And she smelled amazing—like champagne and strawberries. He gave her a tentative smile, yearning for a taste of those red lips, then began their drive.

"Hello," she greeted, sounding chipper, placing her shawl in her lap along with her bag. Her smile was bright, and unlike him, she appeared to be well-rested. While he was in torment. "What's on the dinner menu?"

"Escargot," he offered, sneaking a glance her way "Escargots de Bourgogne to be exact. We're going to a French bistro." He struggled to sound unbothered. But he was bothered at how normal she sounded. That ripped at his confidence.

She swung her head his way. "You expect me to eat snail?" She patted her belly. "My stomach is real sensitive."

Despite his inner turmoil, Maddox laughed. "Don't knock

it till you try it. The delicacy is well prepared and cooked with garlic, herbs and butter." His voice sounded strained to his ears, but Tia hadn't seemed to notice.

She rolled her eyes and settled in for the forty-minute drive. When they arrived at La Fable, they were led to a private area. The table was dressed with white linens, and there was a bottle of bubbly cooling in an ice tin.

"This is nice," she said, then thanked him for holding out her chair. "You go ahead and order whatever you're having for me."

He put in for the escargot as an appetizer and then two orders of the truite amandine.

While they waited for their meals, the owner of the establishment came over to greet him and asked Maddox for a photo. Maddox complied, but he was happy when it was just him and Tia again. He needed to make up for lost time and maximize every minute in her presence.

"How was your day?" he asked to make conversation. Tia wasn't her usual talkative self. She might've been waiting on him to explain his mood shift yesterday. And he would as soon as he thought of what he could tell her besides the truth.

When their appetizer arrived, she eyed the escargot resting in a bed of herbs with a smirk. "I don't know if I can do this."

"Just follow my lead." Maddox picked up the tongs and special forks needed to eat the delicacy. He demonstrated how to retrieve the meat, and she followed suit.

"To answer your question, my day was pretty good, actually. I made an appointment to check out a storefront tomorrow." She eyed the meat on her fork quizzically before popping it into her mouth.

"That's great news." He waited for her reaction.

"Oh my. It tastes just like chicken."

Maddox cracked up and had some. "I have to agree." For a beat, neither said anything. He hated how formal things were with them and knew he had to clear things up. "Last night, I had a lot of things on my mind and I was exhausted. I love being around you—please know that." To him, his words didn't make sense.

She bit on her lower lip. "It's all good. I understand that I can be…intense. I get it if you needed a break from me." Her evident insecurity made him feel like an even bigger heel. "But I figured you would contact me at some point about the couch."

"Did you hear what I just said? Yes, I do want to see the couch, but I love being around you. All the time. If I could take you to work with me, I would. I wish I could put you in my pocket and take you with me everywhere." Maddox saw her shoulders relax and her eyes fill with relief. He reached over to take her hand in his. "Yesterday was all about me. I was in my feelings about something. Please know that. You are a wonderful, remarkable woman, and if anybody thinks you're intense, it's because they can't handle you. They can't handle your passion. I want all you have to give." *Especially your heart.*

She then gave a wide genuine smile which made his heart somersault. "Whew. Okay. I thought I scared you off wanting to be around you too much."

"Nope. I'm the one who's scared." *Scared I won't be able to let you go.* Maddox cleared his throat. "I have a gala to attend in a couple weeks. I wondered if you would want to come with me?"

"I'd love to," she breathed out.

"Awesome. It's formal wear."

"Oh, so I get to play dress-up." Her excitement thrilled him.

He then went on to explain the event. "My mom attended an HBCU, as did I. We have given them a generous contribution every year since its inauguration. This will be my first year doing this without her, so…" Maddox missed his mom. He drew in a deep breath, surprised by the extent of the gash in his heart. This was a wound that would never heal. He could go days and be all right, and then, bam—grief would strike him when he least expected it. Evangeline had been tough, more so once his father had died, but she'd meant only the best for him.

Tia gave his hand a squeeze. "I'll be by your side the entire time." They finished the rest of the meal, and the drive home was filled with laughter and joy. His heart sang. He returned to her place and walked her upstairs. She opened her door and turned to face him.

He looked up at her from under his lashes. "May I kiss you?"

"Yes, and you can do more than that if you'd like." He kissed her and then some. And later, as they lay snuggled in her king-size bed, Maddox dreaded the moment he was going to let this woman, this light walk out of his life. She was a butterfly and didn't want to be pinned down, and since he loved her, he had to allow her to be who she was. Even if doing so broke his heart.

Chapter Ten

That Thursday, Tia paced outside the storefront, waiting for Maddox to arrive. She had ditched her sundress and had chosen a pair of black capris with one of her newly designed company T-shirts. She had pinned her hair up in a ponytail and slapped on a pair of sunglasses. Maddox had texted her that morning to say he wanted to go with her when she toured the place—even though there wasn't much to see.

Charlie pulled up and parked next to Tia's pickup and got out, giving Tia a hug. Charlie was dressed in a tank top and biking shorts along with some sneakers, having just come from the gym.

"So, I take it everything is all right with you and your new boo?" she asked. Tia gave an exultant nod. When Maddox had turned down her invitation to hang, Tia had called Charlie in panic mode. Charlie had told her to calm down, pointing out that Maddox could just be tired, like he'd said, and that Tia should wait to see if he contacted her the next day.

It had been a long day until his text had hit her cell phone, but Tia was glad she had taken Charlie's advice. Because yes, all was right in her world. Maddox was a lot of fun, and she was enjoying his company.

"I can't wait for you to meet him," Tia said.

"Yes, I'm excited to meet the man who has captured your heart."

Charlie's words hit her with full force, and she took a step back. "Wh-what?" she asked, breath shaky.

"I've never seen act this way before about anyone. You are smitten with this guy."

"*Smitten* is a strong word," she sputtered, her heart in denial. "Yeah, he's cool and I like him, but this is very much a short term situation. We're both kind of using each other until we figure out who gets the couch. Then after that we go our separate ways. As friends." That knowledge ripped her gut, but Tia refused to explore why.

"Yeah, y'all can keep telling yourselves that this fling is all about some inanimate object." Charlie chuckled. "Because what's going on with the two of you is very much real." She wagged a finger at Tia. "I don't know this dude, but I know you. You wouldn't sleep with him if there wasn't something stronger lurking underneath. I know it hasn't been long, but I don't think it takes forever to recognize your soulmate. This is your frog."

"Are you listening to yourself?" Tia shook her head. "I think you're mistaken. My sleeping with Maddox had everything to do with lust, not love. This is attraction, nothing more." But her words lacked conviction.

"I think you need to rewatch *The Princess and the Frog*." Her knowing singsong voice made Tia grit her teeth. "You'll see."

"Newsflash—that's a fairytale." She pointed to the storefront. "This is reality. Once we open these doors, it's going to take hard work and lots of sweat to make a real profit. I won't have time for anything else."

Charlie gave her a look. "I'm going to be right by your side making that moolah, but I've never heard of money making a great blanket."

Fortunately Maddox arrived, so that ended their conversation. The first thing he did when he saw her was compliment Tia on her business shirt. Her cheeks warmed under his praise.

When Charlie met Maddox, she was all charm, but behind his back, she gave Tia a thumbs-up and mouthed *He's a keeper* before pointing at the blue silk tie featuring frogs. Tia could only nod as Charlie's talk of love filled her mind.

Maddox gave her a quick peck on the cheek, but she was too self-conscious and covered it up by saying, "Let's go see the inside."

The owner took them on a tour. The front area was a big, open space, and she could picture her pieces placed just so. The narrow hallway led to an office and a bathroom with a huge storage room in the back. It needed new carpeting, some painting and window treatments, but she could see herself working out here. There was a back door that led to decent-sized backyard.

"A little TLC and this place will be perfect," Maddox said.

Charlie's head bobbed. "I think you should take it."

Tia's heart pounded. Signing a lease was a whole year's commitment. It meant she felt sure enough in her talents that she could make the rent. Thinking about her last two sales and the potential restoration income for the Italian pieces, Tia made her decision and rushed to complete the paperwork.

"I can't wait to let my parents know I'm moving out of the garage."

Charlie got teary-eyed. "They are going to be so proud."

"You are going to be nothing short of amazing." Maddox drew her into his arms and rocked her. "Let me know if you need help painting or anything. I'm happy to help you fulfill your dream."

Those tender words turned her heart to mush, turning on the switch to her heart. Dang it, if she wasn't in love before, she would be now. Love blossomed like a peacock spreading its wings, catching her off guard. It felt amazeballs. But with Charlie's keen eyes darting between them, Tia played down the significance of what Maddox said and what she was feeling. She cuffed him on the arm like he was one of the boys. "I'll most likely take you up on that, friend."

He squinted, his brows furrowed, before giving her a nod. Then he said he had to get back to court early. Tia stuffed the pastrami sandwich she had made for him in his hand and gave him her cheek when he bent over to kiss her. Maddox's eyes held confusion mingled with a little hurt. But Tia felt like the words *I love you* were painted all over her chest, and she had to deal with all these new emotions bubbling up inside her for which she was not equipped. She was not equipped for the outpouring. She didn't want to blurt out those words to him and risk rejection because she had gotten too intense.

So though her lips tingled to connect with his, Tia gave Maddox a two-handed wave (way too high and way too much) to prove she was A-okay. But she wasn't.

When Maddox drove out of the lot, Charlie watched her for a beat before extending her arms. Pouncing into her embrace, Tia broke down and cried.

Charlie patted her on the back. "There now, there now. It just hit you, didn't it? Love swooped in and knocked you on your tail feathers, and now you all discombobulated, but you'll soon find your love legs."

Tia sniffled and sobbed some more. "I feel awful. He's going to leave me if he finds out."

"Finds out what?"

Really? Charlie was being cruel right now. Tia pulled out of her friend's arms and stepped back. "I'm falling apart, and you're trying to make me say the words? That's heartless." She wiped her face. Charlie bunched her lips like she was trying not to laugh. Tia folded her arms. "Are you having fun at my expense right now?" she spat. "My chest is literally hurting. Hurting. And you want to laugh?"

"It's all a part of the process," Charlie nodded, trying to

be solemn. "I've been there. Soon you'll find nothing but joy. Once you accept it, that is."

Tia inhaled. "This sucks."

"Yep."

"I can't say those words to him. He would run in the other direction."

"Would he? Only one way to know that for sure."

"Naw. I need to let this marinate for a minute. Then I'll test the waters."

"You saw that tie like I did, right? That man is literally wearing his feelings on his chest. Pretty evident you might not be the only one riding the lily pad in love's murky waters."

Tia snorted. "Would you stop with the corny analogies already?"

"What? I'm only playing my part as your trusty sidekick." She grinned. Then she grew serious. "Talk to Maddox tomorrow. Be upfront. If you're too much and this is too soon, it's better to know now and not waste any more time."

That was some good advice, and after sharing another hug, Tia said, "I'll go talk with my parents."

"And I'll stop at the department store to grab some packing boxes, and I'll meet you by your parents'. We had a couple special orders come in this morning, but I can call and see if they will wait for us to move and get settled."

"That's great. Thank you."

Tia entered her pickup, her heart heavy. Falling in love felt like getting hit with a sack of bricks, and recovery felt a long way off. She cut down a side street and used some back roads to get to her parents' property.

Her father was on his riding lawn mower. Though her parents paid for weekly landscaping during the summer months, Clint still liked to cut the lawn on occasion. As soon as he spotted her, he stopped the engine.

"How's my princess?" he said, giving her a tight hug. "I see your T-shirts finally got delivered."

"Yes, that's the last time I order from online because these took forever to get here." She held a hand over her eyes to shield them from the sun's glare. "I'm doing good. Real good. Actually, I found a place." Tia wanted to tell him about Maddox, but she figured her moving out was a much more pressing topic.

"You're moving out?" Clint wiped his brow. His shirt was slick with sweat and dust. Grass stains splintered his jeans and boots. "Are you sure? You don't have to rush."

"Dad, it's been almost three years. It's time. Don't you think?"

"I see your point. But your Mom and I are okay with waiting as long as needed."

"Aww." She gave her dad another hug. "I'm ready to go. The place I found needs a little fixing, but I'll be putting up my grand-opening signs on my door in no time."

"Sounds good." He kissed the top of her head. "Sallie is going to be ecstatic because she wants to move her knitting business into the garage."

"Knitting business? I thought she was all about golfing these days."

"Well, you know her hobbies never lasts. Kind of like…" Her father stopped abruptly, and Tia sucked in her cheeks to keep from asking if he was talking about her. That comparison hurt a little.

"I'm serious about this career, Dad. I'm not going to quit this like I did medical school."

Clint patted her arm. "I know. I didn't mean that. I love that you're willing to try new things. And I'm here to support you no matter what."

Her mother came outside, the screen door slamming behind her, holding two glasses of lemonade. She was dressed in typical golf garb along with socks and tennis shoes. "I figured you guys could use some serious hydration. This sun is intense. I hope you're both wearing sunscreen."

Tia looked at the woman from whom she had inherited her hair, eyes and skin tone, right along with the freckles beading her skin. "Thanks, Mom." She accepted a glass and took a sip. Goodness. This was so good. No one made lemonade like her mom. "I'm packing up the garage starting today."

Her mom's eyes went wide. "You found a spot?"

"Yes."

Sallie did a two-step. "Go on, my girl. I can't wait to come check it out." Then she touched Tia's curls. "Then once you're settled, you can find a man, get married and work on getting me grandbabies."

This was her cue to tell them about Maddox. Her parents had started off as friends and grown to love each other over time. They wouldn't understand about her falling in love within seventy-hours of meeting someone. Not that they would voice their displeasure, but Clint and Sallie might run off Maddox by grilling him with questions about his background, his teeth, his grades—nothing was off topic.

But since she hesitated, her father jumped in. "Sallie," her dad warned. "Ease up now. Tia's got time for all that soon enough."

Her mother pinched her cheek. "Yes, but she's not getting younger and we're getting older by the minute. I want to be able to run after my g-baby, not hobble."

Tia wasn't going to continue that discussion thread. Instead, she joked, "Well, how about you run your way to the plant shop? I could use some plants for my office."

Her mom didn't even hesitate. "Consider it done."

Chapter Eleven

Maddox leaned back in his chair, rubbed his temples and sighed. If he could rewind and start this day over, he would. Not only had the woman he loved given him a cold shoulder, probably because her best friend was around, but Jefferson hadn't shown up for community service. And the teen hadn't answered his calls. Maddox didn't want to forfeit this option and impose the fine because he knew this family couldn't afford it. He groaned. See, this was what happened when he deviated from being the Iron Fist. There was a strong possibility that he was getting taken advantage of.

Then, he had overheard a couple of the other judges talking about him during a Zoom-call meeting for an appellate case, saying Maddox had gotten this job due to his mother's finagling, never mind that he had experience and had graduated law school. The men hadn't realized that he would be one of the judges on the case since another judge had called out sick.

Talk about an awkward situation once they discovered his presence. Maddox had shrugged it off, but the damage had been done. He had provided input then left them to make the final decision.

Plus he had spilled water on the sandwich Tia had given him. So, he hadn't eaten all day. Now it was close to the end of his shift and all he wanted to do was go see Tia, but he wasn't sure he would be welcomed. So far, his biggest revelation about being in love for the first time was that love was pure misery.

The defendant for the last case had skipped bail, so Maddox ordered a habeas corpus and retired to his chamber.

A glance at his cell phone made his heart sing. Tia had texted, inviting him to dinner at her place. After sending her a quick reply in the affirmative, he dashed out the door.

Dinner was a box of pizza and buffalo wings, but he was quite okay with that. He and Tia settled on the couch to eat, and she sat at the opposite end with her feet propped in his lap. Maddox took a bite into the slice and moaned before leaning back. "This is heavenly."

"Now you know the reason why I moved above the shop." Tia also took a bite, but she ate the crust first.

"You never do the expected, do you?" Maddox observed, fascinated.

She licked her lips. "Not if I can help it."

He swallowed. He was pretty sure she didn't know how appealing she was. How appetizing. She reached for the box of wings off the coffee table and rested them on her lap. It was tilted against her thigh in a way that made him nervous, but Maddox stuffed another piece into his mouth to keep from saying anything.

"So I've got a question. What's up with all the green? And the frogs on your tie?"

"It started as a joke, but now…" He shrugged, unable to meet her eyes. "I don't know."

"I think that's sweet."

She bit into a piece of the boneless wing, the buffalo sauce staining her hands. That was it—he couldn't take this anymore. He tapped her leg and stood before going into the kitchen to get a sheet of paper towel for both of them.

When he returned to the living area, he stopped short. Her butt was perched in the air, and he took a moment to appreciate that fine derriere before he realized her hand was moving back and forth like she was scrubbing something. Oh no. He dashed over to where she stood. There was an orange stain on the edge of the couch. *The* couch. His mother's couch that she had commissioned right before getting sick. The one she'd made him promise to take care of. The very best care.

Maddox took a deep breath. "What happened?" The scent of baby wipes filled the air, and he noticed there was a box of wipes on the coffee table.

"I—I don't know," she sputtered. "I went to pop a piece of chicken in my mouth, and I—I missed." She kept on rubbing with furious strokes.

"You missed?" He clenched his jaw. "You missed?"

She whipped around to face him. "Don't worry. I'll get it out."

He bunched his fists, struggling to keep calm. "There is no getting it out, Tia. It's ruined. You ruined it. I knew I should have said something, but I didn't want to come off as too anal, too uptight, and look what happened!" A thought occurred, and he narrowed his eyes. "Did you do this on purpose?"

Her eyes went wide. She stepped back. "Wait. Are you accusing me of sabotage?" Her tone held disbelief, and a silent warning to backtrack hit his mind. He should apologize immediately before this escalated any further. But all he could see was the...imperfection.

"Yes, as a matter of fact I am. You wanted this couch so bad, and you knew if you did this, I would let you win. Then once I conceded, you could just repair it."

Tia placed a hand on her hip, and her neck snapped from side to side. "I can't believe you would fix your mouth to speak to me like that. You are unbelievable, and I suggest you quit before you write a check your butt can't cash."

They stood for a beat, both chests heaving before he rubbed his head. "I'm sorry. But you have to admit my reasoning makes sense."

She exhaled. "If you think I would damage something so beautiful on purpose, then you don't know me. And to think I believed I—" She shook her head. "Never mind. Look, Maddox. I suggest you leave before I say something I can't take back."

"You're kicking me out?" Dread lined his stomach.

"That's what *leave* means. Yes." She grabbed the pizza box and the rest of the wings before storming into the kitchen to dump it into the trash.

Maddox followed behind. "I overreacted."

"You think?" she shot back. "You're questioning my integrity, my honor. How would you like it if I came out my face like that to you?"

Regret filled him. He lowered his head. "I wouldn't." He rushed over to take her hand. "I owe you a big apology."

"Accepted." He would be relieved if her eyes didn't look so cold. "I genuinely hate that I was too laid back about eating on the couch. I knew better, but I did it anyway. Now, to me the couch is an object, and it was more about cuddling with you and just chilling. But I should have been more careful. I get that. But your reaction showed me that we moved too fast... With everything. Maddox, I think this has to be it for me." Her voice hitched. "Yeah, I think this is best. We need to part ways now before things get ugly."

Tears misted her eyes, making his gut twist.

"Just like that?" He ached to put his arms around her, but he could tell from her stance that physical contact wouldn't be welcomed at the moment. "I knew I was out of line," he pleaded, "but I..." The urge to spill how he felt welled within him. But Maddox stopped before uttering the words *I love you.* If he voiced them now, it might come across as manipulation. And the first time he spoke that sentiment to a woman, Maddox needed her to believe him. Because he didn't know what he would do if Tia rejected him for being a jerk.

He was messing up at love big time.

"Please leave," she said, like she was struggling to breathe.

He could see she was hurting, and it pained him deep within to know he had caused that hurt. It was probably best to retreat until she had calmed.

"Okay, I'll go. But I'll reach out tomorrow." Maddox started down the stairs, but she called out to him. He turned back, hopeful. She took a couple steps until she was facing him eye to eye.

Her lips quivered and she squared her shoulders. "Don't. Don't reach out tomorrow. I… I need time."

"All right." He swallowed, his gut twisting. "I look forward to your call."

But when he got home the next day and saw the couch had been delivered, fully repaired, Maddox knew he had lost her. He had won the couch four days early, but he had lost the girl. She was gone like a feather in the wind.

Chapter Twelve

"If you play one more sad love song, I am going to scream," Tia said, putting the vase on the display table in a corner of the room of her shop.

"All right, all right, I'll turn it off," Charlie said, using the remote to switch the song on her Pandora playlist. The previous renters had been in the music business and had installed an intricate surround system, so wherever Tia went in the store, she had been subjected to listening to most heart-wrenching lyrics surrounding love and living without love.

She had had to cover a few sniffles and hide her reddened eyes with eye drops earlier that morning so her friend didn't know the havoc love was doing to her insides.

Love was not for the weak.

It was exactly fourteen days since she had last spoken to Maddox. Fourteen excruciatingly long days. She dreaded the night like she dreaded a visit to the dentist. Tia should have gotten over Maddox by now, considering it had only taken her a couple days or so to fall for him. But she hadn't. Not even a teeny bit.

Love ached.

In her defense, she might move forward quicker if Charlie would stop pleading with her to call Maddox, as if ending things with him had been easy. Maddox had respected her wishes and kept his distance, but he had sent Jefferson to assist with painting the place twice last week. Tia had welcomed the teen's assistance and had been happy to sign off on his community-service hours. Of course, Charlie made sure to exclaim about Maddox's thoughtfulness. Loyal friend that she was, though, Charlie didn't bring him up when Tia's parents were about.

Tia wouldn't be able to handle their hovering. Because even though they would be skeptical about the whole *love practically at first sight* thing, they would ply her with sweet treats, insisting on not leaving her alone. Then she would have melted like ice cream in the sun, wailing about how much she missed Maddox—and the couch. Tia hadn't been able to eat a sandwich since then. Getting up every morning had been a chore, but she had a business to relaunch and her friend was depending on her for a paycheck.

"I did the right thing," Tia said, as if she could convince herself by saying it aloud.

"It wasn't the right thing. Not for you." Charlie placed one of the house plants on a coffee table. "And you shouldn't have returned your couch."

"It was a fluke, and it wasn't my couch. I gave it back to him."

"If you were wearing pants, they would be on fire."

Tia moved to set up her computer now that the internet was connected.

Her father entered the store holding a box of her tools. "Where do you want this?" he huffed.

"You can put it in the back. I'll sort through those later." Tia cupped the mouse and opened up her email to see if Mr. Romano had approved the preliminary ideas she had sent on the restoration. She had even included sketches for some art pieces she could design for the museum showcase. Seeing he had responded, she pumped her fists and clicked on the message.

Tia scanned the words on the page before she gasped. "Mr. Romano pulled out of the deal." Her heart pounded. "He is thinking of going with someone else from New York and should be meeting up with them at the HBCU Gala."

"What?" Charlie ran to her side.

"Said his investors preferred someone with a little more clout."

Charlie gave her a knowing look. "Someone male."

Tia placed a hand across her chest. "I can't believe this." This money would have paid up her rent for at least six months. Her shoulders slumped. "I'm going to lose my business before I even begin. And I've got to be able to pay you," Tia said, biting her lip. "Maybe I'll ask—"

Charlie lifted a hand. "Don't say you're going to ask your parents for a handout." She placed a hand on her hip. "You've got this. Don't forget you've recorded your trainings. We just have to release clips on TikTok and link them to your website."

"Yes, we can put those out, but it will be months before we get the capital from that." Hopelessness filled her chest. "If I talk with the landlord, I might be able to—"

"Nope. You're not quitting." Charlie was firm. "You're done bailing."

"You're right." She squared her shoulders. "That was a momentary lapse. Old ways are hard to kill. I'm not quitting. We will figure it out. And Mr. Romano said he was thinking about it—not that he has decided. So, there's still a chance."

"Yes, but you can increase the possibility," Charlie exclaimed. "You've got to go to the gala tonight. Maddox sent you the ticket, so you need to go. Meet up with Mr. Romano in person and get him to change your mind."

Doubt reared. "I'm not sure…"

"Listen to me. You can do this. You give up too easily."

"I don't know if I can face Maddox." She couldn't see him and not touch him, not want him. And what if he had moved on? A thought occurred. She placed a hand to her mouth.

"What if he brings a date? I don't know if I can bear seeing him with someone else."

Charlie did a two-step. "Sashay your way over there and lay it all out there. What do you have to lose?"

"Um. My dignity?"

"You give you up too easily. You've got to fight for what you want, and you love this man. Get to that gala and fight for this commission. And to answer your question, if he's on to the next one already, then he wasn't your frog."

Charlie was right. She couldn't quit now, not when her dream was within reach for her business. And potentially for her heart. Tia glanced at the clock and jumped to her feet. "I've got to go."

"Really? You're running away?"

"No, you don't understand. The mall closes in an hour. I've got to get a dress." She darted to the door. "Tell my parents I'll call them later."

At those words, Charlie smiled. "That's my girl." Then she yelled, "Make sure it's green!"

Chapter Thirteen

Maddox held the bubbly in his hand and surveyed the throng. It seemed like anybody who was anybody was here tonight, dressed to impress. There was a band playing oldies, and everyone was getting down. Maddox had donned his black tuxedo along with a crisp white shirt and cummerbund. He had greeted a lot of socialites he used to hang with, but he kept his eyes peeled to the entrance. There was one person he hoped to see, and she had yet to make an appearance.

Unless she wasn't coming. That possibility crushed him to the core.

One of the reasons he had made it through the past fourteen days was that Maddox banked on her showing up to this event. He lifted a hand to adjust his bow tie, which suddenly felt constricting. His dark green frog cufflinks winked at him. They were made of sterling silver and set against an eighteen-carat gold-plated background, which gave them a warm glow. Subconsciously, he reached for small bulge in his pocket.

Maddox couldn't lose hope. The night was still young.

A young man dressed in a gray suit and light pink shirt and coordinated tie walked over to him.

"Thank you for paying for us to come, Your Honor," Jefferson said. "My mom is having a good time." They both turned to look at his mother, who was helping herself to the appetizers.

He lifted a hand. "What did I tell you? As of four o'clock this afternoon, it's just plain old Maddox now."

"Sorry, Mr. Maddox. It's going to take some getting used to."

"Well, get used to it. You'll be seeing me at the foundation every day after school until graduation."

"Yes, sir." Jefferson twisted to eye his mother, who was now dancing real close with a dude in a hat. "Um, I'd better go break that up. See you tomorrow."

Maddox chuckled. After Tia had sent the couch back, he had spent the weekend in that huge house, alone. When the sun had come up, he'd realized he had no desire to go in to work that Monday morning. Or ever again for that matter. Then Jefferson had called in a panic. He and his mother had gotten evicted. Maddox had taken the day to help them secure housing and gotten them situated in their new place.

When he'd left them, Maddox had been exhausted and hungry, but he had felt such…joy, such satisfaction that he knew he could get up the next day and do it again. Help people.

And he thought of Tia.

Now, he truly understood why she had left medical school. She was searching for this feeling, this level of contentment.

He had picked his cell to call Tia when he'd remembered that she didn't want to hear from him. So, Maddox had given his two weeks' notice to his Supervisor and celebrated by making a fried bologna sandwich—which was not as good as hers—and he had eaten every last drop on the couch. He had placed a blanket down though because…small steps. Then over the last few days, he had purchased an abandoned business space in Dover, which happened to be close to Tia's place (not really an accident), and Maddox had gutted and cleaned and painted as he had never had before in his life.

Hard work had been his therapy, but during the nights… Tia had stayed on his mind.

Tonight he would announce the grand opening of the Hearts and Homes Foundation—a planned strategy, since many here had deep pockets—and he would get the girl. That was what he had told himself. He squeezed the box in his pocket again, and that was when he saw her.

His breath caught.

All those copper curls were piled high on her head, and she was exquisite in that green-sequined gown. Heads turned, and his chest puffed with pride, especially since she had spotted him. With a smile, she started in his direction, but then she cocked her head and walked over to that slick-looking Casanova that Jefferson's mom had been dancing with before. That man was working the room.

Reminding himself that Tia was free to do as she chose, Maddox decided to ask an old friend to dance.

Really?

While one part of her brain focused on schmoozing with Mr. Romano to convince him to give her the project, the other part fumed at Maddox all wrapped up in some temptress's arms. The woman had a stunning head of glossy gray hair and a form-fitting black number. Tia would have been all right with it if he hadn't tossed his head back and laughed. Laughed, while her heart had ached for the couple weeks they had been apart.

But she kept talking. Kept dealing, until Mr. Romano agreed.

"Let's shake on it," he said.

She shook his hand, all business. "Once I receive the deposit, I'll get started." Then, putting all the sway she could in her hips, she strutted over to cut in on Maddox and the diva. The band had started up a tango, a dance for couples. The other woman gave her a sweet smile, and then Tia and Maddox squared off.

"You look ravishing," he said, marching.

"So do you," she shot back, keeping in step with him.

"I have plenty to tell you."

"I do too."

He held out his hand. "I'll go first. I left my job and started a foundation."

She gripped his waist and held on to his hand as they strutted across the floor. "That's a bold move. I will definitely need to know more."

"It was time." Maddox closed his arms around her, and she exhaled. This was where she belonged. "I haven't been able to sit on that couch without you."

"Good." She smiled. "I still have an empty space."

"Your turn." He spun her around and dipped her low.

"I've fallen for you," she said, tossing her head back.

Maddox stopped in the middle of the dance floor and pulled her against him. Tia drew in a sharp breath. Being in his arms was exhilarating.

"What did you say?" he asked, voice gruff. He needed to be looking at her to make sure he had heard her right.

She touched his cuff links and licked her lips. "I'm in love with you."

He took her hands and walked her out onto the balcony. Then he folded his arms. "You just had to beat me to it, didn't you?"

The light breeze felt good against her neck. "I have no idea what you're talking about." She bit back a smile. Her heart felt light watching Maddox regroup. Her honey really hated when things didn't go according to how he'd planned. "What did I beat you to?"

"Telling you how I feel." He groaned. "I had this whole speech planned and everything."

Tia hugged him. "It's okay. I want to hear what you have to say."

He laughed. "But I should have known. When it comes to you, Tia Powell, I have to expect the unexpected." Maddox took her hand. "I was walking every day under a cloud, and I didn't know it. I didn't know how gloomy my existence was or how mundane. And I would have spent the rest of my life content, not knowing the truth if it hadn't been for you. You brighten my life. You quicken my heart. When I met you fighting for ownership of the couch, you pushed me out of my comfort zone, you challenged me, you completed me."

Tia released short, choppy breaths. "Whoa. That was—"

He placed a finger over her lips. "I'm not done. I love you, Tia Powell."

"I love you too." She puckered her lips, but Maddox reached in his pocket for a small square box. Tia put a hand on his chest. "Wait, what are you doing? No. No, we're not ready for this. We actually need to date and play catch-up and all of that."

"Will you just look, princess?" Maddox opened the box and held it up.

She gasped as the tears came to her eyes when she saw the green pendant that matched his cuff links, suspended on a rope chain. "Oh, Maddox, I love it."

He smiled. "I thought you would. The frog is pavé-set in tsavorite, and its eyes are made of garnet." Maddox snatched her close. "And I love you for all the moments we have had and the moments we will have. If you will have me, I will give you my heart for always, and you will have unlimited couch visitation." He cleared his throat before looking around and lowering his voice. "If you want me, I will be your frog."

"I do. I do." Then she kissed her frog, and they began their journey to happy-ever-after.

* * * * *

Special EDITION

Believe in love. Overcome obstacles. Find happiness.

Available Next Month

A Fairy-Tail Ending Catherine Mann
Their Unexpected Forever Laurel Greer

....

Tying The Knot Brenda Novak
Road Trip Rivalry Mona Shroff

4 brand new stories each month

Special EDITION

Believe in love. Overcome obstacles. Find happiness.

MILLS & BOON

Subscribe and fall in love with a Mills & Boon series today!

You'll be among the first to read stories delivered to your door monthly and enjoy great savings.

MILLS & BOON SUBSCRIPTIONS

HOW TO JOIN

1

Visit our website
millsandboon.com.au/pages/print-subscriptions

2

Select your favourite series
Choose how many books. We offer monthly as well as pre-paid payment options.

3

Sit back and relax
Your books will be delivered directly to your door.

WE
SIMPLY
LOVE
ROMANCE